DESTINY'S FALL

MARIE BILODEAU

DESTINY'S FALL

MARIE BILODEAU

ACKNOWLEDGMENTS

Destiny's Fall would not even exist if not for the foresight of Dragon Moon Press' Managing Editor, Gabrielle Harbowy. It started with a full rewrite of the original dark and conclusive epilogue to *Destiny's Blood*. I was asked to make it a bit less final, to let the readers imagine the characters had some sort of future (and not just death. Go fig). After providing the new epilogue, Gabrielle and I had a discussion that went like this:

Gabrielle: So, when do I get books 2 and 3 of the series?
Me: …series?
Gabrielle: Yes. Series.
Me: …series? …really?
Gabrielle: Or another book project. But we like Destiny.
Me: Series! I love it!

And that's how *Destiny's Fall* came to be. Thanks, Gabrielle.

Thanks to the rest of the team at Dragon Moon Press for their support and for turning the book from good to awesome, including Gwen Gades, Publisher extraordinaire, and Kari-Ann Anderson, who returned to the world of Destiny to create this second wonderful cover.

My family, as always, is vital to any creative endeavour. Special thanks to Suzanne Desjardins, Gilles Bilodeau and Nicole Caouette, Jean-François Bilodeau and Jessica Torrance, Karen and David Henderson, Katherine and Martin Gallant and my ever patient Roomy, Kerri Elizabeth Gerow. Special thanks to George Henri, Ada-Marie and Xander, whose births and everyday growth breathed life into Ardice Delamores.

I would be remiss not to also mention Nicole and Marc Soucy, Mary Pletsch and Dylan Blacquiere, Kathryn Hunt, Sophie Chisogne, Rob Uhrig, Sarah Watts-Rynard and Utnapishtim III (Utnois). And, last but certainly not least, my writing group, the East Block Irregulars: Derek Künsken, Hayden and Liz Trenholm, Matt Moore, Geoff Gander and Peter Atwood.

DEDICATION

À mon papa, Gilles Bilodeau, qui m'a inoculé son amour des mots et des histoires, et qui me prouve sans relâche qu'il n'y a pas, heureusement, de remède contre cette maladie.

Translation: To my dad, because he's cool.

CHAPTER 1

THE CHILD'S FIRST cries pierced the night and Mirial, First Star and mother of all ether, quivered in response.

Layela Delamores leaned back, exhausted, fighting the nausea of hours of labour and biting back the tears. The ether around her danced with joy, responding to her first daughter's screams in ways it never had for Layela herself. Ardin leaned down and kissed her forehead, his lips energizing her weary body, wisps of his auburn hair escaping his ponytail and brushing her face.

The child screamed again, and Layela tried to shift, to see her more clearly. She already knew, without seeing her, that one of her eyes would be sea green and the other twilight blue. Just like hers, except that Layela had lost a sister to gain that mark.

Her daughter came into this world already courted by a strong Mirial, a strength cultivated by Layela's care over the last few years. Years of hard work, of mastering what little she understood of the ether, years of sacrificing her own dreams and trying to see Mirial as her home, regardless of how she felt. But her daughter was already reaping more with her pure cries than Layela ever could in a lifetime.

A whole being.

Layela stifled a sob and shifted, trying to get more comfortable in the dirty bedding, her gown clinging to her. She needed to change and go announce the birth of a daughter to the awaiting court. She needed to tell them of a secured succession—that Mirial would be tended to. That they were safe.

But her daughter's screams crashed and echoed in her mind, triggering the ether within her, visions gripping the edges of her sight. Mists danced around the room, half-formed visions wisped to life as the mists caressed and coated individuals in the room, allowing Layela a glimpse of their final moments, or at least an impression. In her vision, her captain of the royal guards, Loran, screamed, collapsing on the ground. Her court advisor first turned white, then coarse black. She dared not look at Ardin, having long ago heard the bells tolling, announcing his final moments…

"Are you all right?" Ardin asked, leaning in, concern in his brown eyes.

She tried to smile, but closed her eyes for a moment instead, concentrating on pushing back the ether that had triggered her visions. She opened her eyes, the ether seeming to dance around her before settling. Layela smiled. Ardice would court the ether much more strongly than she ever had. But Layela would need to be vigilant until her daughter proved strong enough to control her own connection with Mirial.

Ardin smiled back at her. "She has good lungs!"

The tolling of the bells resonated in the far edges of her mind. *It is a faraway future*, she repeated over and over again as she looked into Ardin's eyes.

Please don't leave me.

"You're right," she said, forcing a small laugh. "She does have good lungs."

Gresko Listan, Court Advisor, stepped up, clearing his throat. Ardin rolled his eyes for only Layela to see, and she fought back a laugh. Ardin stood. Gresko was as tall as Ardin, but was a stick, his dark royal robes barely held up by his thin, bony shoulders. His face was gaunt and pale. When Layela had first met him, she had assumed his features were due to lack of sunlight and good food, as most Mirialers had suffered during the Great Darkness, but five years had passed and still he remained the same. Beside him, Ardin's shoulders seemed broader. If he stepped up and flicked a finger at Gresko, he would probably break him. Layela had to look down to stop from laughing. The laughter vanished in an aching desire to be alone, with only Ardin and their daughter at her side.

"The daughter should be presented to the court, as per tradition."

Ardin rolled his eyes again and Layela steeled herself. She looked at Gresko imploringly. "It has been a long, a long…" she turned to one of the midwives.

"Thirty-six hours," she quickly said. She looked just as exhausted as Layela.

"Thirty-six hours," Layela repeated. "Is it necessary to put on a show now for the court? Can they not be satisfied to know that it is a girl and their lineage is safe?"

He shook his head, raising an eyebrow. "Surely my lady understands the necessity of the court's demands. After all, my lady did refuse to reveal the gender of the child beforehand."

Layela sighed. Of course, she hadn't wanted the gender of the child to be known. She herself only knew because of the ether, and hadn't allowed any scanners or imaging devices to be used on her child. Had it been a boy, they would have callously shipped him off, as per the generations of women before her. But she had refused to give them that power. Just as she refused to pretend Ardin didn't exist, that he wasn't the father of her child.

"How long will this 'show' take, Gresko?" She spoke harsher than intended. She looked down at the baby, her beautiful face still red and wrinkled, her eyes closed. She was perfection. Fragile, helpless perfection.

"Just a few moments. You simply need to introduce her to the court. Quite a few have gathered, waiting."

Ardin raised an eyebrow. "They've been here for the entire labour?"

The Court Advisor managed to look down at Ardin, despite their similar height.

"The birth of Layela's daughter ensures the safety of Mirial. It is the single most important event that will occur until her daughter's daughter is born. Mirialers understand this," he added with disdain.

Layela's daughter. She could see Ardin's muscles stiffen, and she spoke quickly to avoid any altercations.

"Then let's do it." She struggled to sit up, Ardin stepping in to help. "I'll change and we'll go introduce her, quickly." She stood and held the advisor's eyes with hers. "Both Ardin and I will introduce our child."

He looked about to protest but, seeing the steel in her eyes, quickly backed down.

"Can you take her, please?" Layela whispered to Ardin. His look of annoyance melted away as he took his daughter, holding her as though she were made of the finest glass. Layela smiled and told everyone else to leave so she could clean and change.

And then she would step out before her throne, to follow a path laid at her feet long before she was even born, a path gilded with tradition and belief that she was something more than just an exhausted new mother who wanted little more than to curl up in bed with Ardin and her baby.

Her sole consolation was the controversy she was about to create with the name of her child.

***

The silk of her dress danced around her swollen ankles as she walked towards the court, Ardin behind her, the little girl quiet in her arms. She cradled her close, the visions in her mind as quiet as the child now, the ether dancing around them, content.

Maybe the ether always freaks out that way at first, Layela thought, pushing against the fatigue to force a smile upon her face. She took a deep breath and pushed through the curtains that lead her into the court.

So hushed was the court that the only sound Layela could hear was the silk of her skirt.

They all looked at her with joy and curiosity. In truth, they didn't know what she would spring on them. The child, swaddled in white, betrayed nothing of its gender to onlookers.

Ardin stayed close to her, gathering more than a few disapproving glances. As though the fathers were no more than mere donors. She still had no idea who her father was, and for all she knew he stood in this room at this very moment. She never would know, this she was certain of, but in her heart of hearts she now accepted it had been Captain Zortan Mistolta, who had died protecting her.

She wished she had asked him while he still lived.

The faces of the court were turning from curious to impatient. Layela waited a moment longer, standing before the great lavish throne. A few of the Berganda had gathered as well, already adults at the tender age of five, some already seeding children of their own.

Layela smiled a large, expansive smile.

"It's a girl," she simply said, and the court broke out into cheers, all but the Berganda who were as taken aback as her by the display. Sun was streaming in. Layela had no idea the sun had risen, or what time it was. The smell of incense and booze tackled her still overly sensitive nose, mixing with the scents of her own blood.

"These people need something else to occupy their time," Ardin whispered as he came close, protective of the two of them.

Layela kept her smile plastered on, the court thankfully celebrating amongst themselves and not imposing any closeness on her. She was exhausted, her arms trembling under the little girl.

She turned to Ardin. "Can you take her for a bit? I'm tired, for some reason."

He grinned at her and carefully took the swaddling, his arms stiff and uncomfortable, his face set in deep concentration. Layela hid a smile, wishing Avienne were here—she would find her usually confident brother's hesitation with the baby hilarious.

She made sure the head was well supported before removing her own arms. Ardin glowed with pride, gently holding his daughter.

"What is the new Keeper's name?" someone shouted, and the room grew quiet again. Layela noted a few pointed looks shot at Ardin, who was carefully holding the baby, barely acknowledging onlookers. Layela stayed near him.

"Her name is Ardice." She paused. She gauged reactions. Gresko had informed her that the child had to be named of Old Mirial, just as Layela's name meant 'night' and Yoma's had meant 'day.' She continued with the formal introduction, certain no one had missed the resemblance to Ardin's name. Let them try and deny him now.

"The new Keeper's name is of Old Mirial, meaning 'flowering field.' May she bring new growth to Mirial, as the sun's rays bring back the rich wonders to grace our landscapes once more."

The Berganda were smiling widely, their green skin and hair shining with pleasure. Basically plants themselves, they seemed to appreciate the idea of more and more vegetation on the once-lush planet. A few others looked happy, as well, but most seemed to be trying to swallow the slight Layela had paid them. She hoped she wasn't blushing.

These were her people, or so she had been told. She should trust them implicitly and only try to do what was best for them. But she wasn't convinced all of these limiting traditions were working out for them, either.

Ardice coughed and then began to scream and cry, her shrill voice bouncing off the walls of the court, reaching every far corner. White mists assaulted Layela's thoughts, clinging to her sight, bells tolling in the far reaches of her mind. She looked up, Ardin's eyes wide and frightened, and the world around her swayed. Ether bounced off the side of the court. The Berganda, more sensitive to it than the Mirialers, screamed and clutched their heads as the ether pounded against their telepathic minds.

Layela took a step forward and grabbed the child from Ardin's arms. She tried to coddle her with small chants, to bounce her up and down, but the screaming only intensified.

"We have to stop her," Ardin came near, shouting in Layela's ear. The whole room echoed Ardice's screams and many of the assembled had fallen to the ground, clutching their heads. Some of the Berganda were no longer moving.

Layela forced herself to concentrate, to soothe Ardice with ether. It seemed to Layela's untrained eyes that the ether was at counter-measure to Ardice, like small sparks striking her daughter. And Ardice fought back the only way she knew, by crying. But her cries were twisting that same ether and it lashed out around her.

Layela cooed and concentrated, commanding all of the ether away from her daughter, forming a protective bubble around her. Ardice, not realizing Layela was trying to help, was fighting back and pulling the ether closer like a protective blanket. Layela kissed Ardice's cheek, the skin-to-skin contact comforting Ardice, and she let go of the ether. Layela quickly closed the protective bubble, her back covered with sweat at the exertion.

Calmer, Ardice settled and stopped screaming, her face red from the outburst. Layela soothed the ether around her, sending gentle urges to the Berganda who were recovering, and softly singing to her daughter.

The bells stopped tolling.

She took a deep breath and the room stopped swaying. She looked up at Ardin, her heart catching in her throat at the worry and fear in his eyes.

"She's just tired." Layela whispered. "We're both tired."

She gave him an encouraging smile and he nodded, though the worry in his eyes didn't lessen.

She turned to the court. The fallen were stirring, the others still in shock.

"I'll take care of this. You go rest," Ardin said. Layela wanted to voice an objection, but she was so exhausted she could only nod. She turned around and walked back through the curtains, hearing Ardin say a few comforting words, some gentle jokes about newborns, and encouraging the tired to rest up. That it had been a big day, and the celebrations were just beginning.

She walked further into the palace, where she herself had been born almost twenty-five years ago and immediately whisked away, where her sister had been born and died nearby, and where now her daughter was born.

And, perhaps if Layela understood more of Mirial and its need for a Keeper, her daughter could choose to leave, to visit the stars and grow her own family amongst them, away from the clutches of the ancient, silent star.

***

Ardin, son of the great Captain Malavant, was going around trying to make light of the fact that the Keeper and her new daughter had almost killed them. Bile splashed in her throat. He had no idea about this planet. He was a full-blood, but as useless as any off-worlder. The last time such a thing had happened at a birthing, Mirial had been cast into twenty years of darkness and fear. And he was trying to make light of it, acting like a new proud father ready to hand out fine grade cigars.

Murl turned her back to him, looking at the fallen around her. She helped a Mirialer up, an old man she remembered from the base camp of Mirial, years ago. He had survived the calamity that had almost destroyed their planet and had swept away most of its people. *The Great Darkness.*

"I'm all right," he said, giving her a weak smile. She smiled at him and spoke gently.

"There are so few of us left, we cannot risk losing you because you are too stubborn to admit you are in pain."

The old man nodded and she led him to a chair, staying with him until a healer came by and took him under her care.

She turned to leave, but the old man clutched her wrist. "Thank you, Murl." He loosened his grip, looking tired. "Your parents would be proud of you."

Murl swallowed the tears and nodded, offering him a weak smile before walking out, past the ether creatures that shouldn't even live on Mirial, past the off-worlders who paraded as full Mirialers, even if they had no idea how to be a proper one. Exiting into the fresh air of day. She was assaulted by the smell of thousands of blooms which lay about the palace grounds and surrounding areas.

If there was one compliment she could pay the new Keeper, it was that she was good with plants. Mirial was starting to flourish again under her care. But mostly around the castle. Other areas, like her home village, would still be without food if not for other help.

But that hardly mattered now. A new Keeper was born, and it was already obvious that the ether did not intend to be soothed or calmed by this daughter of Mirial.

Mirial had been broken once too many times. She rebelled against her off-world Keeper, against the lack of respect for her history. There was no way to re-instil the peace that had always prevailed on Mirial without first dealing with a few issues.

If the Keeper couldn't protect them, Murl knew someone else who could.

She glanced back, caught the eyes of her brother. He grinned and she smiled back, the smile not fading as the earth began to shake. Murl ran back into the hall to help the old man and the healers escape. She ignored the Berganda, who were writhing in agony. The angry ether was tearing them and their powers apart.

The old stones of the palace cracked, echoed by screams of terror. A moment of complete silence followed before another crack and more screams. Nobles and servants began pouring from the throne room, the air crackling with their fear. A red-dressed elderly woman managed to grab a child before the frenzied crowd trampled him. A roar exploded from within the palace, thickening the air and smothering Murl's senses. Everyone around her fell to the ground, trying to cover their loved ones or making themselves as small as they could. Murl remained standing by her brother and she listened beyond the roar. She could clearly hear the sound of a crying child riding the waves of the ether.

Mirial could be, would be, strong again.

CHAPTER 2

AVIENNE MALAVANT CLUTCHED her drink as though it were the last water left in the universe. It wasn't water—was too precious to ever be called that—but rather a mix of ales she had come across on her latest caper. Two portions of something-aquiesque, one shot of some pink thing and two pinches of carefully weighed astium, which could otherwise easily be a poison.

But it wasn't when mixed this way, and turned out it was delicious. *Of all the ways to go,* Avienne thought, *astium might actually prove the most pleasant.*

She clutched the drink and leaned forward heavily, mesmerized by the pink and green hues swirling in her thick glass. She wasn't sure if she should down the drink or just stare at it. The bar around her was bustling with activity and she wanted no part of it. She was known in these parts, so no one would bother her—unless they were interested in bleeding, of course—but the problem was not with her entourage.

If she drank this stuff, which she loved, she'd get friendly. She'd laugh, she'd slur a few jokes, possibly make out with some ugly trader, possibly throw a knife to show her finesse, and then possibly kill someone. It had happened on Thalos IV, which was why she now avoided that planet like the plague. Thankfully the man she had practically swallowed, kissing him so hard (a one-eyed fuzzy half-naked middle-to-late-aged man with a belly she could use as a mattress) turned out to be the same one she had showed her prowess to, neatly embedding her knife in his forehead as a "show of her ability." His death had been a small blessing, since at least it meant he couldn't brag, but she still flushed red at the thought of enthusiastically making out with that man in front of everyone, and *then* missing her shot. Not just missing a little bit. She had been targeting a glass of ale on the opposite side of the room from him, but her fingers had been loose with drink when she had swung back to prepare her throw.

The missed shot was much worse, she decided. She didn't mind having her taste in lovers questioned, especially since she questioned it herself, but for her ability to throw knives to be questioned was not something she could live with.

Avienne sighed and leaned back, still clutching the swirling drink. A large man sat with a Slont nearby, winking at her when she looked his way. He was missing most of his teeth and she was pretty certain that, although it was difficult to tell in this light, one of his ears was missing, too.

Just my type. She pushed the drink away untouched and looked up at the dark ceiling. She would definitely not be drinking tonight.

She wished she knew where to go next. Well, she knew where she was going next—to Mirial, where her niece/nephew or what have you should be born by now, or Layela should be really large and downright cranky. She wanted to see her brother badly, but she didn't, at the same time. Every time she saw him it was the same story. He was settled, happy, fulfilled. And now with a bouncing baby he would be even more insufferable, she imagined.

She didn't begrudge him his happiness. Part of her, a petty, small part she tried in vain to keep locked up, was angry with him for having left her. They had been partners forever, watching each other's backs, going on adventures, and he would never do that again, she knew. Yet a long time ago she had been the one wanting to settle and he hadn't even been able to fathom the idea. Not until meeting Layela, anyway. Of course, the *Destiny* was long gone by the time he settled with Layela to grow Mirial and their relationship.

And, she admitted, the two had tried. Layela had taken her in, allowed her to design her own quarters in the palace as they rebuilt, welcoming her like a sister, even though Layela still reeled from the loss of her twin sister, Yoma. And Avienne had tried, too. It had been thrilling at first, living on such a beautiful planet, marking days by sunrises and sunsets and making a new family. But something had been missing.

All of the tomorrows were the same. The same chambers, the same people, the same sunrises, the same gardens with their slowly growing flowers. Avienne had always wanted to stay in one place and to breathe unrecycled air for long periods of time, but once she was there, she felt bored and restless. Layela and Ardin had understood her desire to leave, of course. Ardin had been supportive.

Almost too supportive, bloody bastard.

Avienne leaned in and chugged the drink, wincing as it burned all the way down. She turned the glass upside down, banged it on the table and burped loudly, leaning back on her chair and winking at the large man who smiled a wide toothless smile back at her.

Blood and bones, that stuff's fast! Avienne stood, the room swaying pleasantly around her. Before she could take a step the door banked open and sunlight poured in. Was it really still day? What was wrong with this wretched planet?

Avienne's mind cleared at the sight of two Solariers—Solarian soldiers were hardly a usual sight in this smuggling port. Only the sun-symbol of Solaria distinguished the colour of their uniforms from the smoky bar. She heard a commotion outside. Something was going on. Avienne shook her head in an attempt to clear it, only to make herself more dizzy.

She could hear some shouting and screaming. The Solariers ignored her and headed to the table with her future lover and the ether creature, a blue-skinned Slont. She looked down. The man was wearing his regulation gloves. That didn't stop the Solariers from walking up to him and grabbing him, slamming him hard into the table as they cuffed his hands.

"I didn't do anything," the man said, his thin voice calm despite the mistreatment.

"And we'll make sure you never do," one of the Solariers responded in a sneer. Avienne took a step closer. She didn't like the sound of that, one bit. Adrenaline pumped through her body.

"Leave him alone." Her targeted lover stood. He was tall and had a deep, booming voice, which pleased Avienne and surprised her, all at once. The men here didn't usually have any redeeming quality, much less two. Without a word one of the Solariers pulled out his gun and shot the man in the chest, sending him flying against two other tables, blood smearing the patrons as they fell under the dead man.

Avienne pulled out two knives and let them fly, making sure to keep her grip firm until it was time to let them go. One of the Solariers fell screaming with a knife embedded in his eye, but she missed the other and hit the wall beside him.

She jumped sideways as a bolt warmed her cheek, and another shot rang out as she fell. She quickly stood back up, knives in hand, but the Solarier was dead, shot from behind. The bartender spat a big glob on the floor.

"No'ne kills ma custamers," he said, spitting again, his grease-ridden clothes catching the glob. Avienne smiled at him and sighed as she looked at the stunned Slont. She winked at the barkeeper. "Another day, perhaps."

He horked again as she bent down and quickly stripped one soldier of guns, ID cards, mission box and a set of handcuff keys. The patrons were making swift work of the other Solarier, taking much more than Avienne would ever even consider.

She was apparently soft for these parts.

"The streets are crawling with them," someone said from the door. "They're taking the ether creatures away!"

"Great," she mumbled as she fumbled with the guard's keys, trying two before one finally clicked open the Slont's handcuffs.

"Where do I go?" the Slont whispered. His eyes were desperately blue, matching the hue of his skin. She looked down at the mission box, quickly going through the latest orders. Her skin turned cold and the last of the booze was washed away in dread.

—Bring all ether creatures to detention chambers. Use extreme caution.—

She grabbed the Slont by the upper arm and pulled him up. She doubted any of Solaria's intentions were good.

"You're coming with me," she said, dragging him behind her as they headed out the back, the barkeeper nodding to them before turning to pour another drink as though nothing out of the ordinary had occurred. She grabbed an encrusted tablecloth and threw it on the Slont.

"Cover yourself. My ship is a ways from here."

She sent a message to her ship, ordering her crew to get ready for departure, but not to make it obvious. The Slont followed quietly and unquestioningly, still looking dazed. She could hear shouts in the distance, some shots and screams…She wished she could save more ether creatures, but there were too many Solariers. One would have to do. *One's plenty for a smuggler, really!*

She stepped out into the streets, sharpened her senses to the treacherous daylight, and sought the shadows that would see them safely back to her ship, the *Desiccate*.

***

Minister Noro paced back and forth, annoyed at the recent outburst and at everything it would mean. Swift, decisive action was required, but he felt old and tired. A younger man should be here, not him. Retirement was a stone's throw away and this was not the last indelible mark he wanted to make.

His intercom chirped to life. "Minister, the collection is proceeding steadily. Gas chambers are also being tested, just in case. We'll be receiving numbers of detainees soon."

"Thank you, Lieutenant," he replied, watching the unit go dead after his response.

On planets across all forty suns that comprised the United Republic of Solaria, ether creatures were being collected.

For the greater good. Strike them, before they strike again. Two hours ago something had happened and the ether creatures had lost control. He didn't understand it yet, but anyone within range of them had either been killed or seriously injured.

Noro looked at his screen. Security footage gathered from across Solaria was playing in a loop. He had reviewed that footage again and again. As Minister of Solarian Defence, he held responsibility for all those planets, and for the safety of its citizens. He had tolerated ether creatures, but they had never truly belonged.

He watched again as a Kilita screamed, and then three Solarian citizens dropped dead beside him. A Slont jerked and five people died. An orphanage of these blasted creatures had left an entire neighbourhood lifeless, the few survivors damaged beyond repair. The time index on all this footage was exactly the same, in Solarian time. Whether it was night or day, summer or winter on the various planets, it had all happened in the same moment. The event had been universal, and he was willing to bet his retirement that he knew its origin.

Mirial.

Something had happened, but until his ship reached Mirial to see what that blasted planet was up to, he wouldn't know what. The Solarian communications network did not stretch that far, and even with the re-established tunnels, their access proved limited. He had sent a message to the ships stationed nearest, but it would take time to reach them.

Noro hated interstellar anything.

His screen changed and numbers began to flicker. Number of detainees. The ether creatures wouldn't stand for this, he knew, and some sympathizers would rally to their cause. And if he couldn't control the ether creatures, he would have no choice but to gas them, to protect Solarians.

But no one would understand that, of course. They would count the dead creatures and never pause to think that the numbers could have easily been turned around and been Solarian numbers, instead.

He turned off his screen, stood and stared at his own tired reflection on its smooth surface, wondering if retirement would be enough to save him now.

***

"Do you know what's happening?" Avienne asked the Slont. She kept a strong grip on his upper arm, grimacing at the feel of the dirty cloth. At least he blended in well with all the other dirty traders. She was the one standing out, mostly clean and with flaming red hair. At least they would look at her, not at her companion.

"Something happened a few hours ago," the ether creature said, then added hesitantly, "We, I don't know, something with the ether. We lost control. I was trying to get passage off this planet, knowing Solaria would panic." He added in a whisper. "And why wouldn't they? Something must have happened to the First Star, again."

Avienne's stride grew wider. He was right. Something was wrong, and Mirial must be the cause. *Ardin.* Something had happened to Layela and possibly the child, she was certain. Layela was due right about now.

I should be there already! Why had she delayed her departure? Why hadn't she rushed there like a good sibling would have? Was she resenting the child for taking more of her brother away from her, too?

"Damn I'm pathetic," she mumbled, dragging the man.

"What?" He asked, turning to her.

"Nothing. Let's just get out of here."

The Solariers were intent on the prey they had already captured, loading them up on land riders and busses and whatever else they had confiscated. A few Solarian citizens were included—no doubt the ones who had stood up for their friends. She was embarrassed by how few there were.

At least I'm not as pathetic as they are, she thought as she ducked into an alley, welcoming the shadows. She could hear the hum of ships in the distance, but no engines were firing. That wasn't a good sign. A huge trading port like this one couldn't afford to have so many idling ships. Traffic had to keep moving, merchandise in and off the ships. Her own ship was almost done unloading their last batch, something her crew was doing slowly, as per her orders, and they would be kicked out as soon as everything was done and all the crew was loaded.

Which meant that Solariers had stopped ship traffic.

Great. This just keeps getting more and more interesting.

They weaved into the alleyways, crossing a few other ether creatures trying to escape. All of them were smugglers, so they knew their way. Avienne didn't feel the need to help them.

She had enough with just trying to save this one man.

"Come on," Avienne said, slowing down. The docks were in view now, ships stacked high on rickety elevators and shafts made of mixed metals—all of them rusty. Avienne hated these docks. If one ship came too close to the structure, the whole thing, all two hundred stories or so of it, would undoubtedly collapse. It would be catastrophic and cost a lot of workers their lives. Yet everyone loaded and unloaded without worry, and crossed on the metal catwalks without pause.

She felt a shiver. She hated heights. And she hated this place.

Her ship was high, too, and they needed an elevator to reach her. There was no way she was climbing all of those stairs. She was a ship's captain, and had one more free pass up.

She turned to the ether creature. "I guess you don't have a pass?" He shook his head, looking up with fear at the docks. She guessed he'd never seen them.

"If you think this is bad," Avienne said as they walked towards them, keeping a close eye out for Solariers, "you should see it on a stormy day. The whole thing sways like it's made out of jelly instead of metal."

The man just nodded, his mouth still wide open.

"Keep your head down," Avienne ordered. He obliged quickly.

She walked towards the structure with confidence, but in reality had no clue how she would sneak him up there. The horizon was covered with docked ships—at least 250, all various sizes, hummed in the sky. Elevators clanked with cargo and people up and down, all of them moving so fast Avienne wondered how none of them crashed. Dock handlers shouted to each other, crew members shouted to each other, dock handlers and crew members shouted at each other… it was chaos. Pure, blissful chaos.

The better to hide someone in.

"Looks like the ships are on lockdown, but everything else is moving. I should be able to sneak you out."

He nodded and continued walking. Avienne looked up, thought she identified her smaller model of a ship, and chose a freight elevator they could sneak into if they were fast enough. It was heading down now, so they'd have to jump into it before it went up. Thankfully, cargo loading and unloading was mostly automated.

She pulled harder on the Slont to get him moving faster, to reach the elevator in time, but he stopped straight in his tracks.

He looked at her pleadingly and tried to get away from her, but she refused to let go as he screamed. Around them others screamed too—ether creatures trying to escape. Solariers tried to apprehend a few, but most fell to the floor, writhing. Avienne could feel ether jump from the Slont's gloved hand onto hers—but as a Mirialer, she had learned, ether creatures didn't affect her in the same way as others. It was to her advantage, now.

"Move!" she screamed, dragging the stunned man behind her. He was light and she was strong. She pulled him along as he worked through whatever was happening to him, his limbs stiff and his eyes wide open, his mouth fixed in a silent scream. Around them the ether creatures stopped, some recovering quickly enough to escape, others downed by Solariers before they could move.

She ran past them and jumped into the open elevator, tugging the man in behind her before the doors closed. Their mad dash did not go unnoticed by nearby Solariers guarding the docks. "Stop!" One of them shouted, but he reached the elevator controls too late. The elevator automatically jerked up, so fast that they both fell to their knees and nausea struck Avienne, who wished she hadn't chugged the swirly drink.

The Slont's limbs went limp and he blinked. His features drooped as though he intended to nap. Avienne hit him hard across the face. He looked at her with wide eyes.

"Stay awake!" she hissed. Below them, the Solariers were getting on another elevator.

"Too slow!" she yelled at them as the door to their elevator opened. She pushed the Slont out of the elevator He stumbled but managed to follow Avienne when she broke into a dead run towards her ship. They were high up, and she could see through the mesh of the floor, a full view of the floor below them, and the next, and the many others… The whole structure swayed, sending them bouncing off the two metal bars that served as guardrails.

The Slont's arm stiffened under her grasp. He was terrified.

Good. That'll keep him awake.

A shot rang past her head and she ducked right. The Solariers were on the same level, obviously not amused. The Slont's head was fully exposed; he had lost the dirty rag somewhere along the way.

"Almost there!" she screamed back, hitting the alert button on her comm unit so that her crew would be ready for departure. She turned another corner, her steps clanging on the old metal catwalk, echoing off the large ships creaking around them. Chains struck the swaying docks. The stringent smell of space-weary metal pinched the air.

She jumped on the small platform that led to her ship, the Slont right behind her. She couldn't make out all of her ship from here, since it was facing the docks to take up less space, but she could identify her ship from the other, larger ones surrounding hers by the rust, scrapes and burn marks. They were so close she could have reached out to touch her ship, but she jumped into the open gate instead.

She closed the door behind her, locking the air docks, and ran up to reach the bridge, not caring if the Slont followed.

It took almost two precious minutes to reach the bridge. She didn't encounter any other crew members on the way up, and was starting to wonder if any of her crew had stayed. But a welcoming shout sounded as she stepped onto the bridge.

"Cap'ain!" her second-in-command, a short man named Larod, screamed.

"Gun the engines, get us out!"

"Solariers are telling us to stand down," said Jaru, her systems analyst.

"And I'm saying the docks need redecorating. Gun the engines!"

The two moved quickly to obey her order. The engines churning to life, the scent of rotten cabbage pumping through the entire ship. The ship jerked once and the engine popped, and her hull vibrated, resonating in Avienne's skull.

"Come on, you useless piece of crap!" She kicked the tactical controls and half the panel lights blinked out.

"Blood and bones, I need to steal a better ship!"

The engines sputtered and the ship stopped vibrating.

"Engines online, Captain!" Jaru screamed. She whooped and switched the viewport on. The entire metal structure of the docks buckled as they pulled free without first declamping, ripping great chunks of metal. The *Dessicate's* engines kicked in full blast, throwing Avienne back into her seat. The docks swayed for a moment when the engine's jet of hot hair struck them, then buckled sideways, and seemed to be righting themselves before suddenly collapsing in a heap of smoke and metal, dragging a few of the smaller ships down.

Avienne hissed. That made a nice, round ten worlds on which she would no longer be welcome. She was running out of planets to do business on.

"Where to, Captain?" Larod asked from navigations.

"Mirial. I believe it's time to pay my brother a visit."

CHAPTER 3

LAYELA WOKE TO Ardice's screams, moments before the earth began to shake. She clutched Ardice and hid under a table, Ardin shielding them both with his body. Layela reached out to the ether, which jumped wildly around them. She tried to soothe it with her own calming waves, but the ether fought back, lashing out at her. She yelped and covered Ardice, her arm taking the brunt of the attack, searing marks and angry welts on her skin.

The cries of thousands, if not millions of ether creatures filled the air, originating from the palace itself to planets far beyond the reaches of the mapped universe. Their lives tiny pinpricks caught in the net of Mirial's ether, which closed in on them and seared them from within, attacking them with the very boon it had bestowed upon them, long ago. Layela held Ardice close and could not longer draw breath as she heard their screams and her body echoed their agony. The wild ether tortured them, and she saw the lives of humans, friends and foes, winking out around them, snuffed out by the storm of ether that threatened to consume the ether creatures.

She forced a deep gulp of air into her lungs, cold sweat dripping down her back, the tips of her fingers numb. She feared either vomiting or passing out.

The ether flashed once around her, a great nova setting everything alight. It trembled and then dissipated, the tremors ending, leaving Layela gasping for air.

The doors to their room flew open and royal guards stumbled in, barely maintaining their footing as they headed toward the huddled family.

"Ssshhh," Layela tried to soothe the red-faced baby. Ardin stood and faced Loran Natwar, captain of their guards, who moved as quickly as anyone else despite her artificial leg.

"What happened?" Ardin asked. Loran fought to catch her breath. Layela stood to face her as well, wondering how far she had run to reach them.

"Not sure," Loran said, mostly looking at Layela. Annoyed, Layela looked away and concentrated on Ardice. They were all fine dealing with Ardin when she wasn't there, but the second she showed up, they all barely acknowledged him.

Loran caught on and hesitantly turned to Ardin. He had led her in a successful battle for Mirial. Surely he deserved her respect. Layela bounced the baby and tried to calm her own rising anger. That would not help soothe the child.

"We think it was simply an earthquake, but we're looking for signs of attack."

"Thank you," Ardin said, obviously dismissing her. Loran hesitated for a moment, but when Layela didn't turn to acknowledge her, she bowed and exited with the other guards in tow. As soon as the door closed, Ardin began picking up the fallen frames and putting them back up on the walls.

"She's an idiot," Layela said.

Ardin shot her a quick grin. "I know, but I'm more concerned about what that was about."

Ardice had stopped crying but now was in full hiccups. "Probably just an earthquake, like she said." Layela said as she cooed the child. What did one do for hiccups?

"An earthquake on Mirial? Is that even possible, without you setting it off?"

Layela stiffened. "What's that supposed to mean?"

Ardin sighed. "Nothing like what it sounded. Just that the planet is controlled by ether." He glanced at Layela. "You're exhausted. Let me take her."

"I've got her, thanks," she mumbled. Ardice was finally calming, her little eyes drooping. Layela sighed.

"I'm sorry. I shouldn't have snapped. I'm just tired."

Ardin gave her a hesitant smile. "With reason. Don't worry about it. Get some sleep, and I'll figure out what happened."

Layela sank into the deep cushions of a chair. "You're right. An earthquake shouldn't just happen. Maybe Ardice triggered it. Maybe it takes some time for the child to adjust. I don't know. Nothing in the histories or legends tells me anything. I guess my mother would have been the one to inform me."

Ardin sat on the coffee table in front of her, balancing his elbows on his thighs as he leaned forward. He reached out and gently touched Ardice's cheek. "We'll figure it out. Every new parent has challenges."

Layela raised an eyebrow. "Planet shattering challenges?"

Ardin grinned. "When the mother is so powerful, why not?"

Layela felt tears gather in her eyes and looked down so that Ardin wouldn't see them. This was ridiculous. She was too tired. She needed sleep.

Ardin stood up and kissed the top of her head. "I'll be back," he whispered. She waited for the door to close gently before lifting her head up again. Her arm was red and angry—proof that she had not imagined Mirial's attack on her. She looked down at Ardice. If she was unknowingly doing this, why would she attack her own mother?

"You're just a baby," she whispered. "You don't know what you're doing." She leaned back into the cushions and let the tears stream freely down her face as she tried to sleep.

***

Layela woke with her chin on her chest, her neck aching. Ardice was sleeping in her crib, and Ardin in the bed. She wanted to kiss him for not waking her. She stretched and pulled herself out of the plush chair, every bone and muscle in her body screaming for attention. Yawning, she threw a housecoat on and walked towards the glass doors that led to her own private garden.

She didn't dare look back, afraid that if she glanced at either Ardice or Ardin, they would wake up and she would lose this moment. Since taking on the mantle of Keeper of Mirial, she had not had the chance for much peace. It seemed someone always wanted something from her, whether a negotiation, an acknowledgement, a comforting word. Half the time she wasn't sure what was expected of her, and afterwards she wasn't sure what she had provided.

Moments like this were her favourite. The quiet times, when she was left alone with her gardens.

I suppose I'll have fewer of these moments now, with Ardice around. Guilt clutched her and she quickly pushed the thought out of her mind. She closed the glass doors behind her and took a deep breath coated with flowery perfumes. She smiled and the weight on her chest dissipated. The sun was just rising, a soft glow cast upon her gardens. She could sense the magic of Mirial infusing into everything it touched, from the flowers to the land itself, to every inhabitant that dwelt here. She tried not to think of the Mirialers. She needed this moment just for herself.

The star seemed to know she was awake and it greeted her with long soothing waves of warmth. She carefully returned the greeting, or hoped she did. Her arm was covered by the long sleeve of the light cotton shirt she wore. The ether seemed content this morning, a white mist clinging to the entire world. Layela stared at it, expecting it to leap up at any second. She glanced back at her room. All was quiet within. Ardice still slept, and if she was the cause of the spikes, then all should be quiet until she picked another fit.

"Please stay calm," Layela implored the ether around her.

When it didn't react, she sighed and redirected her attention to her garden, crouching down to work on the flowers. She didn't need to weed, at least not here. Just as she could encourage a plant to grow, she could discourage certain types from taking hold in the soil. To stop her more precious flowers from being smothered.

But the plants still needed her. They sometimes needed water, and other times to be trimmed. They needed encouragement to grow, or sometimes to sleep. Layela had always been good with plants, which was what had inspired her to own a flower shop—it felt like a lifetime ago. But on Mirial, where the earth was infused with ether she could control, her garden was by far the most beautiful patch of plants she had ever managed to grow.

To the right, a plant seemed slightly out of place. Layela sighed. "Good morning, Elsa."

The Berganda rose from where she had been sleeping, looking embarrassed at having been found. "I'm sorry, Layela. I just…wanted to be closer to you." Eyes downcast, she grew quiet.

Layela walked towards the Berganda. "Are you all right?"

Elsa nodded, but Layela could see terror in the young woman's green eyes, still frightened from the ether's strike just yesterday. Guilt tackled her chest. The Berganda were daughters of her best friend, children who relied completely on her as though she were their mother. They had lain writhing on the floor, and she had not even bothered to check up on them, too concerned with her own need for sleep.

"It's okay to be scared, Elsa," Layela took a step forward and gathered the Berganda close to her. The bare flesh of her arms came in contact with Elsa's. A slight prickling sensation, not entirely unpleasant, spread where contact was made. Ether creatures affected humans in strange ways, but Layela was now barely affected.

Elsa returned the hug, still tense in Layela's arms.

She broke away. "What happened, Mother Layela?" Her eyes were wide and white against the green skin, green hair tumbling wildly around the slight face. Elsa was the oldest of Josmere's children, and had already seeded children of her own, but still Layela saw her as a little girl.

Which, at five years of age, she really is.

Her first instinct was to lie, but she stopped herself. If Elsa was about to sprout daughters of her own, if Solaria was about to pay Mirial a visit, as was inevitable now, it would do no good to keep the Berganda in the dark.

"I don't know, Elsa." She paused. *Such an enlightening statement.* She managed a slight smile. "I guess that's not useful. But I honestly don't know what happened to the ether. Ardice's birth must have shifted some of the power, but I don't understand how."

Elsa didn't nod this time.

"Could it happen again?"

A pit burned through Layela's stomach. "I hope not, Elsa. I'll do my best to stop whatever it was."

Layela strained to hear Elsa's whispered words: "The children felt it."

Layela closed her eyes, the tears threatening to overwhelm her. *How could one small child do all of this?*

"Are they all right?"

Another whisper. "I think so. I soothed them. But they would probably gain strength from your songs, as well."

A slight breeze toyed with the flowers and shifted the perfumes surrounding them. Layela smiled. She had sung to Josmere's firstborns practically every day before they had sprouted. Elsa swore she could remember, though Layela wasn't convinced. Still, an unsprouted Berganda might not be like an unborn human. The Berganda had grown quickly, after all, and were sentient and aware of the world around them from the very beginning.

Unlike Ardice. Ardice, who had already harmed so many without understanding what she was doing.

Elsa broke the silence. "It felt like I was reaching out of my skin, while it crumbled around me." She bit her lower lip. "It hurt. Why would Mirial hurt her own children so?"

Layela resisted the urge to gather her in her arms again. "I'm sure Mirial did not mean it to happen."

Elsa nodded. Layela kept the fake smile plastered on her face, no longer certain if she was putting on an act for the Berganda or for herself. She could see the Berganda, and then meet with her Court Advisor. That would cover the entire day. With any luck, she would get a few moments with Ardin and Ardice.

"Come on, let's go see the Berganda." Elsa seemed to take heart and returned the smile.

Layela sighed as they quietly headed back inside the room. Her flowers would remain unattended for another day.

***

"She cares for the plants and the planet," Murl listened to her oldest brother argue. He hunched his large frame forward to add intensity to his words.

Her younger brother quickly interjected, motioning all around him with thin his arms, as though to encompass all of Mirial. "But what about the people? It is the people that make Mirial. Not its vegetation and worms."

Murl grinned and took a swig of water. She could drink ale instead, but after a lifetime of being deprived of pure drinking water, it was too refreshing to pass up for that yellow filth.

Her panel beeped near her and her breath caught in her throat. She leapt up, as did her two brothers. The land around them was still and quiet, a small cave in one of the many scorched deserts of Mirial. Her village jutted from the ground several hours' walk away. A few houses and gardens for food, surrounded by endless desert. Murl had not dared set up the equipment near her village, in case the signal should be followed and their village attacked. The beep sounded again from where the communications equipment lay perched on a rocky shelf.

A light flared to life.

"Is that them?" she asked in a whisper. Her youngest brother walked up to it and looked down, turning to grin at them. It had worked.

They had managed to intercept Solaria's incoming notice of their arrival. She allowed herself a sigh of relief. Contact with Solaria was theirs, and not Layela's. The Keeper's fragile alliance with their galaxy's greatest power would be crushed and reformed under their vision, giving them ultimate power over Mirial's destiny.

Now that they had secured her political connections, it was time to tighten the noose on her greatest power, her only power: the ether of Mirial.

CHAPTER 4

SOMETIMES LAYELA STILL felt as though she would awaken from a dream at any given second. Not that she'd ever known dreams, really, aside from her own dark visions, but she had always imagined they would very much feel like this room. Warm and velvety, and as cushy as the pillows on this chair. She leaned back into them, letting herself be fully supported. Gresko frowned and paused, but surprised Layela by simply continuing his lecture without reprimanding her posture, as he usually would.

Maybe giving birth and everything that followed actually won me a reprieve!

Plenty of what she had done had left a bitter taste in her advisor's mouth, she was certain. He droned on, quoting historic texts and listing off ether races she had never even heard of, who would more than likely ask to be received in court to meet their future Keeper— their queen, by any other name. Layela flinched a bit at that. She was queen of very little, in reality, guardian of a planet with low population and no trading power. But the ether races considered her their queen, at least in title.

Layela interrupted. "What happens when a daughter is born, Gresko?" He frowned, either at the question or the interruption. "I mean, I know it means that the throne is secure and Mirial is safe, but what does it mean to the ether. How is responsibility passed down from mother to daughter? Is anything written down?"

Gresko visibly tried to smooth the frown from his forehead. He cleared his throat. "Mirial sees to that, Lady Layela. When Mirial is ready, you will know."

Layela sighed. She had learned by now that this was Gresko's standard reply for anything that he didn't understand or that wasn't written down in the histories. The advisor proved useful in very much the same way a good reference program did, but she wished he possessed the ability to combine information and deduce from it.

Layela felt a tug at her mind, and a stream of gentle visions began to invade her thoughts. Nothing made sense, mostly colours and noise. She understood it to be Ardice playing with the ether.

Layela stood abruptly, and Gresko jumped to his feet, sending papers flying.

"Thank you for your counsel as always, Gresko," Layela said, trying to remember some of what he had told her. "Please make preparations for those who will be coming, and make sure that all those who need to be invited to meet Ardice are, in fact, invited. I leave it in your capable hands."

He nodded. Layela gave him a strained smile and walked quickly back towards the room, two guards trailing her silently. She wished she could be permitted peace and solitude, but those could only be found in rare moments in her garden.

She turned to the guards. "Kyle, Murl," she addressed them, nodding to each. "I wish to see Loran. Could you please ask her to join me in my chambers?" Kyle bowed and immediately turned around. Murl followed suit.

The final conflict for Mirial. *The Great Darkness.* Those words sounded strange to her now. Only yesterday a child was born with the power to change everything, again. Layela suddenly understood that there had never been a final conflict for Mirial. And there never would be. Mirial, source of all ether, would always be a source of conflict.

Layela's stomach turned into a river of acid. She walked to the gurgling child, the nanny bowing her head respectfully before leaving quietly. Layela bent down and took the child in her arms.

Ardice gurgled and looked straight back at her mother. Layela looked at the green and blue eyes, at the dimple on her right cheek, the small round mouth and tuft of dark hair. She looked and the baby looked back until her daughter grew bored and started looking elsewhere—the rich curtains of their bed, the light streaming in through the window, the portrait of Ardin's old ship, *Destiny*. And Layela wanted to whisk her away, far away, where Mirial could never find them again.

Layela had fought hard at first to survive, and then to exist. And she still fought to survive and exist, smothered by Mirial's ether and her court's traditions. She held the child and saw the future laid out before her, without Layela's wild escapes and sketchy childhood, but rather with the certainty of ruling a planet, actions dictated by the traditions of women centuries or even millennia dead. Layela looked at her daughter and felt overwhelming love and fear—Ardice would grow up to be little more than a symbol.

Layela had not cared about Mirial's history, about her own past, until yesterday. Now it affected more than just herself, and she didn't know how much she could protect her daughter. Would Ardice grow up content with just being a symbol? Remembering her sister Yoma's antics and passion, the same sister who had given up everything to see that Layela survived, Layela knew she had to offer options to her daughter. It was the least she could do, as a mother. Ardin would understand, she was certain. She would discuss with him later how to do that, without creating too much of a backlash. She wondered if the Keeper was really necessary. Why have all of the powers of the universe dependent on one fallible human?

She needed answers. She needed to start to unravel the ribbon of destiny that was beginning to tangle them all.

***

A soft knock came at the door. Layela threw on a cloak to ward off the morning chill. Ardice slept in her crib, her rosy cheeks matching the down that covered her. Layela blew her a kiss and prayed to Mirial that she would remain calm.

She opened the door to find Loran waiting patiently. Loran had been second-in-command of Mirial's flagship, *Victory*. She was now in charge of security, even if the title had mostly been awarded to her for her courage and loyalty. She was infuriatingly traditional at times, especially for someone who had grown up off planet, but Layela still trusted her above most other Mirialers.

Layela smiled at Loran. "I wish to go to the temple, and I would like for you to stay with Ardice and protect her."

Loran stiffened. "You're going alone?"

"You may provide an escort to the bridge, but no further." Layela summoned her most queenly tone of voice. "This is not up for debate."

Loran bowed stiffly. She turned to Murl. "Escort the Keeper. Remain at the bridge until she returns. If you hear anything that needs investigating, enter the temple." Loran shot a quick look at Layela to see if she would argue, but Layela held her peace. She could only ask so much of her royal guards.

She could feel the ether dancing around her daughter, and needed answers sooner rather than later. At least she knew Ardice would be safe with Loran. The woman could be thick-headed at times, and sometimes refused to acknowledge Ardin, but she was loyal to a fault and would ensure Ardice's safety before her own.

The reports had been trickling in from Solaria and from the other ether creatures, who were terrified after their brief loss of control. *Like a beast devouring our bodies from within,* some had said. *Excruciating.* She had felt their pain and tasted the deaths that had surrounded them. She pulled her cloak closer.

Solarian ships were entering her solar system and, even if they had not yet made signs of attack, Layela feared it was only a matter of time. Especially given the death counts on Solaria so far.

She needed answers, fast. She needed to stop the occurrences, or at least ensure she could protect Mirial in case of an attack. She needed to know that she could trust Mirial and the ether to protect her and her people. Right now, she wasn't certain of any of it.

But she knew where to find the answers. She had connected with Mirial so strongly once before that her control over the ether had allowed her to even bring Ardin back to life. She was certain it had been due to her location. Mirial would speak to her there again, through the temple, the strongest point of ether and most sacred area on the planet.

Which was also her sister's final resting place, after the final bargain with Mirial that had sealed her fate.

CHAPTER 5

GRESKO LISTAN REMAINED in the sitting room long after Keeper Layela's departure, glancing at the richness around him. The room itself dated back more than a millennia, and had suffered almost no damage during Mirial's latest trials, unlike most of the rest of the palace. Its lofty arches were said to be maintained by ether, the stone and glass fragments constructed at dangerously sharp angles which should not have held without bonding materials. And yet there were none, just carefully cut and assembled rocks and sky-coloured pieces of glass locking into one another, reflecting the sun from the high windows, angled just right so that rain never infiltrated, no matter the direction or ferocity of winds.

Buttresses on the walls mimicked the ceiling, also casting light from windows placed beyond them, giving the palace the illusion of being light itself, from a distance. The room did not adhere to a simple four-wall pattern, but instead many smaller walls and buttresses jogged all around them, forcing the furniture towards the middle of the room. Only plants adorned the walls, fitting given the light here, and the Keeper's eternal love of plants.

The throne room next door shared many of the sitting room's features. Viewed together from high above, they formed the symbol of Mirial. Every other room in the palace worked in unison to support the symbol, as though Mirial's fate rested on the inhabitants of the palace.

And few understood that symbolism as well as Gresko Listan. For generations, the daughters of this family most graced with ether had tended to the people, plants and life force of Mirial. And, in turn to all of the ether creatures, in a carefully balanced, nurtured ecosystem. The entire universe depended on this.

Even the carefully maintained records of Mirial failed to mention, deliberately or not, why Mirial needed Keepers, and why this particular bloodline had been chosen. But Gresko understood that they were just as human as anyone else, despite their ties to limitless power. Some were more powerful than others, some were more godlike. The current queen's mother, Kilasha, had been a rock, almost a goddess in her own right. She had been more than a queen; she had been a powerhouse. He had begun his career under her, working with her and the captain of the royal guards, Zortan Mistolta, to bring unity to Mirial. He had not always agreed with her methods, but he had known she would bring great change to Mirial.

Or so he had hoped. He looked up at the sunlight streaming near him, the warm sun of Mirial hitting the red velvet of the chair right beside his. He had sat here with Queen Kilasha, long ago.

Before she had given birth to twins. And then, in a moment of what he could only attribute to insanity, she had doomed them all by betraying that which she had vowed to always protect. She had insisted that both twins be saved, instead of ritually killing one at birth, as the law decreed.

The law existed for a reason and it had been Gresko's job to maintain it. But he had been a fool, trusted his queen, and agreed to stay outside the birthing chamber, truly believing only one child would be saved. If one had been a boy, as the queen's first labour had been, he would have whisked the child away, as he had done before. And if female twins, he would have taken care of killing the second child, as was his duty as principal advisor to the throne.

And so he had waited, in this very chair. Like a fool, he had believed everything would work out. That the Keeper, *his* Keeper, would continue to perform her sacred duty. And, like a fool, he had failed in his duty.

The Keeper, weakened by childbirth, had assigned the captain of the royal guards to take the daughters far away. And he had. His loyalty, unlike Gresko's, had been to the Keeper. Gresko's was sworn to Mirial herself.

And so Mirial had perished, struck with storms of ether so great it was hidden for twenty years, until the twins, Yoma and Layela, returned to save them. But still, one of them had to die. The story still had the same ending, because Mirial had written it so long ago. Why had it been necessary for so many to die and suffer for their Keeper's inability to act out her duties?

Gresko had lost everyone, that day. He continued to serve the throne without fail, providing the best advice. Lady Layela was his third Keeper. Had she been brought up on Mirial, chances are she would have been excellent. But she clung to the customs and traditions of Solaria. Had she given birth to a boy, he was certain she would have kept him, too. She insisted on announcing to everyone, or at least making it painfully obvious, that Ardin Malavant was her chosen consort. The ladies of Mirial always hid such details— the Keepers were meant to be like queens—like gods—and their dalliances were not for mere mortals to know.

Yet the Lady Layela insisted on clinging to the life of a mortal, as though not understanding that she was meant to be so much more. Gresko had begun to suspect that her almost twenty Solarian years away from Mirial had ruined her beyond repair.

He ran his hand on the soft velvet, up to the dark wood of the armchair. He had just sat here once, a long time ago, when he could have been preventing Mirial's downfall.

He stood up, pulled his jacket straight and lifted his chin, and strode out of the great sitting room which formed half the symbol of Mirial.

He did not intend to make that mistake twice.

***

The temple stood before her, the symbol of Mirial etched into the highest point of the roof, the stone still collapsed in certain areas. Its sides were scorched with the fires that had almost swallowed the planet of Mirial whole on the day of Layela's birth.

The palace had been restored over the past five years of Layela's reign, but she had yet to allow the workers to touch the temple. It had always been sacred to those of Mirial, but for Layela, it was the graveyard of her sister, Yoma, as well.

She looked up towards the temple, which had once been part of Layela's darkest vision, harkening her death or her sister's. The bridge before the temple had been reinforced to make it safe, to stop stones from falling into the chasm.

And it was just about here that she had been stabbed, to bleed out in her sister's arms as she carried her across the bridge to the temple. The temple was more than her sister's graveyard—it was hers, too. She had died here, only brought back by her sister's gamble to exchange her soul for Layela's. Layela shivered, remembering the moment of extreme pain and fear, and then the warmth of death, of being welcomed into Mirial herself. And then being ripped away to awaken to a wounded body, a dead sister, and a final battle that had almost cost her Ardin.

The temple was not a place of contemplation or love for her, as she imagined it had been for generations of women before her. She hadn't dared return since her sister's death.

She took a deep breath and walked towards the bridge. The wind was picking up, promising a storm, her purple velvet cloak billowing in the wind around her. She lowered her head to hide her face and make sure her hood stayed on, and walked onto the bridge. She sensed she was no longer followed. The royal guards stayed their ground on the bridge, but she was certain Murl and her soldiers would come racing in if she cried for them. It gave her little comfort.

She could swear she could still see faint traces of her own blood, as she had bled her last on the threshold of the great temple of Mirial.

She focused her attentions on the temple ahead, instead. It must have been formidable in its prime. The three great pillars adorning the front were carved in stylized depictions of the Three Fates. Their flowing robes billowed and formed the base of the pillars, and upon their heads rested the great arch with the symbol of Mirial.

The first Fate looked back towards the temple, the second sideways, and the third straight towards incomers. Layela was uncertain why that was, but she knew that legends accorded them power over the destinies of all creatures. It was one of the few myths consistently spread across time, planets and belief systems, as far as Layela knew.

She crossed by two of the Fates and walked into the darkened temple. As soon as she crossed the threshold, light infiltrated again from the broken roof. The temple was simple, with a stream hugging its interior walls, where Yoma had been laid to rest. And petrified trees still jutted, silent guardians of this cemetery.

Layela pushed back her hood and hesitated. She wanted to talk to

Mirial, to reach out to the First Star, to find out what was happening with the ether and how she could help fix it. The only place she had ever truly known Mirial to be listening had been here, at the temple.

Layela shivered and forced herself to focus on the altar ahead, where Yoma had mixed her blood with Layela's to summon Mirial's energies.

Of course. The blood was the link. She crossed the stream to stand near the altar.

The knife that so long ago had killed Layela and doomed Yoma was still there. Its jewel-encrusted handle would have been considered beautiful by anyone else, but Layela knew that the knife's sole purpose through the ages had been to slay a twin, should one be born to the queen.

With ice crystals forming on her spine, Layela reached for the handle. The blade was still encrusted with old blood. Fighting back the onslaught of grief, Layela quickly brought up her other hand and sliced the palm, watching her blood trickle down into the altar.

CHAPTER 6

PATROS PACED THE cramped quarters, wrinkling his nose at the strange smell that seemed to permeate the entire vessel. His room was small but not uncomfortable, and he knew he should be grateful for being saved, even if his saviour was rather unconventional. He sat back down on the coarse, old blankets on the bed. He hoped he was just imagining the layer of dust pirouetting up into the air.

His fingers were tingling, so the old, rough wool was a comfort. He could feel it through the numbness. His throat was slightly clamped and his lungs sighed deeply with each breath. He lowered his head into his hands, his elbows resting on his knees. What had happened to him? How could he have lost control so easily? And to what? Was something happening to Mirial again?

"It can't be," he mumbled, his spine tingling with a gripping chill. Slonts were one of the longer-lived races of Mirial. He was fifty, and could perhaps live for three or four centuries. Though he was young, for his people, and had left home only recently, he recalled the ether wars of thirty-some years ago. He recalled how so many of his brothers, his cousins and his own father passed away. His mother had never been the same. He also remembered twenty years of being cut off from the ether, powers dwindling, the ability to connect to other ether creatures blocked. Even the elements had ceased revealing their properties to his people, a thin layer of powder sheltering the very finest of details from their eyes, until they could no longer see the properties of objects, but rather just their appearance.

It had been…terrifying.

But the new Keeper had changed all of that. She had freed the ether and saved so many of Mirial's children—the ether races that the humans feared so much.

He sighed and stood, flexing his muscles. The flow of blood would return. He took a deep breath and concentrated on the wall of the ship, until his eyes revealed the simplest compounds and the intricacy of the metal. It was manmade, of course. Humans loved to show superiority over a world they didn't, couldn't fully grasp, by changing its natural order. But he could see this was still interesting work. He was one of the few of his race able to appreciate the complex beauty of these synthetic materials, which was why he had embraced leaving home, and not feared it as so many of his people did.

A chime, mere seconds before the door slid open.

"Name's Avienne. How are you?" the red-headed captain of this vessel said, the grin on her face not hiding the concern in her eyes.

"Um, Patros. I'm well, thank you." He nodded slightly. He did not know humans well enough to read them as effectively as he read their ships, but she seemed genuine enough. And she had saved his life.

"And thank you for saving me."

She shrugged. "Seemed like the thing to do. Sorry about your friend."

"My friend? Ah, yes. We were more like business partners," he answered quickly, automatically.

"Ah, I see. You're one of those ether creatures, then."

"What?"

"The ones who are too good to make friends with humans." She sighed expansively. "I was hoping for a friendly one."

"I'm not…I mean…" He flushed, and knew his skin would glow blue. Her laughter bounced off the walls.

"Don't worry. I don't take it personally. You're cute in full blue, though." She winked at him, and he could feel his skin's flush deepen. She grew serious.

"Do you know anything about ships?"

His turn to shrug. "I'm not a sailor, but I know enough to get around."

"Good. Then you're needed on the bridge. I didn't realize most of my crew had deserted when I hauled you on board."

"Your crew deserted?"

She winced. "Well, we haven't been turning a profit, I fear. Nothing personal. Just business. Or so I'm told. But a few stayed!" she added defensively. "Well, two, anyway."

Not knowing what to reply, he kept silent. The ship shook slightly, and the proximity alerts went off. Avienne pulled out a leadcom. She whistled as she looked at the update.

"We've got company. Let's go."

She turned on her heels and was gone, leaving Patros to stumble after her, wondering what he had gotten himself into now.

***

The tunnels, usually empty save for a few trading vessels, were filled with ships. And they were all headed in the same direction as Avienne. She accelerated slightly to keep up with them, her proximity alarms pulsing softly on the tactical control panel. Most ships had transponders, well-registered and stored in the Solarian databases. Jaru, the systems analyst, mumbled in a corner, his hands flying over his station. Only pausing to chug coffee, he fed her the information on all of the ships.

Some belonged to ambassadors from random worlds, no doubt come to welcome the new heir of Mirial and try to get in good with Avienne's brother and Layl. *Fat good that'll do you.* Her brother had about as much patience for cheap shows of solidarity as she did.

But it wasn't those ships that worried her. Those were fine. Predictable, even. It was the few unmarked ships, of unknown models and origin, which worried her. Well, those and the few Solarian military ships. Those were worrisome, too.

She shook her head. They'd mobilized too quickly. They must have been anticipating problems when the heir was born. Or they were planning on attacking all along, while the planet was celebrating the birth of her niece or nephew.

She narrowed her eyes at the closed shutters. She wished she could just open them and have a look at those unmarked ships. She needed to know where they hailed from. Maybe a symbol would betray them. Perhaps they were from Mirial, too? Her blood tingled with excitement even as it boiled at the sight of the Solarian fleet. Her first officer, Larod, a broad shouldered middle-aged man from a seafaring world, was casting curious glances her way.

She opened the lines of communications to see if anyone was

chatting, but all was dead silent. Unless some of the ships were chatting on closed frequencies, it seemed everyone was just intent on reaching their goal.

The elevator doors slid open. The Slont! He'd finally followed her up, looking apprehensively at his surroundings.

"I need your help," she immediately said, grinning.

"Okay." He couldn't have seemed less willing if he just turned around and run off the bridge.

"You can look out at some of the surrounding ships, and you won't get seizures like the rest of us would. I'm bringing us beside an unmarked ship now. Have a look at it and tell me if there are any marks on its side."

He just nodded this time and walked near the viewing port. Good enough.

"Larod, open her up," she ordered. Larod shook his head and mumbled something to Jaru. They both looked down as the shutters opened, the light of the bridge throbbing blue and white, giving the impression of being underwater during a sunny day, except the pulsation was wrong. It was too rhythmic, too fast, and too unnatural. Her pulse accelerated.

"Well, what do you see?"

"It's hard to make anything out, the light is bouncing off everything. I think most of these are Solarian."

"Most of them are," she snapped. "The one on our left. What make is that?"

He paused. "There's nothing there."

She almost looked up before lowering her head again. "What do you mean, nothing there? I can see them with our sensors!"

"Well, it's not there," he sounded just as annoyed as she was, now.

Avienne risked looking up quickly, glancing to the left. He was right. All she could see were blinks of white and blue, pinpricks of brilliant light forming the tunnels as the ships rode them to distances far away.

She looked for only two seconds, and next thing she knew she was on the ground, Larod's concerned face leaning over her. She swore he always smelled of salt and fish, even if he'd given up the sea years ago. She tried to speak but choked instead.

"You shouldn't have looked," Patros said as he leaned beside her. "I wasn't lying when I said there was nothing there."

Avienne managed a half laugh and grabbed his gloved hand so he could pull her up. He was stronger than she would have imagined, easily hauling her to her feet. She wasn't heavy by any means, but she was tall and muscled enough to realize the ether creature was not frail. As she let go of his gloved hand, she wondered what powers Slonts possessed. Like all other ether creatures, most of their powers seemed to derive from their hands, and skin on skin contact. Hence the regulation gloves—a Solarian initiative against something they perceived as threatening.

Larod reached down and closed the shutter. "Never a dull moment."

Avienne's head played the drums to which her stomach somersaulted.

"So we have invisible ships, then," she said, mostly to shift the cotton in her mouth.

To his credit, the Slont did not suggest she lie down or, even worse, seek medical help.

"Invisible to the eyes only. At least our sensors can perceive them."

"For now," Avienne mumbled.

"What do you mean?"

"They're probably just caught in the wake of the tachyons, like the rest of us, and are letting us see them so we don't bounce into them," Jaru said. "Or they can't stop the tachyons from licking their hulls and revealing them. I mean, the sensors can pick up giant spots without tachyons in them. Maybe it's a combination of both?"

The Slont looked worried. "What do you think they want? Will they make trouble for the Keeper?"

Avienne managed to stop her eyes from rolling. She was worried too, but hearing a perfect stranger worrying about Layela because she was "Keeper" was both weird and annoying. This was family business, not random blue stranger business.

"Probably," Avienne said, and then she grinned at him. "But don't worry, we'll help."

He looked at her sceptically but again kept his mouth wisely shut.

"Sit down and relax," she suggested as she sat, herself. "We're not going anywhere for a few hours." She added in a mumble, "Well, I mean, we're going to Mirial, but we're stuck in this tunnel."

"I've never seen Mirial," Patros whispered wistfully. Avienne didn't respond.

What could she say about the homeworld that she kept running away from?

***

As soon as they cleared the tunnel, Avienne opened the shutters. Patros hissed as he looked upon Mirial, the sunlight filtering into the ship and outlining the sharp contours of his face. His skin seemed bluer now, even though they were only at the edge of the solar system where the sun barely shone.

"It's beautiful," he whispered. Avienne doubted they were seeing the same things, her eyes too human to perceive the myriad of ether she suspected he saw. Still, she agreed that it was beautiful. The sun was calm now, but unlike other stars, it didn't seem definite in its colour. It wasn't yellow, or red, or even white. It was a mix of colours, sometimes yellow, other times blue, and then purple. It wasn't an invasive shift in colour, only noticeable at the outer edges of its fires, where the ether left the sun to drift out toward the rest of the universe. But it marked this sun as different than any other.

"Larod, bring us to Mirial," she ordered, and he set a course for the planet bearing the same name as her sun, the only planet left in the solar system after the ether had gone wild more than twenty years ago. A wildness that Layela now ensured would not reoccur.

Avienne had last left Mirial two months ago. And now she was rushing back, with Solarian ships deployed around her, diplomatic ships from planets she hadn't even heard of, and invisible ships. She checked her sensors.

"We can't see them anymore." Avienne mumbled. Patros kept silent. He looked intently towards the approaching planet.

Avienne flicked on her outbound communications and set it to the proper channel. She grinned at Jaru, who returned the smile. Mirial was his home, too, even if he'd lived in exile for twenty years. "Mirial, this is Avienne Malavant from the *Dessicate*. Permission to approach palace for landing."

Patros' eyes grew almost as wide as his face. He hadn't expected them to receive access to the palace. He had no clue who she was. An advantage of Mirial's obsession with keeping Ardin's name out of their communications and histories. No one knew the consort's name, or that a consort even existed, so no one could guess she was related to the royal family of Mirial.

She shot him a grin.

"*Dessicate*, this is the Mirial Palace Port. Please enter atmosphere and begin approach. You're cleared for landing. Transmitting approach vector." A pause, and Avienne held her breath, waiting for the customary greeting. "Welcome home, sailor."

She smiled, surprised at the tears gathering in her eyes. She quickly looked down so Patros wouldn't see them.

How could she love a home so fiercely she wept every time she reached it again, and yet hate it so deeply she could never stay longer than a few days?

Blood and bones, she needed a drink.

***

The air of Mirial was so fresh it made her lungs ache. Sweet nectar and blooming flowers scented the air around them, even in the docks, where usually the stench of worn metal and leaking combustibles reigned.

Patros walked with her, not too near nor too far. He wasn't a coward, but hardly a fool, either. She suddenly wondered how old he was. He didn't strike her as overly young, yet he seemed innocent to her, or perhaps simply too accepting. And it would be hard to find out more in any Solarian database. There was still a tentative peace, in the wake of the Ether Wars, but not because of attempts at understanding between the races. She looked down to his hands, covered by leather gloves stamped with the insignia of Solaria, and she couldn't help but wonder how long the ether creatures would be content living under a treacherous rule.

A worry for another life. She hoped.

He caught her looking at him and arched an eyebrow.

"You still haven't explained to me why we have access to the palace."

She grinned. "I have family here. And it looks like they're going to need help. I'm not convinced all of those other ships were friendly. Especially the invisible ones."

He nodded and looked away. She walked towards the palace entrance and he followed her, looking at every detail as though drinking pure water for the first time in his life.

"Avienne!" She heard the shout before she saw her brother walking towards her, a grin on his face. The gap between them was quickly closed and they hugged, his taller frame picking hers up, making her grunt.

He let her go and although a grin still graced his lips, she quickly noted the dark rims under his eyes and the poor hue of his skin.

"You look like shit," she said nonchalantly. He grimaced.

"And I don't even need to be drunk all the time to look like this."

She laughed. Blood and bones, it was good to see Ardin again.

"Who's this?" He enquired. He shot her a speculative look and she shot him one of warning. Laughter danced in his eyes.

"This is Patros. He's a Slont. Patros, this is my brother, Ardin."

The Slont lowered his head slightly.

She chimed in before Ardin could speak. "Patros, you're free to go, too, wherever you'd like. We can find you transportation."

He pondered for a moment. "I would like to stay on Mirial, for now." He looked around longingly and took a deep breath of the fresh air. He gave a smile, showing perfect white teeth, which surprised Avienne. "I have waited a long time to meet the Mother of All Ether."

Avienne nodded. Ether talk made her uncomfortable. She turned to Ardin.

"And I've waited a long time to meet this child of yours. Um, boy or girl?"

He forced a smile. "Girl."

"Ah. Let the celebrations begin, I guess."

Ardin's smile thinned. She had hoped, for Ardin and Layela's sake, that the first child would be a boy. Less pressure on everyone involved.

"I'll take you to her. You have to tell me what's happening out there, too. We've been receiving so many conflicting messages that we're not sure what to expect anymore."

"What about that small Solarian fleet surrounding you?" she asked casually.

He shrugged. "Not surrounding us yet. They're still at the edges of the solar system. Only twenty ships at most. We've sent them a welcoming message, and they've responded politely. We'll see."

She nodded. She didn't ask, but she doubted Mirial had much of a fleet. It would be an easy victory for Solaria. But, then again, Mirial was full of ether. She noted the guards nearby and could hear the sound of construction. She doubted these were further renovations, and knew her brother would be fortifying the palace against attack.

Defences were good, but a good offensive would be better.

"I'll come find you later, Patros," she said as they began walking away.

"Feel free to explore," Ardin added. "The gardens are beautiful, and ether creatures always find them soothing. They're Layela's specialty."

Avienne noticed Patros grew still, but she didn't bother wondering why. Ether creatures were mysterious at the best of times, and these weren't the best of times. Perhaps some time to relax would loosen him back up.

She quickly forgot about him as she followed her brother into the palace, flowering vines clinging even within the walls, a gift of the Berganda, no doubt. She saw a few wandering, looking lost, their green skin and hair slightly yellowed.

"Are they all right?" she whispered to Ardin.

He looked at her grimly and whispered. "Things have been strange with the ether since Ardice's birth."

She glanced back at them, remembering a Berganda she had befriended long ago, who had sported the same yellow hues before passing away.

Being on Mirial always brought back random tidbits of the battle five years ago. Friends lost; her beloved home, *Destiny*, burning up in the atmosphere; her brother almost dying. Her skin crawled with bits of unwanted memories.

They reached the private quarters of the royal family, the sheer purple curtains dancing in the hallway with the gentle breeze, casting shadows and light from the magical star that had taken so much from them all.

Given them life, but taken so much in return.

CHAPTER 7

THE BLOOD SPLATTERED into the altar and Layela looked at it, keeping her palm over it, the wound still bleeding. She waited, holding her breath as a tiny pool formed within the worn stone bowl, blending with its encrusted blood. She imagined the stench of blood coating her entire body. She could sense the ether in everything. It danced around her, flourished in the great silent trees behind her, skimmed in the river below her, and nourished the very air around her. Yet it did not respond to her summon, did not even flinch at her blood.

Nothing happened. She had been wrong. She couldn't contact Mirial this way. This channel must have been closed long ago.

Feeling sick and relieved, Layela closed her hand on the wound. Water dripped from the ceiling into the rivulet that circled the inside of the temple walls. The sound made Layela's stomach lurch. She turned from the altar and focused on the courtyard—the great trees just as dead as the last time she was here, the stone walls still unkempt, the water stiller than it should be. She was responsible for this.

She still knew so little of this land and its traditions. But Mirialers were hesitant to teach their Keeper their own ways, as though she should automatically fit in and know them. It was foolish, and it wasn't helping her represent them adequately. Only Gresko counselled her, but mostly at her bequest. The only advice he offered on his own was to tell her she had overstepped bounds, or ignored tradition, or that her posture was poor…

"Oh Yoma, how did I get into this?" She paused and continued in a whisper. "And why am I being so difficult about it? You gave up your life so that I could live. I promise you I'll find a way to make you proud."

Layela looked up at the dead trees which adorned her sister's grave. She summoned the ether, its warmth flowing easily from her to the petrified oaks. She let the ether revitalize the sap, the bark, the very molecules that were at the core of the trees' life. She encouraged their roots to absorb the water below, where their strength led them deep.

The trees responded, their desire to live still clamped firmly, as though they had been waiting for the Keeper to awaken them from their slumber. Tears gathered in Layela's eyes. She should have come here before. Not because she had a problem to deal with, but rather to pay homage to her sister's life. The gardens of the temple were dead, and she had done nothing to bring flowers here. She, who had once owned a flower shop! What better tribute to her sister than to fill her resting place with beauty and colour?

Layela reached deeper into the well of ether, to pull more from it and feed the dormant gardens. The seeds hidden deep within could perhaps be made to stir, with the right coaxing. The ether flowed through her until she felt lightheaded and unable to breathe, as if an invisible hand had grabbed hold of her throat. She gasped, her hands rising but meeting only empty air around her neck. She tried to force breath into her lungs, but only managed to squeak. Her face was hot and her eyes stung. When she tried to scream for help, she couldn't even manage to repeat the squeak. She ran her hands around her neck, but still could feel nothing of the invisible assailant.

Then she sensed it trickling away, dancing back towards the trees and rivers… *the ether.* She leaned back and caught herself on the altar.

What was happening? She had never been attacked by her own ether. Had she done something to offend Mirial? She tried to cut off the flow, but it pounded into her instead, like a great wave of boiling oil. She managed to scream, but the sound was so weak she doubted her guards could have heard.

The temple cracked and dust streamed down around her. More cracking, and Layela lost her footing as the ground began to shake. She fell beside the altar, clutched it and pulled herself under it, tucking in her limbs as great stones collapsed around her. She tried to soothe the trembling ground, whispering to it, fighting off the intrusive ether with waves of calm, using the same lullaby she so desperately used on Ardice, who seemed taken by the same temper as Mirial…Was Ardice doing this? Was she hurt?

A great piece of wall fell near her and Layela screamed. She closed her eyes and forced her breath to calm again, and imposed her will on the ether around her. She imagined it was but a child, but a baby, afraid and alone, and she sent soothing waves down into the earth.

The tremors ended as abruptly as they had begun. Layela swallowed hard before standing. Her guards were rushing in, weapons drawn. Layela ran to them and then past them, to find Ardice before another attack came. What was her daughter doing? What was happening to her?

"Lady!" Murl cried as she passed by, her eyes wide.

"I must reach my daughter!" Layela cried, and the guards followed her closely. She ran, ignoring her exhausted body, wondering why Mirial seemed bent on destroying her.

***

Patros stood in the gardens outside the palace, looking at the ether dancing on the plants, running a gloved hand over delicate petals. It was unlike anything he had ever seen. The gardens were lovely, of course, but they also glowed with ether, so much so that it made his heart ache. All memories of desperately thirsting for the ether were washed away in the sight of these gardens, brimming with the life-giving force.

Movement caught his eye and he looked towards a Berganda, walking away from the palace. She was beautiful, in a pure kind of way. Her dress danced about her, a gauze that seemed almost sheer from a distance. Her hair danced playfully in the slight breeze, but it was her hands that drew his attention. Her hands were naked, laid out for anyone to see, or touch. A shiver ran down his spine. When he was a younger man, before the Ether Wars, he used to walk around with his hands laid bare. But now, even removing the gloves to wash seemed like a risk. Solaria held no safety and no guarantees.

But on Mirial…

Patros looked around instinctively. He looked at his hands and back to the Berganda, now vanishing on the horizon. He took a deep breath, his heart thumping his chest as he removed the gloves and secured them to his belt.

He wasn't sure what to do. The breeze licked the sweat from his hands, the soft breath of Mirial welcoming his freedom. He held his hands before him and examined them—the deep lines of his veins, the calluses where the gloves repeatedly rubbed the gentle skin that grew between Slonts' fingers, the smooth curb of his fingers where most races had yet to shed their nails.

He stared at them for some time, the hands seeming foreign to him, as though they belonged to someone else entirely. He looked down at the plants, the ether dancing invitingly.

He hesitated for a second longer and then, unable to resist, he reached down and touched a cool, smooth leaf. Its dew was cooling, and cleansed his hand.

He closed his eyes and focused on the ether and the colours and sights that exploded through his hand all the way to his mind.

***

Elsa Berganda, first sprouted daughter of the legendary Josmere Berganda and adopted daughter to Queen Layela, Keeper of Mirial, walked back to Lake Feathers, still shaken by the recent quakes. A thousand lights had flashed in her mind at once, as though Mirial pounded her repeatedly. Her sisters had felt it too, their thoughts frightened. Never in their short collective memory had Mirial been anything but a hospitable and welcoming land. But their collective memories only expanded since her birth, five years ago. The Keeper would take care of them, as she always had.

She could see the lake in the distance now, a vast expanse with the sunset rays of Mirial playfully shimmering on its surface. Beside it houses built of wood and plants composed the small Berganda settlement. The queen said that someday the Berganda would be able to coax the plants into creating a village for them, to create shifting houses like the one her mother and her mother's mother had lived in, but Elsa could still not see how. With time, the queen insisted. And then she would delight them all with stories of their mother.

Elsa smiled at the thought of Josmere and the Keeper, who were the mothers of Berganda now. She let her mind relax and felt the presence of more than two hundred sisters, a constant background hum in her mind, now filled with worry. She sent out soothing waves, and she could feel them hush, her words like water after a drought. As eldest, she had always had that impact, which was encouraged and cultivated by the Keeper, too. She cared for all of the Berganda, and knew that they were stronger with one of their own taking care of them, and not always under her care.

Especially now that they were full grown.

A pit was growing at the bottom of Elsa's stomach, to borrow a very human expression, and she couldn't quite figure it out. The chatter and hum was the same, and yet, something was missing…something so important.

A noise she hadn't heard since the recent quake.

"The children!" she screamed and broke out into a run. She couldn't sense her children anymore, just days from sprouting into full Berganda!

She ran, and her thoughts propelled the other Berganda to run, her fear so thick it now smothered the entire telepathic stream, their fears only adding to hers.

The Berganda did not usually speak much, or so they had read. But their mother used her voice with her human sisters, and Queen Layela could use telepathy but chose words instead, out of habit. So when Elsa heard one of her sisters scream to the full potential of her voice, to be followed by another and another, she knew it was over.

She reached the birthing gardens, fell amidst the yellowing children and joined the screams, shedding tears she had not even known Berganda possessed.

***

Layela reached the room as the screams slammed into her, her own scream catching in her throat as her knees buckled. Ardin held her up.

"What? What is it?" he asked calmly but firmly. Layela knew her eyes were wild. Their daughter began to scream, and Layela cooed and pulled the ether into herself, away from her daughter, forming a protective field with her body.

The mists clung to her but she forced herself to see beyond them, to keep walking, one foot in front of the other, trying to push the mists away from her daughter, the screams of the Berganda bouncing in her skull, soaking her with grief.

"Layela, what is it?" Ardin insisted, holding her shoulders to force her to focus on him.

"The Berganda," she managed to say, her voice hoarse in her ear. Ardin nodded and grabbed his sword, calling to the few royal guards to stay with her as he ran up ahead to the Berganda, not asking Layela for any elaboration. Layela followed him, but couldn't keep up with his pace, following as fast as she could, the guards uncertain what to do except to flank her.

The ether began to calm again as Ardice's breath lengthened into sleep, and Layela kept cooing and pushed the ether from her, the laments of the Berganda so strong on the wind she could taste them.

By the time she got there, so exhausted she could barely stand, the lament had fallen to a soft plaintive cry, its horror replaced with chilling acceptance. Ardin came out from the birthing gardens, shaking his head, looking as though ten more years had found him. She walked towards the garden gates.

"You don't need to go in there, Layl," Ardin said, but she shook her head and continued walking. He wisely moved out of her way and let her go through. Ardice stirred and Layela began to sing the lullaby she had sung to a dying Berganda what felt like lifetimes ago.

She sang and sang, her soft voice bouncing off the walls of the garden as she stood amongst the withered and yellowed remains of the Berganda that should have sprouted but days from now. They had been dug out by their mothers, desperate to see their children's promise of life.

Had her daughter done this? Had she wreaked such havoc within days of being born?

She sang as the tears ran unchecked down her cheeks, cradling her daughter more closely than before, assailed by a mix of love and hatred so fierce that she choked on the lullaby and fell silent. Closing her eyes, she let the mourning song of the Berganda wash over her.

CHAPTER 8

ARDIN PACED BACK and forth in the throne room, having left Layela and Ardice to rest. Avienne sat on the throne, her feet up on its side, flinging knives up and snatching them back out of the air in a lazy motion. She acted bored, but he knew her well enough to see how the deaths of the Berganda young had shaken her. Josmere had been a friend, too, and Avienne was loyal to a fault.

"This was worth the trip," she said and snatched the knife again, making it vanish with one flip of the wrist. She stood and stretched.

"Are you going to pace all day, or are we going to do something more exciting?"

Ardin stopped and looked at her. He shrugged. "I guess we could go look around the city. You could see some of the new additions, if you'd like."

Avienne arched an eyebrow so high Ardin imagined it vanishing into her hairline. "You have a fleet hanging just outside your solar system, strange rips in the ether that are shaking your planet, apparent genocide," Avienne swallowed hard, "and you suggest we go for a stroll? Unless this stroll is a pub crawl, I'm just not that interested, Ardin."

Ardin grinned. "Blood and bones, I missed you, Avienne. But stay out of Mirial's official business. If it was up to you, we'd be at war with everyone."

Avienne's laughter bounced off the high ceiling. "True. So very true. All right, we can take a walk first. I have a flask with me, and I suppose I could use some unrecycled air."

"You don't have to walk with *me*," Ardin suddenly said, looking away from Avienne to hide his grin.

"What do you mean?" She sounded genuinely confused, which entertained Ardin even more. Avienne could be really sharp but really dense, too. Especially when it came to men.

"I mean the Slont." He paused and turned to face her. "I'm more than happy to see you go on a nice romantic walk with him." He continued gravely. "You have my blessings, if that's what you came here to get."

Avienne hit him on the shoulder and grinned. "I like blue, it's a nice colour. But seriously, I saved his life, so I think he feels indebted or something."

"Slonts are like that. An honourable bunch. You wouldn't know."

"Oh? How come you know so much about them. Are you a scholar now?"

Ardin sighed. "I've had to learn a few things while on Mirial, Avienne. The whole ether thing, remember." He stretched. "I need a break from politics. Are you coming with me, or did you want to find your blue lover boy?"

A voice sprung out from the other end of the throne room. "I'm actually much too old to be a boy."

Avienne's face turned beet red. Ardin turned to face the Slont, amazed he managed to keep a straight face. "It's a pleasure to see you again, Patros. I take it your rooms are to your liking?"

Avienne snorted, already recovered. Ardin felt himself flush now. He only now realized how much he'd changed to accommodate his new role, while his sister was still pretty much doing the exact same thing they had grown up doing. Except she seemed to be an even worse smuggler than the crew of the *Destiny* had been.

"I am very grateful for your hospitality," he seemed to want to add a title, but not knowing what to say, simply nodded.

"Call me Ardin, please," Ardin said. Avienne mumbled behind him. "Or consort."

If the Slont heard her, he gave no indication of it, for which Ardin was grateful.

"Ardin," the Slont said, as though testing out the name to see if it bit. "I have concerns I wish to share with you."

Ardin sighed. "Everyone is concerned, Patros, but Layela is doing everything she can."

Patros lowered his head but kept his eyes fixed on Ardin. "I am certain the Keeper is doing everything in her power to protect Mirial and her people, but I have noted something strange that occurred with the quake."

"You mean stranger than the planet shrugging?" Avienne said.

The Slont did not crack a grin. Ardin wondered if he knew how.

"I," Patros hesitated, looking at the siblings. "I had my gloves off at the time."

Ardin sighed. "You don't need to wear those barbaric things on Mirial. We're not Solarian territory, nor do we ever intend to be."

The Slont nodded and looked down at his gloved hands, as though embarrassed by something. He did not remove the gloves.

"What do Slonts do, anyway?" Avienne asked, either to break the discomfort or out of genuine curiosity, Ardin wasn't sure.

Patros looked at her again, losing his scolded boy air. The Slont's ability to seem both old and young at once was distracting. Ardin supposed part of it was that his skin showed no sign of aging, and so Ardin had no clue of his age.

"We see clearer with our hands, with our touch." The words tumbled out faster as he grew excited. "We can see the molecular construct of items, of anything, really! It's like looking at life itself, not at the colours and shapes that our eyes see, but rather at the elements, at the basic building blocks of everything. Some of them are pure and simple, like gold, and other items are vastly complex, such as plants, or the alloys humans are so fond of creating. They claim their own beauty, too." He paused for breath and looked momentarily embarrassed by his outburst.

Avienne saved him. "That sounds wonderful."

He grinned and nodded. "It is, if only you could see…" Growing serious again, he continued. "When the quake struck, I was touching some of the plants that the Keeper encouraged to grow. They bask in ether, and I can see it too, in their basic construct. It's as if once it's in, the ether becomes part of their being. But something strange happened. It wouldn't show to your eyes, but they changed."

"Changed? How? What do you mean?" Ardin said.

The Slont struggled for words. "I've seen ether used before, I've touched it in items, and it's always constant, like a light that animates the nucleus of the molecules. But when the quake hit, that light flickered. It didn't come back in some parts of the plants."

Ardin shook his head. "What does that even mean?"

"I'm not entirely sure, but it seems that some ether vanished with the quake. I checked around the gardens. Most of them are that way. But I think it was just the plants. I didn't see ether withering from the rivers or anything else." Patros shifted. "My observations were limited to a small section of Mirial, of course."

"The ether vanished?" Avienne injected. "Can it do that? I mean, maybe it just went elsewhere? Or it just needs to be put back."

"Maybe," Patros said, looking sceptical.

"We'll have to ask Layela to try, at least," Avienne said.

Ardin didn't reply. Maybe that was what had happened to the Berganda. Too much of the ether was robbed from them, and ether creatures were more susceptible to loss of ether. Especially unborn ones. He shivered. The sight of all the unborn corpses would haunt him to his grave.

"Is it affecting ether creatures, Patros?" Ardin whispered. Avienne's eyes grew wide and she swore.

Ardin exchanged a glance with Avienne. "Things might be about to get a whole lot worse for the ether creatures. We have to either strike a deal with Solaria for their safe transfer here, or figure out a way to save as many as possible."

"Figuring what's going on with the ether might be a good first step," Avienne mumbled.

Ardin's face darkened, and Avienne held her peace.

"Patros, find out what you can about the ether creatures. The Berganda might be able to help." Patros simply nodded. "Avienne, come with me. I need to hear everything you know and saw from Solaria. I think it's time we start negotiations in earnest, before more people die."

CHAPTER 9

LAYELA'S LIMBS FELT like lead. She concentrated on her feet, and only her feet. *Lift heel, lift rest of foot, move forward, careful to avoid other leg, place down in front, bear weight, repeat with next foot.* As she did so, her arms rocked Ardice, the baby still red from her latest fit. She wasn't sleeping yet, her eyes opening intermittently to peer around. Her strange, wonderful eyes.

"Shh, shh." She was too tired to mutter the words of a lullaby, too heartbroken to even try. She had sung to Josmere before burying her, still alive, in the gardens that the Berganda had claimed as theirs. She had sung over the grave as her friend bled out below her, to save her race. And it had worked. But now her children's children had perished.

"Shh…" Layela looked down at the tiny form. Her tired eyes stung from pooling tears. She took her daughter's little hand, letting tiny fingers wrap around her finger. So small. So fragile.

So dangerous.

She sat, hoping Ardice would be content enough to sleep. As soon as she relaxed back into the cushioned chair, she began to drift. Clouds of ether seemed to dance in her blurry vision, almost assuming shapes, like ballerinas at a great concert. Whenever one came close to revealing its features, it vanished into fine dust again.

Ardice hiccupped. Layela's eyes snapped open, the dancers vanishing. She blinked a few times to work the remaining dust from her eyes. Ardice was adding sobs to her hiccups. Layela gathered her and stood, bouncing her as she resumed pacing, but to no avail.

Layela's heart accelerated.

Please stay calm! She pleaded silently. But as Ardice's screams intensified, the ether began to gather around them, turning from usual soothing mists to angry storm clouds, spiking with each of her daughter's screams.

"It's okay, it's okay, it's okay," Layela tried to hush Ardice and she tried to hush the ether around her, too, forcing waves of calm outward from herself; calm she did not feel.

Ardice scrunched her face, as though deciding whether to blow up or calm down, and the ether around her seemed to wait as well. It was opaque in some places now, with jagged edges. Layela waited for the storm.

But Ardice calmed instead, settling in Layela's arms.

The ether dissipated back into its usual mist. Layela looked down at Ardice.

How was she managing to manipulate it without even touching it? Was she that much stronger than her mother?

Layela's head jerked up at a slight sound coming from the garden. Her gardens were always quiet, and even the Berganda made no sound. Would Elsa be back now? Layela reached out with her mind, but nothing greeted her. She took a step towards the gardens before thinking better of it and turning back around to put Ardice down first. She was debating whether or not to call her guards when a knock came at the doors of her chamber. Layela sighed with relief.

"Lady Layela?" She recognized Gresko's voice.

"Come in." She did not turn to greet him, still intently looking outside.

"Lady." He paused. "Is something wrong?"

"I thought I heard something from the gardens," she said, and Gresko quickly crossed the room to verify. Layela felt silly. "It's probably nothing. Just my fatigue."

Gresko turned to face her and nodded. Layela looked at her advisor as though seeing him for the first time. He was gangly and tall, with sharp features. But his usually clean-shaven face showed some shadow, and his eyes were outlined dark, as well. She had seen her advisor troubled before, but never quite like this.

"Sit, Gresko," she invited him. He hesitated for a moment before collapsing in one of the large chairs, leaning heavily on the pillows as though they were absorbing him. He quickly recovered his posture and sat up with his back erect, a slight flush creasing his features.

"I have some news," he said, carefully choosing his words. "There is some discontent, Keeper. The people do not understand what is happening with the young Lady," he looked down at the sleeping Ardice, and his sharp features softened for an instant. "Nothing like this has ever happened before, Keeper."

Layela spoke without bite in her words. "I wouldn't know, Gresko."

The advisor leaned forward. "I think I may have a solution."

"Oh?" She looked up with interest, feeling hope re-energizing her.

"Give me the child. I'll make sure she's safe, but perhaps separating you two will lessen her intake of ether."

Layela's hands grew cold.

"No."

"Keeper…"

"I said no, Gresko." She bit back harsher words. "I am in no way abandoning my child, to you or anyone else. Besides, I was nowhere near her when the last attack came." She grew softer at the thought of the Berganda. "If I could have saved them, Gresko, don't you think I would have?"

The advisor looked down, not meeting her eyes. He was not a bad man. Staunched in tradition and set in his ways, but he wanted what was best for Mirial. She could not fault him for that.

"Gresko, we will find a way to make this work. If Mirial needs a Keeper and Ardice is to become that Keeper after me, than surely Mirial will embrace her. In all of the history of Mirial, I'm certain there were other events like these. The family just probably didn't talk about them, right?" He looked up, as though considering her words. "Come on, Gresko, you know as well as I do that the royal family, my family, probably held many secrets not shared with even their court advisors. They figured this out, too, and so will I. I just need more than a couple of days to adjust to being a new mother and to having a child that can handle ether, that's all! Once I've done that, we'll be fine."

He nodded slowly before speaking. "Still, the people, Lady. They are discontent and afraid. They fear Mirial suffering again, and losing what little they have left."

Layela lowered her head. She wasn't sure what to do. She needed to think, and her chambers felt too stuffy.

"I'll think about it, Gresko. I promise." She stood and he quickly followed suit.

"I'll take a walk around the palace. Perhaps if the people see how beautiful and innocent she is, they will fear the ether less."

He looked unconvinced.

"It's worth a try, right?"

He nodded, and she walked out, having regained some energy from their talk. She heard him instructing the royal guards to stay close, and others to keep an eye on her chambers. She shook her head.

An army of Solarian ships was gathering at the edge of her solar system, ships she had no fleet to fight against, and Gresko seemed to think the greater danger lurked on Mirial herself.

***

Elsa sat in the back of the birthing gardens. The children had been buried to one side. Flowers bloomed over their graves already, thanks to the Keeper's will. She was alone. Her sisters all stayed away from the gardens, now. Their chatter buzzed at the back of her mind, but today she didn't care to join.

They would rebuild. Her people were survivors. Their mother had died to give them life. Elsa dug her feet deep into the earth until stones cut her, a bit of blood escaping. The ether of Mirial danced, absorbing the blood. In a few months, another Berganda would be born. The new daughter would be the oldest of her generation, as Elsa was. Because her sisters were still too afraid to bleed, to give life again.

But for Berganda, if sprouting was not their life goal, than what could possibly be?

Someone cleared his throat and she looked up. At the entrance of the gardens, by the half broken wall, was the blue ether creature that had come on Avienne's ship. She looked at him with curiosity, but couldn't muster any conversation. He was very blue, and she couldn't help but stare.

He cleared his throat again, hesitated and then came to sit beside her, his back stiff against the stone of the garden wall. He looked down at her feet and leaned his head back.

"My name is Elsa," she finally said.

"Patros," he replied. She found his presence comforting. He was older than she, despite his physical appearance. The ether danced around him more, which took years to happen, or so Layela had always said. Without thinking, she reached out and placed her hand on his arm. His skin was smooth and hairless, and she felt the ether tingle, soothing her.

His eyes grew wide with surprise and she quickly removed her hand, embarrassed. "I'm sorry…" she started saying, but he quickly shook his head

"No, it's fine." He cleared his throat. "You wouldn't know this, not being from Solaria, but an ether creature touching another with no glove is deemed, um, very personal." He flushed bluer.

She looked down, feeling her own face grow warm.

"I, um," he hesitated again. "I came here to see how you were. Ardin was concerned."

She tried to put on a brave face, but doubted it would convince him. Taking a deep breath, she managed to nod.

The Slont analyzed her with his deep blue eyes. She didn't shy away, though she desperately wanted to. He squinted and seemed to be peering beyond her, down to her very soul. He held his gaze for a few moments, and then he looked away.

After a time, she whispered, "What did you see?"

The silence clung to the gardens for a few moments before his answer came. "The ether. It's mutating around us. Within us, too."

She looked down, where her blood had been absorbed into the earth, the ether a light mist clinging to the ground. She placed her hand on it, though she couldn't see what the Slont saw. She could peer into the minds of humans, but not into the construct of the world around her.

"Show me?" she asked. He hesitated, but then placed his hand over hers. His ether struck her own and slammed into her mind, the world coated with the scent of rotten fruits. She bit down a cry and took deep breaths, concentrating on the images transmitted through his ether. The ether of Mirial was different, she understood, but only because of his shared thoughts. She had never peered so deeply into it before, and could not compare. But his mind was linked with hers, now, and she could gaze at pieces of it. It was dark, frightening, catching glimpses of things she had never before imagined.

She forced herself to concentrate on the ether. Dancing madly and wildly, the depths of the mists were no longer as they had always been, calm, and soothing. Instead they seemed out of control, like an animal madly trying to scratch off fleas. The Slont removed his hand

and she missed the warmth of the ether instantly, even though she was glad of the weight lifted from her mind.

"Will my child be all right?" She looked at the Slont.

"I think so," he said, but she could see the hesitation in his face. *Will any of us be all right?* She wanted to ask, but could not word the question. Instead, she gently sang to her newly seeded child, burrowing her hand in the dirt and letting the ether dance around her skin, fighting back her growing fear and concern.

The Slont waited a moment longer before standing, leaving the gardens without another word. She understood him more sharply, now that she had felt the horrors he witnessed. His fear of losing the ether again, the consequences and pain of its loss, clung to her like a spider web. She stopped singing and was still, feeling the breeze of Mirial. She had lived here her entire life. She had never lacked for anything, especially not ether, the lifeblood of her race. Before today, she could never have imagined the thirst, the fear, the hopelessness she had felt clinging to the Slont. The need for survival.

She forced herself to breathe, bringing up her dirt-coloured hand to her face, examining the spot where the Slont had touched her. Like a second skin, feelings she had never known now coated her.

Survival. Maybe this was the other ether creatures' advantage. They wanted to survive above all else, understanding so well the consequences of losing the ether, or a war. Were the Berganda at risk from their own calm, peaceful upbringing? Could her hands do what would need to be done to survive?

Alone in the gardens, no longer bleeding into the earth, Elsa wondered if the Berganda race was meant to survive at all.

***

Gresko maintained a steady pace as he walked with his hands clasped behind his back and his head lowered as though in deep contemplation. He nodded amicably to some of the few guards and servants he passed. With Layela walking the gardens of Mirial, the traffic in the royal chambers was minimal. Perfect for some preliminary examination.

He passed once before the door of the royal bedchamber, two guards walking past. He took a deep breath and continued into the small library next to it. He looked at the old, withered spines of the books. Gently, he ran a finger on several of the spines, the cracked leather dry and scraping his skin. He lowered his hand and sighed.

He had explored, read and re-read all of these volumes from front to back. Since Layela's ascent to the throne, since reclaiming the surface of Mirial—including this palace—he had gone through each and every one of them, making careful notes on anything he felt could prove useful to Layela. She held the title of Keeper, but she had not been brought up to be Keeper. He sympathized that it wasn't an easy role to fill, but he also had a duty to perform.

Not only to counsel the Keeper in her royal duties, but also to ensure the preservation and survival of Mirial. And nothing in these books, not even a stray sentence or small handwritten note, had prepared him for the consequences of Lady Ardice's birth. The ether seemed almost to reject her, though he couldn't understand why. He exhaled sharply. Even should one of these books hold the key to what he sought, some detail he had dismissed because he wasn't anticipating this issue, it was too late to peruse them all again. They were old, and the history of Mirial had never been digitized for quick search. The books were sacred, handwritten by each court advisor, a history recorded by those closest to the throne. They encompassed every detail of a reign—from trade negotiations to scientific exploration to artistic contributions. Every detail except personal ones, such as the sons that had been born and whisked away, or the daughters who may not have spoken with the ether. When an heir was weak in her connection, a younger heir, should Mirial gift the Keeper with one, would take the throne instead. It was a simple system, and the only personal business recorded in the histories.

He reached the end of the row of histories, where he came to the fresh volumes holding his accounts of The Great Darkness, his careful penmanship marking the years of Mirial's reign on the paper spine. Leather was still too much of a rarity to waste on books, he had been told.

Throughout the difficulties, he had maintained his duty and up kept the records. Yet, right after the last volume, which ended with Lady Layela's ascension, an empty spot marked the shelf. He had not yet written of her in power. To anyone else he would say that he had been too busy reviewing the histories and counselling their young and inexperienced Keeper. Not that anyone else would ask, since he didn't think anyone but himself ever paid attention to the rich history of Mirial.

But he knew why he had not yet filled the first volume of Layela's reign. Aside from notes regarding the reconstruction efforts, trade negotiations and agricultural revival, he had very little on Layela. Part of it was the change in Mirial herself. There were so few of her people left, and so their artistic and scientific contributions were not as prolific as they had once been. The planet had no fleet to speak of, and no political power. There was nothing to write. It would be like recording the daily events in a newborn's life—tedious and dull.

He took a deep breath of dust and ink. The other reason he had not written of her reign was his own lack of understanding. He had tried to understand Lady Layela, at first. But her motivations lay outside his realm of comprehension, limiting his grasp of her decisions and his ability to influence her. He should have remedied this long ago. The need to understand and influence his Keeper to do the best job she could was more important than ever. He needed to ensure she would select Mirial above all else, and right now, he didn't even know how to retain her attention.

He straightened his spine and walked back towards the royal chamber. No one was in sight. In one quick motion, he opened the door and entered, closing the door softly behind him. He exhaled, not realizing he had been holding his breath. He shouldn't be found here, but if he were, he would simply come up with a plausible explanation. He'd let his wits work for him in the moment. They usually did.

Looking around the small room, he decided to begin his hunt at the desk. If he could find some sort of personal account written by Layela, perhaps a journal, he could acquire insight on her thoughts and decisions. The shame that had threatened to still his hand when he had first come up with this plan remained tucked away. He had promised himself he would not allow Mirial to fall again on his watch, and he would do whatever proved necessary to keep that promise.

A few papers were strewn about the desk, but nothing important. A few notes written by Layela on the loss of her sister, which he dismissed. A few love letters from Ardin, which he read with curiosity but also dismissed. Next, he moved to the nightstands by the bed, one on each side. He tried to ignore the fact that both were obviously in use, as the consort lived with the Keeper.

The first nightstand held nothing but a few books from Solaria. He was headed to the second one when a sudden blast sent him flying to the ground. Glass and stone flew around him, the stench of burnt plants and wood reeking in the scorched air. He looked up and through the smoke he thought he saw a few figures jumping over the garden wall. A breeze cleared some of the smoke, revealing the words "For Mirial" painted on the rock.

Guards ran in and gave chase, others helping him up. Loran's face was dark as she surveyed the damage. She did not question his presence here.

"Where is the Keeper?" she asked.

"This way." He half-ran towards the gardens at the front of the palace, down the long corridors, not caring that he looked a shambles and his usually carefully-arranged robes were laced with dust.

He would not find a way to influence Layela this day, but Mirialers, it seemed, were not so judicious in their methods as he was.

CHAPTER 10

ARDIN WALKED QUICKLY down the corridors of the palace. What his little his sister had told him rang uneasily in his ears. Gathering and detaining ether creatures had led to war, once, thirty years ago. He turned down a corridor, nearly hitting guards who leapt out of his way. Avienne followed close behind, her footsteps silent.

He needed to find Layela now. Negotiations with Solaria had to become their priority, to get the ether creatures to safety. He turned down another hallway, his mood darkening with every step. He could contact them, but they might be insulted that the Keeper herself hadn't initiated contact. This had to be done right and it had to be done fast.

Another turn and he struck a servant, sending the woman and a pile of linens flying. He bit back an angry retort before helping the apologetic woman back up. He let her deal with the linens.

"This isn't going to get solved any faster if you knock everyone in the palace down, Ardin," Avienne said softly. Though she kept pace with him, he slowed a bit, and exhaled.

"I know. But…blood and bones, Avienne, we should have seen this coming, or at least planned for it! The Berganda children are all dead, and so many more might die…"

"I know," Avienne said with uncharacteristic tenderness. "But you might not be able to save the ether creatures, no matter how hard you try."

She was trying to prepare him for the blow, he understood. But his fists still curled and his pace picked up again. He could see Layela just outside the palace, walking the gardens with Ardice. Love mixed with his anger as he approached her. She was exhausted, he knew, and had mostly been concerned with Ardice, but now Mirial and all of the ether creatures were her responsibility.

Our responsibility. He corrected himself. She needed to know what Patros had said about the ether. Perhaps if she knew, truly understood that its nature was changing, she could somehow stop it, or at least ease it. Patros joined them, practically running to keep up with the siblings.

Ardin looked at him, and the dark look in Patros' eyes told him what he needed to know. Ether creatures had been affected by the change in the ether, probably for the worst.

A smile fluttered and vanished just as quickly from Layela's lips as Ardin reached her. Gresko reached her at the same time and spoke before Ardin could. The prim advisor's robes were dusty and unkempt, and he sported a slight scratch on his cheek, though he seemed unaware of it.

"My Lady," the advisor said, out of breath. "We need to get you inside. To safety."

"What do you mean?" Ardin asked.

"The unrest is…growing. Things are moving too rapidly—even from when we spoke, barely an hour ago." He lowered his voice. "The people are frightened, my Lady. They fear the young Ardice is cursed, that she brings ill omens, that you have lost control of the ether."

"That's ludicrous," Layela spat. "My daughter is not cursed! She's just a child."

Gresko lowered his head. "Of course, and I agree, Lady. But regardless, we must take every precaution to see you safe."

"Gresko speaks truth," Loran said as she joined them. "I have relieved several maids whose tongues cut too deep." She shared a quick look with the advisor and continued, her voice softer. "We cannot risk you now. I will place you in the protection of my best and most trusted, Lady Layela. But you must come with me."

Ardin's worry for the ether creatures exploded into fear for his family's safety. He put a protective arm around Layela. "No arguments, let's go. All of you."

"No." Layela planted her feet. Ardin turned to object, but she faced him. "Ardin, we must address this now. We can't just run away at the slightest sign of unrest. We must stay and make peace with the people."

"Layela…"

"I've made up my mind, Ardin." She looked down at Ardice. "They need a Keeper. They need us. They're afraid, that's all. I don't think they're bad people. They're just trying to protect their own."

"But you are their own, and they're turning against you."

Layela sighed. "Am I really one of them, Ardin? Are you? We didn't go through what they did. We can't understand what they've been through."

His worry imploded into a chasm in his stomach. He swallowed bile. The familiar steel was in Layela's eyes; he could not sway her now. "All right. But let's first get Ardice to safety. At least until things have calmed down."

Layela looked down, obviously not keen on the thought of letting her daughter go. Without thinking, Avienne said: "I'll take her."

Ardin, Layela and pretty much everyone looked at her with disbelief in their eyes. She shrugged. "You need someone you trust to take her." She raised her hands defensively. "Don't get me wrong—I'm suggesting I'll take her AND a nanny. Even I'm not insane enough to just take the kid. We've just met, after all. But I can watch over her if you're worried about her. We'll wait in my ship. If anything goes wrong, we take off."

Ardin nodded, a grin playing on the corner of his lips. Avienne lifted his worry like no one else, even Layela. He was glad she was there, even if she probably didn't feel that way at the moment. "All right, Avienne. But you won't have to wait in your ship." He shot Layela a look. She gave him a strained smile and turned to Gresko.

"I assume there are leaders to these malcontents."

The court advisor nodded uncomfortably. "I believe we could find them easily enough."

"Bring them to court. Tell them I wish to speak with them and discuss the situation."

Loran whispered to the guards, several of whom vanished immediately. They would prepare security. Ardin didn't argue the point. He had issues with the woman and she with him, but she was still good at what she did.

Layela kissed Ardice gently. Ardin took her and did the same, letting his lips rest on the warm skin, letting his senses be enrobed by the fragility of this new life, still in awe that this was his daughter. He looked at her beautiful eyes and she gurgled as he carefully passed her to Avienne, who held the child awkwardly. "Come on." Ardin said. "You won't wait in your ship. You'll wait in something better."

Avienne was about to protest when her brother took off, leaving her to follow. Patros hesitated a moment before following them. Loran was half dragging Layela inside, Ardin giving orders to the guards escorting them.

He needed to get Ardice safe, and then run back to Layela. The sooner he had his entire family safe with him, the sooner he could breathe normally again.

***

"If things go sour, we'll put you in a high security facility at the other end of the palace. It was built long ago for the royal family," Loran said as she herded Layela. "But you must trust me, Keeper."

"Don't you think that's a bit of an overreaction, Loran?" Layela said, out of breath. She had yet to recover from months of pregnancy and still carried the baby weight. Keeping up with Loran was proving challenging.

"I don't think so, Keeper."

"All this for a few malcontents?"

Loran didn't reply. Layela shot her a quick look. "Loran, what aren't you telling me?"

Loran sighed and slowed a tiny bit, giving Layela some reprieve.

"There was an attack on your chambers," she said. "Had you not been out walking, I fear…" She let the thought drop. "We do not understand how they got past our security so easily. Several of our guards were on duty."

The world spun out of control around Layela. Her daughter had just been born, and now her people were trying to kill her? Guards took flanking positions around her and kept close. Close enough to take a hit for her.

"Where they after me, or after Ardice?" she whispered.

"We won't know until we apprehend them. But your safety is our first concern."

Layela nodded and walked faster. Or perhaps they had been after Ardin? Had she angered too many people by breaking tradition? They would not risk not having a Keeper, not after the events of the past twenty years. But they hardly needed a mother and a daughter—one Keeper was enough. And Ardin…

She felt light headed. Who would do this? She was perhaps not the best Keeper, but she had tried…had she spent too much time worrying about the gardens of Mirial, while her people withered around her? Tears gathered in her eyes. What type of ruler was she? Resentful of a throne she had never craved, for which her sister and best friend had died?

Was that who she had become? Someone her own people considered worthy of assassination?

Her arms longed for the weight of her daughter. This should have been one of the happiest times of her life, not the scariest. Yet here she was, terrified. More royal guards fell in line around them as they walked.

Layela hurried to keep up, barely breathing, wondering when the next strike would come and which one of her loved ones would be the target.

***

"My ship's on the other side of the docks!" Avienne said. "I don't know what you have in mind, but I know I can trust my ship."

"I've seen your ship, Avienne, and she bears her name well!" Ardin said. He turned away from where Avienne pointed, down a metal corridor. The old stones of Mirial's palace faded away behind them.

"We taking the scenic road?" she asked.

"Faster," he replied, not slowing his steps, obviously anxious of returning to Layela's side. Avienne's arms were growing tired from the strain of holding Ardice. It wasn't that she weighed much, but rather that Avienne was tense, afraid to drop the child.

"Great. Faster to what?"

"You'll see in a second."

Avienne turned a corridor and finally saw the ship, in a separate indoor bay. A huge bay, for she was not a small ship. Her steps faltered and she stopped, mouth gaping. Ardin stopped beside her, grinning.

"I wanted to show you earlier, lazy ass, but couldn't get you out for a walk." He took a deep breath. "Avienne, meet *Destiny II*."

Avienne would have known had Ardin not told her. *Destiny*. Their home for twenty-odd years, traveling with a generational crew bearing the secrets and loyalties of Mirial. A ship that had been destroyed in the final battle for Mirial, laying to rest Captain Calan, their adoptive father, on Mirial.

She had been a legend in her day, the flagship of the fleet of Mirial, a mix of art and military might.

But this ship, this ship was just as magnificent. Mimicking some of *Destiny's* more intricate designs, her hull took on the shape of an old sea ship, and she could make out masts and sails lovingly detailed into her perfect metal. The symbol of Mirial was not just etched on the front, but it was woven into each tiny detail, reminiscent patterns on the slightest bent of her hull, the incline of her bridge, the curves of her sides. She shone. Not literally, but her metals were so new and had never known the stress of re-entry, never had to keep a crew's oxygen from the unforgiving vacuum of space.

She was sleeker, and a bit smaller than the original, but none of the details or artwork had been compromised with size.

"She's beautiful," Avienne whispered.

"And she's ours, now come on!" Ardin ran ahead.

Avienne had to tear her gaze away, never wanting to stop looking, for never again would she see *Destiny II* in its pristine glory.

Soon, unless events on Mirial stopped their steady climb, she would earn an entirely different type of beauty. One of experience, one of survival.

Avienne grinned.

She would become an even more magnificent ship.

CHAPTER 11

LAYELA STOOD IN the sitting chamber, which gave way to the throne room. Nearby was the birthing chamber where her daughter had been born. It seemed several eternities ago, even though it had only been two days. Her mouth was dry and her mind covered in spider webs. How much had she eaten and slept since Ardice's birth? She could hardly recall; she remembered only the destruction and death, burned in her memory like nova flares.

Gresko stood near a window, his arms clasped together behind his back, the tightness of his jaw betraying his worry.

She wanted to comfort him. They needed a Keeper. *No harm will come to me.* But her words felt hollow, and in no scenario could she guarantee the safety of those who would stand with her.

She reached out to Mirial, her body suddenly warm as if lit by the sun, even though she stood inside. Balls of sunlight clutched to her eyelashes and she blinked lazily, relaxing under the feel of a summer day. Bright daylight erupted behind her eyelashes and she closed her eyes. She wanted to just lie down and sleep.

"My Lady?" she heard Gresko say. She blinked and turned to look at him. He was holding her up and she was half reclined. She had actually fallen asleep. She shook her head and stood up, flushed.

"My apologies." She mumbled. "I guess I'm more tired than I thought."

He said something she didn't quite catch. She smiled and forced herself not to show how shaken she actually was. Was Mirial trying to comfort her, or put her out of commission before this important event? How big a mistake was this meeting? Should she have run as the others had suggested?

The weight of ether lay heavy upon her mind. She felt slow, cotton in her mouth.

The doors opened and Loran stepped in, her jaw clenched and her eyes a little bit wider than usual. Layela forced herself to focus on her.

Loran gave a quick bow. "I'm sorry, Keeper." She paused and chewed on her lower lip before catching herself and standing tall. "Many of the guards have deserted. They rally with the traitors." Her eyes sought out Layela's. "What are we to do?"

Layela reached out for the ether but felt nothing, save the same heaviness. Mists danced on the edges of her vision, but Mirial kept this vision from her. Her heart fluttered and her head pounded. Was Mirial betraying her, too?

She clutched to the mists, tried to force them to reveal what was about to happen in the next room. *At least show me who is about to die, if anyone!* She thought she spotted Loran falling beside her, but the motion was too quick to be certain. The mists writhed for a second, slowed and seemed to pirouette before vanishing completely.

Layela gasped. They were gone.

She tried to reach out again, but it was as though a wall now stood between her and the ether. She knew it was there, could almost sense it, but couldn't reach out and touch it. Was she so nervous she was blocking the mists?

Perhaps nothing will happen. She failed to convince herself. Had she not heard the bells for Ardin but moments after Ardice's birth? She closed her eyes and took a deep breath.

"Lady?" Loran enquired again, tension lining her face and limbs.

Layela straightened her shoulders. "Let them do what they will." She gave a short nervous laugh. "This is ridiculous! Surely we can just discuss this and figure it out!" she added, as though an afterthought. "Mirial needs her Keeper."

Loran nodded and stepped aside, to stand beside the door leading to the throne room. Layela intended to be at the throne when the discontents entered. She did not intend to be intimidated by them. They were the ones who had insisted they needed a Keeper, and that she was the right person, the only person, to assume the role.

She had never wanted the role, slipping into it out of assumed necessity and loyalty to her dead. But still, she'd be damned if she let them get rid of her so easily. If Mirial wanted her gone, Mirial would do so herself. Ignoring the missing warmth of Mirial, Layela stepped out into the empty throne room.

***

Murl stood outside the throne room, her short sword quiet at her side. She ran a finger gently down the pommel. *I should hand this back in.*

The scent of a thousand blooms assaulted her senses, the breeze shifting in the courtyard. A crowd had gathered, the uprisers summoned by the Keeper herself to discuss with them what was happening, undoubtedly hoping to stop events that had been set in motion long before she had ever set foot on Mirial.

But Layela did not know that, and Murl felt sympathy for her for a moment—just for a moment of weakness. Layela was young, did not know what she doing, nor did she crave doing it. And now, with the wards set by Murl's brother, Layela would not be able to even draw on her one strength. Even should she break them, they would ensure Layela would not draw on Mirial, which would split the power between Murl and her brother.

Murl looked at the people around her. Sallow, deep-set eyes told of sleepless nights. Yellow skin where even Mirial's sun had failed to heal old wounds. The taste of fear in every whisper.

They were terrified. And the Keeper should have seen to soothing their fears long before her daughter had ever been born.

She should have cared for us as much as for her plants.

Fists formed at her sides. Regardless of what she thought of Layela and her poor, useless judgement, Layela still occupied the throne of the Keeper, and Murl was betraying the Keeper. Murl's brother stood beside her, tall and strong, his face hidden by the cowl of his cloak. He shifted minutely, the movement signalling his anticipation. They would enter soon.

She grasped the hilt of her sword and set her jaw. Layela would not be Keeper for long, and Murl's sword would soon be called upon by the new Keeper. If Mirial did not wish this to be, then Mirial would have to stand up for Layela in the throne room.

She doubted that would happen, now.

***

No sound travelled the length of the throne room, not even any noise from the crowd Loran reported had gathered outside the doors. Layela wrung her hands, debating what to do. She could lie to them, she supposed. Maybe even invoke some sort of military action, except most of her guards had deserted her and they had no standing army.

Which Ardin had always insisted should be changed. But she had believed Mirial and her people had survived enough recent battles and needed a new, peaceful beginning. Apparently Mirialers did not think as she did.

Fool!

"Where's Ardin?" Layela whispered, more to herself than anyone present.

"On his way," Loran answered. There were a few guards around, forming a line before the Keeper. Layela hated the break it would cause between her and her people, but she understood the necessity and doubted Loran would agree to move them. Still, with so many of their own rank having deserted, could they fight their comrades to protect her?

"Let them in," Layela said impulsively. Perhaps it was best that they enter before Ardin arrived. His presence might throw fuel on an already burning fire. Loran crossed the floor quickly, putting more weight on her artificial leg, using it to propel herself faster with an uneven gait. She glanced back once across the vast throne room and pulled the doors open, then walked back to her position near the throne. The rays of the sun of Mirial streamed in, creating a carpet of light waltzed upon by dust.

Layela straightened her back and stood on the stone slab that held her throne, high enough to grant her full view of the room, but not so high as to make her tower over everyone and seem inaccessible. She did not sit. It would be too insulting to her guests.

Seconds trickled by, each seemingly longer than the last. Loran joined her and stood before the stone rise, to the side. She nodded to the other guards, a few of which Layela knew by name. They formed a loose half-circle in front of the throne. Layela quickly counted sixteen. Sixteen, from her original forty. She hoped more hid in the shadows or outside the room.

The stillness made her nervous. They had come, had they not? They would at least speak with her, would they not?

A shadow sliced the beam of sunlight, reaching all the way to the throne. Layela looked up. A cloaked figure walked in. From the width of the shoulders, she could only imagine it was a man. He walked with purpose towards her, joined by a multitude of followers who streamed in silently. Layela had anticipated anger and fear. This calm front chipped away at her confidence.

She pleaded for Mirial, a swell of longing spreading across her chest. But still, the sun was quiet, its blanket of light only covering the intruders but not reaching her. The room was smothered with the lack of ether.

The cloaked figure stopped before the beam of light ended, a few metres from Layela's guards, who stood tensely before them.

Layela opened her arms in greeting. "Welcome. I trust that, together, we can find a peaceful solution."

She folded her arms back down, not letting her spine curl or her eyes lower, as she desperately wanted to. She wished she could see the face buried in the shadows of the cloak. She noticed Murl stood very close to the man, and Layela's anger boiled.

Words were about to escape her lips when the cloaked man spoke, a whisper which echoed like a thunder clap.

"Mirial demands that you step down."

Shivers crossed her spine. She wanted to laugh the man's demands away, but couldn't. She had felt powers in his words. Not the power of being right, or of certainty, but rather a power she herself courted.

Mirial.

Mirial was courting this man. Layela was shocked at her own repulsion. Mirial lore claimed the star only courted women, but why would she think that true? Why did the breaking of this one tradition repulse her when she had purposefully destroyed so many herself?

It hardly mattered. The Berganda, the people of Mirial and Mirial herself had entrusted her with this throne. She couldn't relinquish it to the first bully. Not when allegiances with Solaria were still shaky and Mirial still had so much to learn of the world beyond its solar system. To relinquish now would be to abandon her people to a possibly mad man hiding under a cloak. He continued.

"Bring me to the temple to relinquish your control of the ether."

Gresko stepped forward. "It's unheard of for a son of Mirial to be the Keeper. Mirial will not allow it."

Murl spoke this time, scoffing. "He was here during the battle for

Mirial and fought for many of us. He wasn't brought up off-planet, like Layela." Layela felt slighted by the lack of title. Had she grown so used to the formalities she claimed to detest?

She steeled herself. Ardin entered from the back and made his way to her side, infusing her with confidence again.

"If Mirial wants me to step down," Layela answered, her voice easily carrying through the room. "Then Mirial can tell me so herself."

She could swear she heard the man grin.

"Then stop me." The last word was still echoing in the room when the ground cracked below them and the room jostled. Layela was caught by Ardin and managed to remain standing for a second longer, but when the second quake struck, it sent them both to their knees. Gresko screamed and Loran tried to attack the man, but was thrown back instead, striking the wall and crumpling on the ground.

Layela focused and reached out, placing both palms on the ground to will Mirial to calm. She did not feel the ether but still she pushed, soothing as much as she could while the ceiling above them cracked. She glanced at the cloaked man. He stood perfectly still, as did his followers. He was focusing the earthquake beneath their feet! Layela couldn't even fathom how to do that, even if she had access to the ether.

Tears of hopelessness welled in her eyes and she closed them, reaching out not to Mirial, but to her sister, Yoma, joined with Mirial years ago.

Only silence answered her.

***

Ardice gurgled on the side, Avienne glancing at her as she made sure all systems were go. The ship's old engineer, a woman named Rose, baby-talked like it was her calling, and Avienne wasn't about to interfere.

The pilot, Clave, a tall, dark and handsome one, was checking systems on his end. "It all looks good here." He turned to her and offered her a slight grin, his deep blue eyes dancing with laughter. "Of course, we've never actually flown her out of the atmosphere."

"Great," Avienne mumbled. "This is getting more and more fun."

Clave turned back to his station.

"Well," Avienne whispered. "If she does clear the atmosphere and makes it into space without exploding, then she'll be one heck of a ship."

Clave and Rose both spoke up at the same time. "Agreed."

Patros sat on a nearby chair, looking uneasy, his blue skin flushed.

"Is this all the crew?"

Avienne grinned. "Larod and Jaru are joining us from the *Dessicate*. Figured they deserved to enjoy a nicer ride, too. And Ardin and Layela will join us. Not that Layela's worth anything on ships, but my brother can captain this thing in his sleep."

Patros looked uneasily around the bridge. Rose said, "These ships are so well built and automated that you only need minimal crew to run them." She paused. "Of course, if we have any major repair work required, that's when we're in trouble." She shrugged. "Well, anything to the outer armour would require a spaceport, I suppose, and we're as good as dead if it's too compromised, regardless."

She went back to gurgling with Ardice.

"And I thought I wasn't the nurturing type," Avienne grinned to Patros, who had turned pale blue.

A crack broke the silence, like a bomb going off in the distance. Patros jumped to his feet at the same time as Avienne.

"Earthquake again," Clave said. "Nasty one." He furrowed his brow. "It seems very localized. Under the palace. I have no idea what's causing it."

"Clave," Avienne said, "cut tethers and break berth. Don't clear port until I'm back. Keep us low-key, as much as possible."

"Rose," she turned to the engineer, quickly crossing the bridge to take Ardice from her. "Make sure our systems are fine. We're going to have to maintain flight within the atmosphere a bit longer than anticipated, and she's big. Let's make sure we don't crash before we even reach space."

Rose and Clave quickly followed orders without questioning her.

"Patros," Avienne said and he jumped up to face her. She put Ardice in his hands. "Keep her safe."

A protest was forming on his lips but he just nodded and sat back down, buckling himself in and holding the child as though she were the last oxygen tank in a dead ship.

Avienne leapt up a few steps to her station, bringing all smaller weapons online. She glanced at the map to see the exit shafts. Close enough to the old *Destiny*.

"Get ready to clear out. I have a feeling Ardin and Layela are going to need to get out fast. I'll go nab them. Be ready to clear down any resistance. Don't hesitate to fire on anyone that gets in your way. And make sure no one else gets on board!"

"What if you don't make it back?" Patros asked, eyes wide.

"Then save my niece!" Avienne jumped into the lift and headed down to the bowels of the large ship, heading to the nearest shuttle bay. Manoeuvring the large ship would prove too difficult and unwieldy in the atmosphere, but a shuttle would be perfect to scoop them up and leave.

As long as the whole palace didn't come crashing down before she reached them.

***

A drop of honey.

The light of Mirial was diffused, like Layela was seeing it through a drop of honey. She wrapped her will around that drop, not caring if the light was muddied and broken. The ether, Mirial, was still there for her. It was just muffled, hiding. Or held prisoner. She was aware of Ardin covering her, of the others in the throne room standing perfectly still, watching as stone came tumbling down from the palace ceiling.

Waiting to see if Mirial would save her.

Yoma, Layela cried through the drop of honey, not caring that she screamed the word out loud.

"Yoma!" She threw her will through the veil covering Mirial's ether. She imagined it swallowed whole and coated. She pushed with ether she could no longer feel, pushing through that barrier, until she was certain her cry had passed through.

It took Layela a few seconds to realize that the ground had stopped shaking. She stood, swaying. Loran and her remaining loyal guards quickly gathered before her.

Gresko stood up and brushed his robes. She cast a glance his way, but his pale and troubled features signalled that he had no answers for her.

Scenarios buzzed around her mind like bees, all drawing the same conclusion: the cloaked man would take Mirial from her. With limited access to her ether, she simply couldn't fight him.

"We need to come to a peaceful resolution. No one needs to die over this," Layela insisted, taking a step forward. Later, she could determine what exactly had transpired and take necessary action. If any actions were necessary.

"Mirial has declared you an unfit Keeper," the man said. "She no longer has need of your blood, or your daughter's."

Murl smirked at Loran. Loran scowled and pulled out her short sword, as did the guards beside her. The crowd that had followed the cloaked man in did not pull any weapons, simply waiting.

"We need to go, now," Ardin said, pulling on Layela's arm. Layela nodded, but stood rooted. The pure stream of sunlight was changing from white to dark red, and everyone standing in it was outlined in coals of fire. Her breath caught in her throat as a scream exploded in her mind.

The Berganda were begging for mercy, their pain pounding into Layela, joined by the cries of thousands, millions of ether creatures feeding off the pure ether of Mirial.

"Stop!" she screamed. "You're killing them!" She pulled back on the ether, but the veil blocking her from Mirial's magic had grown too thick for her to pierce, smothering her instead.

She choked and fell on her knees, gasping for breath.

"It ends now." The cloaked man pointed at Layela. Red and black mists exploded from his finger and sped towards her like a javelin. She tried to move, but Mirial's thick blanket dulled her senses.

Mirial wants me to die.

Ardin tackled her to the side, but instead of collapsing on the wall, the mists boomeranged back around and attacked from behind. Ardin saw the mists first and tugged Layela out of the way, but was too slow to move out of the way himself.

His left shoulder absorbed the blow, sending him flying into the air and tumbling into the guards blocking the cloaked man. Several collapsed under his weight.

Layela ran to him, fighting the guards who tried to keep her back. She lashed out, hitting her court advisor and sending him down. She kneed a guard and punched another, striking wildly at whoever tried to pull her away from Ardin. The intruders were approaching them, knowing there was no escape for Layela. She hit another of her guards and managed to grab Ardin's limp arm, but two more guards pulled her back.

"No!" She screamed and tried to kick back, doubling her hold on him to drag him along as they dragged her. She spotted the cloaked man from the corner of her eye, and memories of another tall, dark mist wielding enemy tackled her senses. *Dunkat.* He had returned to destroy them! To destroy all that she loved, as he had tried to do so long ago, when he had succeeded in ripping her sister from her!

Please! She pleaded with Mirial to help her, to give her just a moment's respite, to at least let Ardin get to safety. Her arms ached from holding on to him, her ribs bruising as her guards pulled her back.

"Enough of this weakness," the cloaked man declared, and even her guards stopped pulling on her, his command stronger than their desire to save their Keeper. Layela jumped in front of Ardin to face the man.

"You embarrass yourself and Mirial, Layela Delamores," he tossed her name with stinging casualness. "This is but another fine reason for Keepers to keep the identity of their consorts a secret. Much more dignified, really."

Murl lifted her chin, a smile playing her lips.

Layela laughed. "Oh? What about the reason for males to be kept off the throne? I'm sure there must be a good reason for that, too!" The words stung even as she spoke them out of anger. The man towered over her and she was certain he would strike her, but she refused to relinquish ground.

The wall to the right suddenly blew up in shards of rocks, and the room exploded in light. Everyone crouched. Layela turned and grabbed Ardin's arms and began pulling him away. Murl jumped on her, catlike, but a gunshot made her back away. Loran stood near, armed.

Layela didn't even think to thank her as she pulled Ardin away, towards the light.

"Come on!" Avienne screamed as she manoeuvred the shuttle closer. She grabbed Ardin's other arm and yanked him up as Layela kicked herself in.

"Loran! Gresko!" She screamed into the light, trying to cover her eyes to see the captain better. Her advisor was nowhere to be seen.

"Go!" Loran screamed from somewhere far, just as the flare bomb ran out of energy and the lights returned to normal. Avienne jumped in the pilot's seat and pulled back on the controls, forcing the shuttle to bank right and head back towards the hole in the side of the palace.

Layela strapped Ardin down and ripped his shirt aside to see his wound, the scorched clothing easily giving way. Ardin was barely conscious, his face pale and taut, grunting slightly. Layela struggled to remain seated while treating his wound.

She kicked the healing kit free from under the seat as she ripped the last of the clothing away from the wound, hoping she had the necessary supplies to at least mend it until they could reach a healer. When she looked at the wound, she sucked in her breath. He wasn't bleeding. The wound was black and shallow, as though the skin had been cauterized while it was shredded.

She pulled him forward, not even needing to remove his coat to see the scorch marks on his back.

The mists had gone clean through.

Avienne swore and pulled hard on the shuttle controls. Layela grabbed Ardin and held him as the ship jostled again, wishing she could feel his breath.

CHAPTER 12

CLAVE, FIRE HER up, we'll board before we clear the atmosphere!" Avienne's crisp voice boomed over the comm unit.

"Aye." Clave punched in the sequence with clammy hands to fire the ship's base engines for the first time, which would help them clear the atmosphere. *Destiny II* lurched to life, groaned, and then settled into a quiet hum as the engine began pushing her up out of its planet-bound port. The ship had been built on the planet and could handle its forces, but its ability to clear the atmosphere remained to be tested. *Destiny II* lurched up ungracefully. Warnings popped up on all stations. Rose handled everything from the engineering console, re-routing power as necessary.

"Nothing much to worry about," she reported, and grinned at Clave.

He wondered if Rose was as nervous as he was. Nothing much seemed to rattle the old engineer.

He focused on his station, turning the ship to pierce the atmosphere nose first. It would encounter too much resistance otherwise. The gravity engines kicked in and kept everyone on the bridge fairly stable as they began a straight ascent.

The lift doors opened. A thin, fast-moving middle-aged man and a more rotund older man entered. The older man saluted. "Jaru and Larod, reporting for duty from the *Dessicate.*"

Rose nodded and introduced herself before turning her attention back to her station.

"The shuttle is in," Rose declared. "All ports are closed, and we're safe for atmospheric exit." Jaru and Larod both took stations, their hands gliding over controls with ease and confidence. The noise of the ship was minimal, only the comforting churn of her engines rumbling through her core.

The child began to cry.

The ship shook and buckled, changing exit angle to a dangerously flat one.

"We've been hit!" Rose screamed. "I need to put up our shields!"

"We won't be able to clear the atmosphere that way—too much resistance!" Clave shouted back, his throat dry. Another blow caught the backside of the *Destiny* and one of her engines cut out. They banked to port.

"We're not going to clear it if they take out too many of our thrusters, either! We need them! We should go further outfield to clear the atmosphere."

The lift opened and Avienne entered, grim-faced.

"Don't change course. Straighten us out, and don't raise those shields," Avienne said as she walked to the tactical station. "Let's give them something else to worry about, instead."

Clave turned, wide-eyed. "You can't fire on the palace!"

Avienne gave him a withering glance. "They don't seem to be hesitating about taking shots at us. I told you, cut through the resistance."

Clave was about to protest but thought better of it and turned back to his station, hands in fists. He could stop her. He had family down there. But his duty was to get the Keeper out of here, to safety.

Everything he had done so far was to ensure she lived.

At least until he was told her survival was no longer required by Mirial.

***

It began like a whistling. A low, shrill hum filled the air, and then expanded until the few panes of glass vibrated.

"They're attacking the palace," Murl said, looking up at her brother. He nodded and held up both hands. The blow came swiftly, her brother grunting as he absorbed the shock and buckled to his knees. The court advisor stood nearby, wide-eyed, looking at the ether flowing from Murl's brother's strong arms straight into the stones of the palace, strengthening them against the blasts of the energy weapons from the escaping ship.

She motioned two of her guards to keep an eye on him and they soon flanked him, though she doubted he even noticed, his features pale in the dark glow of her brother's ether.

The air vibrated with power, yet nothing broke. Not stone cracked, no pane of glass shattered, no one even felt the ground shake. He was in complete control of the ether swirling around him. Not that she could see it.

She tried to imagine it. He had described the mists to her often, as he protected them against so many forces. As he protected them now from their own Keeper.

She felt hatred burst to life within her. She was firing on them. On her own palace! On her people! What kind of Keeper could Layela claim to be? Who stood on Mirial now, controlling her ether and keeping them safe, as always?

It was not Layela.

It had never been her.

The whistling ended and her brother buckled to his knees. She knelt beside him.

"We cannot let them win," she said, and he nodded, sweat dripping from his face, pooling on the ground before him.

"I will not let them win, brother."

He reached out and put a strong hand on her shoulder. She felt his strength flow into her.

I will not let you down, she whispered in her mind. The sonic boom of the *Destiny II* reaching Mach 1, breaking the atmosphere to be propelled into space, washed down over them.

Murl stood. There were few places that ship could hide. She would find it again.

Her hands shook with adrenaline, fear, and hatred. She had to leave, soon. She had never left Mirial.

But it was part of the greater plan. As soon as the signal came, she would go.

She glanced at Loran, who was trying to stand despite obvious damage to her synthetic leg. Another off-worlder, come to claim Mirial as her own.

A lesson in freedom would be forged with her blood.

***

Destiny II cleared the atmosphere, the ship propelled by the remaining combustion before engaging her energy engines, which rumbled somewhere deep below her decks, leaving her crew with only a hint of noise travelling her metal hull.

Avienne sat at tactical controls.

"Where to?" Clave asked, not turning around. Avienne didn't immediately answer him, fixated on the darkness of space before them. It wasn't the hollowness of space that haunted her, but the darkness of the wound that had pierced her brother and seared his flesh closed, trapping whatever evil now festered within him.

Space, what lay before them, was not dark.

It was lit by distant flickering suns, comet trails, nebulas and objects not yet reached or identified by any explorers within Solaria and its border worlds. The space before them was not dark because it was filled with promises of adventures, hope, blood, multiple days occurring on different suns at various speeds, in a slow celestial dance answering to no discernible conductor.

Nothing was planned, only balanced. Someday, Avienne imagined, the whole universe would tip the wrong way and just disappear. Everything that seemed so carefully planned, so constructed, so maintained, would vanish in the blink of an eye, and no one would ever realize it had ever existed. Because no one would be left.

Avienne sighed. She was making her own head hurt.

There were few places to go that could be reached quickly enough.

"Head to the tunnel. Keep debris between us and Mirial as often as possible to hide our trail. Let's hope Solaria will let us through without any problems."

She wasn't interested in a fight, another useless battle in the vastness of space. She needed to escape, but she didn't know where to go, or who could help them. For all she knew, Ardin was already dead below, in the depths of the ship.

Space suddenly seemed a lot emptier to Avienne.

***

Loran recovered from the shock to see that the Keeper and her family had escaped. She forced herself to get up, to stand, but a pressure held down her prosthetic leg: Murl, leaning heavily on it with one leg.

"Get off, Murl," she ordered, fear tingling to life in her heart. The fear blazed into panic when she saw the cold smile spread across Murl's face.

"Your parents might have been from Mirial, but you yourself are a disgrace. You're not even whole."

Loran kicked out with her good leg, but Murl caught it and bent it back, spraining the knee badly. Loran screamed and fought the tears. Now was not the time to break down.

"They've escaped," Gresko said. He stood, brushing his robes.

Murl shrugged. "They'll get them. There's really no escape."

Gresko met Murl's eyes with no hesitation. "The sooner, the better."

"Gresko?" Loran didn't believe what she was hearing. He was the man most loyal to the Keeper, had been the right hand of three Keepers.

"My loyalties lie with Mirial herself, and not all Keepers live up to her needs," he said, keeping his eyes on Murl. "But the Keeper and the heir should not be injured. It is imperative that they survive."

"We don't need your advice," Murl said, hitting down on Loran's prosthetic leg as though bored. Loran bit back a scream. The shock resonated into each nerve ending.

The dark cloaked man hovered near the throne, gently running his hand on its wooden arm. Gresko shot a look at him. Loran knew Gresko well enough to see he was choosing his words carefully. Guards were near the advisor, but the cloaked man and Murl seemed undecided what to do about him. Unlike herself—Murl had already obviously made up her mind about Loran.

"I'm not convinced you won't need my advice, and I'm sure you'll need the Keeper to survive," Gresko said, standing tall. "And tradition is tradition. We must ensure Mirial is satisfied with her Keeper, no matter who it is, and that the bloodline is passed the correct way." He paused. "To ensure only the true Keeper remains."

Murl laughed. "Is there a tradition of court advisors betraying the Keeper?"

Gresko was stone-faced as he answered. "You would be surprised what is not written in our histories."

At that, Murl nodded. Gresko held his peace. Loran swallowed bile to see how easily he had accepted these traitors as his new allies. She had always thought highly of the court advisor. Before now.

A noise crashed in the hall, like a sonic boom, seconds before the ground shook fiercely. *Another ship has left the atmosphere. But which one?* Murl lost her footing, and Loran took the opening and struck out, hard. Murl went down. Loran tried to stand, but her wounded knee sent her back to the floor, biting back a scream.

She reached for her sword, but she was too slow. The tip of Murl's sword rested under her chin. Loran remained very still. Gresko voiced no objection.

I guess no one but the Keeper and heir are necessary for Mirial, she thought bitterly. She did not regret having dedicated her life to the Keeper, and Layela, although a bit strange at times, had always been good to her. Her bitterness was directed at the fairy tale of a Mirial her parents had woven in their stories. She had truly believed Mirial would be different. Somehow above it all, and full of respect and honour and everything else she fought so hard to find every day.

"Do you still claim Mirial as your home?" Murl asked. "If not, I would be willing to let you go." The lie danced in the crease of Murl's thin smile. Loran was not remotely tempted to lie in return; there was no point. She might as well go down for what she had always fought for and always sought—an honourable and caring Mirial.

She held Murl's gaze. "Mirial will always be my home."

Murl gave a quick satisfied smile, raised her sword and struck down.

CHAPTER 13

HAVE TO GO to Ardice," Layela whispered to Patros, her eyes reflecting the grief in her voice. Patros nodded and looked down at the unconscious Ardin. Layela leaned down and kissed his forehead, standing slowly before making her way resolutely to the lift.

Patros watched her go. The ether creatures were not as involved in the life of the Keeper as the Mirialers, and not as caring of the traditions that surrounded the role. He himself had never had an opinion about the new Keeper's choice to break traditions, though others of his people had been vocal with their disapproval. He now knew enough of Layela and Ardin to know that he wanted to help them, as much as possible.

Ardin was still breathing, though his breaths were shallow. Patros knelt beside him and pulled the bandages free, the wound slick from ointment. It was black—more black than just burned. The skin itself wasn't scabbed. It wasn't a burn. He had no idea what it was.

"That's ugly," Avienne whispered as she crouched beside her brother. Patros started. He had not heard her enter, too concentrated on the wound.

"I think I can help," Patros said. Avienne looked up, meeting his eyes. Patros looked embarrassed for a second. "I…lied to you. We don't just feel the molecular composition of objects. We can manipulate it, too, though it's very dangerous. Our own original homeworld was destroyed by a careless handling of elements." He took a deep breath. "I may be able to stop this, whatever it is."

Avienne was nodding. He continued before she could speak. "But, you must understand, it's very dangerous." He ended in a whisper. "I may just kill him."

Avienne stopped nodding and looked down, her red hair falling to cover her face, only Ardin's broken breaths filling the silence.

"He would want a fighting chance. Do it." She held his eyes for a moment and he nodded, pulling off his gloves.

His hands fell on his lap and he looked at the wound, took a deep breath and steadied his nerves. He placed his hand directly on the wound, which felt slick to the touch, and cold. A tickling skirted his palm before an outright assault of ether struck him, his head snapping back and his eyes growing wide. A scream formed on his lips but he held it in, forced his eyes to close, and lowered his head, the creases on his face deep with shadows.

Through the haze of ether, he heard Avienne's voice like a distant whisper.

Blood and bones, if he makes it, I'll even give up drinking. Confused as to whether she was referring to himself or Ardin, he shook off the words but took heart in her nearness.

I'm not alone.

A second wave of ether slammed into him, blocking all thought and knocking his breath from his lungs. His entire body tensed beyond his control, his muscles shrieking in agony. He felt like a balloon filled to the brim, about to explode. His senses were overwhelmed and then smothered, blocking his ability to see, hear, sense…he felt trapped within his own body. He focused down, tried to identify the tips of his fingers, where the ether was pounding into him.

He found it, where the floodgates were wide open and ether was greedily invading his body, which acted like a sponge. He visualised the floodgates closing. Blinded, he waited for his control over his own ether to return, slowly chipping away at the force of what was in Ardin's wound.

He could feel the cool air of the ship on his balmy skin, smelled the booze that Avienne was consuming and he squinted at the light. His body felt like his own again, his spine releasing the tension, his head rolling forward. His hand was already shaking. He put his other hand on the wound to stabilize the first.

His vision blurred. At least now it was fatigue instead of ether.

He carefully examined the wound with his ether, closed his eyes and concentrated on what his hands told him. The wound was strange. Unlike anything he had ever encountered. It wasn't a wound, really. The basic makeup of the organs and skin had not been compromised, still retaining function and shape, no rips, no molecular inconsistency. From what his ether could see, there was no wound to speak of. But the attack on his own ether proved that there was a dark force at work within Ardin.

He looked deeper, into the cells themselves. He started with a surface cell, in direct contact with his hand. A skin cell, half-dead, ready to fall off. The ointment was slimy under his palm, and he wished he'd have thought to ask Avienne to wipe it off. He tried to ignore the viscous sensation as he peered into the heart of the skin cell. He kept his defences up, twisted ether greeting his ether's embrace. The cell was riddled with dark energy, which was multiplying, like a cancer.

Patros looked deeper, examining cell by cell what he now saw as an invasion. The dark ether had latched onto the cells, much more strongly to the newer ones than the half dead ones. Patros tried to coax the dark ether into moving, but nothing made it shift. He wondered if the Keeper, who could actually channel ether, might be able to help him. All he could do was see it and interact on a basic level.

Perhaps a blast of pure ether would save Ardin.

That was not something he could do, but he could help slow down the progress. The dark ether was moving too quickly right now, jumping from invaded cell to normal cell. But it needed the spark of energy to be able to latch on. Patros needed to create a shield around the already invaded area, a moat of some sort, to stop the darkness from spreading. It was already dangerously close to Ardin's heart. Patros began carefully snuffing out the life of the cells surrounding the wound. He began with skin cells, turning slightly gray around the dark wound. Then he pierced deeper, not certain what he was affecting, not familiar enough with human physiology to predict the consequences of his actions.

He dug deeper, cutting off small blood vessels at first, then larger ones, grateful no artery was in the path of the dark ether. He cut off as few muscle cells as possible, hoping he would not render the arm useless. Bone came next, large chunks of bone cut right through. He hesitated less, not certain but guessing, or at least hoping, that the ribs would prove able to take the damage. He cut off the cells, watching them wither, forming a barrier.

Beneath that, he reached the top edge of the left lung. He took a deep breath, feeling the cool air coat his own lungs, knowing this was irreversible, but necessary, damage. One by one, he snuffed out the cells around the dark ether.

Ardin's chest heaved and he coughed. Avienne turned her brother's head to the side, and Patros smelled blood. He closed his eyes, ignoring the pain he was inflicting, and carefully travelled the length of the wound, seeing no bridge, no gap line, no possibility of escape. He was grateful the wound was contained in his body and did not extend to the edge of his shoulder or side. He hoped he had not sacrificed limb for life.

Satisfied, Patros opened his eyes and removed his hand.

Ardin coughed once and his breath came in regular and deep, as though he simply slept. Layela knelt beside Avienne now, holding Ardice close, her eyes closed in silent prayer.

Avienne looked up and mouthed a thank you, tears gathering over her green eyes. His heart skipped a beat. He prayed he would prove worthy of Avienne's gratitude, and not become a cause for great sorrow.

***

Solarian Defence Minister Noro stepped off his ship and took a deep breath. So this was what Mirial smelled like. Flowers and fresh water. He didn't even care. If Solaria could make headway with Mirial, a rich retirement would await him. And he was aching to retire. The mistakes of a Solarian colonel greedy for revenge had cost Noro dearly in the battle for Mirial. He had never succeeded in regaining his foothold.

But now, invited here, on a planet in full insurrection, he could certainly pass a treaty much to Solaria's advantage. He was certain of it. There were not that many Mirialers left, most destroyed by their own ether. They were weakened, and without a Keeper, they were terrified. When he had received word from these insurrectors to wait before engaging with the Keeper, he had been more than happy to oblige. All the more to his advantage.

A woman of medium height greeted him. Her sandy hair was cut short and her handshake was firm. Her eyes were cunning. She was a survivor, of that he had no doubt.

"Welcome, Minister Noro. I'm Colonel Murl, of the Mirial military."

Noro tried to look impressed, even though he knew she had only just formed this "military" and was probably its only officer as of yet. Still, this woman seemed capable of rallying the troops and might prove an asset. If she could be controlled.

"We appreciate your invitation, Colonel. We would be happy to provide any help in this unstable time for you."

Murl nodded. He doubted the woman was very politically-savvy. It would make things easier for him. Much easier.

He could almost taste the fresh strawberries he would enjoy during his beach life retirement. He just needed to finish this.

"Have you found the Keeper yet?" Murl asked. Noro refrained from telling her he was not under her command.

"No. Our fleet is spread out and looking, but it is a big solar system, with lots of debris."

Murl nodded. Noro was fascinated. He wondered if she cared that some of that debris included planets that had once held life, that they were all blasted to nothing by the sun that still shone in the sky above them. He guessed that she did know, but was too concerned with her own survival to worry about something as poetic as space debris.

He could appreciate that.

"Here is every code, access code, identification and communication or otherwise that the *Destiny II* and her shuttles emit. If she enters your space, or if her crew tries to fool your sensors, you should be able to identify her with these, regardless of their tricks." She paused and looked disgusted. "The Keeper's…mate is a smuggler. He has tricks, but none that can hide every ID chip in those ships."

Noro nodded and accepted the chip she handed him. That would simplify things if the Keeper came to Solarian space, which she more than likely would do. Solaria covered more known inhabited worlds. Once he'd captured her, then he'd simply have to decide how best to politically leverage her.

"It would be best for the Keeper not to be…destroyed," Murl continued. "Our preference is to collect her alive, as well as the heir."

"It is imperative," a tall man said. Noro had not even noticed him until he spoke. The thin man's features were pale and drawn. Neither his eyes nor his lips, nor any tension in his limbs, betrayed what he thought.

If I'm not more careful, I won't even make it to retirement.

"Minister, this is Gresko Listan, Court Advisor," Murl waved his way, ignoring the formalities. Gresko lowered his head slightly as a sign of acknowledgment. Noro did the same.

"The Keeper needs to be retrieved alive, as well as the heir. Mirial depends on this." The court advisor reiterated. Murl seemed annoyed by his opinion.

"Do what you can, Minister, to bring us child or mother alive. We don't necessarily need both," she said in almost a growl, as though warning Gresko to be quiet. The tall man narrowed his eyes slightly, the only sign of his annoyance. He would be a bigger political challenge. The girl was reckless and impulsive, and therefore easier to fool. But the court advisor was shrewd. He had dealt with queens and politics his entire life. He would not be easily convinced.

When Noro answered, he looked at the court advisor. "We will do everything in our power to bring back the Keeper, and the heir, alive."

The advisor nodded, but Noro could see he was not fooled. And why would he be? It was to Solaria's advantage that Layela Delamores die. Without her, the ether races, a thorn in Solaria's side, would perish within a few generations, without Solaria having to sully its hands or deal with anti-genocide softies. And Mirial would become part of the Solarian empire. Without ether for protection, it would be powerless against Solarian might.

His retirement was in sight.

But first, Layela Delamores had to die.

***

As soon as the lift doors opened, Avienne jumped up.

"You shouldn't be standing yet, you stubborn oaf!"

"Blood and bones, Avienne, I'm fine!"

Ardin was pale but moving with relative ease, only his left arm tense at his side. What she could still see of the wound through his ripped clothing had been covered up by fresh bandages. Layela followed him close, her face red and her lips thin.

"We thought we had lost you," Layela whispered, her voice trembling. "And we might yet, if you're not more careful!"

"We should be so lucky," Avienne mumbled as she walked to her station. Signals lit up as she reached it. "Blood and bones. Argument over. We've been spotted. Of course!"

Ardin sat in the captain's chair and Layela sat with Ardice at one of the empty stations, a reflection of just how undermanned they were.

"They're mad!" Avienne shouted as a Solarian ship veered course and headed straight for them.

"All right, no point in hiding anymore, gun it for the tunnel entrance," Ardin ordered. Clave manoeuvred the ship towards the tunnel. They picked up speed and within seconds reached velocities much greater than the old *Destiny* could have handled. And Avienne couldn't even feel it. She whistled appreciatively. This ship was impressive, to say the least. Her fingers danced on the control panel to ensure the weapons were calibrated correctly. It was difficult to make sure without firing, but she was certain she'd be able to test them soon enough.

"Two of them are heading off to block us." She brought the image up on the viewscreen. "Ugly things," she mumbled.

"Clave, keep us running straight towards them." Ardin said. "Avienne, prepare to fire on them and anything they send our way. All hands, prepare for possible impact."

He sat stiffly in the captain's chair, focusing on the incoming ships, his features taut and still slightly gray. Avienne raised the front shields without waiting for him to ask. She wondered how strong this ship's hull was. *Destiny* could take a good beating even with shields down. She imagined this descendant could, as well.

"Torpedoes incoming!" Avienne said, returning two shots and destroying the incoming weapons. No more shots were fired on either side.

"Were they testing us?" Ardin mused. The ships seemed to be waiting for them.

"They're directly in our path." Clave reported. The door to the bridge opened and Avienne watched Rose walk to the engineering station, mumbling as she did so.

"Should we shoot them?" Avienne asked, itching to blast them out of their way.

"Two more are appearing behind us," the engineer reported, her voice granular.

"Avienne, clear the path," Ardin ordered.

"Happy to!" She hit the final command to fire the highest level energy weapon, two high-velocity proton cannons…but nothing happened.

"Avienne?" Ardin asked, turning back to look at her. She swore,

trying again. Nothing happened. She triggered another set of weapons.
Nothing.

"Blood and bones!" She fired all weapons in all directions, and still nothing.

"Nothing's working! I just want to shoot them!"

"Rose?" Ardin turned to the engineer.

"They seem to be creating a dampening field from the four ships surrounding us. I'm not sure how." The woman didn't turn around, her fingers gliding effortlessly over the controls as she tried to analyze the incoming data.

"This shouldn't be possible," she mumbled just loud enough for Avienne to hear.

Her console flashed a warning.

"They're firing! All of them. Of all the crap…shields aren't responding, either!"

"They're managing to dampen our defensive and offensive capacities. Anything that relies on systems outside our hull is down," Rose reported.

"What about thrusters? Do we still have some power there?" Ardin asked.

"She's dead in the water," Clave reported.

"Brace for impact!" *Destiny II* shook with explosions. Avienne clutched her station, but the missiles mostly just rocked the ship.

"Now that's an armour!" Avienne exclaimed.

"We need to figure out how to get out of here!" Ardin said, jumping up to take the navigation station. He quickly switched the commands over to engineering, mimicking Rose's panel.

Fancy. That was a nice touch. The ability to move stations was important, especially when they crapped out, which had happened several times aboard the old *Destiny*. Avienne concentrated on her own station, looking for any functional weapon, any way to activate the shields, all to no avail. The only functions they had control over were whatever remained within the hull. She looked up towards Ardin.

"We blow up something in the bay," she said. Ardin looked at her, his eyes lighting up.

"Something big enough to blow the door and propel us forward!" He turned around. "Rose?"

The engineer shook her head. "Although I love the thought of setting off explosives in our ship," she coughed deeply, "we don't have anything that would propel us all the way to the tunnel. And I'm not sure we can even get the shuttle bay doors opened, either."

Warnings flashed across Avienne's screen. Her eyes grew wide. "They're charging their anti-proton guns!"

Ardin whipped around, eyes also wide. "What, who? Which ship?"

"All of them." She looked up from her station. "They're all going to fire at once."

***

Layela could feel the ether dancing around her, crashing against her, waltzing wildly around the ship. Ardice stirred, her face collapsing. Layela held her daughter and reached out with the ether, to the threat that now surrounded the ship. The ether was increasing around her, growing thicker with each passing second. She feared it would smother her and Ardice.

She closed her eyes and pushed it away, gently. It refused to go, rippling instead—away, and then returning to her. Ardice began to sigh heavily. She would soon be in full tantrum, and Layela feared what she might do with so much ether at her disposal. Layela grabbed hold of the ether and let her mind ride it, seeing both out of her own eyes and her soul's eyes, following the white mist beyond the hull of the ship, into space itself.

The mist was thick and spread thickly through space. Layela could see the Solarian ships beyond them, her mind blinded by the knowledge of what they were doing. The ether was frantic around her. Was it trying to warn her?

Layela grabbed as much of the ether as she could, but she could not wield it effectively. The mists seemed too heavy for her to move. No matter how much she pulled and pleaded, she cried and begged, the mists simply continued rippling with fear. They refused to obey her. She could touch them, but not move them, still.

What's the point of warning me if you won't help me! she shouted in her mind, frustrated, grabbing one final time and pulling the ether before those guns fired and ripped through the ship's hull, dragging everyone she loved into cold, merciless space. She willed the ether to grow thicker, to absorb the energy of the weapons, to slow it, to stop it, her fear mutating into multiple desires and commands, each less specific to the last, each building to the same message: *Stop!*

Layela's concentration was broken when she felt a strike against her face, sending her flying down. She panicked, looking for Ardice. She had been holding her! Where was she! Ardice's screams pierced the air and she looked up. Rose was coddling the child and trying to soothe her. Avienne stood before her, both angry and concerned.

"I don't know what you were doing, but it's not working. Stop it," Avienne snapped at Layela and then glanced at Ardin, who sat white-faced and clutching his wound, his eyes filled with fear and concern as he looked back at Layela. He coughed and turned his head, but Layela still saw him spit blood. She felt numb. Not only was the ether not listening to her, it was also hurting her loved ones. She stood up, shaky, and went to take Ardice. Rose handed her over without a word, but Avienne shot Layela a look of warning. Next time, Layela doubted Avienne would just slap her back to her senses.

But what could she do? They were about to be destroyed, and none of the gathering energy was of any use. They would die regardless. She held Ardice closer and tried to soothe her, mumbling the words over and over again: "I'm sorry. I'm so, so sorry."

***

Ardin sucked in his breath and coughed once more, swallowing with difficultly. Avienne rapped her knuckles on her station. They couldn't count on the ether or Layela for help. And their armour could have absorbed the blow of one proton weapon, maybe, but the heat generated by four would undoubtedly destroy them.

"Open communications channel. Tell them we surrender." Ardin's dark eyes met Avienne's. She could see anger in them—he hated giving this order. "We can figure out how to escape later." Avienne nodded, trying to show a confidence she didn't feel. If she were Solaria, she'd make sure they didn't walk off the ship alive. She opened the lines of communication and waited for them to do the same. She hailed them again, her fingers turning to ice as she entered the command over and over again.

"They're not answering," Avienne whispered. She looked up at Ardin as her panel beeped its final warning: the Solarian ships were firing.

"Weapons fired. It was fun," Avienne said as the energy beams rushed towards them. The beams seemed to slow for a moment, taking longer to reach them. Avienne held her breath. Something was stopping them. Layela?

But then the strange slowdown stopped and they resumed their speed, faster even than before. Avienne exhaled slowly, tracking the energy beams' progress towards them.

A great flash of light blinded them all, but the *Destiny II* didn't even rock.

"What happened?" Ardin asked at once.

"A ship got in the way, it seems, extending their shields over us," Rose answered.

"Mirialers?" Ardin asked.

"Not like any I've ever seen," she brought it up on the screen. A ship, made visible only with by the weapons fire dancing around on its shields, was turning away from *Destiny II* and heading towards the Solarian ships. The Solarians fired torpedoes at it, missing almost every shot. The energy from the anti-proton gun vanished and now barely licked its shields into visibility. And whatever shots did strike barely seemed to have an effect. The ship manoeuvred at a ridiculous speed, turning at sharp angles that should have been impossible considering its velocity. Avienne had never seen anything like it before.

The ship opened fire, and with one sweep, destroyed both ships standing in their way.

"Blood and bones! Now *that's* a ship!"

"Systems back online," Rose said.

"Clave, get us to that tunnel, now!"

The *Destiny II* roared to life.

"Activating tachyon shields," Avienne reported, the familiar blue aura forming around the ship. She closed the shutter as they approached. Clave could use the computer system to navigate easily enough.

The ship shuddered, and then seemed to move ahead of its own accord, which was accurate enough. They would basically surf the trapped tachyons to their destination.

"No signs of pursuit," Avienne reported.

Ardin turned and added darkly, "At least none that we can see."

CHAPTER 14

ELSA STOOD IN the middle of the gardens, where her freshly seeded sproutlings were already growing. The wind was soft and the sun warm, the scent of blooms and vanilla dancing on the winds around her, her dress billowing gently. It would have been the perfect day, had they not heard what had happened at the palace and seen the great ship leave the atmosphere, with a sonic boom and a trail of smoke.

The constant chatter of her sisters filled the back of her mind. There wasn't as much worry as she might have expected. The Berganda were weary still from the loss of the children, which dulled their fear.

She turned sideways. On the horizon, to the south, she could see the tallest towers of the palace, three of the stone pyres reaching up towards the sun of Mirial, representing the Three Fates. On most days, Elsa found the sight comforting. But today, it left her feeling cold and empty.

What do we do? The question floated in Elsa's mind over and over again. Layela had once told her to trust her instincts—that she was an ether creature and in touch with the universe around her. That, even though she couldn't see the future, her survival instincts were guided by Mirial herself and would not fail her.

But Mirial had failed Layela. From the snippets she had heard, from the ripples she had felt in the ether, she knew it could no longer be trusted.

She needed to put her trust in herself, and her sisters.

Come, she sent out a wave, which rippled back in agreements. She didn't know what plans the insurrectors would have for the Berganda, but she knew the old Mirialers didn't look too kindly on the ether races, even though they were also children of Mirial. She didn't dare take a chance, even if it meant abandoning the gardens of their birth.

At least for now.

She sent soothing waves to the earth. The saplings, still so small and tiny, responded in turn. *Be still,* she comforted them. They grew still and quiet, and she hoped they would avoid detection.

She reached out to the plants surrounding the gardens—the elm tree to the right, the great oak to the left. The bluebells lining the ground, mixed in with buttercups. The Lacile flowers which glowed gently, hiding now from the sun. The grass all around them, the wildflowers peeking through between the blades, the roses and their thorns, the poofy orange plants whose names she could never recall, and the bushes that held tiny leaves and pink flowers when spring was fresh and new.

She called out to all of them in the sunlight, to take care of the gardens, to protect the sproutlings of the Berganda in these uncertain times, while their mothers fought for peace on Mirial. Wave after wave of hope and need left her and filled the plants. With her all-too-human eyes, she imagined the plants standing a bit taller, but she knew it was only her imagination; they gently swayed in the wind around her.

Her own mother had been able to communicate with the plants and bend their will to hers. Or seal them to her with friendship, she wasn't certain. Her own mother would have stood by Layela and fought, even giving up her life for her and the Berganda. Elsa hid her forming plans deep in her heart.

She had never known her mother, but she intended to live up to her legacy.

Protect our children, she reached out one last time with her mind, her heart heavy as she stepped out of the sunlight and, with her sisters, vanished into the darkness of the surrounding woods.

***

Loran could hear water dripping from somewhere near. Gresko had negotiated for her life, and then for some mercy. The drugs administered by the healers made her memories foggy and her mind dull.

Murl.

She would kill her at the first opportunity. Loran had never taken another life, unless you counted monsters created from ether. But in this case, she believed she could.

She shifted and pain cut through her despite the drugs. She clenched her jaw, put her hand on her eyes to steady herself, and focused on counting the drips. The pain passed. More or less.

She would never be without pain. It had been bad enough with her prosthetic leg. It had taken weeks to get the proper treatment, Mirial still recovering from its twenty years of exile. Weeks while her nerve endings repaired and her skin tissue reformed. She had been in agony. The Keeper visited her often, as did the Malavants, to her surprise. They spoke to her even when she was in too much pain to speak back. Sometimes they just sat there quietly, which had also helped.

The Keeper had wanted to help her, but even her powers couldn't regrow a leg. And to heal the wound fully meant that she would never receive a proper prosthetic. And so she had begged the Keeper not to heal her, to just help her face the pain. And she had. When Layela had been there, Loran had sometimes cried from the relief. But it was not something the Keeper could maintain. The pain always returned, worse than ever.

By the time the proper equipment, parts and doctors flew in their great ships to help the wounded of Mirial, her leg had had almost a month to heal. The destroyed tunnel leading to Mirial had slowed progress down too much.

The doctors hadn't even wanted to give her a full prosthetic. But she had insisted. She needed something she could control more. She wanted to fight, to be of use to the Keeper, to be there for Mirial. She couldn't imagine doing so without a fully functional leg. So they had re-opened her wound, and attached the device to her nerves as best they could. But the wound was too old. Her new leg never quite worked the same as her real one, and the pain never stopped.

It was bearable, for which she was grateful. When she was near the Keeper, it was lessened. She imagined Layela knew and didn't make her ask for relief, simply giving it. Loran wanted to protect the Keeper for the ether she could control and for the kindness she chose to use it for.

Loran gave a bitter laugh. She had tried, but failed. The Keeper was out there, somewhere. And Loran would die here, a useless wreck of someone who had once believed in something.

She shifted again and almost threw up. Tears began to stream down her face. Without the Keeper, there would be no more relief, no more hope. She hated herself for her selfishness, but she needed those few moments where she felt like herself.

But now…Her prosthetic leg was still attached, but uselessly broken. She couldn't even send signals to it anymore to move it. She would need a full replacement, and she had a few available on Mirial now, of course, but no one would bring one to her and no doctor would approach her, not as long as Murl held her here, in the dungeons, underground.

She took a deep breath. She wanted to see, but didn't. She closed her eyes.

Face it, soldier.

With a sharp intake of breath she propped herself on an elbow. A thousand tiny suns exploded before her sight, but she managed to remain conscious. She opened her eyes again, light-headed and on the verge of passing out. She had lain here for too long. Hours or days, she just couldn't tell. The slight light revealed what she suspected Murl had done. With a sob, she fell back down, her entire body wracked as she cried, the sounds of her grief echoing off the deep walls.

Murl had taken all she had left. Her good leg was gone, only a stub remaining, and doctored just enough that Loran wouldn't die from it.

Loran would find a way to kill her, even if she had to crawl to her to do it.

★★★

Gresko heard the sobs bouncing off the walls and knew Loran was awake. He looked up from where he sat on a damp rock. He had been waiting for hours for her to awaken. He didn't know where else to turn. Loran was still loyal. One of the few.

He waited until the sobs subsided a bit, to spare both of them the embarrassment, and then he stood. The caves of the old dungeons were dingy, damp, broken down and downright barbaric. Murl had enjoyed leaving Loran here to contemplate her fate.

The whole idea left a very bitter taste in Gresko's mouth. He had known Loran's parents and disliked the thought of their little girl being treated in such a manner. No loyal Mirialer had ever been meant to see the inside of these dungeons.

And certainly not a royal guard of the Keeper. He walked slowly towards the back of the dungeons. The cell had been left unlocked. It had amused Murl. Another way to tease Loran, to know she was free and yet couldn't leave.

His chest tightened. He had never before felt old, but for the past few days he could feel no other way. Murl was a product of a dark time. She could have been better, perhaps, born under different circumstances. The Lady Adina had tried to protect and provide for her people, and she had mostly succeeded at the first. A feat in itself, considering the times.

But Murl was a product of the Great Darkness, living proof that Mirial had failed to give necessities of life, like proper morals. He was old, and he was starting to see it. So few of his generation had survived. They needed the young to remember and understand all that Mirial stood for.

Loran had an advantage, growing up off-planet. She had not been raised in constant fear and starvation, in constant need and without light. Perhaps the off-world children were more like the old Mirialers, in a way.

He walked very slowly to Loran's cell, he realized, buying himself time. He was not a violent man and had rarely witnessed violence of human on human. The sight of Loran's blood, and Murl picking up the limb as Loran lay there bleeding to death…he wondered if he had been too selfish in saving Loran. Perhaps death would have been easier.

He steeled himself. He would never believe that. Life was better, no matter what.

Mirial will greet us only when our time has come.

He walked in the room, Loran lying in the middle of it, on a rock. Her features were pale and drawn. She was probably trying to stay conscious.

Her broken prosthetic lay at a strange angle, the foot jutting unnaturally to the side, the knee bent backwards. He did not look at where her other leg should be.

Pulling out his small healing kit, he sat beside her.

"Loran, it's Gresko. I've brought you medicine."

She swallowed and took great effort to speak. "No more drugs."

"It will help you heal."

She furrowed her eyebrows and her lips grew thinner. She managed to croak another protest.

"All right, no more drugs. Let me at least give you antibiotics. Your body is too weakened right now to fight even the slightest infection."

Loran didn't protest and he took that as consent. He prepared the shot. He had already given her antibiotics after she had been wounded. He gently pierced her skin with the needle and pumped more pain killers into her, combined with extra sedatives. Her breath soon lengthened and her features relaxed.

Gresko sat with her for a time. He needed a doctor willing to help with the prosthetics. Loran was respected on Mirial, and she could rally the off-worlders. He needed her to live.

He needed her to carry out her duty to ensure the throne of Mirial remained strong.

CHAPTER 15

LAYELA WISHED SHE could access the gardens of the *Destiny II*, as she had once on the *Destiny*, to let her thoughts be refreshed by the scent of fresh blooms and multicoloured flowers, or at least just to be in a place where once a garden had been maintained. But the gardens had not yet been planted, and no oxygen was being pumped in that section. The space was as dead as what surrounded the ship.

Instead she wandered into the mess hall, grabbing supplies to bring back up to the bridge. It didn't look like anyone was about to move from their stations, even though the tunnels were free of any resistance so far. She had left Ardice with Ardin. Her heart had ached at the sight of the two of them, his holding her so tenderly, even though his left shoulder pained him so.

She had almost killed them both. Well, maybe not. At least she could take comfort in the fact that she could access her ether, even if using it proved too great a risk. Perhaps her distance from the planet was proving beneficial. Had the strange cloaked man managed to ward her on Mirial? Was such a thing even possible? *Dunkat.* Could it really be him?

Her hands turned to fists. She would kill him again. And again, and again, and as often as necessary to keep her family safe.

And she would do so without ether, if she had to. With her bare hands.

"Excuse me, Keeper." She turned to see Patros standing at the entry to the lounge. She forced a smile.

"Patros, please, call me Layela. It was my name long before I became Keeper of Mirial and, under the circumstances, perhaps a more adequate way to address me."

"You are still Keeper." He practically spat. She started, taken aback by his aggressive tone. He had only been a supporter and calm, up to now. She suddenly realized he was terrified. His hands were even shaking a bit. He was terrified that she would abandon Mirial and leave his people to suffer. Leave all ether creatures to suffer and perish.

"Of course, I will not abandon Mirial," she whispered, knowing full well she would abandon it in a heartbeat if she could afford to do so. But she didn't want to get into a full-blown argument. The day had been taxing enough. "But the journey will be long if we don't use first names, Patros." She paused. "I would appreciate you treating me as a friend."

His eyes grew a bit wider and he nodded slightly. She changed the topic. "I haven't had a chance to thank you for saving Ardin. I don't know how to repay you."

He lowered his head. "No need for repayment…Layela." He bit down the syllables of her name awkwardly. "Simply continue to do the best you can for Mirial, and I shall always be in your debt."

He hesitated, looked down, then his eyes met Layela's with certainty. "The wound is not healed."

Layela's limbs went cold. "But it's healing, right?"

He hesitated again and this time did not look her in the eyes when he answered. "I don't think so." He sighed heavily and ran his fingers through his hair. "It's full of dark ether. I'm not sure what it's doing. It's trying to spread and take over his entire body. I put safeguards into place, damming it in, but…I just don't know how long it'll hold. The dark ether is very powerful."

Layela looked down at the food she had gathered. "Is there anything we can do?" she whispered.

"I'm not sure. I noticed on Mirial that whenever a quake would hit, some of the ether would leave the plants, and darker ether would infiltrate." He paused and continued in a whisper. "In the ether creatures, as well. I'm not sure. In Ardin's case, it's like the ether was pushed out and the dark ether replaced it, leaving him contaminated. Maybe you could change the ether in his cells?"

Layela looked back up. "I don't know. Using the ether was hurting him and Ardice. What if I remove the dark ether and kill him instead? Is that better?"

"I guess there's only one way to find out."

Layela shook her head. "It'll affect Ardice, too, and I'm not sure how much. The ether around her…it hurts her. Or she pulls at it. I'm not sure anymore. She doesn't seem to be on the same wavelength as it, anyway." She continued in a whisper. "I couldn't risk her well-being for Ardin. He would never allow that."

Patros seemed frustrated. "Then what do we do? Do we just escape Mirial, let it fall to darkness, and watch Ardin and all ether creatures die?"

Layela flushed. He was right. She was coming up with so many reasons not to act, but she wasn't coming up with a lot of plans on what to do next. *Ardin.* Holding Ardice, keeping her safe, loving her dearly. And being there for Layela, no matter the situation or consequences. Believing in her when no one in the world did, especially after she became Keeper, still reeling from the loss of Yoma and Josmere. She would be all alone, if not for him.

"No," Layela piled the food in Patros' arms and walked back towards the lift. "We'll try, at least, to save him."

She'd already given up too much for Mirial.

***

Ardin tried not to shift to get more comfortable. His shoulder throbbed and he could barely move his fingers, and drawing too deep a breath flared pain in his chest bone, as though as knifeblade resided there. His sister watched him like a hawk, and he didn't intend to give her any room for arguing his presence on the bridge. He needed to keep busy. To keep moving.

"The Solarian ships broke formation just before we entered the tunnels," Avienne reported.

"Where are they headed?" He leaned forward a tiny bit in the captain's chair. The pain proved just enough to make him rethink a full shift of position.

"Some are heading to Mirial. Others are breaking in a sweep pattern."

Ardin looked darkly at her. "Why can't I help but think they had something to do with Layela being chased out of Mirial?"

"Would explain why they didn't make a move when they got here. They were just waiting. Blood and bones, I hate this politics crap! Can't we just shoot everyone?"

Ardin gave her a thin smile. "I don't know that we have to do anything, at this point."

The lift opened and Patros practically spat his words: "You mean you would abandon Mirial?"

Layela stepped out from behind him, and Ardin looked at her as he spoke, his voice low. "We owe nothing to Mirial. It's Layela's choice, and hers alone."

Patros seemed ready to walk up to Ardin and start a fight. Avienne crossed the bridge and stood before him. "Do yourself a favour. Back away now."

Larod, his sister's plump second-in-command, took a step towards the ether creature. Ardin's respect for the man grew, though he wondered what he would do if the Slont fought back.

Patros stood rooted in place, staring darkly at Ardin. Then he nodded stiffly, turned, and headed back into the lift. Avienne watched him until the doors closed. She turned back to Ardin.

"Do you think he knows which floors have oxygen?"

"Lift won't open on the others."

"That was a joke, Ardin. We have enough serious going on without having to be all serious ourselves."

He felt Layela's presence beside him and his mood lifted. He turned to look at her, able to ignore the pain in his chest when she was near, quiet strength and determination. Her two-coloured eyes looked up at him, her dark hair framing her pale features. With a light touch he brushed a stray strand of hair away from her face. She closed her eyes and leaned into his touch, and his hand lingered there, the bridge dropping away as though they were the only two people left in the universe.

Ardin wanted to say something to her, about how beautiful she was, or how proud he was of her, or how he wouldn't leave her, but all of his words rung hollow as the pain intensified in his chest. He gasped, unable to stop himself from flinching as mountains seemed to collapse on him, crushing his lung, his muscles, his ribs…Ardice was crying, screaming in the background, and Ardin understood. Layela's features were set in deep concentration, her features drawn and pale.

He grabbed both of Layela's hands in his. "You're hurting Ardice," he whispered in Layela's ear. Then he added. "And me."

The influx of ether stopped as quickly as it had begun, taking most of the pain with it. Sweat coated his body and he ignored his shaking hands as he drew Layela close. Rose was soothing Ardice, their daughter's sobs breaking and growing less frequent.

"You can't risk hurting her," he whispered again, to reinforce his words.

A sob parted Layela's lips. "I don't want to lose you. Either of you."

"You won't," he said, his voice lacking conviction.

Layela stayed in his arms for a moment longer before pulling away, her eyes shining with unspent tears. She looked at him for a few seconds, then at Ardice, before turning determinedly to the lift. She was gone without a word.

"Sit down before I make sure you can't get up again for a long time," Avienne whispered beside him. He didn't argue, practically collapsing on the captain's chair. He looked to Ardice, asleep in Rose's arms. He wanted to hold her and feel her warmth against him, but he feared the dark ether might contaminate his fragile daughter.

He leaned back against the chair and stared out into space, waiting for the pain to ease.

***

Layela ran ungracefully down the corridor, catching up to Patros before he entered his room.

He looked at her with disgust. "I thought I'd been dismissed."

Layela tried to catch her breath. "He's in pain, Patros. Try to show some compassion."

"He doesn't seem concerned over my people!"

She drew herself up as much as she could and held his gaze. "I care about your people, Patros, and I won't abandon them." His eyes narrowed as though judging the truth of her words. He stood over her at least a head, and had proved to be quick footed. She suddenly wondered if following him had been a bad idea. What did she know about him, anyway?

He needs me, she reminded herself. Without a Keeper, without Mirial, the ether creatures were dust.

When he didn't speak, she continued. "I will not abandon your people, but I need to understand the dark ether. It's at the root of all of this, that much is clear. And to understand it, I need to be able to understand Ardin's wound." She almost bit her lower lip before catching herself. "I couldn't heal him, Patros. The ether, my ether, it hurt him instead."

Patros sighed and she looked back up. He offered her a slight grin.

"I guess we all have a lot to lose."

Layela nodded, accepting his peace offering. "If I can't help Ardin, I need to find someone who can. Do you know anyone, Patros? Old ether races? There must be knowledge amongst your people that Mirial has long since forgotten."

He shook his head. "My people were very insular. Our homeworld was long ago destroyed, and we lost many in the Ether Wars. I'm sorry, Keeper, but we have limited lore and knowledge with which to help you."

"Do you know of any other races near you that might know more?"

He shook his head again. "My people are long-lived, but nowhere near as long as some of the other ether races. But we lost knowledge of their names and locations a long time ago."

Locations… She smiled, hope settling into her chest.

If legend or lore still sung of their presence or location, she knew one man who would know where to point her.

***

"You want to go where?" Ardin said, his eyes almost as big as his forehead. Layela looked down at Ardice, who slept peacefully in her arms. What they needed were answers. Knowledge that no longer existed on Mirial, but that perhaps existed elsewhere. Another ether race.

"We need Gobran," she said. "He'll be on Thalos IV still, gathering his maps." Gobran Kipso, captain of the *Victory*, given honourable discharge after the battle for Mirial. He had wanted her dead, once. Because of his loyalty to Mirial, not for personal reasons. He had since become a great ally. And, most importantly, he was a map collector. He had once described to Layela how many maps he had. Hundreds, if not thousands. Some digital, but many on old parchments and materials that only resisted decomposition through careful handling and regular maintenance.

He had left, months ago, with his daughter Alecya, to show her the world and his map shop on Thalos IV, where he and Layela had first met. He intended to find all of his maps again, and carefully store them for transport back to Mirial. And he would show Alecya some of the worlds beyond Mirial. She had never travelled off-planet, and they were excited at the prospect of a journey together.

Ardin cocked his head. "Thalos IV. In Solarian space."

Layela mimicked his look. "Are you telling me that the best, newest ship in all of Mirial can't avoid a little detection?"

A slow smile spread across Ardin's face. She wanted to kiss him when she saw the light in his eyes.

"Thalos IV it is."

Layela smiled. The ship continued its journey through the tunnels, the shutters all closed to avoid seizures. She reached out to Mirial, far away now behind them, Ardice calming and falling asleep in her arms. Mirial responded with a wave of peace and warmth, unjudging, uncaring, just being. The waves danced around her. Layela could not reach out to touch them, for fear of hurting Ardice or Ardin. But she had managed to shift them, even if just a little bit. She feared what would happen if she could touch more of the ether, pierce the wall that still seemed to stand before her, although now thinner than it had been in her throne room. She would find a way to shatter it, but not at too high a cost.

Even if Mirial needed her and her ability to cultivate its energy so that it could grow and pollenate other life, just like a garden.

Layela wondered if the garden could grow wild and still live, or if she had foolishly allowed too many weeds to grow while she had tended only to her prized roses.

CHAPTER 16

MURL TESTED EACH weapon carefully. She started with her own short sword, infused with ether from her brother. Its energy pulsed in her arm and throbbed in her muscles, a warmth spreading deep into her tissues. Her pistol, well-loaded with bullets, strapped to her hip opposite the short sword. And a plasma gun on her lower leg, below it. Plasma guns were outlawed on Solarian worlds, but useful in battle. Besides, she had no care for Solarian law.

Knives and several explosive devices were strewn across her body. She had cast aside her official uniform and donned her black clothing of old, her long sleeves covering the burn scars on her arms. Worn, maybe, but in this clothing she had been at her best as a warrior, at her fiercest. When she had survived what killed more than ninety percent of her planet. She could still smell tar and her own blood, from battles long ago. She had fought demons, monsters, Mirialers gone mad.

And now, she would fight her own Keeper.

No. She was not fighting against the current Keeper. She was fighting for the next Keeper. Layela just happened to be standing in the way. Responsible for her escape, Murl felt it necessary to go after her, herself.

The weapons on her body were powerful and would prove useful, but the ones on her ship, built for rescue operations, were what she was counting on. Her fighter ship was small, extremely fast and manoeuvrable. She had the maps and design specs of *Destiny II*. The new flagship of Mirial was strong and impressive, but not without its weaknesses.

By her orders, her own ship had been outfitted with weapons that could take advantage of those weaknesses. She wouldn't be able to destroy the flagship, but she could lower her shields and pierce her hull, granting her access to its precious contents.

She felt a presence behind her and turned, weapon in hand. Her brother smiled at her.

"Always a quick one, Murl."

Braken's hood was lowered, since it was just the two of them. He hated the hood, she knew. It was hot, and itchy, and hid the world from him. But he had chosen to wear it, so that Mirialers would not fear him. Murl remembered his face, growing up. His eyes of sea green were still piercing, but his features, once handsome, looked as though they had melted from his bones. Blisters still made frequent appearances, as though the fires that had claimed most of his body still burned from within and would never stop.

Murl placed a hand on his cheek, the skin warm and soft and pliable. It reminded her of pig's fat. She fought down the thought as she stood on her tiptoes and kissed his other cheek, sleek, as always, with sweat. It was the fires from within. The ones she intended to smother.

"I won't be gone long. I'll be back soon, I promise."

He nodded. "Be careful, sister. Layela is dangerous. She's already begun breaking her wards. If she figures out how to safely tap into the ether, she could do you serious damage."

Murl nodded and took her hand away from his face, resisting the urge to wipe her palm on her pant leg. "I will be careful. I promise. You be careful, too. There are still some here who would be loyal to Layela, like the Berganda."

It was his turn to nod. "I will take care of them. I have enough loyal soldiers and power to deal with a few weak rebels. Our next steps must be achieved, Murl. We are so close!"

There was such longing in his voice that it made her heart ache. They were close. After years of work and mastery, of ensuring the right elements were in place, a new Mirial could be born. Stronger than before. Able to withstand the calamities of nature and Solaria.

"You must not fail." Her brother reiterated, placing both hands on her shoulder. "I will be with you." Her shoulders grew warm as he pumped ether into her body. *Do not fear, sister,* his voice echoed in her mind.

I don't, she replied, as pain ripped through her, lightning from fingertips to toes, the cracking and shifting of her bones echoing in her skull. She gritted her teeth and braced her legs to remain standing. Her mind opened with light and her brother's mind whirled within her, her within him, an endless possibility of ether and light. She reached out, wanting to stay in his warmth, to settle there and never know pain or loss again, but he gently guided her back to her own mind, like a father scolding an overly eager child. She did not argue nor hate her sorrow, for it made her stronger to have seen the full light and lost it, then never to have seen it.

The pain left suddenly, and she felt as light as a cloud.

She opened her eyes, swearing she could see more sharply, feeling her brother's power throb within her, concentrated on her chest. He had gifted her with Mirial herself. She could not fail. Braken gently wiped tears away from her face. She looked down, embarrassed, not having realized she was crying. She noticed a glow under her shirt, where the warmth spread.

"I will be back, with Layela and our friends in tow." Her own voice sounded foreign in her ears, so thin and tired. She wanted to lie down and sleep and run a marathon, too. "I make no promises for the others, however."

Her brother grinned. His teeth were still as white and straight as ever, looking out of place on his disfigured face.

"They don't matter. Kill them all. Just bring her back, and we'll celebrate the birth of a new Mirial with her blood."

He turned and left, pulling up his hood as he exited the room. Murl watched him go, her big brother, wishing she could take his pain away. But she couldn't, not now, and she knew that.

Still, she could lessen it. But she intended to do whatever proved necessary to help him, and Mirial, be born again, stronger.

No matter the cost to others, or herself.

CHAPTER 17

WE'RE NEARING THALOS IV," Clave reported.

Avienne whistled. "I never get used to the efficiency of this new tunnel. Best in space, they say!"

"The faster to reach us by," Ardin said quietly, looking down at Ardice. "She's doing better?"

Layela smiled. It had only been a few days with a difficult baby. Granted, one that could easily tear apart the fabric of creation, apparently. Still, it had felt like a lifetime.

"She's better," Layela answered, hoping she wasn't cursing her daughter's improved mood.

"If we're gonna get out, we should do it now. We'll be in Solarian territory soon." Avienne said from the back, half of her words mumbled through yawns.

"Right. Pull us out, Clave."

"But that'll leave us light leagues to travel outside the tunnel!"

"Pull us out or I'll jettison you, Clave," Ardin spoke the words softly, sending a chill up Layela's spine. It had been years since she had seen Ardin at the command of a ship, and even then, he had never had to assert his authority on the *Destiny*.

Clave shot a look to Layela. She sighed.

"Ardin is captain and in charge of this ship. And he's a man of his word, so I'd do as he says."

Clave nodded and pulled *Destiny II* outside the nearest exit port. The viewport cover slid up, and the blue hues of the tachyonic shields washed away in the emptiness of space.

A few meteors floated before the great solar system of Thalos. All planets in Thalonian space aligned every second month, solidifying trades. From their vantage point, the seven planets were on their end of the solar system, adding ease and speed to their journey.

"Keep her hidden," Ardin ordered Clave. "We'll head to the planet by shuttle. We'll return soon with a guest in tow." He turned to Avienne.

"Don't even think of leaving me behind!" She leapt into the lift and was gone. Ardin shook his head and turned to Layela.

She spoke before he could. "You'll need me. I have more connections on Thalos IV than either of you."

"Five-year-old connections," he said. "How do you know any of them still exist, with Solaria in the mix now?"

Heat rose to her face but she forced herself to meet his gaze. "They're good connections. Besides, do you even know where Groban's shop was?"

He sighed and looked down at Ardice. "Well, we can't bring her, and we can't exactly leave her here alone."

Layela flushed. She knew he was right, but she had really wanted to see Thalos IV again. To go there would be like going back home. She could see some of her old haunts, and feel closer to Josmere and Yoma. It was hard remembering much more than their deaths some days on Mirial, considering they had both basically gone there to die.

But that was her past, now, and she needed to concentrate on the future. She bit her lower lip and took Ardice from Ardin's arms.

She forced a smile. "I understand, of course. Please be careful."

"I will be. You, too." He stood straight, and if not for the slight slope of his left shoulder, she might have believed he wasn't injured at all. She tried not to think of it.

"We'll walk you to your ship," Layela offered, and they headed down the elevator.

"Larod, you have control of the bridge until I return."

"Aye, Captain."

"And Larod, Clave, Jaru and Rose," Ardin added before the doors to the lift closed, "if anything happens, anything at all, save Layela and Ardice before anyone else, understood?"

Larod turned and nodded just as the lift doors closed.

***

Avienne flipped a knife as she walked down the corridor. She hated to admit it, but she was nervous about heading into Solarian territory. Both Ardin and her had discussed it last night, and decided it was best for Layela to stay here with the crew. Ardin wasn't happy about leaving her without his protection, but they had little choice. Avienne needed someone else she could trust, and the only other person with direct Solarian experience and knowledge of Thalos IV was either him and Layela.

She had also suggested that he stay here with Ardice and that Layela come instead, but he had been against the idea. Which worked out great for her—better her brother, a seasoned smuggler and good with multiple weapons, than an ex-flower girl and thief.

Still, she was worried about heading down with Ardin. Her brother had entertained a very different lifestyle over the past five years, and although she was certain he had maintained his fighting skills, how much practical experience could he still possibly have? He had been basically ruling a planet. Not to mention the wound that he tried so hard to keep hidden.

She sighed. She'd have to trust that he wouldn't put himself in a situation he couldn't handle. She laughed. Of course he would. She doubted that much had changed.

Her unit beeped. She was in front of the right door. She grinned and stored the small comm unit away. It was great. She could control the bridge from here, undertake onboard and offboard communications, access ship maps and systems and, her favourite, track down guests and crew members.

She pressed the chime to the room. Seconds later, the door opened, with a dishevelled Patros standing there.

"Sleep well?"

He half grunted and waved at her to come in. She did, sitting down ungracefully on the second, still-made bed. Crew quarters were so dull and practical. The royal quarters and posh touches she imagined were part of the final schematics had not yet been incorporated into the ship.

Shame.

"Ardin and I are heading to Thalos IV," Avienne said, foregoing preliminaries.

Patros nodded. "I will come," he simply stated. She grinned.

"That'd be fun, but it's Solarian space now, remember? Your presence would make too much trouble."

He nodded but looked disappointed.

"I do have a favour to ask of you, however," Avienne continued, leaning forward and placing her chin in her hand as she rested her elbow on her knee. The Slont remained perfectly still, and only the slight narrowing of his eyes betrayed his concern.

She smiled sweetly. "We're leaving Layela here, with Ardice. I need to make sure no one tries to hurt her," she continued.

Patros hesitated for a moment before speaking. "She's on a Mirial ship. Who would dare try to hurt her?"

Avienne shrugged. "I don't know. I just don't know these people enough, or at least some of them. I hope no one, but the fact of the matter is, I don't know."

"And you trust me, even after the…blow out?"

She shrugged. "Emotions run high, sometimes. Let's face it— you're the best I've got. And you obviously remember what happened the last time Mirial was without a Keeper. I give you enough credit to make sure it doesn't happen again. Layela can help you and Mirial, but you'll have to trust her."

Avienne stood. "And remember also that if anything happens to her while she's in your care, there will be no safety for you in or out of Solarian space."

He stood to face her. "No need for threats. I already saved your brother, remember?"

The smuggler peered into his eyes. It was harder for her to tell if ether creatures were lying to her, but his eyes seemed truthful enough. And her gut told her she could trust him.

"And I appreciate that, thanks!"

She stood on the tips of her toes and surprised him a quick kiss on the mouth.

"See ya!" she called as she walked out of the room, counting her weapons and planning what to pack for the shuttle.

The mission seemed easy, even simple. Go down, grab old man with maps, come back up. But, in her experience, the easier the mission, the greater the danger to her and Ardin.

They would definitely need more weapons.

***

The shuttle bay was almost identical to the original *Destiny*'s. The main difference lay in the number of shuttles. This one still had a full complement, whereas *Destiny* hadn't even had enough to evacuate its entire diminished crew.

"We'll take something small and quick, that both Avienne and I are familiar with. We'll each be able to pilot, so don't worry about anything."

"Right," Layela said. *Two to pilot in case someone is incapacitated.*

She placed her hand on his chest, near the wound. He held his breath but said nothing. She could feel it, the dark ether. It whispered horrors in her mind and warmed her finger until she had to remove it, for fear of getting burned.

Ardice stirred, awakened by Layela's awakening of the ether. Ardin took her hand in his, brought it to his lips and kissed it. A thin coat of sweat covered his face from her simple probing. He looked deep into her eyes.

"I will come back."

Layela nodded. He kissed her again and took Ardice in his arms, speaking soft words to her. He handed her back and headed for the shuttle, just taking the time to shoot a quick grin to Layela.

Avienne walked past her. "I'll make sure he makes it back," she said, winking. "I promise." She stopped and added. "I asked Patros to keep an eye on you. He's okay, just worried."

Layela nodded slowly. Avienne and Ardin were best equipped to get Gobran and bring him back safely. They would be fine. They would be back in no time.

The Malavant siblings boarded the shuttle and a few instants later, it headed towards the decompression chamber. She watched until the great doors closed behind it, and she heard the sounds of evacuating oxygen as the outside doors opened. Onto space.

Ardice began fussing. Layela bounced her and started towards the lift. She needed to study the plans of this new ship, and the controls for these shuttles, just in case she and Ardice needed a quick escape.

Staying on *Destiny II* might be the right decision for now, but she had no intention of being caught unprepared if a quick escape proved necessary.

CHAPTER 18

AVIENNE NAVIGATED THE shuttle close to space debris, keeping her energy signature insignificant, using only blasts of compressed air to shift their direction. It would take longer to reach Thalos IV without full-on engine power, but avoiding detection was more important. Ardin sat next to her, letting her do most of the piloting. His gaze moved from sensor readings to the expanse of space outside the viewport.

He was distracted. She broke the silence. "Are you sure you're up to this?"

He started to protest, but then he gave her a slight grin. "I have no idea. I haven't been traveling the stars like you for the past five years."

Avienne grinned. "Been missing out, Ardin."

He smiled back. "You, too."

She felt like hitting him, but sighed instead. They were shadowing the debris of a huge broken ship, at least twice the size of *Destiny II*. The ship's metal caught glimpses of the faraway sun, revealing a combination of silvers and golds, and some red metals Avienne had never seen. The ship would have been beautiful if not for the hole that had ripped her almost in half, turning her into a crypt for her crew. Avienne didn't even recognize the symbols. It was at least a few centuries old.

The shuttle was following it like debris, caught in its wake. The best part about the Thalos system was that it was an old space-faring system with lots of wars, especially among the royal family. This entire section of the system was littered with debris and corpses of ships.

Useful for hiding.

"And your wound?" She hated to ask. She wanted to ignore it. But to ignore it might mean to lose Ardin, and she wasn't willing to do that.

He shrugged the question off. "It'll keep."

She felt like hitting him but sighed and leaned back in her seat instead. "We should get extra supplies on Thalos IV. Maybe some underground medicine could prove useful."

"Sounds great. Illegal drugs from Thalos IV? Sounds like a great idea!"

Avienne sighed. "Well, the theory is sound. Maybe we'll find something."

"I thought Solaria had cleaned the planet up?"

Avienne laughed. "You've been out of the circuit too long, Ardin. There are still healthy smuggling pockets. Besides, the alliance between Solaria and the Thalos royal family is still shaky, and I don't think it'll ever get stronger. They're like oil and water, one obsessed with order and rules, the other, with its throne and lineage. I'm not sure what Solaria sees in Thalos, really. Seems like loads of wasted resources for a system that doesn't offer much else but debris and intrigue."

"Solaria likes expanding. I think they'd love to be the only military might in the universe."

Avienne cast a sideways glance at Ardin. "You're worried about Mirial, aren't you?"

Ardin didn't answer, leaving his sister slightly disappointed. Part of her had hoped ripping him away from the planet would rekindle his love of space. She realized that she'd harboured the fantasy that he would join her in space again, so the journeys wouldn't be as long and boring. Not to mention lonely.

She laughed softly. He looked at her quizzically and she turned to face him. "We'll figure this out, Ardin. Once Ardice has calmed down and we can safely bring her back to Mirial, maybe we can convince the people to calm down. Not to mention taking down that big cloaked maniac. We'll figure it out."

Ardin kept his peace, though she could see uncertainty dancing in his eyes. She wished she meant what she said. Part of her just wished Mirial would burn and free them all.

***

Thalos IV was quieter than anticipated. The planet loomed before them, with only its basic security grid in place. Ardin entered a code and Avienne watched the ship's outbound signals change from a Mirial shuttle to a Collar transport ship. An old smuggling trick.

She raised an eyebrow at him. He grinned. "Old habits die hard."

"That's good to hear," she replied, keeping an eye on all readings anyway.

They began entry into the atmosphere without being challenged.

"This seems easy," Ardin said. "Has their security gone that far downhill? I mean, we can alter signals, but anyone looking out a viewing port would recognize we're not from Collar."

"Never underestimate the power of avoidance of extra paperwork. Besides, I think most of the Solarian fleet is around Thalos III. The royal family might still be trying to keep Solaria out of its 'trading' system."

Ardin nodded and grew quiet. He leaned forward and kept punching the same buttons to show him the same readings, so that he would see immediately if someone had signalled their presence. Of course, the ship would alert them if outbound readings changed or if they had been spotted. Avienne was glad they were already almost in port. She might have to hurt her brother if he kept it up.

"Let's go to our old haunt," Avienne said. "Last I was here, it hadn't changed. Should be safe enough."

Ardin nodded, pulling the ship towards the old, broken docks that boasted more smuggling trade than anywhere else in all of Solaria.

A light flashed on the panel in front of Avienne. "Great."

Ardin cast a quick glance at it. "Who's hailing us?"

Avienne raised an eyebrow. "No one friendly. Solarian Security, apparently."

"Nothing on our sensors," Ardin said. "Maybe they're hailing from the planet?"

"Um, I don't think so," Avienne said as the proximity alert flared to life. A great shadow blocked the sun above them and Ardin swore and pushed hard on the shuttle controls. Avienne was grateful for the seatbelt that stopped her from flying off her seat.

"Weapons armed!" she cried as the six cannons broke free from their shuttle's hull.

"How did it get so close?" Ardin's voice was strained.

"Dunno. Blocked itself, somehow. Blood and bones, there's two of them! And they're big!" Avienne swore. Their six guns suddenly seemed insignificant against the two large Solarian attack ships shadowing them.

"Think they're overdoing it," Avienne mumbled.

"No turning back now!" Ardin said, not slowing as they approached the busy docks, targeting one of the main landing stations. It was a huge dock, with vendors and bars galore. A perfect place to hide, as long as they escaped quickly enough.

Avienne aimed for a higher wall, in the hopes no worker would get hit by her incoming fire. She fired just as the Solarian ships struck from behind, the entire shuttle jerking. Ardin missed the hole created by Avienne's shot, trying to veer the shuttle sideways so they wouldn't slam into the wall. The hull groaned as it scraped against the side of the metal docks and Avienne returned fire.

"Our shield are already out!"

Ardin gritted his teeth. "Fire away, we're going in!" Avienne hit every weapon release, not caring where she was firing as long as enough of them struck forward and cleared a path. Ardin forced the shuttle sideways in a tailspin, straight into the second floor of a warehouse.

Ardin hit the communications button, hoping *Destiny II* would receive the message. "They knew we were coming, identified us too easily. It's too dangerous—leave Thalonian space now!"

Shards of wall exploding around them, they struck, metal screeching as the shuttle absorbed the impact. Avienne held on to her seat, to the controls, to anything she could grab as the panel flared in sparks before her, the shuttle skidding and moaning until its floor gave way and her seat went flying up.

Frantically she tried to undo her seatbelt, but the seat dragged her backwards, outside the shuttle. She tried to grab hold at Ardin, who stayed stuck, thinking she heard her name as she flew back and struck something hard.

***

Ardice woke up suddenly, whimpered once, and her entire face collapsed. She turned red and shrieked.

The air around Layela turned acrid. Her arms overheated and chafed. She heard bells tolling.

Bells… the vision of Ardin's death clutched her mind, and she remembered long ago hearing those bells, heralding his end. Her heart broke with each strike of the bell. A life without Ardin. *A life alone.*

She held Ardice tightly and let herself collapse as she fought back sobs, the bells crashing in her mind. Ardice's screams managed to pierce the tolling. Layela snapped back, opening her eyes. The world was covered in the mists of her vision, still. She could see very little except for Avienne, standing tall, her red hair billowing in the winds of Layela's vision, laughing as she looked at her. She winked and was gone, as were the mists.

Layela tried to stand, but she was too weak.

"What happened?" Rose asked, her voice cracking. Layela realized the engineer was holding her from behind, supporting her from falling over. She quickly straightened. Rose didn't seem fazed, wrinkles surrounding the old woman's calculating and concerned eyes.

"A vision," Layela whispered. Ardice was calming; her eyes, shining with awareness, sought out her mother's. She could feel waves of warmth coming from Ardice, as though her daughter was trying to comfort her. Layela teared up. How aware was her daughter? She was so young, so little still, just a few weeks old, and yet in her eyes shone an awareness that should not yet exist.

What am I supposed to do? Layela despaired. Her daughter would suffer regardless. But she had to at least stop the physical pain caused by the ether.

"What happened?" Rose asked again, her voice even softer.

Layela snapped back to attention. "Ardin and Avienne are in trouble. Something went wrong. I'm not sure what."

Clave and Rose shared a quick look. "What?" Layela stepped up.

They hesitated. "Tell me now, or I'll throw you both out the airlock!" She hoped she sounded somewhat intimidating.

Clave spoke up. "We received a message. The Malavants' shuttle was attacked—Solaria knew they were coming. They ordered us to leave this area." He shot Rose a quick look and then stood tall before Layela. "What do you need us to do?"

Layela looked up, surrounded by what she hoped were allies. She didn't know Clave, but something in his dark eyes told her she could trust him. Rose was warm and loving, her wizened eyes holding only comfort. Patros had been sworn to protect her, and she didn't believe he would betray her. Not as long as Mirial needed her.

She looked down to Ardice. One green eye, one dark blue eye. Night and day. She was amazing. She would grow up to be amazing.

"I need to go down there," she whispered. "I think I can help them, or at least find them."

The silence on the bridge was smothering. She pressed on. "I need someone who can fly a shuttle to come with me," she paused, swallowed hard, "and I need someone here to take care of Ardice."

Clave shrugged. "I can fly the shuttle better than anyone else. But I've never flown in Solarian space."

"I can help you," Layela said. "I don't know the controls, but I know Thalos IV."

"What guarantees do we have that you'll make it, if the Malavants didn't?" Rose asked. "Avienne seemed pretty seasoned to me."

Layela bit her lip and looked down, then forced her chin back up. "I hope I can use some ether once I'm away from Ardice and Ardin."

Rose narrowed her eyes. "Are you sure that's wise?"

Layela flushed. "I don't know. But I can't think of any other ideas, can you?" She looked around at those gathered on the bridge around her. "Can any of you?"

No one spoke. She relented a bit. "I won't use much. Enough to disguise our approach. Stay far, and keep Ardice safe."

Rose's face softened. "I'll walk you to the shuttle."

"I'll grab some supplies and meet you there," Clave said, heading for the lift.

"I should come with you," Patros argued. "I promised Avienne I would keep you safe."

"Your presence would be too noticeable on Thalos IV. Stay here, keep Ardice safe. That is more payment than any of us could ask."

He nodded and stayed behind as Rose, Layela and Ardice entered the lift. Layela held the small bundle of life and tried to remember every feature, the curve of the small lips, the slit of her eyes, the colour of her few hairs.

In case this was good bye.

***

Rose wished she could gather Layela in her arms and take away the worries. She couldn't, she knew, partly because the two women didn't know each other well, partly because Layela was Keeper of Mirial, and too important to be comforted by mere mortals. Or so it used to be. Walls erected long ago seemed to be crumbling around Layela and her personal, human touch.

She was just a young woman, a mother terrified of leaving her newborn behind. Afraid of losing her beloved.

It was a terrible choice to be given, and Rose could only imagine. She had had children and grandchildren once. The grandchildren would have been about Layela's age. They hadn't survived the dark ages. Not one of her three children or five grandchildren. She had once believed she would be smothered under the weight of her own grief, losing herself into tinkering with machinery, trying to keep whatever technology Mirial still had running and functional. Her work had earned her recognition after the rebirth of Mirial, and Ardin himself, who had heard of her work, had approached her to help build the *Destiny II*. She had protested at first, knowing very little of spaceships.

But he had insisted she at least try and she had never regretted accepting his offer.

Before being an engineer, before losing herself in the love of details and mechanics, she had been something else, however. And she had had family, once, too.

She looked sideways to Layela, her face set in grim determination. She was no great beauty, but had a definite practical prettiness about her. She decided to reach out to the young woman who stood beside her. Not see her as anything more than what she was: young, afraid, and lost. There was no point in telling her everything would be all right. None of them knew that, and those useless words would ring hollow. She could offer her some comfort, however. Something she could have told Layela a long time ago, but fear or remaining embarrassment had stilled her lips. She looked at the lift door before her as she spoke, not looking at Layela.

"I had a sister once, too, and I lost her…like you." She began, her mouth dry. Layela turned her head slightly. She said nothing in turn, probably waiting to see where this would go, but she didn't tell Rose to be quiet, either. And so Rose continued, her heart fluttering. She had never told anyone this story. She had never imagined she would need to. She imagined the girl beside her was one of her grandchildren, or children, or at least a close friend. Not one of those Keepers of legend. The words rolled more easily as she did so.

"I loved her very much. We didn't always get along, but we always loved each other. She left, one day. I was so ashamed by her deeds, or by what I suspected she had done, that I changed my name to disassociate myself from her, just in case her story was ever found out." She was rambling, she knew. She was nervous. Memories flooded her mind and clogged her words. She wished she could oil her neurons, sometimes.

She took a deep breath and continued. "I guess what I'm trying to tell you is that your daughter will be safe with me." She paused. "My sister knew your mother. She once took care of her children, and kept them safe, as best she could."

She forced herself to turn and look at Layela, whose lips were slightly parted, as though wanting to say something, but uncertain. "Her name was Lisak Delamores. You took her name, and my family's name, in turn. That makes you family, Layela."

Tears were gathering in Layela's eyes, and Rose had to look away, to hide her own tears. "My name is Rose Delamores. I was ashamed for so long that my sister had agreed to take you away, that she had betrayed Mirial. But now that I know you, and I see how you've turned out, I'm glad she was brave enough to do the Keeper's bidding."

She faced Layela again. "I swear to you I will take care of Ardice and protect her with my life. It's the least I can do for my family."

Layela looked down at Ardice and whispered as she spoke. "She was kind, the old woman. I never remembered her first name, but she gave us our family name. She died when we were very, very young. I'm so sorry."

Rose smiled and reached up to wipe one of Layela's tears away, surprised at how natural the motion seemed. "Don't be. She lived a good life, and many sorrows have since clouded that one. With your permission, I would like to take back the Delamores name. I never should have forsaken it, and I've lived with shame too long. I'm sorry."

Layela nodded and smiled, laughing a little. "I should be the one asking you to continue using it." The doors opened and they entered the great shuttle bay. They waited in silence until Clave arrived, and when the time came, Layela gently kissed Ardice, hesitated for only a moment, and handed her to Rose.

Rose took the little bundle. She was so fragile it made her heart ache. She had seen what horrors could befall fragile young children.

Layela placed a hand on Rose's arm. "She's your niece, for all intents and purposes, Rose Delamores. Keep her safe, above all." She whispered the last few words, so only the two of them would share them. Her voice trembled. "If you must, do like your sister. Vanish. I will come find you, if I can. Promise me you'll have the strength to follow in your sister's impressive footsteps."

Rose nodded. Layela eyes shone, one green, one blue.

Keep my daughter safe, she pleaded with those eyes. *Above all else, Mirial, the ether creatures, even Ardin and Layela, keep Ardice safe.*

Just as Layela's mother had probably once asked of her sister, before vanishing into the great canopy of stars.

She nodded.

Some legacies were worth following. No matter how many had died, or how many demons still haunted Rose's nightmares. This was about the living.

And the legacy of the Delamores would not be about how many died because of the Keeper's decision. It would be about how the Delamores family always chose to protect the living and the innocents, above all else.

RDIN ALMOST LOST consciousness, but the pain in his wound spread as the belt pushed against it, and it jerked him awake. The shuttle skidded to a stop, leaving him upside down and struggling with his belt. He managed to unbuckle it, and fell sideways on the command panel. Grunting, he pushed himself to his knees. Avienne was no longer in the shuttle. That entire side of the shuttle had been ripped off, and even her seat was gone. Ignoring the scent of burning and the splatters of blood, he stood and staggered out of the shuttle.

He blinked. It was dark—they were inside a bay. It was quiet. Either it had already been empty, or it had been deserted at the first sign of trouble. He could hear ships hovering outside. He had to get Avienne and move out, fast, or they would fall into Solarian hands.

He stumbled to where her seat had landed.

Empty, the seatbelt ripped.

He could hear footsteps now, coming up some rickety metal stairs. "Avienne!" he tried to cry, but his voice cracked.

Banging at the other end. He was out of time. He ran as quickly as he could to hide behind some crates. He continued scanning the room, but still he saw no sign of his sister.

"Avienne!" he hissed. No answer.

Solariers entered the bay and Ardin shrunk back in the shadows. He would be easily found. One well aimed beam of light would reveal his presence. He steadied his breath and tried to plan an escape. Except he lacked knowledge of the area, and he was still looking for Avienne. He couldn't leave her here, in whatever state she might be in. *Alive.* He realized he hadn't even considered the option that she might be dead.

After all the risks she had ever taken, after all the stupid things they had done together, it would seem so stupid to die in a shuttle crash.

"Found one!" someone cried. His blood went cold. "Still alive, too!"

"Pretty thing, even if banged up." Ardin risked looking around the crate. Avienne had landed on some crates on the other end of the bay, having flown further than Ardin had believed possible. He could barely make her out, the dark cargo bay lit by streams of sunlight filtering in, turning everything grey and dusty-looking.

But as the Solariers crossed a beam of light, he saw they carried someone, the red hair flaming in the sunlight.

His heart sank.

He grabbed his gun and stepped forward, wondering if Avienne would survive a direct attack. He hesitated for a split second and a hand reached out in the darkness and pulled him back. He turned around, gun drawn, to come face-to-face with an orange-eyed Kilita, holding her hands up in pleading.

"I've come to help," she whispered.

Ardin narrowed his eyes. His encounters with Kilita had been unpleasant. But he had little choice. "Help me get my sister, then," he whispered back.

She shook her head. "Too many. You'd die trying. But there may be another way to get her out, if you trust me."

Ardin's skin crawled. He looked back around the crate. There were a lot of Solariers, at least twenty, now looking at the shuttle. They were debating its origins, and whether Avienne had been the only crew. Beyond it, they were loading the unconscious Avienne onto a prison shuttle. His hand tightened around his gun. He wouldn't let them do anything to her.

The Kilita held his arm. "If you want to die, that's fine. But die a better way. We can free her, still."

Ardin took a step back. The shuttle door closed and took off. He had noted its numbers, symbols, and the faces of every guard. He would hunt them down to find Avienne and, depending on what had been done to her, kill each and every one of them.

His wound throbbed down his arm now. He ignored the pain and stepped back into the shadows.

***

Avienne woke when the shuttle took off. Her hands were fastened behind her back and she was seated between two guards. Two bulky, smelly guards. She kept her breaths long and steady so they wouldn't know she was awake. Her tongue twitched with the effort not to gag.

Where was Ardin? Had he been taken, too? She didn't dare look around the shuttle. It might be to her advantage for them to think she was still unconscious. As long as they weren't interested in that kind of thing, anyway.

She paid attention to the sound of the shuttle, trying to gauge direction, speed and distance. It might help her get her bearings later on, when she escaped.

And she would escape. Blood and bones, she didn't intend on finishing up as Solarian meat.

***

"Where are we going?" Ardin asked. They followed a tunnel of carefully placed freight boxes and crates, ships and walls. They were far beyond the bay now, he was certain, though he had no idea where exactly.

The Kilita turned back and frowned, indicating with a finger to her lips that he should be quiet. He exhaled impatiently. The female Kilita looked a lot like the male Kilita. Strong built, broad shoulders, large brow and coarse hair, all tinted orange, with a face that didn't record the smiles she might have given. If she had ever had occasion to smile.

Her steps were broad and certain, her large feet surprisingly quiet on the metal floor. He followed close. Having lost Avienne, he didn't want to now lose what could be his only ally on the planet. He hoped she was an ally, anyway.

For all he knew, she was leading him into a trap worse than the Solariers.

They reached another empty bay and she quickly opened a crate and motioned for him to enter. He looked at her sceptically but she jerked her head towards the crate again, insisting. He stepped in. She followed, closed the door, and they were both cast in darkness, in uncomfortably close proximity.

He heard a hiss and was blinded by the Kilita's torch. He was about to protest when she whispered: "Quiet. Follow."

He squinted his eyes open, tears gathering as they grew used to the harsh torchlight.

A door now stood before them, leading down a dark corridor which smelled of musty earth. He had never before smelled anything resembling earth on Thalos IV.

He stepped in and followed her down the corridor. She closed the door tightly behind them and, after a few minutes, decided it was safe enough to speak quietly.

"I'm Litras. You?"

"Ardin. What is this?"

She turned and gave him a grin. "It's a tunnel to escape. Used to be for smuggling, but handy now to help ether creatures off Solarian planets."

"Has it been that bad?" he asked. He had heard nuggets of stories in reports, but hadn't followed up. Ardice's birth and Mirial's defences had pressed heavily on his mind. He felt guilty now, for not looking into it and perhaps negotiating safe passage for the ether races. Not that it would have done them any good, with the recent events.

"It's been bad," the Kilita answered simply.

"Where are we going? I need to help my sister."

"You're from Mirial," she stated. His first instinct was to deny it, but he couldn't think why. Besides, the shuttle had been clearly marked with the flower symbol of Mirial.

"We both are. My sister and I."

The Kilita continued for a bit in silence. "They'll know, too. Bring her to the camps. Mirialers and ether creatures alike, though a lot more of us than of you."

"There are other Mirialers in the camps?"

She nodded. "I'll show you." She stopped and turned to face him. "The camps are bad, Ardin of Mirial. If you want to get your sister out, you must do so quickly. Or you'll never get all of her back."

A shiver down his spine and his hand tightly on his gun, he followed her down the rest of the dark corridor.

***

Thalos IV.

The planet covered the horizon before them, its gray atmosphere hiding the lay of the land below. Layela knew it well enough. She punched in coordinates and hoped her memory was holding better than her nerves.

"The atmosphere isn't helping us see any ships," Clave spoke up for the first time since they had left *Destiny II*. "Our sensors can't even pierce it."

Layela gave him a weak smile. "It adds to the challenge, I suppose."

Clave returned her smile and turned back to his console. "How do you want to do this?"

"Without difficulty, I hope." The joke fell flat, though Clave did give a chuckle to humour her.

She sighed. She had to get her stretched nerves under control. Was she not supposed to be the Keeper of Mirial?

"Keep going straight towards the coordinates. I'll try to hide us." Those words fell as flat as her joke. How was she going to hide them? By calling on the ether that may or may not obey her—or, even worse, might hurt Ardice or Ardin?

She closed her eyes and steadied her breath, ignoring the erratic beating of her heart and the sweat beading across her brow. Mists clouded her vision as she re-opened her eyes. Mirial answered her calls this far, at least.

"I think another ship pierced through. I can't see anything, though," Clave said. Layela ignored him, concentrating.

She encouraged the mists to gather and come closer, to weave themselves like a protective cloak around the shuttle, to hide them through illusion and shadows. The mists shivered, and for a moment Layela thought they might do as she beckoned. But then they collapsed and all but vanished. She gasped.

"What is it?" Clave asked, looking sideways at her.

She turned to face him but couldn't form the words. The ether had failed her again.

"I'm turning us around," Clave said, pulling back on the shuttle controls without waiting for her to answer. As Thalos IV was streaming off their main viewport, a blast shook the shuttle. Layela screamed and grabbed hold of the control panel.

"Is it Solaria?" Clave asked, punching the shuttle forward as fast as it would go as several other shots struck them. Layela took over tactical, firing up the main shields and charging weapons. She analyzed the sensor reading for the ship, which was identified in their main computer.

She furrowed her brow. That was strange. They didn't have access to the Solarian database so there were only a few ships that would be identified by their registry. Layela looked at Clave, not believing the words even as she spoke them.

"It's a ship from Mirial. They came for us. Mirial is actually shooting at us!"

Clave swore and veered down, towards Thalos IV.

"What are you doing?" she asked, firing back at the ship.

"Taking them away from *Destiny II*." Layela nodded. She suddenly understood.

They had managed to separate her from her daughter, after all, and their current Keeper had suddenly become disposable.

She didn't argue with Clave. Better her than her daughter.

CHAPTER 20

THE SHUTTLE VEERED directly into the atmosphere of the planet known as Thalos IV. Murl pulled up what data she had on the planet, and it didn't seem to be welcoming. She needed the Keeper alive, not flat on a planet somewhere.

She turned in pursuit, her ship faster than *Destiny II*'s shuttle. Her brother had ensured that she had the spacefaring advantage, regardless the size of her ship. She caught up with them just as they pierced the atmosphere, flames licking the hulls of both ships. Punching in a few commands, she extended her shields over *Destiny II*'s shuttle, protecting her not from the atmosphere, but from the planet's security sensors.

Based on the same ether technology that used to keep Mirial hidden from most of Solaria, they were fairly certain the technology would still hamper Solaria. Certain enough to chance it, anyhow. Murl ran her hand against the dash of her ship. It was old, pre-dating the Great Darkness by quite a few years, sporting technologies whose secrets had long been lost to Mirialers. A vestige of how great her civilization had once been, and how great it could be, once again.

Murl's hand went to her chest, where a jewel had been stamped in the tender flesh. It was now as much a part of herself as her skin. Beneath its red glow spread the ether gifted to her by her brother,

Braken. The skin around the encrusted jewel was warm, but nowhere near as hot as Braken's skin. No sweat even gathered around it, more of a sensation than an observable fact.

They broke through the atmosphere. Murl fired a beacon onto the other ship's hull, extending the protective shielding while allowing Murl to keep track of them.

It was fortunate she had located them again before landing on a planet. It would make it easier to capture the Keeper without destroying her.

***

Layela maintained a constant eye on the sensor readings, fearing detection at any time. They had entered Thalos IV too quickly and violently, and would have brought attention to themselves. Yet no communications signalled their presence and no ship came to stop them.

"The Mirial ship is backing off," Clave said, punching in several strings of commands.

"Why is it doing that?" Layela asked, checking the sensor readings again. "And where are the Thalonian security units?"

Clave shrugged. "Maybe they haven't spotted us yet? Or you're hiding us from them using ether."

Layela doubted the first and knew the second to be false. Clave's experience with Solaria was limited, but Layela knew that they could easily and effectively cover an entire security grid when necessary. That they chose to let them slip through worried her. Especially since Ardin and Avienne had not made it, and both were seasoned smugglers.

Layela looked out the viewing port and bit her lower lip. She didn't know where the Malavants were. She had hoped her ether would work, and she could use its mists to guide her to her friends. But her instincts were still dull and the mists courted only her peripheral vision.

"There's a smuggling cove not far from here. We should be able to get through without being spotted, and vanish into the crowds. We'll find more information that way."

Clave glanced her way and nodded. He didn't comment on her failure to mention the ether, but she was certain he had noticed.

***

Murl watched the shuttle land and entered another nearby shuttle bay. So long as Layela tried to access the ether, Murl's own abilities should be able to track her presence.

The landing attendant approached her, a rough looking bald man who smelled worse than the swamps of Mirial. Murl scowled at him.

"Payment, honey," he said, holding out his hands and pulling back his shoulders to show his full size.

Murl scoffed. "Honey?" She flipped up a knife and threw it deep between the man's eyes. Shock didn't even register on his face before he crumpled. She grabbed his large wrists and pulled him towards a trash chute with a grunt. She heaved and pulled him up, managing to get his arms and head caught in it, and then she grabbed his legs and pushed him the rest of the way in. She cursed. She had left her knife implanted in his skull.

What a waste.

From the stench of this place, the chute was rarely emptied. Murl would have plenty of time to retrieve the Keeper and return before any foul play was discovered. And even if the man was discovered, she doubted she would be suspected. Too many people around here, and her knife held no definitive identification marks.

She took the stairs all the way down, not trusting the rickety lift.

First person I meet on another planet, and he's dead after hello, she mused. They were soft, despite arguments that this was one of the toughest planets on Solaria. Compared to Murl, who had grown up while under siege by dark creatures, they were jelly.

She stepped out of the stairwell, her senses assaulted by a thousand scents she had never before encountered. Bile rose to her throat and she fought back the urge to vomit. The day was hot and sweaty. There was no breeze, no sunlight, just this gray, sickening haze, and the sound of thousands of people all trying to be heard at once.

She had not expected that. Mirial was always quiet compared to this, its entire population in the thousands. It boasted sun and fresh air, water like mirrors and plants that shone even under moonlight.

This place was like a giant trash can.

Murl pulled up her scarf and tied it around her nose and mouth to block some of the treacherous scents. She took a deep, disgusting breath and steeled herself before walking out into the thick crowd.

An elbow caught her gut and she quickly retaliated, feeling the satisfying snap of bones under her own elbow strike. The man swore and nearly fell. She continued without glancing back. The crowd grew thicker and someone pinched her behind. Her hand whipped back, caught the hand before it vanished, and snapped the wrist. A scream. She continued. She met each person's glance with a piercing stare of her own, and people started giving her a wider berth, the crowd parting before her.

Good. She could sense the Keeper, not far. The trail was faint but present. She would collect her and leave this infested hole of rot.

She curled her nose in disgust as she passed a meat merchant. The cuts didn't even look like animal meat.

The sooner she left this Mirial-forsaken place, the better.

***

They landed, paid, and vanished into the smelly crowd, walking silently. Clave kept his head down though Layela could see him shrinking from the travellers, looking up with wide eyes once in a while.

This is his first time on another planet, Layela thought. Clave was elbowed in the gut by a passerby and he reeled back. Layela hooked her arm in his, keeping him close.

"Keep your other arm in front of you to block any blows, and avoid eye contact. And make sure to keep an eye out for Solariers. Solarian soldiers," she added, just in case.

He nodded, but his entire body was stiff and awkward. Layela sighed, but didn't let go of him. He would have to get used to her as just a person, not a mystical Keeper. Especially since they had to work together.

She pulled him into a side alley, which would lead to Groban's map shop. Maybe he could help them find Ardin and Avienne. Regardless, the shop was near one of the Dark Knights Network's access points. Well, where one used to be, anyway.

There certainly weren't any guarantees that it was still there, or that the Dark Knights themselves even still existed. Events had always moved quickly on Thalos IV, and information networks rose and fell regularly. Bartering systems changed daily and smugglers struck it rich, never to be heard from again. She had spent years on this planet, but the only knowledge she possessed that would prove useful was her understanding of how quickly things changed.

And how careful they would have to be to make it off alive.

Several streets later, they cleared the docks and markets, and the crowd had dissipated. Layela let go of Clave's arm and shoved her hands in her pockets. The day's warmth vanished with the crowd.

"We'll head to Groban's shop first," Layela informed Clave in a low voice. "See if he can help us."

Clave nodded but didn't look her way, his hands deep in his pockets. Something was bothering him, more than just being on a new planet, away from everything that was familiar to him. He looked down at the pavement, not even interested in these new surroundings.

Outside the overcrowded docks and market area, Thalos IV did have quite a bit of charm. The entire planet was a city, which was why its markets were so crowded with imports from other planets. The only large piece of green land she had ever seen here had been Josmere's home, long ago abandoned by the Berganda.

The city was broken up into sectors and communities, not formally indicated or acknowledged, but well known to the planet's inhabitants. They were now in a working class neighbourhood, which many dock workers called home. It was a dirty neighbourhood, too close to the docks' entry and departure paths, resulting in soot and evacuated waste from ships trying to avoid extra docking fees. But the inhabitants had adapted. The streets were covered by a giant canopy, large flower patterns gracing the textiles. The old houses were mostly brick, which was rare in these parts. Concrete or synthetics were easier and cheaper to transport and use. But this neighbourhood had been built long ago, before Thalos IV had drained its own resources.

The houses were two-storied, with multiple cracks covered with concrete and often painted in the same bright colours that were used on shutters, doors, and the few metal exterior staircases. The people here cared about their homes, even though they could collapse if the wrong ship passed overhead too quickly or too closely.

Just like Mirial is my home, now. The words didn't resonate within her. She had never had a home, never known enough roots, to feel overly attached to one place. Places were temporary, homes could be destroyed, landscapes changed. Only those she loved, those she battled for, were her home.

She glanced sideways at Clave. No wonder he seemed so distraught. For her, she was chasing after her home, her loved ones. But for him, he was running away from the only home he had ever known, in the hopes that Layela would come back and bring peace to his world.

She wondered if she would let him and all of Mirial down, in the end.

CHAPTER 21

OLD, DEAD TREES and still vines surrounded Elsa and her sisters, their spider limbs casting dark shadows on the mossy ground. The Berganda were quiet around her, not even communicating with one another telepathically. Elsa's breath fogged before her. A few birds chirped nearby.

Elsa looked up ahead at the increasing darkness, walking on a soft patch of moss, her sisters' footsteps making no noise around her. The silence proved unnerving. The trees around her were still strong with ether—the good type of ether that didn't attack or hurt anybody. Elsa ran her hand against the great trunk of a tree as she walked by, feeling the tingle of Mirial on her fingertips. It reminded her of Layela and tears sprang to her eyes. Angry at herself, she clenched down her jaw and picked up the pace.

Mother Layela could not help them now. She was far away and running for her life. The Berganda were adults now, and she and her sisters would fend for themselves and make her and their mother proud.

One of Elsa's sisters, Slita, slipped in beside Elsa, who was now well ahead of everyone else. Elsa slowed and they walked in silence for a few moments.

"I think we're being watched," Slita said. Elsa began looking around, but her sister's calm hand on her arm stilled her. "Do not look, sister. Let us continue walking. They have not yet attacked, so we may be safe."

May be. Elsa nodded. Slita was using her voice instead of their mind to communicate, so their other sisters would not hear. Where Elsa was the most impulsive of her sisters, Slita was by far the bravest.

"What should we do?" Elsa asked. She had no weapons, and although Slita sported a gun secured at her hip, most of their other sisters were unarmed, as well. And as far as fighting was involved, only Slita really knew how to defend herself. The rest could easily be picked off.

Elsa's breath was coming in short bursts. She had doomed her sisters. It had been her idea to take refuge in the woods and abandon the children. She had led them here, to their graves.

Slita's calming hand fell on Elsa's upper arm. "Calm yourself. The others will sense your worry. If they had wanted to attack, they would have already."

"What if they're leading us into a trap, or an ambush?"

Slita shrugged. "We'll fight as best we can."

Elsa's spine contracted at the thought of her sisters going against armed assailants. It would be a slaughter. Concentrating on what to do next, she missed a step and caught herself on a tree, the soothing ether loosening her muscles. Vines gently slid sideways to comfort her, a gentle brush of the arm. Mirial's forests were old and so riddled with ether that, like all plants on Mirial, they seemed sentient and responsive to the ether creatures.

Elsa reached back and touched a vine, the coarse woodsy plant shuddering in delight. Then it struck her. They weren't that helpless, after all.

She reached out to Slita. *Sister, show me where they are. I have an idea how to stop them.*

Slita's surprise was palpable. Within seconds she had regained her composure and sent waves of thoughts to Elsa, who furrowed her brow and concentrated.

It wasn't a clear picture. Berganda telepathy was dependent on moods and impressions. Slita's mind was clearer than most of the Berganda, honed as a warrior would sharpen a fine blade. Elsa could easily trace the pattern communicated to her because of that clarity of thought. She soon had a full vision of the encroaching enemy. Her hands curled and she forced them to relax. Slita's clarity was accompanied by an overwhelming sense of urgency and the desire to fight.

Elsa forced the thoughts away. She feigned exhaustion, leaning on a tree, and reached out to grab a vine. The ether began tingling in anticipation as soon as she touched it. Elsa took a deep breath and closed her eyes, concentrating on Slita's positioning of their enemy and on the forest.

Help us! she implored, words spoken so strongly that they rippled through the forest's rustling leaves and settled in the vines. Her sisters all heard the imploration, while Slita's request for them to remain calm held off their growing panic.

The vines' reaction was immediate. The ones Elsa held twitched and then the rest began to move. Screams soon bounced off the great trees around them and some weapons were fired. The Berganda all crouched instinctively, Elsa included. All but Slita, who pulled her own weapon free and, with a shrill she hadn't even known Berganda could make, ran off into the trees, towards the enemy.

"Slita!" Elsa screamed as she charged after her, keeping low to the ground. She heard a confrontation up ahead, and then the forest grew quiet and still, save for a few moving vines.

Elsa passed through two trees, the moss covering the noise her feet might have otherwise made. She spotted her sister, who held a gun at a man standing before her.

"We mean no harm to you," Kyle, guard of Mirial, insisted as he held his arms up. He cast a frustrated look towards Elsa. Slita turned her head only slightly to give her sister a grin. Elsa responded telepathically.

Can we trust him?

He says they're loyal to Layela. But common loyalties hardly mean allies.

Elsa nodded, and immediately wished she hadn't done so. She wondered if Berganda of old, who grew up amongst each other and not with humans as guides, had been devoid of such obvious gestures, relying on their telepathic link to fully communicate with one another.

"How do we know we can trust you?" Elsa asked. Slita tensed beside her.

"We fight the same enemy," Kyle said, casting an annoyed glance at Slita.

"For now," Slita voiced.

"I agree. How do we know your loyalties won't shift."

Kyle raised an eyebrow. A very human gesture that Elsa still struggled to master. She loved the look of it.

"How do I know yours won't? I'm of Mirial. I follow one Keeper, as chosen by Mirial herself."

"Many don't seem to feel that way," Slita added, but Elsa noticed her grip on her gun loosened.

"We can help each other," Elsa said. "We can command the forest around us, and you have the knowledge of the landscape we lack. If we work together, our chances of success are greater."

Kyle raised his eyebrow only slightly this time. "Success for what? We plan on taking down the usurper. What do you wait for, Berganda? Will you stand and fight for Mirial?"

Elsa hesitated. She hadn't thought that far ahead. Her first instinct had been survival. Running had been necessary. But fighting? She felt Slita's warmth and strength flow towards her, comforting her. She was terrified, and Slita knew it. All the Berganda were terrified.

But the Berganda had not always been so timid, and Mother Layela needed their help. They couldn't lie in wait for her to return and rescue them. They, too, had to act.

Elsa reached out with her mind and asked the forest to release the other soldiers. The vines lowered them to the ground, unbound their limbs and released their mouths, allowing fresh air into their lungs. The soldiers gathered around Kyle, most without weapons, looking to him for guidance. They were not all guards of Mirial. Some were servants, others peasants.

Kyle looked to Slita, who holstered her gun. Kyle picked up his own and did the same.

The others followed suit, and they all quietly began slipping back into the forest, towards their safe hold. Elsa and Slita reached out to their sisters and together they all followed the last resistance of Mirial into the shadows of the forest.

***

The forest grew thicker around them, the spider vines wrapped around the trees and blocking out more and more of the sun until it was so dark that Elsa began fearing for her sisters' safety. Had they fallen into a trap? She reached out to Slita, who sent back comfort and confidence. Her sister did not seem to think so.

The air grew musky and damp, the ground slick with plant decay. Elsa chose her steps carefully, letting her senses guide her more than her eyes, which were now useless in the complete darkness. The silence around her grew oppressive. Save for a few mutters from her sisters, no other noise seemed to travel the length of the forest.

The ground below her changed to slick stone and the darkness above changed in quality.

"Stop," she heard Kyle say and she stopped. The Berganda shared a single ripple of worry.

Lights were turned on and Elsa had to look down and cover her eyes, tears gathering in them. She counted her breaths and looked up, still squinting her eyes against the light.

They were in a cave, which had been outfitted with spotlights and computers. To the left were a few hover-ships, perfect for forest travel. Other Mirialers milled about, looking with curiosity at the Berganda. Some looked with open disdain. Elsa tried not to shy away from their looks, but she found herself turning her head regardless.

"What are they doing here?" The man was so large that Kyle had to look up to meet his eyes.

"They're on the run, too, Trusk. Like the rest of us."

Trusk barely turned his head to look at them. He snorted and turned back, walking away. "Just make sure they don't get in the way!"

Kyle turned to the Berganda. Seeing Slita's narrow eyes, he gave a slight smile. "Sorry. Some Mirialers are still getting used to having strangers here."

Elsa spoke before she thought better of it. "We've been here our whole lives. It's our only home!"

Kyle's smile faded. "Yes, but you weren't welcome in the beginning. If the Keeper hadn't been so fond of you, you would have been chased off long ago." Elsa took a step back as though stricken. She knew the Mirialers disliked her and her sisters, but she had never realized that their hatred ran so deep.

Kyle ran his hand through his hair, at first looking apologetic, then annoyed. Elsa couldn't tell if his anger was at himself or the Berganda.

"We can be of help to you," Slita said, her soft tones husky for a Berganda's, almost male in pitch. "You saw how easily we prevented your attack in the forest, Kyle. We may not be of Mirial," the sarcasm dripped from her words, "but she certainly seems to understand and welcome us."

"Don't say things like that," Kyle hissed. "I agree you can be useful. We need to convince the others of it, that's all." He gave Slita a slight grin. "I've seen you fight, Slita. That alone would prove useful. Add the ether on top, and we may just have a shot at beating the usurper."

Slita smiled back but Elsa felt a hole explode in her stomach. *Beat the usurper.* The idea of actually running off into battle, of fighting an enemy that even Layela could not beat, terrified her.

"Just stay low until the time is right," Kyle added before walking away, shouting at some soldiers.

Slita placed a hand on Elsa's arm. "Don't worry, sister," she said, smiling at her. "We'll find a way to win this day."

Elsa forced a smile and nodded, wondering how her sister could remain so calm. Especially knowing that the only person who truly welcomed them on Mirial was now gone, and everyone else either tolerated them or wanted them gone—or worse, dead.

Elsa gritted her teeth. Their mother, Josmere, had found life on this dead planet. They were her legacy. They would find a way to survive.

They had to.

***

Mirial's old bases and outposts were still around, and some were even operational, but they were hardly undetectable. To most technology they were, sure, but they were fighting ether too, or whatever deviance the usurper wielded. Kyle was nervous enough already, having so many warm bodies in one place. Add all the shouting, and he was downright worried.

He glanced towards the Berganda. Most of them were huddled together in one corner. *I guess they're not very warm blooded.* He felt momentary embarrassment at knowing so little about them or the other ether creatures. It had been his team's downfall in the forest— he had no idea Berganda could communicate with trees.

Of course, now that he knew, he wasn't at all surprised.

Two Berganda were off to the side from their sisters, staying close to the shouting resistance. Slita seemed taller than the rest, though Kyle suspected that was a matter of perception. She held herself like a warrior, proud and tall. Most other Berganda had learned to make themselves small when around Mirialers.

Kyle sighed and walked towards Slita and her sister. He couldn't remember her name. They all looked the same to him, except Slita. She had wanted to be part of the royal guards, working harder than anyone else he had ever known. But, in the end, too many objections—and several threats made against her sisters—had overshadowed her desire. But regardless, she was a fighter. She had never stopped watching the practice from the shadows.

He nodded as he joined Slita and her sister. She returned the gesture, but suspicion lined her eyes.

"They're getting restless," Kyle said, not sure how to open the conversation.

"It's barely been two days," Slita's sister said with incredulity.

"Kyle, this is Elsa. Elsa, Kyle."

"I know who he is." Elsa was obviously annoyed. "He's one of those idiots who decided to keep you out of Layela's guards. You! Who better to protect the Keeper than one of her daughters!"

Kyle felt his anger bubble but he kept it in check. There were enough hot tempers around. He didn't need to inject his own into the situation.

He ignored Elsa's accusation. "Mirialers learned long ago that swift action is the best method of survival. They fear the usurper will grow in strength unless he's stopped now. They intend to attack soon."

Slita scoffed. "They will get themselves killed. You weren't able to stop him from chasing Layela off the planet. How do you expect to fight him back now?"

Kyle felt his cheeks grow warm. "That traitorous Murl had her own troops on duty at the time. We weren't ready—we were off duty. This time, we'll be ready."

Elsa and Slita exchanged a quick look, then turned back to Kyle. Elsa kept her voice soft. "How do you know Murl has no other traitors amongst you? Do you think she isn't already aware of you?"

Kyle's skin turned from hot to cold. Of course. Murl was shrewd— she would have planned for every possibility, including this one.

He forced himself not to turn around. "We don't know that," he whispered.

"Exactly," Slita said. "So we plan something on our own. The three of us," she nodded towards Elsa too, who nodded enthusiastically.

"You're not battle trained." Kyle felt his control of the situation slip away, if he ever had any.

Slita raised an eyebrow, a very human gesture. He fought back a smile.

He lowered his chin in acknowledgment. He had seen her fight. She would prove a worthy ally.

"Elsa is firstborn. She's strongest with the ether." Slita said, and Elsa's head raised slightly, pride gleaming in her eyes. "She'll prove invaluable."

Kyle turned to look at the shouting Mirialers, working themselves up to a battle they would probably lose. Slita was right. A traitor was more than likely already in their midst.

He turned back towards the two Berganda, who waited expectantly. "What do you propose?"

CHAPTER 22

LET GO OF me, you tri-footed ugly-faced latrine turnip!" Avienne tried to kick sideways but failed to connect, and was tossed aside like a bag of potatoes. She landed hard against a wall and fell to her knees, the pain vibrating up her spine. Her hands were tightly bound behind her back, the metals cuffs cutting her skin. She continued struggling, hardly caring about the pain.

They had taken her weapons, those bastards. Her knives, her gun, her small explosives—all gone. *At least I left my good ether knives on the ship.* The thought brought little comfort.

She was trapped, somewhere in a holding cell. She hadn't seen where they had taken her, and the guards were growing annoyed at her constant attacks.

Smarten up, she could hear a small voice in her mind protest. But she squashed it down.

She was bound, surrounded, in a dingy concrete cell that smelled of urine and blood. Never before had she been held by anyone, and she didn't intend to make it easy on them.

Unfolding her legs, she leapt forward to head butt the nearest soldier, but something pulled her back to the wall and she snapped back against it, the air knocked out of her, her shoulders almost tugged out of their sockets by the strength of the bonds.

She slid halfway to the ground, but the chain held her up at an awkward height. She looked back and could barely make out a restraining system. The cold clamps tugged on her bloodied wrists. She bit back a cry.

Like I'd give them the satisfaction.

"So?" the leader of the little troop asked. "Looks human enough." He smirked. "That shuttle of yours. Marked from Mirial. Better hope it's something you stole. Thieves get off easier than Mirialers, in these parts."

Avienne's blood grew cold. She couldn't feel her fingers anymore, the clamps were so tight.

"We know how to check, you know. And I think you're worth checking."

She glared at them, pleased to see a few shift nervously. Let them try to "check out" anything, and she'd deal with them accordingly. Ready to pounce, regardless of her bound hands, she was surprised to see them turn their backs and leave the cell.

The door opened again and a man was thrown in, stumbling to the ground. He was an ether creature, that much was obvious. A Kilita, from Avienne's reckoning. Their race had once been strongly affiliated with Solaria, a powerful warrior race sought after for their cunning. But the man before her did not look cunning, folded over on himself.

Before Avienne could ask the man if he was all right, he looked up at her and straightened his torso, while remaining on his knees. His eyes were orange and half-slit, a giant scar running down his left cheek.

But it was his hands that held her attention. His right hand was badly patched up with bandages, or what remained of it, anyway. It had been cut clean at the wrist.

Avienne hissed and her hands turned to fists. She hoped she'd get a chance to fight her way free.

***

Layela kept her head down, the streets here familiar enough not to warrant full attention. They were in a quiet neighbourhood, far enough from the docks that the overhead skies were quieter. More than two hours had passed since their landing on Thalos IV, and still Layela struggled with the ether.

She focused on the kernel of Mirial she knew must still exist within her. She visualized it as Yoma, but still received no answer from the First Star, save for a gentle whisper on the winds. She could sense it near, but it was out of her grasp. *I need you!* she implored, tears of frustration clouding her vision.

Why did the First Star seem at times almost ready to grant her requests, and at others so distant she couldn't even feel her warmth?

Clave, who had been walking quietly beside her, broke the silence. "You grew up here?"

She almost snapped at the interruption, but forced herself to smile, instead.

"I did. For a while. This is the place I lived the longest, anyway."

She didn't elaborate. She had not left Thalos IV under the best circumstances, and those were memories long overshadowed by more painful ones.

Clave was quiet for a moment longer. "You lived here with your sister, right?"

Layela stared. Mirialers rarely mentioned her sister. The very mention of her name seemed forbidden, as though her twin had defied the will of Mirial by having lived so long. But Yoma had died to protect them all. Layela's face flushed red as she realized she didn't speak of Yoma all that much, either, taking her cues from the Mirialers.

She took a deep breath.

"Yes. It was Yoma, myself, and Josmere, a Berganda." She smiled at the memories, the familiar sights, sounds and smells of Thalos IV suddenly welcoming and comforting. "I miss them," she added, without meaning to.

Clave nodded. "I had a brother. A twin. He was lost to me a while back. I miss him, too."

"I'm sorry," Layela said, glancing at him.

Clave turned and gave her a tentative smile. "I guess we all lost something, or gave something up, for Mirial."

Layela smiled back. It was the closest any Mirialer had ever come to acknowledging her own grief, and not just her duty as Keeper. She turned back to the streets.

"I don't intend to lose anything else. We're getting Ardin and Avienne back. We're here," she said, keeping up her pace as she neared the store front. Clave looked up with interest. "Don't draw attention to yourself," Layela hissed. "Keep up pace. We'll walk by once. If everything looks all right, we'll go back and enter the shop. I'll go in, you keep an eye out on the streets."

Clave nodded, his eyes betraying his worry.

"We have our comm units, so if anything suspicious happens, let me know. Most of these places have back exits or secret access points, and the stores are fronts. I'm not sure about this store, but I imagine it's the same deal. If anything happens, I'll escape through the back, and we rendez-vous back at our shuttle. You remember how to get there?"

He nodded, but Layela doubted he could. The streets of Thalos IV were an unplanned jumble, unlike the few, planned centres of Mirial. But he could use the comm as a tracker, so she wasn't worried about him.

They passed the map shop, shivers traveling up Layela's spine. The last time she had been here, her sister had been inside. It seemed as quiet today as it had on that day. She tried to reach out with her ether, but sighed. She hadn't always had this power. She'd have to trust her ability to get out of trouble with her old skills.

"I should be the one going in," Clave said. Layela shook her head.

"You have no idea who you're even looking for. And besides, Mirial aside, this is my family. Stay out here. I'll be right back."

She turned towards the dusty window displaying maps behind sun-filtering glass. The store name, *Starborn Maps,* clung to the brick surface despite cracks in the paint.

Layela took a deep breath and walked in. She turned to watch Clave vanish into a back alley, not noticing the second shadow that followed him.

***

"I'm sorry," the Kilita said as he looked up. An ugly scar ran down his left cheek, having robbed him of one eye.

"They're not exactly good jailers, are they?"

The Kilita snorted, in what Avienne hoped was a laugh. "They're good at what they do."

Avienne cocked her head. She couldn't argue that point. "And what do you do?" As she spoke, she struggled with the cuffs behind her. She couldn't push her hands through, and she was no lock picker. She sighed.

At least he's in a chatty mood.

"I can unlock whatever powers you possess. Mirialers generally just have the ability to resist ether, and that's pretty much it." He gave a short smile. "Humans often die screaming."

"Wonderful. Is that what cost you your hand?"

He shrugged. "That was for killing a guard. Thought we could make it out. That's what they do here. If ether creatures don't obey, hands chopped off. Most of them die from the resulting infections. Doesn't take long."

Avienne shook her head. This was ridiculous. "How long have these camps been up? I haven't heard of them at all."

"Been up for a while. A year, maybe? Called them jails for unruly creatures. Now that Mirial is acting up, they're using it as an excuse to round up everyone. Lots of soft ones here, now. No good for them."

"I guess you're not one of the soft ones," Avienne mumbled.

Another shrug. "Nah, but I have nothing against people. It's soldiers who get me. Took out the wrong one, is all."

"Fair enough. So how about we call this a day and you let me go? I can help you escape."

The Kilita broke out laughing. "I like you, girl. I hope you're not human and you live. Oh, you'll die in the camps, anyway. Doesn't matter. It's been fun."

He closed the gap between them faster than she would have expected, his cold hand reaching to her face. She felt nothing. Nothing at all.

But his eyes filled with terror and his head snapped back so far that she could no longer see his head, only the bulging artery pounding his neck. A spasm shook his entire body, his limbs, head, and chest all jerking for a few seconds before an ear-scratching scream ripped from his throat. He fell like a rag doll and lay motionless on the floor.

She stared, stunned, as Solariers threw open the door and pointed guns at her heart while looking over the Kilita.

"He's dead," one of the soldiers declared. He turned to Avienne, wide-eyed. "What are you?"

Avienne recovered enough to shrug and look disinterested. "A young maiden dealing with a Kilita whose hand you chopped off and left to heal on its own?"

She had barely finished the sentence before the soldier moved forward and butted the side of her head with his gun.

Stars flashed in front of her eyes. She managed to cling to consciousness for a moment, but the second hit almost wrenched her still-tied arms from her shoulders and she slipped into tarry darkness.

CHAPTER 23

LAYELA PULLED OPEN the door of the shop, the metal of the handle cold to the touch. She was not surprised that no one was manning the desk. This section of the shop was fairly organized, with maps of Solarian space, tunnel access points, Thalos IV and its communities strewn about for purchase. Useful for tourists or smugglers.

Dodging a few precarious large maps dangling from shelves, Layela walked to the back of the store. The door was cracked opened. She took a deep breath and gently pushed it the rest of the way, grateful it didn't creak. Cement stairs greeted her, and she took them one at a time until she reached the bottom. She moved past the bookshelves that hid her view of the small downstairs room. The place was a mess. Maps were strewn everywhere, several bookshelves were toppled over.

Layela pulled her gun free and carefully walked forward. Someone had been here, looking for something. That much was evident. But were was Gobran?

She winced as she stepped on Gobran's precious maps. She kicked something that gave some resistance. She looked down, where a map shifted. A foot.

A naked foot.

It was not a man's foot, but rather a woman's, sleek and pale. Her stomach churned. A bookshelf, laying at an angle, was on most of the rest of the body. She walked around it apprehensively, already suspecting what she would find, or rather who she would find.

On the other side of the bookshelf she could see a svelte hand sticking out at a strange angle from under the mess of maps, familiar hair jutting from the side. *Maybe she still lives…*

Layela leaned down and barely touched the hand. So stiff and cold. She turned sideways and threw up bile.

Alecya Kipso, long-lost daughter of Gobran, had survived almost twenty years of the Great Darkness as a member of Mirial's army. She had lived through all of that, only to die under a bookshelf on a planet far, far away.

She saw no evidence of Gobran, but part of her hoped he was dead and would never have to know how his daughter had passed.

Layela stood back up. Her skin crawled with disgust and grief. She swallowed acid and looked around her. In a corner she could see blood. She didn't approach to examine it. It might be Alycia's. She had no way to tell.

She needed fresh air. Layela ran up the stairs and banged the door shut. She closed her eyes and leaned against the wall, taking deep gulps of air. It was filled with the dust of the store, and tasted like blood.

Her own personal grief washed over the grief for Alecya. Without Gobran and his daughter, without her ether, how was she supposed to find Ardin and Avienne? How could she ensure Mirial's survival, and her daughter's peace? Should she simply stroll into a Solarian base and ask? She crouched down, lowering her head to her knees. Clave was out there, waiting for the Keeper of Mirial. She needed to compose herself.

Screw the Keeper. Her own internal protest shocked her. She took deep breaths which broke into sobs. Her fingers wrapped around her legs, but the sensation of Alecya's dead hand, like a log, persisted. She forced air into her lungs and kept her head down, focusing her thoughts.

Break down on your own time, her sister's familiar words teased her mind. This wasn't her time. This was Ardin's time. Avienne's. Ardice's. Mirial's, even. If she only existed for her own sorrow and fear right now, a lot of other people would pay the price.

Then it struck her.

There was no smell of rot. Layela had seen enough dead bodies in her day to be familiar with the strong bittersweet smell of decomposition. She was only a few hours dead, then, if even. If Gobran was still alive, his time might be limited.

She stood back up, quickly, heading to the desk. There was a comm station there, a small, mostly useless computer. But still, if she could break into it and access Solarian databases… *I have no idea what I'm doing.*

She lowered her head in frustration. Even if she had been good at breaking encryption codes on computers back in her less-than-favourable days, it had been years since she had even considered doing so, and the technology would have only advanced that much further beyond her skills. Her lock picking skills she had maintained, mostly out of boredom on Mirial, but technology had moved so far beyond her hacking abilities that it made her want to cry.

What next? She needed to head out that door and have a plan ready by the time she met up with Clave. She needed to know where to go, if not for victory, than at least for answers. The Dark Knights network was her only chance.

She needed to find sign of their passage, and buy the information she needed. She wished she had brought more money with her, but she'd have to find a way to make it work.

A sudden explosion shook the ground, fireballs lighting the sky outside the shop, shattering the store window. Layela ducked and covered her head, pieces of glass cutting her flesh. The heat from the blast seared her skin as another explosion thundered through the sky around her. She managed to remain on her knees and forced herself to look up, to see what had happened and if another attack was imminent. The building in front of the shop was toppling sideways onto the one next to it, bricks and glass raining into the street. And crushing the alley where she had left Clave.

They were being chased! Of course they were. Why had she been too stupid to realize it? Layela clutched her gun so hard it cut her hand. She ran outside, before the easiest exit out of the map shop became even more dangerous, not daring to waste precious minutes looking for a back exit. No one greeted her, to her surprise. She hoped Clave had managed to survive, and that he would remember his way back to the ship. Without ether, she couldn't know, and didn't dare linger. Solarian troops would be here soon. Her eyes made her entirely too recognizable.

Turning down the first dark alley, Layela maintained a long, steady stride, hand resting on her holstered gun, listening for any sounds of pursuit and praying that a trap did not lie in wait.

***

Braken stepped into the temple of Mirial, its ancient walls silent sentinels around him. He did not need to be in the temple to speak to Mirial; he simply enjoyed the formalities of this location. The power of hundreds, if not thousands, of Keepers backed this moment. The strength Mirial had chosen to infuse him with years ago, as they fought the armies of darkness, was an undeniable sign of the legacy he was meant to preserve.

He took a deep breath, lowered his hood, and let the scent of decay and new leaves wash over him. That was his Mirial. Reborn and still dead. A balance yet to be achieved.

He sent his mind forth, beyond himself, beyond the walls that surrounded him, and reached for the centre of Mirial herself. She was beautiful. Pure light and darkness dancing with each other, waiting for one to tip the balance in a battle of chemical reactions and knowledge long lost to his people.

The light was no more good than the darkness was evil. Both depended on the desires of his people. His heart swelled as he reached out to her, his desire to save Mirial riding a wave of ether all the way to the great sun. He sensed her response, at first welcoming. He basked in the warmth, no longer sensing his own breath, letting his consciousness be absorbed in her soul.

Then the light gathered around him, and before him stood the Keeper Layela. He blinked, surprised. Green eyes looked at him, a cocky smile turned the Keeper's lips, and he realized it was not Layela, but someone much like her. The light pummelled from her into him, sending him reeling back to his own body.

"No!" He screamed, falling to his knees and hitting the ground with his fists until they were bloodied. He needed all of Mirial behind him, and as long as the Keeper had allies protecting the sun, he could not stop her.

But Mirial would be his.

He remained on his knees, looking at the etchings around him on the wall, seeking out answers. If Mirial was to accept him as full Keeper, which he was certain she would, he needed Layela to relinquish her hold fully.

He feared Layela's death would not prove sufficient. What he needed were more answers than he had. Answers that might not be found on Mirial herself.

He stood. Layela would be trying to find a way to heal her lover. To do so, she needed to be rid of his ether, implanted deeply in Ardin's shoulder and chest. He had used it to ensure Layela would not use her own ether, for fear of destroying him, which was good as the wards were almost completely gone. But as long as Layela remained alive and clung to her stubborn ideals, she would be looking for a way to heal him, with or without ether. And, whether he liked to admit it or not, Mirial currently courted her more strongly.

Allowing himself a smile, he pulled his hood back up and walked outside the temple, reaching out for his sister through the ether.

They needed answers—the same ones Layela would seek. The sooner she found them, the better. They needed to keep her motivated to move fast, and lie in wait for her.

If there was one thing he could bet his life on, it was that Layela would stop at nothing to save those she loved. It would prove her downfall. He would make sure of it.

***

A few blocks away from the exploded map store, Layela had to slow down, her calves complaining at her speed. Her body, still recovering from pregnancy and then childbirth, was nowhere near the shape she had once enjoyed. The day was growing short and the shadows long. It would be night soon, which could be a blessing and a curse. With few resources, Layela feared the night would prove more dangerous than handy.

She needed a place to hide, to rest, to figure out her next steps. She stepped onto a main road, near the docks and markets. It was crowded here, and she needed to blend in. She tucked her jacket over her gun and her hands into her pockets, keeping her head down. She avoided eye contact at all cost. If she could access the ether, covering her one green eye to become blue would be easy, but without it, it would prove impossible.

Of course, a simple pair of sunglasses would have also sufficed. She sighed at her own reckless tendencies. The thought of losing Ardin had been so terrifying that she had rushed headlong onto Thalos IV, with poor planning. No planning, really. What had she hoped for? *A sign from Mirial.* Her entire plan had foolishly hinged on ether that no longer communicated with her. She had acted like a desperate young girl, diving head first into danger to save the one person who still seemed to understand her. The one person who bothered to know her as more than just the Keeper.

Clave. He seemed to have cared, too. He might have been a friend, but he had waited behind as she had requested, between buildings toppling onto each other…

She curled her fingers and turned down another crowded market street, letting herself surf along with the mass of bodies cramming into her, the scents of sweat rivalling that of rotten meats. Her stomach was still queasy, and she tried her best to ignore the assaulting scents.

She had not been paying attention to her direction, but suddenly realized she was nearing the ancient home of the Berganda. That was it—a safe place to spend the night. Tomorrow, she would resume her search, and this time she would not stop until she found them. She needed to rethink her strategy. She couldn't let anyone else down.

Despite living on Thalos IV with Josmere for a long time, she had only once visited the great home of the Berganda. Or, what had been their home, when many more of them had lived. It was a large space, full of greenery and beauty, and protected by plants that had long ago befriended the Berganda.

If she could convince the vines to open the gates for her, she could slip inside and be safe for the evening. She glanced behind her in the crowd. As far as she could tell, she was not being followed. With any luck, she had already lost whoever had blown up the building.

Clave.

She had just left him there, just like Alecya.

A trail of bodies marking her passing.

CHAPTER 24

ARDIN FOLLOWED THE Kilita down several tunnels, through gates, some sewers, and then, out of the stones of the tunnels themselves, an entire city seemed to sprout. At first he noticed a window, with a faint light inside, then a door, and now, still underground, streets jutted off in various directions, houses with gables standing like silent sentinels around them. Some signs hung before certain houses, but they were written in a dialect Ardin had never seen.

A few torches were burning to light the way, the flickering light making the underground town even more eerie. Litras turned to him and gave him a sharp-toothed smile.

"It's an old city, supposedly populated by ether creatures long before the Thalonian empire expanded to the entire star system." She didn't bother whispering, her gruff voice bouncing off the walls. "Apparently humans weren't even part of this solar system at first. Then they came and took over Thalos III, which was inhabited. With time, I guess they thought this planet looked pretty good, too."

Ardin gave an appreciative whistle. "But why keep this city under the streets of Thalos IV?"

The Kilita shrugged, her low, broad shoulders hiding her neck for a few seconds.

"It was a Kilita town. We're not fans of the sun." She gave him another grin. "Hurts the eyes after a while. More like stone. Not soft like the Berganda."

Ardin bit his tongue. He'd known some Berganda who could easily beat a Kilita. But he didn't dare anger his host and end up abandoned in the middle of this strange city.

He gestured to the writing. "Is that your dialect?"

She nodded. "We don't even know how to read it, anymore. Too much human around, I guess."

Ardin let the matter rest. He had grown up believing he was as human as the next person, not understanding Mirialers had small but important traits that drew them apart from the rest of humanity.

"Like locusts," the Kilita grumbled. "Like locusts, those humans. Spread over everything, take over everything. Multiply worse than rabbits."

Ardin hid a smile. "Why don't you just have more babies to ensure there are more of you."

The Kilita snorted. "Stupid question from a Mirialer. Only so much ether to go around. Only so many ether creatures can exist."

Ardin grew quiet again. He hadn't known that. It explained why there always seemed to be so few ether races, even though certain races, like the Berganda, could reproduce quickly and bring many to children to life at once. Of course, they also enjoyed much shorter lifespans.

He pushed any thought of the Berganda side. They would be safe on Mirial. Surely no one would hurt them. Besides, he had more pressing matters to address.

"I need to get my sister out, Litras. Can you tell me where they've taken her."

Litras was quiet for a few moments. "There are a few options. None of them good. The closest slave camp to where you crashed is tough to get anyone out of."

"I'll take my chances." A shadow moved to his left. He noticed that Litras nodded slightly. They had been spotted, and he hoped that Litras' signal indicated that Ardin could be trusted.

He ignored the signal.

"Where is the slave camp?" he insisted.

Litras stopped walking. He stopped short behind her.

"Are you really from Mirial?"

Ardin sighed. Why could it not, for once, just be easy? "Yes," he answered unflinchingly. Shadows detached from the walls around them, jumped out of windows, and even dropped from rooftops.

Bright orange eyes flickered in the torchlight.

Litras stood before him. He didn't bother reaching for his gun. He was sure they would have him down long before he had managed to fire a shot.

"We're going to have to make sure, you understand." His hands grew numb, but still he stood his ground.

He nodded. "Then you'll tell me the way to the slave camp?"

Litras smiled, except this time, the sharp teeth looked entirely more menacing.

"If you are from Mirial, you can head there yourself after we're through." She removed the glove from her hand. "In the dead Bergandas' old home, by the market."

She closed the gap between them.

***

Layela neared the Bergandas' home, relief already flooding through her at the thought of a quiet night. And at regrouping her senses. She crossed another street and accessed a quieter one, off the markets. She would be nearing the gates very soon.

Tomorrow morning, she would head towards the central part of the smuggling hive, which was past the docks, maybe an hour's walk from here. It wasn't the safest place to be, but better to fall in the hands of smugglers than Solariers. At least there, no one would betray her to Solarian authorities.

She'd find a way to blend in. She was good at that, blending in.

No wonder I'm not great at being a Keeper.

She allowed herself a brief smile and looked up. The gates of the Berganda home should be to her right, inconspicuous in this neighbourhood. They were old, made of a metal that that looked just like obsidian. For all she knew, it was obsidian, and the Berganda had managed to shape the stone in that manner.

She neared them, but frowned. No vines were holding on to the gates. She drew closer to get a better look, but a Solarier stepped in her view. A visor hid his face and weapons adorned his belt.

"State your intentions!" His voice was metallic. He was wearing a gas mask, as well. Layela feared she might throw up again and felt lightheaded at the rush of adrenaline. She tried to erase the fear from her eyes.

"I'm sorry, but I was looking for the Meta Meats Market. Is it not down this road?"

The soldier looked at her for a moment longer. She didn't dare look down, for fear of looking suspicious, but tried to glance sideways, instead, as though looking for the market.

It was such a lame story she doubted he would buy it. But it was the best she could come up with on the spot. Sweat began dripping down her back and the sides of her face.

The soldier pointed back to the street. "Back there, turn left. Follow the scent of rotting mammoth."

Layela managed a weak smile and mumbled a thank you. She turned around, as quickly as she could without breaking into a run.

"Nice eyes, but I like this view more!" He screamed after her, whistling. She didn't acknowledge him, keeping her head down as she walked back into the crowd with no idea what to do next.

***

Murl couldn't believe the Keeper's luck. Either Mirial still favoured her, or she was blessed by another force. To so easily slip through Solaria's fingers was nothing short of amazing.

Still, she was being too slow. If she wouldn't leave without the Malavants, Murl either needed them dead, or rescued.

Murl kept her hood up and followed Layela, the Keeper unaware of her presence. She was shielded by her brother's ether, and very little would be able to detect her. Although Layela was on the right track, she was too slow.

They needed answers now, and only the Keeper could unlock them. She was annoyed at the necessity to keep Layela alive longer. But her brother had been insistent. She sighed and looked up at the unfamiliar sun, angry that it would now be much longer before she stood beneath the sun of her forefathers once more. At least the child heir would be theirs soon. She would destroy Layela as soon as Braken had what he needed.

Apparently the Keeper needed something on this planet. Something that the Malavant siblings had been willing to risk their lives to get.

Still... the Malavants were Mirialers, and would be connected to the ether, whether they knew it or not. Their link was weak, and they certainly couldn't control any of it, but they would leave a trace. Murl ducked into an entryway to get respite from the crowd. She concentrated on her own ether, a hand on her chest. Letting it flow outwards, she could clearly feel Layela, delving deeper into the crowds and away from her. But she hardly mattered right now. To make Layela move faster, she needed the Malavants. At least the man, though Layela would not leave without the woman, too.

Her senses spread around her until she found both siblings—one deep under the city, and the other…she grinned. The other was just next door, past the guard that had turned Layela away.

Murl let the Keeper go and focused on the nearby sibling instead. She couldn't tell which one was which, but their signature was recognizable. They were both surrounded by ether creatures and even other Mirialers.

Ardin's wound would ensure Layela kept moving, and that she would refrain from using her powerful ether. Eventually Layela would find a way around the wards Murl's brother had set in place. The extra security of Ardin would then be required.

But his sister, Avienne Malavant, was useless in this journey. Murl would just have to make sure to bring back evidence of Avienne's death to get Layela moving again, away from this wretched planet.

CHAPTER 25

AS FAR AS Avienne could tell, the prison, camp, or whatever she had been tossed into, was just another impressive display of Solaria's disorganization. The ether creatures were shuffling about, some doing assigned chores, others tied in a row, just sitting on the ground. She recognized more of the creatures, mostly Kilita, but others she had never seen.

Must be good at hiding. But not good enough.

She wondered what sorts of powers they possessed. Their hands were all fastened in gloves, secured at the wrists by metal cuffs.

Guess I won't find out anytime soon. The three guards herding her had left her own hands free. She doubted she could make good her escape, even if she tried. She'd have to keep an eye open for the right opportunity. She glanced sideways at a wooden building in shambles. Trees were cut down, and half of an actual prison complex, albeit a small one, was built. A few flowers remained underfoot, but most of the grass was brown and over-trampled.

The air was thick with noise from the construction, huge slabs of metal being welded together, sparks flying as great ships lowered various sections and walls to hold them all together. It wouldn't be fancy, but it would be functional within days at the rate they were going. She could smell the welding from here.

The metal walls worried her. They were very thick, with only one entry point—a large door right at what she assumed was the front. The systems installed seemed simple, so it wouldn't be a full prison complex with judging chambers, as usual. This was different. She turned her head to look, to be rewarded with a hit to her lower back from one of the guards.

"Head straight."

She lowered her head and winced. She didn't even want to know what her face looked like after being smacked around. She'd need several drinks to forget that one and get rid of the raging headache.

Wait, did I really promise to quit drinking if my brother lived?

She sighed. *If. For all I know, he's dead, now.*

A chill ran up her spine and she ignored it. The soldiers would have teased her with his death, had they found his body. He was still alive, somewhere, and undoubtedly looking for her. Of course, that hardly meant she intended to wait around for him. A girl had to look out after herself, and Ardin might have a hard time finding her.

Another ship appeared, more of a shuttle, and lowered a large tank to tack on to the side of the building. Avienne resisted the urge to look sideways, glancing as far as she could without betraying her interest to the guards. She wasn't keen on being hit again.

The tanks were lowered, three of them together, and fastened to the side of the building.

Three tanks… Avienne's blood grew cold. She remembered sharing a drink with an old Plast years ago, an ether race that had once had the ability to communicate with wooden-looking large winged animals, until the last of them had been slaughtered in the Ether Wars. He had gone on for three hours about the horrors of the war, which Avienne had tried to ignore as she downed her drinks. It had taken three hours to knock herself out.

But one thing he had told her she remembered above all else—the description of the gassing chambers. Some small ones in the regular prison complexes, and other large mills, erected for the sole purpose of mass extermination of the ether races. Theirs were resistant races, until the discovered mix of three strong gasses, which proved the easiest and most effective combination to eradicate any of the ether races so far encountered by Solaria.

Avienne swore under her breath.

Three gasses, three tanks. No exit.

It was too bad the Three Fates didn't seem interested in intervening.

***

Murl scaled the wall and dropped silently to the ground. Crouching behind the remnants of a dead tree, she glanced through some branches. There was barely any coverage, and the scene spread before her. A giant building, which she didn't care for. Lines of ether creatures tied down, some seemingly half-dead from lack of water. She didn't care for them, either.

She gave a small smile as she spotted her target, red hair practically glowing in the sunset. They were bringing her towards a kind of shack. Or a home, maybe. A small home.

She could easily kill her now. Summon the ether, which she was curious to do, and hurl a fireball at her. But that would draw too much attention, and she didn't need all of Solaria after her as she herself pursued the Keeper.

There would be time enough for playing with her dark ether, soon. Now, she only had to wait for night to crawl in, and she could sneak past the guard and slit the Malavant's throat. She had done much worse and much harder before, and she certainly would not fail.

She sat in the grass and stayed as immobile as possible, wisps of ether dancing around her. This land had been strong in ether once. It was pathetic now, but still, if Murl closed her eyes, she could pretend she was on Mirial.

Except she wasn't on Mirial, and never would be again if she let her defences down to pursue whimsical ideas.

She set her jaw and waited for darkness to cover her passage.

***

Avienne stumbled into a wooden building, the guards pushing her in and slamming the door behind her. "Friendly lot," she mumbled.

"Avienne?" an old, familiar voice asked. Avienne looked up. The rays of sunset cut through the crooked boards of wood which formed the walls. She could make out a few people around her, some huddling together, others hiding in darkness. She couldn't distinguish which one had called her name.

"Um, yes?" she asked in a whisper, so as not to draw the guards' attention. She didn't care for another hit. At least not right away.

"Avienne Malavant." She heard a chuckle. "I'd recognize that fiery voice anywhere."

"Gobran!" She followed the sound of his voice and the slight movements of his shoulder as he chuckled. She knelt beside him and clasped his hand in her own. "We've been looking for you," she said, trying to see him better in the darkness. His hand was shaking rather violently and felt old and frail in her own.

"Gobran," she whispered. "How long have you been here?"

He coughed and wheezed. She didn't think he was laughing. "Not long." He paused. "A lifetime."

A guard shifted outside, no longer blocking the sunset rays from reaching Gobran. Avienne looked up at his face and had to stop herself from crying out, though she caught her breath loudly.

"That bad?" Gobran wheezed again. Avienne couldn't speak for fear of her voice cracking. His face was taut, and where his two eyes had been, there was only blood and puss covering his eye sockets. They had removed his eyeballs and left him to heal on his own. Avienne felt her stomach turn.

"That bad." Gobran said, squeezing Avienne's hand a little bit. Angry tears ran down her cheeks. She brought Gobran's hand to her lips and kissed his fingers. She ignored the taste of blood on her lips.

"Don't worry, child," Gobran said, opening his hand and feeling around her face, wiping away the tears on her right cheek. "It's a blessing."

"How can you say that?" Her voice broken. She clutched his hand.

He wheezed again. "It was either that, or…" His shoulders began to shake. Avienne put her hands on them, not knowing if tears could even escape the ravaged eyes.

"Don't speak, Gobran. It's all right. You don't have to say. I'll get you out of here." Her words tumbled out of her mouth. He ignored them and continued, his voice rising to a pitch.

"It was a blessing, they said, so I wouldn't see what they did to my daughter." He broke into dry sobs. "Alecya, oh, my baby girl," Avienne grabbed the old man and hugged him hard, whispering soothing words in his ears, not even knowing what she was saying, just trying to calm him down.

"Quiet!" the guard screamed from outside. A few of the figures whimpered and huddled deeper in the darkness. Avienne held on to Gobran, still whispering to him. She would kill every single guard here, this very night.

And then she'd get medical help for Gobran and a drink, several drinks for herself.

Oaths be dammed.

CHAPTER 26

LAYELA REACHED THE meat market and kept her head down, walking through the dissipating crowd. It would be night soon. She didn't need to sleep but her body ached, and she was no closer to finding either Ardin or Avienne. For all she knew, they were dead.

No. They wouldn't be. They couldn't be.

She realized she was nearing the shuttle. Maybe her shuttle was linked with the Malavants. It was from the same ship, after all, so it only made sense that some sort of tracking mechanism would exist. She felt like an idiot. All these hopes and delusions of using her ether had only blinded her to such an easy and simple answer. An embarrassed smile crept across her lips. She walked faster and forced herself not to break out into a full run.

She kept her head down, her steps energized by hope. Of course she could find their shuttle. She visualized the controls in her mind. It was probably near the general sensors. She just had to figure out their signature, which was undoubtedly marked into the computer. Why would you even expect people to remember something like a string of code identifying a shuttle? The onboard library would store that information, surely.

Layela hopped up the cement stairs leading to the shuttle, feeling lightheaded and almost giddy. The Fates were finally favouring her. Or she'd smartened up, anyway.

She jumped on the last step and walked into the high ceilinged, multi-level garage. A shuttle flew past, the sound of its engine resonating in Layela's ears for several minutes. The stench of exhaust clung to the walls and floor, made of cement turned patchy black.

Layela didn't care and didn't even cover her nose to block out the scent. She needed to reach the shuttle now and test her theory.

It would work. It *had* to work!

She neared the spot where she was sure she had left the shuttle. Another shuttle was idling there, much uglier than her own. She walked by it and pushed ahead. In her worry for Ardin and Avienne, she mustn't have been paying enough attention. She turned down another row and looked. She was certain it had been closer to the exit. She wheeled around and went back.

She had definitely been there, where the idling shuttle was. Spots were sometimes hard to find right beside the market, with so much interstellar and local traffic, so she wasn't surprised that her spot would have been filled right away.

But where was her shuttle?

"Can I do something for you, little girl?" Layela wheeled around. A broad-shouldered man was smoking near the shuttle, taking long drags and puffing them back into the air, as though the cigarette smoke was oxygen itself.

She smiled, making sure she seemed more confident than friendly. "I seem to have misplaced my shuttle," she said.

The man took another long drag. He was in his early forties, she guessed. The tattoos on his arms revealed several smuggling rings she was familiar with and knew well enough to avoid. But she recognized none of them as slavers. A small comfort.

"Lots of shuttles get stolen around these parts."

Layela felt her hope blow away with the man's smoke. She nodded and began walking away, but he called after her.

"It's your lucky day, though!"

She turned slowly to face him again. "Your shuttle's the one with the flower symbol on it?"

Layela swallowed and nodded. She doubted he knew the symbol of Mirial, and hoped he would know nothing of the Keeper, or her strange eyes. The man threw down his cigarette butt and stomped on it before walking towards Layela.

She held her ground, looking up to meet his eyes.

"I saw the guy who took it. Was waiting for the spot." He paused and took out another cigarette and lit it. Layela wanted to scream at him to finish his sentence, but didn't want to lose the one person who could provide much needed answers. He took a long drag and blew it to the side. Enough of the smoke blew on Layela to make her cough. He gave her a thin smile.

"Dark hair, dark blue eyes, thin and tall-ish. Was wearing a dark jacket. Didn't even look like he had to break any locks. Just walked up to it and opened that door like he'd had the codes all along."

Layela mumbled a thanks. The man nodded and walked back to lean against the idling shuttle, still smoking, as though he had never been interrupted.

"You know him?" He suddenly called after her in a drawl.

She forced a smile. "Yes. He's a friend."

The man's lips curled at one corner. "Not a lover, I hope. Had another lady friend with him. Walked him right to the shuttle, and gave him a long, and I mean looong, hug. Didn't board with him, though. Maybe he'd already got the goods?"

Layela's blood ran cold.

"What did she look like?"

"I love helping cat fights along," the other corner of his curled up. "Not my type of girl. Shorter, sandy hair. Looks ready to kill everyone, except her lover boy. Called her Murl."

Murl.

Layela mumbled a thanks and walked until she was out of his sight. Then she ducked between two large shuttles and leaned against one. Her euphoria crumbled to dread. He had described Clave to a tee, and Murl had been with him. If Clave had left with the shuttle, that meant he was heading back to *Destiny II*.

Her mind somersaulted with possibilities, making her dizzy. But all scenarios pointed to one likely outcome. Why else would he not want her to know he was still alive, if not to break away from her and not have her pursue.

He was going after Ardice. She couldn't think of any other reason why he would abandon her here, why he had not been in the alley and survived, and why he had not come to find her, or waited for her at the shuttle as agreed. It must have been his plan all along.

"Idiot!" She punched one of the shuttles and regretted it immediately as the skin split across her knuckles. "Idiot," she whispered again.

She leaned her head against the cool metal. There would be no reason for the others to suspect Clave of treachery. He could waltz in and take Ardice. She doubted he would hurt her. She was too valuable, still. If they'd abandoned her, that meant they were edging their bets on the new Keeper.

And Murl was somewhere on Thalos IV, hunting them, no doubt.

Idiot! It was too late to change what had been done. She closed her eyes and reached out with all her grief, her worry for Ardin, her fear for Ardice, her love for both of them and even her self-loathing at having trusted those she should not have.

She reached out and implored Mirial, her raw emotions spreading from her chest, turning to anger at the injustice that had been dealt to her—worse, that she had let be dealt to her!

Like the first rays of sunlight, she felt Mirial's response from far away, a trickle of water in her dry throat. The First Star responded weakly and flickered out almost immediately, but she left Layela with a sense of direction, of where she had to go next.

The ether was gone. Layela didn't even try to grasp it again, following her instincts now, knowing Mirial guided her footsteps as surely as she had so often.

She ran down the street, not caring for the attention she might draw to herself, not caring if Murl intended to gun her down right now, only knowing that she stood to lose everything she loved.

***

Murl was still crouched by the tree when she saw the ether around her ripple and then return to its placid nature. The jewel throbbed on her chest, the ether crashing onto it and making her gag. She lowered her head and shifted her feet to steady herself.

Someone had thrown a stone in the pool of ether, and it could only be Layela. She didn't know what had amplified the Keeper's determination to use the ether, knowing the danger for Ardin and Ardice. That Layela had broken down the ward was no surprise. They expected she would be able to, as soon as Clave left her proximity. Maybe Layela had figured out Clave's plan already? She didn't know, and she didn't care. Regardless, Layela was powerless to stop them now, unless she intended to sacrifice Ardin.

Murl looked back up and carefully stood. She seemed steady enough. Layela had buckled the ward, not broken it.

Still, it showed the Keeper's strength remained intact. Murl needed to move now, if their plans were to succeed.

Starting with the death of the red-headed daughter of Malavant.

***

The Kilita lowered her hand and backed away from Ardin to join the ranks of the other Kilitas. Ardin was growing impatient. It had been hours since the Solariers had dragged his sister away, and he'd had enough of hiding.

"Are you going to help me or not?"

Litras shrugged. "You're Mirial enough."

"How is that even a test?" Ardin's voice didn't hide his annoyance. Touch his skin, and that was it?

"Mirialers don't react to ether."

Ardin squinted. "I know for a fact that's not true. My wife's a Mirialer, and she was hurt by a Kilita, once."

Litras frowned. "Before Mirial showed up again, things were different. Mirialers were as affected as the rest of the ether creatures. Weird thing, that lack of ether. Or too much, I hear." She paused. "You're really going after your sister?"

He nodded and stood his ground. She burst out laughing, and so did the Kilita surrounding him. "You're a foolish man, Ardin. Tell us, how will you get her out of a slave camp? And how will you escape the planet? Your shuttle was destroyed, remember."

Ardin ignored the frost creeping into his blood. "That's for me to figure out. In the meantime, tell me what you know, please. Give me a chance to rescue her."

Litras grew serious again. "The camps are dangerous, and well guarded. They've killed many of ours, and the gassing chambers will assure many more will die."

"And I need to get her out before that happens."

"Might already be too late. Might not. But we can at least help *you* escape, if you drop the idea of saving her."

"Not going to happen."

Litras shrugged again. "Good. Not enough loyalty in this world of ours." She paused. "If you survive, try to find us. We're in the shadows, helping others like us escape Solarian space while time remains. We'll help you escape and bring you back to Mirial."

"Don't bring anyone there," Ardin hissed.

Litras looked surprised. "Where else are we supposed to go? The Keeper will take care of us, and keep Solaria away. If not the Keeper, than who?"

Ardin felt deflated and looked down. He debated lying, but saw no need for it.

"The Keeper is no longer on Mirial."

The silence grew so thick it was smothering.

"What do you mean?" a male Kilita asked from the shadows.

He blew out a frustrated breath. Everything was going so wrong. "The Keeper had to leave. Some…Mirialers blamed the ether spikes on her, and she left for her own safety." The wound of his chest throbbed and sweat broke out on his temples.

"How do you know this?" Litras asked in a whisper. He had no idea what the ether creatures thought of him, or the fact that Layela did not keep the identity of the father of her child a secret. Or if they were even aware that Ardice had been born. He decided to err on the side of caution.

"We're traveling on her ship. She's not far and needed to seek help from this planet." He quickly wove on a lie, seeing an opportunity. "My sister has what she needs, and without it, the Keeper may be in even more dire trouble."

He didn't give her a chance to reply. "I once heard that the Kilita were a brave race of warriors who had no equals for enemies. And I see that you are honourable, too, for setting up the network that has saved so many, and risking your lives for the safety of innocents." He paused for effect, looking around to meet the eyes of the gathered Kilita. "Will you stand for the Keeper today? Will you help ensure Mirial's survival, and the free flow of the ether you rely on to survive?"

He paused and held his breath, hoping he had not pushed too far into the melodramatic. He'd heard none of those things and had simply made them up. He loved the idea of the Kilita helping them out, regardless of negative past associations.

"What has the Keeper ever done for us?"

Litras replied before he could. "You seemed willing enough to go to her for protection a second ago!" She looked at Ardin with slitted eyes. No other protest sounded. She was obviously one of their leaders, making Ardin even more grateful.

"If you lie, I'll kill you myself." She looked at him a moment longer before turning around, shouting: "Gear up!"

The Kilitas followed and Ardin waited, hoping his newfound allies would not prove to be his enemy.

CHAPTER 27

GOBRAN SHIFTED FITFULLY beside Avienne, moaning in his sleep. Avienne leaned against the wooden wall of the shack, her arms resting on her knees. The place smelled of death, disease and human waste. A few of the others glanced her way. She had spoken to some, at first. Some just seemed unable to speak and, from the bloodstains, she guessed they no longer had tongues.

All things considered, the bruises and cuts on her face seemed very palatable, now.

The prisoners were all human. It didn't take her long to figure out that they were all from Mirial. A few had told her they had never even been to Mirial, and were just second-generation citizens. Solaria had apparently kept fairly decent records, and the collection of Mirialers had started as soon as the ether blips had begun.

She looked at the fading light. She had been observing the guards for almost an hour. There were two that stayed right outside the door. There was no other entrance or exit from the cheap building. A great many more guards were busy with the gassing chambers and ether creatures. The Mirialers, it seemed, were of little worry.

I'll have to teach them better.

Avienne sighed. It sounded great in her head, but she had no idea how to get out. Oh, she could make a good show of it and maybe die a horrible death trying to escape. Something they'd sing about while downing shots for years to come! But to leave here would mean abandoning Gobran, or losing all hope of speed.

The old man was more than likely a dead man with those wounds, but she couldn't bear the thought of leaving him here, at their hands. He had made her cry, even! She hadn't cried in, well, she didn't remember. She apparently had a soft spot for old, blinded men.

Isn't this a lovely journey of discovery?

A woman stood. Avienne raised her head just a little bit to see her more clearly. The woman crossed the floor without making a sound and sat down beside her. Her skin was pale brown and complemented her green eyes.

Avienne remained seated, waiting for the woman to speak. Or to just sit there.

The woman shifted a bit. She glanced sideways at Avienne.

"You're a friend of the Keeper?" she whispered in grainy tones.

A slight grin graced Avienne's lips. "I'm the aunt of her child, so ya, we're friends."

The woman looked away and leaned against the wall. Avienne didn't feel the need to break the silence. The only thing worse than being trapped with a bunch of Mirialers on Mirial was to be trapped with a bunch of Mirialers in a small, guarded hut.

"Is she coming for us?"

Avienne sighed. "Why don't you just think about helping yourselves? Wouldn't that be more practical than daydreaming?"

The woman flinched, as though struck. Avienne shook her head. She looked like a Mirialer that had lived through the Great Darkness. Her posture was calm, but her gaze was quick and furtive, like a deer ready to escape at any second. Old pale scars marked her dark skin, and Avienne thought a few fingers were missing, though the light made it difficult to tell. "You spent how many years surviving monsters attacking your home, and you survived, to come here and die in a small hut, surrounded by Solarian soldiers who probably never even fought a single real battle?" Avienne gave a low laugh. "Pathetic."

The woman didn't reply for some time, sitting very still, breathing heavily. Avienne had struck a nerve.

"You think we can take them?" the woman said. Avienne cocked her head.

"I do. But I don't want to abandon my friend."

The woman nodded. "I'm Elice, by the way."

"Avienne."

"How do we go about doing this?"

"Carefully?" Avienne grinned. It was nice to have an ally that wasn't just moaning. "I'm not sure. Do you have any weapons?"

Elice closed her eyes and sighed. "No. They took everything, of course."

Avienne joined her in a sigh. "Well, that'll complicate things."

She jumped when Gobran suddenly reached up and grabbed her arm. "Are you all right?" she whispered.

"Boots," he said.

"Boots? You want me to take your boots off?"

He gave a slight smile. "No one ever checks the boots of the old blind man for weapons."

Avienne grinned. She crawled to his feet and reached into his boots. She came away with two knives. Two guards, two knives, two women. The tides seemed to be finally turning. She handed one to Elice.

"You know how to use this?"

From the slow smile spreading across Elice's face, Avienne doubted that would be a problem.

***

The Kilita had "geared up" quickly, although gearing up meant less clothing, more weapons, more war paint. He wondered how effective it would prove on Solarian soldiers. The women didn't bother covering their chests which, as Ardin quickly noted, didn't much matter.

"You need weapons, Ardin of Mirial?" Litras asked, brandishing a spear. It wasn't wood, at least, but rather some sort of sleek metal.

"No thanks, I'm good."

Their hands were all uncovered, and a few of them had fierce, sharp nails. Their hands were made of a coarse, nail-like substance, like a horse's hooves but with sharp claws. He'd heard they were deadly weapons. The Kilita who had been wearing gloves, like Litras, had short, dark nails on orange fingers, completely different from Kilita that had never trimmed their nails to accommodate the gloves.

Litras noted Ardin's gaze. "Gloves make our hands sweat, stops the skin from thickening."

"Some of them have never been to surface?"

Litras grinned. "Of course they have. In the shadows. Few people pay close attention to the shadows of Thalos IV."

He nodded. "Are we ready?"

It was her turn to nod. "The sun is almost set. We'll be at an entrance under them by the time night falls. We're good at shadows." She grinned and began the trek into the darkness. He followed, ducking to avoid jutting rocks as they left the underground city.

"Under them? There's an entrance under them?"

She didn't turn as she answered. "The Berganda and Kilita were close as ether races, or so our legends say. We had direct access from our underground realm to their aboveground world. Met halfway, in a moonlit cavern. Or so our legends say," she repeated.

"We're not far. Stay quiet, now."

Ardin nodded and followed in silence. It was infuriating how little he still knew or understood of ether races, and how little they themselves knew or understood about themselves, too. The Ether Wars had long been over, but between those years and the ones marking Mirial's disappearance, most of their collective history had been erased. Or they'd chosen to forget.

But it didn't matter, for now. He had allies, which he had needed, and they seemed to have a plan to help him get his sister out of that forsaken camp.

Or so he hoped.

***

Layela had to slow her progress on the crowded streets. The kernel of instinct gifted to her by Mirial faded with each step, and she required all her concentration to continue using her internal compass.

Please don't leave me now! Her heart skipped beats and she felt flushed. It was as though the ether remained just within her reach, but something still stopped her from accessing it. She concentrated on what remained within her, following her instincts until she crossed another street and realized where Mirial was taking her.

She hopped into the shadows of an alley, leaned against a wall and took a deep breath.

If Mirial meant for her to go into the Berganda's former home, the least the star could do was provide her with some sort of ether or protection.

She closed her eyes and gathered her wits, if not her courage.

***

"Gobran," Avienne whispered in his ear. "I know you're hurting, but you have to be ready to move, okay?" The old man made a noise that sounded close enough to agreement.

Elice had warned the others, though some didn't look like they'd ever move again. They'd leave them behind. They had to. It would already be hard enough dragging the wounded who wanted to make it out of here.

Their one blessing was that the door didn't face the large building. Guards from afar would still spot their escape if they looked at the exact right moment, but with any luck, they wouldn't. The sun was almost set. The time to move was now, while the shadows were longest, and before the guards turned on the large security spotlights.

They couldn't help the trapped ether creatures, but she could live with that. Getting herself and Gobran out was her main goal. She hoped Gobran lived at least long enough to give Layela the information she sought.

Elice stood and caught Avienne's eye. The woman nodded, and Avienne returned the gesture. She pulled the knife free, careful not to let the blade gleam in the fading light, pleased to see Elice equally careful. It boded well. Avienne walked towards the door, hoping to draw the guards in on some pretence.

Should really have worked that out first.

She reached the door, but couldn't see the guard. Either one of them. She looked back at Elice, her eyes large and wide in the growing darkness.

The door began to open. Caught by surprise, Avienne took a step back as the wooden door grazed her face. A woman stood in the entryway, her face covered by shadows.

"Avienne Malavant?" the voice hissed. Avienne did not respond, clutching the knife more tightly. That voice sounded familiar, and it wasn't a good familiar.

The hairs on her arm stood at attention and Avienne jumped sideways, narrowly avoiding the dark ether crackling past her, killing two Mirialers behind her and taking out the back wall. The roof buckled and half of it came crashing down. Elice recovered her senses faster than Avienne, stabbing the intruding woman in the arm. She shrieked and stumbled back. Avienne slammed the door on her, knocking her backwards. She didn't wait to see if she would get up again.

She heard orders being shouted at the other end of the camp, and the security spotlights beamed on them like rain.

"Let's go!" she screamed, losing all hope of stealth. The sound of approaching soldiers rang in the night.

Avienne grabbed Gobran and helped him up, looping his arm around her shoulders and half dragging him through the wall at the back. She heard others following. Avienne stumbled and swore, almost tripping on a guard. His glassy eyes stared back, his throat slit.

"Hang on," she mumbled to Groban as she bent down and grabbed what she could from the soldier. His gun was gone, but at last he had a comm unit on him. She'd need to get in touch with her ship again, eventually.

Glancing back, she saw Elice dragging someone else, running as fast as she could.

Not fast enough, Avienne knew that, with the wounded, none of them would make it out quickly enough. But she had no intention of leaving them behind. None of the ones who still wanted to live, anyway.

***

Layela felt a ripple in the ether seconds before she heard the crackling of wood and shouts. She peered around the corner. The guards were running in, abandoning their posts to deal with the commotion inside. She could hear more shouting and the cracks of weapons fire.

She grasped at the ether, but the wall blocking her from it had reformed with a vengeance. The gates were wide open, and only one guard had remained at his post. He was pulling the gates shut again. If she was going to act, it had to be now.

She slipped out of the shadows and walked towards him, ignoring the fatigue of her bones.

"Excuse me!" she cried in her friendliest voice. The guard jumped and wheeled towards her. She held up her hands.

"Sorry, I didn't mean to scare you." She smiled. She didn't think it was the same guard as before. She had tried not to look too closely at him, but this guard seemed shorter.

"Ma'am, this isn't a good place to be." He turned back to the gate. She followed him.

"Are those the old Berganda gardens I've heard so much about?" She stood on her tiptoes to peer over him.

The guard left the gate and turned to face her. "Ma'am..." He didn't get to finish. Layela kneed him in the crotch, and then double-fisted him in the face as he leaned over in pain. He fell down, knocked out.

Layela shook her hands. She had forgotten how painful punching could be.

She bent down, grabbed his gun and key cards, took a deep breath and entered the gates.

***

Avienne dragged Gobran as she ran, shots firing around them. The old man lolled near unconsciousness. There was little Avienne could do to absorb the shock or slow down, so she just hoped he would survive a while longer. She wished she had a gun. The knife seemed useless now.

She didn't dare turn around to see the progress of the guards, or how many Mirialers had survived. Elice ran even with her, grinning at Avienne. A bullet caught Elice in the knee and she stumbled, her scream cut short as another shot hit her in the head. She crumpled in a bloodied heap on the ground. Avienne swore and pulled Gobran back to some cover behind a stone wall covered in brambles. The old man's breathing was laboured and his right eye socket oozed.

Avienne took a deep breath and did a mental count. "This doesn't look good for us, Gobran," she whispered. The soldiers were approaching, calling out for their surrender.

"I've lived a good life," he said, squeezing Avienne's arm in comfort.

The soldiers suddenly stopped firing. For a few moments, the silence was smothering as Avienne awaited the enemy's next move. Then shots turned to screams, rippling across the night, echoed by screams from the other prisoners. Avienne propped Gobran up and chanced a glance around the wall. If that crazy woman was up and attacking them with her dark ether, she at least needed to know her whereabouts.

She squinted in the dark night, pushing back a stray strand of hair. Soldiers were falling, running in a disorganized heap. She could hear screams, and… "Are those spears?"

"Avienne!" She heard Ardin first, then spotted him as he shot a guard. She laughed. "Ardin! You're slow!"

He ran up to her, grinning, and hugged her gently around Gobran.

Avienne looked back at the field, where the ether creatures were now being set free by… "Are those naked Kilita?"

"Geared up Kilita, I'm told." He glanced at her face. She was sure she didn't even want to see how black and blue she was. "You all right?"

"Better than him," she indicated Gobran with her chin.

"Let's get out of here." Ardin supported Gobran from the other side, and the three ran. The gates loomed before them, opened, for a change in their luck. Ardin swore, and Avienne looked up.

Up ahead, just before the gate, Layela walked in, gun in hand.

"That can't be good," Avienne mumbled, pressing forward. Behind them, the crackle of ether began to lighten the night as the last rays of sunset vanished.

***

Layela barely noticed Ardin and Avienne running towards her, seeing instead the looming darkness behind them. The night crackled with it, tiny lightning bolts of dark purple, almost black themselves, gathering in the sky over them. It was a concentrated attack, and it was directed at the Malavants.

She broke into a run to meet them. Ardin was screaming at her to get back but she ignored him, concentrating on the imminent danger they couldn't see.

"Keep going!" she screamed at them, and Ardin swore, making it clear he had no intention of leaving her here.

"At least get behind me!"

They did at least that much, stopping just past her. The ether gathered and grew in size, forming a cyclone around them, her hair dancing in its wind. Others were running towards the gate, mostly ether creatures, many of them Kilita.

Layela's blood turned cold at the sight of them. *It was only one Kilita, not the entire race, who attacked me.* She forced the memories deep as the ether creatures ran towards her.

"Behind me!" she screamed again.

"Keep running!" she heard Ardin add. The sky seemed darker yet lighter all at once. The stars were hidden from view although the night was clear, but her skin, the plants, the ether creatures— everything that had come in contact with ether, everything that had been infused with it, glowed in the darkness.

"Hurry!" she screamed. The dark ether crashed down before her, killing dozens of ether creatures and sending her to her knees. Ardin grabbed her arm and pulled her to her feet. "We have to go! You can't fight this!"

The gates slammed shut behind them.

"Blood and bones!" Avienne screamed, throwing herself against the gates. They didn't even budge.

"Not time to go just yet," a familiar voice said. Layela turned and her blood ran cold. Murl. Her eyes glowed black and her fingers sparkled with unspent ether. Dark ether.

"That ether is dangerous," Layela said in warning. "You have to let go of it."

A guttural laugh escaped Murl's throat. "It is a gift from Mirial herself, and you dare insult it! You are no longer Keeper, Layela. We no longer need you!"

Layela braced herself. Murl was drunk with power, her mad laughter whipped around them by the winds.

"Keeper!" A half-naked Kilita woman screamed. "Escape, we will buy you time!" She ran before Layela, lance in hand. A few others joined her.

"The blind loyalty of the ether races is sickening, at times," Murl said. "And where will they escape to, with the gates closed? I thought the Kilita were smarter."

Ardin grabbed Layela. "Litras, come on! This is foolish!" Layela held her ground.

Only Mirial could save them all. Would Mirial really let her fall? Would she really let her just die like this, by tainted ether?

"We can't just leave them!" Layela screamed.

"Think of Ardice, Layela. She needs you!"

Tears welled up instantly in Layela's eyes. *Ardice!* Helpless, and Clave was coming for her. She nodded and let Ardin drag her back, Avienne trying to open the gates still.

"We'll have to climb!" the Kilita said.

"He won't make it!" Avienne screamed back as she looked to Gobran, leaning heavily on the wall by the gates.

"Gobran!" Layela chocked on his name and had to look away from him.

The ether sparked and the winds picked up. The Kilita screamed what must have been a war cry and attacked, only to be tossed back like rag dolls.

Murl's eyes lit up with darkness, a deep silver lined with insanity. She lifted her hand and the dark ether funnelled towards them like a tornado, absorbing the ether from the plants around them, planted with careful care by the Berganda generations ago. The ether mixed in, turning dark as it twisted into braids. Layela could see it clearly, the tornado coming towards her, towards them all.

She glanced at Ardin. He screamed, the words snatched away by the growing winds. But Layela could hear their echo from earlier: *Think of Ardice.*

She steeled herself and stepped in front of everyone, calling on Mirial and on the ether of the land, infused with the Berganda's will. She willed Mirial to heed her and protect them, pushing so hard the glass that shielded the First Star from her shattered into thousands of shards, glistening with darkness before collapsing on the ground. *Dark ether.* They had managed to ward her ether with the darkness.

She held up a shaking hand, grasped her ether and flung it into the heart of the tornado.

The dark ether was thick, absorbing her light. Layela stood her ground, bracing her legs to absorb the strength of the wind around her, ignoring her hair whipping her face. A rock flew up and struck her arm. She grunted and kept it raised, to help her focus the ether, regardless of the fact that she could do so with only her thoughts. She forced it back, further and further, the sky an explosion of light.

A scream exploded behind her and a shout for her to stop. Layela was pulling back the ether when she was struck in the back of the head and she fell to her knees, gasping, the pain exploding down her spine and up into her skull.

The ether faded, the night quiet once more. Murl was nowhere to be seen. The gates cracked open behind them.

"We're going to have all of Solaria and Thalos on us, soon!" Avienne shouted, pulling her up. "We have to go!"

"You punched me!" Layela accused her.

Avienne turned from her and pulled her brother up, who was unconscious. "Figured I'd give us all a chance to escape."

"Let me carry him. Kilita are stronger than humans," the Kilita woman, Litras, offered. Avienne nodded and let her handle Ardin. She flung him across her shoulder as though he was merely a sack of potatoes.

Avienne helped Gobran back up and Layela braced the other side of him, trying to focus on the fact that she had saved them all and could still save Ardice.

If she could do so without calling on any more of her ether, she might manage to save Ardin, too.

CHAPTER 28

A SINGLE SOLARIAN SHIP cut the atmosphere of Mirial and headed for the palace. Braken watched it approach and pulled his hood up. The most important lesson he had ever learned was not to trust strangers. And anyone born off planet, anyone who had grown up away from Mirial, fell in that category.

The guards Murl had left for him were waiting patiently outside. He could sense some of their indecision. His presence changed things. He was a man, first of all, and not the declared Keeper, yet Mirial answered his summons with ease and eagerness. He could feel the First Star now, caressing his burnt skin. He welcomed the warmth and comfort.

The Solarian ship made dock. He could see her from where he stood, on his room's balcony. Layela had chosen a low-level room to be closer to a garden, but Braken had gone back to the larger room that had served generations of Keepers before him.

He straightened his shoulders. He *was* Keeper, now. Layela had run in search of answers; answers only she could find. Murl would make sure to get them from her. The child would be brought back here, for sacrifice in the Temple of Mirial, to end that particular line.

Layela would be killed by Murl once she had what was needed, as would the Malavant siblings. Clave was his back up, in case any of it went wrong. Then, Clave and Murl would return home to live out their lives in peace.

As long as Solaria left them alone, of course.

Braken turned in one swift move, his cloak swirling at his feet. He pushed the door open and kept a steady stride, the guards struggling to keep up. He allowed himself a slight smile.

Solaria thought it had the advantage, now. For five years he had watched signs of their planned invasion, even though Layela insisted on ignoring those signs. The tunnel they had rebuilt on their money, even though no trading power existed here and they were well out of Solarian space.

But nothing remained between Solaria and Mirial, not since Mirial's shields had wiped away the closest solar system. Mirial was the next logical target. The next step to expansion, especially considering the wealth of ether.

Solaria had sent a few delegates. Some researchers had come to study ether. Layela had allowed it, as long as they shared all their findings. He could understand the Keeper for that move. She probably longed for their help to understand a system her feeble mind failed to grasp. She had at least declined Solaria's offer to set up an embassy on Mirial, stating the fragile state of her planet and people following the calamity of the Great Darkness.

Her planet. *Her* people.

He had listened in on that statement. He had tapped the palace's communications lines long ago. A wise move on his part. It had fortified his resolve to remove Layela's hold on Mirial. She would have thrust them into another era of darkness, one that Mirial herself could not stop. Mirial could not change politics, nor could the First Star sway the hearts of lesser beings.

Mirial was power, pure and simple. She was the source of all life, and the end of it all, if she so chose.

For Mirial understood, as he did and Layela did not, that sometimes to ensure the growth of a beautiful garden, certain weeds had to be destroyed.

***

Gresko paced his chambers. He had developed a pattern over the last two days. Around his bed, then his favourite chair, then past his two best paintings, and then around his bed again. It kept things more interesting than just going back and forth, but did nothing to lessen his frustration.

He had not been invited to the historic meeting with the Solarian representative. He was not surprised. His role as Court Advisor seemed a bit passé now that Layela had been effectively chased off Mirial and an unnamed male heir sat on the throne.

Gresko knew who the male was, of course. He was not a fool, and only wished he had the means to tell Layela. Or that he would have told her before. She had deserved to know. She should have known already, but he had kept his secrets, as he was meant to.

But his loyalty to Layela's mother should not have surpassed his loyalty to Layela. It had, he could now clearly see, and it made him feel ill to think of it. He was Court Advisor. He was meant to advise the current Keeper. His full loyalties should have been Layela's, but they hadn't been, and because of him Mirial was in danger of much more than just cultural clashes. Layela had needed him more than any other Keeper had. She had not known the history, the culture, the traditions…and yes, she was unconventional and did as she pleased, but with a little more effort on his part, he still firmly believed she would have grown into a fine Keeper.

But he had not insisted, keeping his own past shaded in secrets and lies, hiding promises made to Keepers long gone.

He stopped pacing, and fell into his chair. Never had he suspected the male would step forward. He remembered the night of his birth. The court had assembled—the queen was having a child, perhaps a promised daughter. He had waited in the sitting room with the captain of the guards. Adina, the queen's sister, stayed with her, as was right and proper.

Then a guard had fetched him. "The Lady wishes to see you."

He had nodded at the captain of the guards. Nodded. And the captain of the guards had nodded back, a slight gesture that might have escaped a less observant man. They both knew what that meant. The Keeper had given birth to a son.

He stepped into the birthing room. The Keeper was already standing and had changed. The Keeper's sister held a cloak for her to cover herself with. The night was cool, and the Keeper's features were pale. Were those tears in her eyes? Gresko said, "It's not your fault, my Lady. Perhaps the next child will be a girl."

Anger flashed in his Keeper's eyes. Then, he had chalked it up to fatigue. Now he understood that the Keeper had loved her children, all of her children. Had the Keeper had Layela and Yoma first, he firmly believed that she would have gotten rid of one of the twins as bound by duty. But the pain and guilt of losing her first labour must have been more than she could bear. He should have seen it. He should have been more aware of his Keeper's weakness. It had been his duty to know, but he had ignored it, or not noticed it. He couldn't tell anymore.

She had walked out into the court, to announce that it was a false labour and to invite everyone to eat and drink regardless, and pray to Mirial for a healthy child. Her sister trailed along.

Gresko had headed to the bassinet, where the child rested. The midwives huddled over it. He cleared his throat, and they moved aside. He had been surprised, he remembered. Surprised that there had been two. Twins.

If one had been a girl, things would have been different. But they were two boys, so he had packed them up, and carried them to a village far away to be adopted by a pre-screened family. The villagers would know, of course. But they would never speak of it. It was the way of Mirial.

He had never told Layela, which he regretted deeply, now.

Looking out his window, he could see the great Solarian ship in the docks. He didn't know what Braken planned. He doubted it would be an alliance with Solaria. He would be a fool to consider that.

He feared it was something much, much worse. But what terrified Gresko most of all was the fact that he didn't know where the second twin was. He feared Layela would find out the hard way about her older brothers.

He stood again. He was Court Advisor, and in the absence of the proper Keeper, his duty to Mirial remained intact. He was not without allies or resources yet.

He hoped.

***

Minister Noro stepped off his flagship in full military uniform. Rare were the occasions that called for him to dress so these days, but his first official meeting with this new Keeper of Mirial certainly seemed to warrant it.

He had opted for a small retinue, understanding that Mirial was still recovering from its "Great Darkness" or whatever the locals called it. The air of Mirial was pure. It was dry, though it held a touch of moisture from the nearby river. Passing over the land he had seen only desert, but around the palace sprouted grass and flowers alike. The last Keeper had been rumoured to have quite the green thumb. He had been more familiar with her, since one of his colonels had pursued her relentlessly to stop the rebirth of ether.

But ether had to return, as Noro had known, and his colonel had perished trying to wage war with an almost dead planet. It had been embarrassing for Solaria, and he had never been as grateful as the day Layela granted forgiveness if they granted her space. The last thing he had wanted was a repeat of the Ether Wars. He had made his reputation the first time, and it was not something he cared to repeat.

Reputations forged in the Ether Wars were not kind ones, though they were quite hefty.

The door to the palace opened and a man walked out, his face covered by a hooded cloak.

How charmingly rustic, Noro thought, adopting his most diplomatic and deferential expression.

"Minister Noro," a low voice rumbled from within the hood as the man stopped before him. He was tall, slightly taller than Noro, who towered over most men. The shadows of his cloak hid his features in surprisingly thick shadows.

"Keeper," he used the title, not certain how to greet a Keeper of Mirial. That appeared to satisfy the man, who seemed to grow taller after hearing the title.

The man was proud, and still uncertain of his role. Noro could use that to his advantage. Still, best to test the waters before pushing forward recklessly.

"The invitation to meet you was most welcome," Noro said, putting some emphasis on *you.* The man nodded. Noro held his peace. He still felt uncertain about why he had been invited here. He hoped this Keeper was more of an advanced thinker than Layela had been. A partnership with Solaria could strongly benefit Mirial.

The Keeper stood silent for a moment longer. "I thank you for accepting my invitation, Minister." His words were slowly spoken and carefully chosen.

Noro lowered his chin in acknowledgement. He waited a moment longer. The sentence had been held in suspense, indicating the Keeper intended to continue his thought without interruption. His palace, his rules.

"I was pleased to hear you had some progress tracking the rogue Keeper, but not surprised to hear she slipped through your fingers." He paused, his great cowl lowering slightly. "Mirialers will always prove stronger, no matter who they are. But no matter. I want to test something important with you now." A black hole formed in Noro's stomach. *Test* was not a word he had ever heard used in delegations. It was not a comforting word.

His guards felt his discomfort and took a step forward. Noro hissed. He didn't want their recklessness to ruin his chances at an allegiance with Mirial.

They shuffled again, their weapons clanging. Noro wanted to turn to tell them to be quiet, but something in the way the man looked towards them stayed his eyes.

"Not with you specifically, Minister. You're entirely too important to waste on tests."

Noro took a deep breath and felt the blood drain from his face. He turned carefully. The soldiers were still standing behind him, but there was no doubt in his mind that they were dead. Their skin had taken on a tarry darkness, parts of the flesh melted to reveal dark bones beneath. Their arms hung uselessly.

"Not bad, for a first test." The soldiers began walking towards Noro. He stepped back, right into the large chest of the Keeper. "Simple creatures, you humans are." He gave a low laugh. "Don't worry, Minister. They'll simply escort you to your quarters, while we figure out a few other details with Solaria."

The soldiers flung their arms, gaining some form of control as their hands closed on his upper arms. He mustered all of his training and control to keep from screaming.

CHAPTER 29

KEEPING THEIR HEADS down, they ducked through dark, small alleyways braced by crumbling wooden buildings. The darkness was thick and smothering, with dust and dirt crowding the air. The camp escapees struggled to control their breath and make as little noise as possible. Litras lead them into an old building, as quiet and dark as the rest. Layela glanced around, unconvinced they were alone.

The Kilita kicked in a loose board at the back to reveal an entrance. They streamed in one by one, careful not to hit the narrow sides. The only casualty was Ardin's head, knocked with a rather large thud. Avienne whispered to Layela that the hit shouldn't leave too much damage, but even she didn't laugh at her own joke.

When they were all through, Litras set the piece of wood back in place, at least as much as she could from the angle.

"Quiet until I say so," Litras whispered. The darkness gathered thick around them. They walked on, carefully feeling the walls around them. Layela heard Avienne whisper something to Groban, whom she still supported. He grunted in pain or laughter, Layela couldn't tell.

The walls surrounded them, silent sentinels, ceilings lost in the shadows, corridors thick with humidity and the smell of mould. Then they too dropped away and the consistency of the floor changed under Layela's feet. The humidity dissipated and cool air licked the sweat from her skin. She reached out to graze the wall, but her fingertips only met air. The darkness made her dizzy and disoriented. She concentrated on the small scuffing noises of her companions, resisting the urge to grab hold of someone and not let go.

After a few minutes of walking, Litras turned on a small light, blinding them for a few moments. Layela blinked away the spots of light and glanced around. They were in a large cavern, stalactites jutting around them. Pinpoints caught the light and held it. *Jewels,* Layela realized.

The cave was riddled with them, from rubies and emeralds to colours she couldn't even begin to describe. Litras glanced at her and gave a slight laugh. "All those smugglers arguing over rotten meat up there, not realizing the fortune they walk on. They've never bothered with a geological survey of this planet, figuring it a useless hunk of rock. They just covered it up with their own junk instead. Humans," she grumbled as she deposited Ardin gently.

Layela dropped to her knees beside him, turning him to be on his back and checking his limbs and torso for signs of blood. Avienne joined her. Gobran's raspy breaths filled the cave.

"Was he hit?" Layela asked. Avienne shook her head.

"Small blessings. He doesn't need that on top of everything else." She met Layela's eyes, but said nothing more. Still, Layela couldn't help but hear the unspoken accusation: *You hurt my brother.*

She pushed the thoughts far away and unzipped his coat. She moved the shirt out of her way to see the wound that cloaked man had inflicted. Touching the wound made her draw her hand back and hold in a yelp. It had stung her!

Avienne looked at her and then quickly reached to move the shirt without wincing. She sucked in her breath. Layela looked down. The wound had doubled in size, at least. The darkness spread up his neck, even, and halfway through his torso. She couldn't see his arm, but she imagined it traveled the length of it, as well.

"It grew." Avienne said in a flat whisper.

Layela didn't reply. It was dark ether. It fed off pure ether, converting it to darkness.

If she called on Mirial again before healing Ardin, she might kill him.

***

Hiding behind the rubble of a house near the camps, Murl could hear the Solarian ships arriving, and soldiers shouting indiscernible orders and warnings. Spotlights scarred the area in bright, large beams. Some soldiers walked by but did not spot her. They were too horrified by what had happened to perform a proper, thorough search.

Murl counted her breaths and hoped her heart would steady. The surge of power had been…unexpected. She had drunk from an endless well of ether and had not wanted to let go. She would have killed Layela, Ardin, everyone on Thalos IV in that split second, and she knew it.

In that moment, the answer her brother sought hardly seemed to matter. With that power, which was only a fraction of what Braken could draw upon, she felt as though she could have taken down all of Solaria with a simple wish. She had connected with everything around her, all at once, and it had all seemed so small and insignificant, including Layela. Until she had pulled upon her own wealth of ether and completely lost control. She had seen Layela and the others cowering, had felt Layela's counter attack. Murl knew she would have killed Layela, killed them all, despite her orders to bring the Keeper back to Mirial. With the power flowing from her talisman to her fingertips…*she could have easily destroyed them.* And ruined Mirial.

She shuddered.

Now she remembered why her brother needed the answers Layela so desperately sought—answers on Mirial, and on the passing of its bloodline. If that power dissipated with the deaths of Layela and Ardice, if the Keeper line was not properly passed down, the consequences could be devastating. Mirial could entirely stop communicating with them, and they would no longer bathe in ether. Regardless of their hatred of the Keeper, Braken had warned Murl that without the answers only Layela could find, their access to the ether would be impossible, as well.

A searching spotlight passed uncomfortably close to her. At least Layela wouldn't use that much ether against her. Surely by now she had figured out how Ardin reacted to her attack.

And if Layela didn't use that much power, Murl wouldn't have to, either.

Which at least slightly lessened the chances that she would kill the Keeper before they were done with her.

The spotlights moved away. She kept to her crouch and followed her instincts into the darkness.

***

Layela's movements were wooden as she pulled Ardin's shirt over his wound. His features were pale and drawn. He was fighting against the darkness that was clutching him. But she didn't think he was winning.

"What do we do now?" Avienne asked, sitting beside her brother.

The words snapped Layela out of her grief. "Ardice. We have to contact the *Destiny II* and save Ardice!"

Avienne's eyes grew wide. "From what? What does that even mean?"

Adrenaline forced Layela to her feet. "Clave. He took the shuttle. I'm certain he's working with Murl. He's gone back to the *Destiny II*. I'm sure he's after Ardice."

Avienne whipped out a comm unit and pressed it. "Avienne to *Destiny II*. Come in, *Destiny II*." Layela could have kissed her.

She waited a moment as static filled the line. "*Destiny II*? Come in." A few more moments. "Blood and bones, pick up or I'm coming up there and turning you into scrap metal!"

"I don't think the ship will respond to threats." Gobran wheezed a laugh. Avienne softened a bit.

"They must be blocking our communications, or that rat changed frequencies before he left. He could have, easily, and no one would know unless they specifically checked. I know I wouldn't."

"What do we do?" Layela asked, her voice hollow in the cave. She couldn't use ether. She might kill Ardin. And yet, what would he want of her? He would hate her for choosing his life over his daughter's.

But…to live a life without him. Layela looked down and closed her eyes, fighting the urge to retch. It was turning into a habit.

"We could fly up," Litras offered.

Avienne sighed. "Our ship is scrap, and hers got stolen," she nodded towards Layela.

"I have a shuttle. I think it works." Litras shrugged. "I'm not a pilot."

"Best we've got," Avienne said. "Is it far?"

The Kilita shook her head.

Avienne helped Gobran up. "Come on, old man." Litras lifted Ardin. Layela followed, battling her light-headedness.

She could save her. If this shuttle didn't work, if it was too slow, if Avienne couldn't make her take off right away, she would still find a way to save Ardice.

Even if it meant sacrificing Ardin.

CHAPTER 30

THE NIGHT WAS quiet and brisk, Elsa's limbs stiff with chill. She huddled in the oversized sweater Kyle had secured for her. Slita ran low to the ground, following Kyle closely. Slita wore a lighter jacket, made snug to her body with the weapon-bearing belt and the extra two guns slung on her back.

The palace lights illuminated the sky up ahead, the blood red moon low in the sky. The sky was clear but the shadows on the land were thick, forcing Elsa to concentrate on her footing to avoid any treacherous falls.

The sky began to hum and she looked up. Slita grabbed her arm and yanked her down beside a rock, smothered by deep shadow. She held her breath as the humming grew louder. A surveillance ship flew overhead, barely metres from them. The warm blast from the engines grazed Elsa's cheeks.

It continued on its way, not even slowing down.

Kyle appeared beside them and crouched. "Let's hope the others avoid detection for some time, too."

Slita nodded and they moved from their hiding place, back into the open air of the desert, having long abandoned the cover of the trees. A few large rocks and ruins provided some cover, but not enough to let their guard down for a moment.

Elsa's breath curled around her in small puffs as she ran behind Slita.

No fear, sister, Slita's voice floated in her mind. Elsa didn't even respond, knowing her sister could easily see through any lie she would cast as an answer. She huffed and followed Slita, suddenly struck by how different all of her sisters were. Ambition had graced Slita, and impulsiveness Elsa. Her other sisters were gifted with other abilities, or traits, like compassion, nurturing, comedy…She had never really noticed until their old world had changed drastically overnight. Now, she and Slita were the only two who had stepped up, showing how most Berganda were peaceful by nature. It was no wonder so many had perished during the Ether Wars.

Pay attention! Slita's command struck her mind and she looked up to see spotlights graze the ground before them. Slita moved to the side to avoid one, Kyle and Elsa following suit. Spybots hovered throughout the landscape.

Elsa held her breath until they were past them. The danger they now faced was evident and crept like ice in her bones. All they had to do was to bring down at least part of the security network to give the incoming rebels more of a chance at success. They had told no one of their plan, not sure who they could trust.

The sky above them cracked as another Solarian ship pierced the atmosphere and landed at the palace. All day they had been landing at regular intervals. If they were to stop Braken, it would be now, before the Solarian forces became too acquainted with the terrain and strengths of Mirial.

"Let's go," Kyle whispered. He stood and ran ahead. Slita followed, as did Elsa, though her legs were having difficulty going as fast. They jumped down a rocky overhang, helping Elsa down in turn. She tried to fight back her fear, but found it difficult making her legs move.

"We can access the palace via these tunnels, which used to lead to the underground palace." Elsa leaned in closer to hear. "It's a big underground network, and Braken has few resources now. Even the Solarian soldiers would be lost and unable to stop us."

He grinned as though to reassure them. Slita and Elsa exchanged a glance.

They entered the tunnel with no light, counting on the bit of moonlight filtering in for the first few steps. Elsa put her hand on the cave wall. There were few plants around her to even summon help from. In the forest, most of her usefulness was based on her ability to charm the plants to life. She put her hand on the gun at her waist, but really had no idea how to use it effectively. She hoped it wouldn't come to that.

They rounded another corner and Kyle turned a flare beam on, the green light floating in the cave ahead. They could see no enemies, but the jagged edges and uneven walls allowed for many hiding places. Kyle motioned them forward. He wasn't ten paces ahead when the wall crumpled right on top of him, large rocks covering him before he could scream. Slita jumped to the side, barely avoiding another explosion which sent rocks smashing to the ground near her. She rolled and vanished in the cavern.

Elsa stood rooted for a moment before the wall beside her exploded and she threw herself to the side, a rock smashing into her arm. She yelped and ran to the other side of the cavern, towards where Slita had vanished.

This way, hurry! her sister implored. Elsa jumped over piles of rock. She saw Kyle's hand jutting out at a strange angle. She ignored it and ran until she spotted her sister in the shadows. Near her, to the left where the rocks blocked Slita's sight, she could see strange men walking towards her. They were soldiers, or she thought they wore a uniform, but in the low light of the cavern, with Kyle's lantern casting a glow from where it had fallen, she could also tell there was something very wrong with them. As though they couldn't quite control their limbs.

Her scream caught in her throat and her mind wouldn't even send a warning. Slita heard the monsters a second before they were on her. She fired her gun, but the monsters kept coming until they surrounded her, arms lashing as though armed with claws. Slita's scream and the pain rippling from her mind snapped Elsa free from her fear. She ran forward, pulling her gun. Too afraid of hitting her sister with the weapon, she stumbled to her knees and put both hands on the ground, imploring the ancient roots to come to their aid.

She found them, all the ancient roots from trees long dead, their essence barely kept alive by the ether of Mirial. They responded slowly at first, but as she poured her urgency into them, they sprang to life. They shifted and broke through the rocks of the cavern, long petrified themselves, and attacked the monsters on top of Slita.

The monsters were quickly pinned by the roots, gurgling but unable to escape. They were soldiers, or had been, but they no longer even remotely resembled human.

"Slita?" She voiced the question, knowing there was no point in calling out telepathically, her skin shivering with the silence and grief already pouring from her sisters. Elsa pushed them all away, forced them all to be quiet, to leave her alone. She cut off the thoughts of the other Berganda as she knelt beside the yellowing skin of her sister, too far gone to even offer or receive comfort.

A sob caught in Elsa's throat, but she was still too afraid to let it escape. What if more of those monsters heard her? She looked down at Slita's blood, flowing freely onto the rocks, pooling into crevasses and hardening, useless and quiet.

No Berganda children would ever be born from her brave sister. At that thought, a sob did escape her throat and she lowered her head to Slita's withering chest.

An explosion above her snapped her head back up.

The rebel attack on the palace had begun.

***

Braken watched the poorly planned attack against Mirial's palace from the comfort of his balcony. He did not even need to unleash his newly formed army. A few well-placed bombs had already scattered the rebels and sent them fleeing back to the forest. He let them go.

He knew where they hid. He knew all of the hideouts of Mirial. But hunting the rebels down was not pressing. They were still under the mistaken impression that Mirial's sanctity could only be preserved by restoring Layela to her throne. They were wrong, of course, and he truly believed they would come to understand that, with time. Especially once the ether of Mirial had properly been passed down to him.

Once the sun hosted his ether and his alone.

He didn't want to kill Mirialers. There were too few left. They would come around out of a sense of self-preservation, if nothing else.

The Berganda, who hid with the rebels, would have to perish. He only needed one to bring Layela back, and from the ripples in the ether from the caves below the palace, he understood which one he needed. Controlling plant life was as easy for Berganda as controlling the dead was for him. And he had found dead beauties on Mirial. Corpses so old their species had long been forgotten, in even the long lore of Mirial.

He took a deep breath singed with sulphur. Smiling, he called to the ether and deactivated every detonation device and trap he had laid out in the old palace of Mirial, deep below. The Berganda would now have clear access to the palace. The Berganda had one advantage over his ether. They were strong telepaths, some of the strongest in all of the worlds.

And they were like daughters to Layela Delamores.

***

Elsa felt something shift in the air around her. She couldn't quite figure it out, but she raised her head to examine the rock. Everything had grown quiet. The attack on the palace seemed to have already ended. The creatures now hung quietly from the roots, no longer gurgling. Her own grief nestled quietly in her heart.

She didn't look back down at Slita, not wanting to replace her memories of her vital sister with the sight of her corpse.

Kyle's lantern still gave off some light, which she followed a bit deeper into the caves. She peered into the darkness and recognized some of the rock formations. She had been here before, but not from this entrance. There was another entrance further up ahead, one that she used to come to as a child with Slita…

Elsa swallowed hard and looked down. She could take that exit, hoping no more traps existed, and just leave. Or, she could try to go further into the palace to see what else she could learn, to help the rebels and convince them that they and the Berganda were on the same side.

With Kyle dead, that would prove more difficult than ever.

For a moment, Elsa was tempted to open up the line to her sisters. To reach out for their warmth and find comfort there. She looked back up and rolled her fingers into fists.

She didn't need comfort, now. She needed action.

She needed to put one foot in front of the other, and never look back.

CHAPTER 31

THE SHUTTLE APPROACHED *Destiny II* without any communications or warning. Jaru mumbled to himself as he chugged coffee.

"Can't get through. Her systems seem fine. She's on autopilot and her shields are blocking our sensors. Could be no one in there, or they could be injured…" Larod blocked him out as he sat down in the captain's chair. It was a comfortable enough seat, but he preferred being second-in-command. Less pressure.

But until Ardin or Avienne made it back, this was where he would have to sit.

"She's a ghost ship, then," Larod whispered, looking off into the distance. He had always dreamt of ghost ships. He'd grown up on an ocean world, one of the rare ones, and had been a sailor at sea, before space. Barely a man, and he'd been out on the water more days of the long years than on the land. Nothing like the roll of the waves under your ship to stimulate poetry. When the fog rolled in, he imagined ghosts and spirits dancing onto the ship, blocking it from the next port, and taking them somewhere far. And magical.

Mirial was the closest he'd ever been to one of his imagined worlds, and he'd left too fast to explore it.

"No such thing as ghost ships…" Jaru put in. He continued mumbling to himself, his words buzzing like the ship's controls. Larod sighed. The systems analyst's mind could move fast, but it played in the restricted field that Jaru considered "reality." Larod couldn't help but think it limited him greatly.

"We could tether them and just drag them with us until we know what's onboard," Jaru suggested. Larod shook his head.

"Could have wounded onboard. Can't risk it."

"Wounded, on a ghost ship?"

Larod cracked a smile. Perhaps Jaru's mind could push its boundaries after all.

"Bring 'em in. I'll go to the shuttle bay and greet them."

"What if they're the enemy?" Jaru asked.

"Keep them in the decompression bay. We'll have a look first. And tell that Slont fellow to come join me. Captain seemed to trust him, and I betcha he's good in a fight."

Jaru nodded. Larod jumped into the lift and headed down. As he passed by the habitat floors, he swore he could hear the child crying, even through the titanium sheets.

That child had some good lungs. Would make for a scary thing to hear coming from a ghost ship.

***

Patros had been resting when the call came from Jaru.

"You're needed in the shuttle bay. Incoming shuttle."

He had wanted to ask questions, but by now knew better than to ask the systems analyst. It would be a long and complicated answer. And would lead to many more questions, he had no doubt.

He jumped off his bunk, stretched, threw on his jacket and headed down to the shuttle bay. He hoped it was Avienne. He was growing worried, and thought more and more that he should have gone with her. She could have used his help. Of course, she had asked him to look after the child.

But the old engineer had her well in hand. Save for a recent crying fit, Ardice had mostly slept and gurgled. The only thing that would attack that child right now were germs.

He hopped into the lift and headed down. It felt good to move. Back home, he was used to constant movement. Not just his own, but the movements of the world around him, as well. To feel the molecules stretching and moving around his hands…he missed the feeling. *Destiny II* had yet to offer him an interesting challenge in molecules. Even her alloys were rather boring.

He craved raw, unspoiled materials. Peering in and seeing their atoms in perfect harmony, unlike anything else he had ever seen. Majestic.

The doors opened. He stepped onto the shuttle bay control centre, where Larod stood. The man was short, but he hardly seemed to care that everyone else towered above him. "Effusively a sailor," Avienne had described him. He couldn't agree more.

"The shuttle's coming in now," he drawled, looking down. There was no tenseness in his muscles, but Patros doubted he would see any unless one of the Three Fates herself walked off that shuttle. And then he'd probably just shrug it off.

Patros hid a smile. He could see why Avienne liked him as a second-in-command. A calm demeanour was a good method of ensuring Avienne's rather no-calm demeanour didn't doom the ship.

"Who's in it?" Patros asked.

Larod shrugged. "Dunno. Gonna know soon." Larod gave him a grin. "You're the muscle."

Patros raised an eyebrow. He was tall and fairly strong, for being so thin, but his race was hardly good in a fight. Which was why most of his people had been exterminated in the Ether Wars. Hiding would have proved a more prudent route for the Slont.

"Here you go," Larod handed him a gun. At least Patros was a fair shot. Larod stuck one in his belt, as well. Patros felt better knowing he wasn't the only muscle.

The shuttle was grabbed by *Destiny II*'s automatic landing system, which latched onto it and powered the shuttle down. Tracks took care of the rest, moving the shuttle into the decompression area. Larod and Patros watched as oxygen was filtered into the room and the internal air maintenance systems were checked to ensure no further decompression was necessary, lest the inhabitants be killed.

Nothing stood out of the ordinary, so Larod pulled the shuttle through the rest of the path. Almost, anyway. He kept the shuttle in the sealed portion of the bay, instead of bringing it to the main area.

"Better safe than sorry." Larod mumbled. "Ghost ships."

Patros shook his head but didn't ask for elaboration. He was quickly learning that acceptance proved the easiest method for dealing with these sailors.

Larod activated the speaker system. "Please identify yourself, or step out of the shuttle."

No response came. The shuttle just sat there, quiet. Its space lights were still on, the bright beams reflecting back on it from the walls, giving it an eerie glow.

Ghost ship, Patros found himself thinking as well. He shook his head. He'd been on this ship too long already, and it hadn't been that long.

"I'll go check it out," Patros offered. "Keep the door locked behind me."

"Good lad," Larod said in agreement. Patros sighed. He doubted there was anything wrong with the shuttle, and he really hoped he wasn't about to get himself killed.

He grabbed the rungs of the latter leading down to the bay. As soon as he landed on solid ground, he pulled his gloves off. He stood before the door and looked up. Larod nodded and pressed the controls. The door opened.

He stepped through, and heard it close behind him.

"Well, ghost," he murmured. "Looks like it's just you and me."

***

"I got this ship off a guy," Litras said proudly as she lead them down another tunnel. "It's good, I hear. He owed me."

No one said anything in answer. Layela made an effort. "Why did you want a ship?"

Litras grinned at the question. "To fly to Mirial, of course! I was going to come up and find the First Star again, when it first vanished, years ago." She shrugged. "Didn't figure out how to work this thing, though I still think flying to Mirial would be neat."

"Today's your lucky day," Avienne mumbled.

Litras either didn't hear or chose to ignore her. They reached a sealed door. A metallic sealed door. "It's in here," Litras said.

"Is that a shuttle bay?" Avienne asked.

Litras looked at her as though she were insane. "Where else are you supposed to keep shuttles?"

Avienne didn't respond, but Gobran wheezed some more.

The Kilita punched in some numbers and the door opened. Litras flicked the lights on, all of them having to look away for a few seconds as their eyes grew accustomed to the light.

"See?" Litras exclaimed. "A ship!"

Avienne swore. Layela looked up in curiosity. She was a ship, all right. A fighting class vessel, she guessed. Small enough to avoid detection, and quick enough to escape. She was sleek and seemed in fairly good condition, but what held their attention was her hull. On its side, etched carefully and in great detail, was the symbol of Mirial.

"This is from Mirial," Layela whispered.

"Describe her to me," Gobran asked. Avienne indulged him. "Kinda small but long, sleek looking. Different than most Mirial ships, actually. Less show-offy."

Gobran was silent for a moment.

"Is her symbol surrounded by small etching? Look like light emanating from it, but when you look closer, they're actually roots?"

Avienne leaned in and squinted her eyes. "Oh ya! I see them. Hard to make out in this light, but definitely there. Much less noticeable than the rest of the symbol, I gotta say."

Groban wheezed slowly. "I always knew she was here, and this was the world he had come to. That's why I settled here, after a while." He paused, and turned to Layela, facing her despite his blindness. "That's the ship I pursued out of Mirial so long ago. The one that took you away from your world, Layela."

Layela sucked in her breath.

Avienne turned to the Kilita. "I'm guessing the man who sold it to you was tall and mysterious?"

The Kilita looked surprised. "Ya, you know him? He was nice enough. Needed some money fast. Needed to get rid of this ship, and didn't want anyone on Solaria or anywhere else to see it for some time. I promised him a year grounded. Figured I'd learn how to fly in the meantime. Never did."

So she had come to Thalos IV right after her birth. The building blocks of her life were falling into place, slowly. But those were not the mysteries that needed solving, right now. Her own past could wait. She was more concerned with her future.

"Can she fly?" She directed the question to Avienne.

Avienne grinned. "She looks good! Gobran, surely you're not about to tell me that the Captain of the Royal Guards would have picked a poor ship in which to escape pursuit?"

Gobran wheezed and Avienne grinned. She jumped up and opened the hatch, pulling herself up through. Within seconds the ship was powering up and the main ramp was being lowered to allow for the others to come onboard.

Avienne stood at the top of the ramp, leaning on the doorway. "Welcome to the, um, the…?" It was Gobran's turn to indulge her.

"She was known as the *Haven* back in her day." He paused. "But we can rename her as you wish, Layela."

Layela shook her head before realizing Gobran could not see the gesture. "Of course not. She bore the name well. Let's give her another reason to serve Mirial."

They boarded the ship as the sky roof opened, and were breaking the sonic barrier within minutes, flying back towards *Destiny II* as fast as Mirial's once-fastest ship could fly.

***

Patros approached the shuttle carefully, feeling ridiculously self-conscious as he did so. What could they possibly expect to find? A monster? An actual ghost? Whoever was inside, they were probably wounded and couldn't use the communications system.

He quickly crossed the floor and looked at the shuttle. He had no idea how to open the door. Absolutely no clue. He reached for the hull and let his senses guide him. Sometimes, by seeing the molecular structure of machines, he could also sense the way power travelled, and he could decipher what wires did, and so on. Rarely, but sometimes. He wasn't mechanically adept, so it proved a much harder task for him than for many of his kin.

Still, he probed the metal, to steal whatever secrets it would reveal…He removed his hand almost immediately.

Ether. Not the Keeper's ether. Something different. Like the wound on Ardin. Either Ardin was in there and in dire straights, or the person who had wounded him was in there. Patros hesitated. He felt like a fool for doing so, but he started backing away from the shuttle.

Larod could mock him all he wanted later on for getting the jitters. He was the one who believed in ghost ships, so Patros didn't think his vote counted anyway.

The shuttle's door clicked open. Patros' hands went numb. He hoped he wouldn't accidentally shoot anyone as he held up the gun.

A second passed before Clave stumbled out, fell to his knees and then collapsed on the ground.

***

Larod was about to go assist Patros with the fallen sailor when his comm unit went off.

"What is it, Jaru," he asked.

"I figured out why the shuttle couldn't contact us," Jaru said, his voice thin over the speaker. The man was actually whispering. Larod did the same.

"Why is that?"

"Because someone changed our hailing frequencies. I just spotted it by chance. I was looking at every possibility."

"Who would have done that, and why?"

Jaru paused for a moment. "Someone who didn't want anybody else to be able to contact us."

Larod nodded and looked down at the collapsed man. He suddenly wished he was safely at sea. In foggy climate, and near a cliff.

"There's something else," Jaru continued, speaking deliberately compared to his usual spewing of words.

"Oh?"

"Whoever did this scrambled all the coding. I'm going to have to rebuild from scratch. Could take a while."

"What's a while?" Patros was waving at him to come help. He waved down.

"A few hours. A day, at most."

"Make it faster."

"Of course!" the systems analyst replied, and Larod didn't think he was even being sarcastic.

He took a deep breath, pulled his pants up and his coat down, and grabbed the first rung of the ladder to go and help the ether creature. Ghost ship indeed.

CHAPTER 32

THE *Haven* **FLEW** like a dream. The skiff had all the functionality of a small ship, yet boasted the sleek simplicity of a shuttle. Her controls mimicked those of the *Destiny*'s shuttles, but with more options to give her greater stealth and tracking capability. Avienne pulled gently on the steer, the skiff responding smoothly, gaining speed. None of its main components had seemed to suffer from being unused. Not even any of her life-giving liquids seemed low—oil, hydraulics fluids, fuel…she was fully packed. Including her oxygen tanks. Avienne had flown in both her main pursuers, the *Destiny* and the *Victory,* and she could see how Zortan had made good his escape on this ship.

Even her hull had been designed to cut through far-seeking sensors, letting them slide off her ship and continue into deep space. A ship would have to be fairly close to actually detect her.

Destiny II hid in a nearby asteroid field, letting herself be carried forward to avoid detection. It was an easy trick, if you were good enough. With Larod in charge, Avienne wasn't worried. He was a tad simple at times, and superstitious, but he was one of the finest sailors she had ever sailed with.

He would keep *Destiny II* safe from detection, but Clave knew where the ship was, and they just couldn't be sure of his intentions. "Damn Mirialers," she mumbled to herself.

Litras sat quietly beside her, in the co-pilot's seat, though she obviously had no idea how any of the controls worked. And she had no reason too, Avienne decided. Growing up on a planet you never left would definitely hamper knowledge of ship controls.

The sensors flared to life.

"What is it?" Litras asked, perking up.

Avienne responded quietly, so the others in the back wouldn't hear.

"A fleet of ships. Solarian, Thalonian, you name it. They're sweeping the area."

Litras leaned back and nodded. She brushed some dust from the control panel, the only sign that this skiff had bid her time. "Can we avoid them?"

Avienne shrugged to hide her worry. "Probably. If she managed to escape the entire fleet of Mirial back in her day, I imagine she can avoid another fleet, as well."

As she spoke, Avienne calculated the proximity of the vessels, and their sweeping pattern. She ran a hand in her hair. At this rate, unless the crew of the *Destiny II* took proactive measures, the fleet would detect them before the *Haven* had reached them.

And she doubted the crew would be paying attention to what was happening outside, considering what she feared was happening within.

***

Patros leaned near Clave. The tall man was pale and drawn, yet he was breathing. Patros stood back up and walked into the shuttle. No one else in sight. Whatever had happened, it had forced Clave to abandon his companions.

Patros turned around and started when he saw Clave standing on his feet. Patros was too shocked to say anything, but Clave spared him by speaking first.

"I'm so sorry," he simply said, holding up his hand in a dramatic gesture. Patros took an automatic step back, but didn't move fast enough to avoid the stream of ether that struck him hard in the chest and sent him flying backwards in the shuttle.

***

Clave still felt groggy. Whatever Murl had triggered by getting over-enthused with the gifts Braken had given her, had rippled throughout the ether and knocked him out. He still stumbled a bit, but knew he had limited time. Layela had fought Murl and won, and she would soon head here. He needed to be gone before then.

One piece of the puzzle lay within this ship, and he would leave with it—her—before the others arrived.

Larod stood outside the control room, locking down the bay.

"I can't let you out, Clave," he said over the comm unit. Clave walked up and stared at him through the clear, thick separating wall. Clave liked the sailor. He was gruff and no-nonsense, and might have been a fine ally, in another life.

"Don't worry about it, Larod." Clave smiled at him as he summoned the ether. It hurt him—it always did. A burning sensation ran up and down his oesophagus, and his chest felt as though someone had grabbed several organs and compressed them. He ignored the pain and pressed on, forcing his body to become as transportable as the wind, or even more so. To be able to slide through other atoms without disrupting either his body's patterns or the wall's.

Larod gasped. Clave could see in his reflection that he had grown translucent. He took a step forward and walked through the wall without difficulty. Instead of continuing straight through and regaining solid form right away, he slipped down a floor, closing his eyes. He hated the sensation of falling. When he felt only air, he allowed his body to grow solid again.

It had drained him, and he was so far from Mirial that regenerating would take some time. But he had limited time to accomplish his mission, and he didn't intend to fail.

***

Larod sounded the alarm. He had seen a *ghost!* Clave was that, and surely nothing else.

He snapped himself back to reality and hit the comm unit. "Jaru! Intruder aboard. Lock her down and warn Rose."

"Aye, Captain!" The alarm sounded and the doors all latched into place. His codes would get him through, and hopefully the lockdown would slow Clave. He didn't know how long he could stay a ghost, but from the pained look on the younger man's face, he doubted that he could do it for very long.

Larod opened the bay door and ran to Patros, the blue creature shaking himself free of the shock. The hit had been minor, it seemed.

His clothes weren't even shredded—it had just been something to throw him back.

"He must be after Ardice." Patros winced.

"I have the ship on lockdown. But that man has tricks up his sleeves."

Patros nodded. "He's accessing ether. Not the pure ether of Mirial, but the ether that I could sense back at the palace. I should have known someone else was manipulating it! It was never Ardice—they just made it look like it was, so the people would revolt."

Larod had no idea what the man was going on about, but it hardly mattered now. "We need to get to the child," he said. Patros nodded, and the two broke at a run, Larod opening the necessary doors and access points to bring them to the lift. If Clave didn't know where Rose was, it would buy them time. But Clave had been involved in the construction of this ship, and knew her as well as anyone else.

Patros and Larod threw themselves in the lift and headed up. The young lass was crying still, he could hear her.

He pushed the lift to go faster. The Slont's knees almost buckled under him, but he didn't complain.

Larod intended to make sure that child didn't have anything more to cry about.

***

Jaru had warned Rose with a quick message. Rose had debated hiding with Ardice, but the child had started crying again, choking and gasping on her own sobs. Something was triggering her. Rose was sure of it. She had started crying just before Jaru's call came through.

She looked down at the small bundle of angry pink. "What do you see, little one?" Rose had locked her door and grabbed a gun. It was the best she could do to protect the future Keeper, and it would prove inadequate, she understood beyond a doubt.

She bounced her a few moments more, and then the pitch of her cries changed. They became more urgent. Rose's stomach fell to her knees. She placed Ardice gently down in her bassinet. She stood before the door, idly wondering if her sister had perished this way, too, protecting someone else's child.

The door slid open, as though security codes hadn't even been in place. Clave stood before her, and she shot without asking questions. The bullet ripped forward and stopped just short of hitting him, spinning before him but not moving forward. Rose lowered her gun.

"Don't hurt her," she implored. She hoped she had not misjudged his humanity, as she obviously had his loyalties.

He nodded. "Stand aside, Rose. I don't want to hurt you."

She believed him and took a deep breath. "You know I can't do that, Clave. You know I can't let you take her." She held out her arms imploringly. "She's just a baby, Clave."

"I know, Rose." He seemed about to tell her something more, but then decided against it and asked her to step aside again.

Rose placed herself between Clave and the child. Clave could destroy her easily, she knew. Ardice's cries were broken now, little sobs. Rose took a chance and walked back to pick her up, and held her close, cooing gently to her.

She turned her back to Clave. If he was going to strike, she'd make sure Ardice was safe. "I'm sorry, Rose," he whispered.

She closed her eyes and waited for the impact, intent on taking as much of the blow for Ardice as she could.

She waited, counting her breath, but still no blow came. She turned around slightly, to at least see him. Clave stood there, his eyes wide, his mouth gaping. Rose suddenly realized that Ardice had stopped crying.

The baby was gurgling contentedly against her. Rose turned fully around. Clave seemed trapped by something, rendering his limbs tight and useless. Ardice looked at him, the colours of her eyes deepening with a wisdom that frightened Rose.

Patros suddenly walked up behind Clave, placing his bare hands on his skin. Clave shuddered once, and then collapsed.

Ardice cooed, yawned, and fell asleep.

Patros exchanged a look with Rose, and then stared intently at Ardice. "Not bad for a newborn," he said. "Already won her first battle."

Larod was close behind him. He knelt and checked Clave's pulse. "Against a ghost, no less."

CHAPTER 33

ARDIN'S BREATHING HAD grown faster and more distressed. Layela placed an oxygen mask on him and pumped some relaxants into his blood. Gobran sat near, his eyes patched and as disinfected as Layela could manage without cutting the wounds open. She had pumped him full of pain killers and antibiotics, in the hopes the old man still had enough battle left in him to survive.

"Is he all right?" Litras asked. Layela was still uncomfortable with the Kilita, but was making a strong effort to hide it. The Kilita had, after all, saved all of their lives.

"What's wrong?" Avienne asked from up front. Layela took a deep breath.

"Someone's using ether. It's hurting him."

Avienne grunted and stayed up front, but Layela felt the shuttle accelerate.

"Is it that psycho?" the Kilita asked. Layela shook her head. "No, her ether didn't pull on him, since it's the same that's in his wound. It's a small blessing."

"Then who's using it?"

Layela didn't want to answer the woman, but knew that she would persist until she knew. Kilita had different cultural barriers, and politeness was not their norm.

Avienne answered from the front. "Ardice."

Layela nodded. "She's managed to tap into the ether. I guess whatever was blocking me was blocking her, too. That's what must have been hurting her so much. Her inability to draw on the ether when she was so terrified of the dark ether."

No one asked what that might mean. They all knew. Clave was on the ship, and a newborn was fighting for her life. Layela lowered her head to hide her grief. Ardin's pulse was erratic, and she looked at the wound, careful not to let the dark ether strike her.

Patros' wards had failed.

She could see the darkness spreading, crawling on his skin, nearing his heart. She didn't know what would happen then.

"That doesn't look good," Litras said. Layela wanted to answer, but knew she would just choke on the words.

No, it doesn't.

***

Avienne tried as best she could to ignore the plight of her brother. There was nothing to be done. She remembered her brother's pride as he had introduced Ardice to her. He would want his daughter to survive before himself. She knew it with such ferocity that it helped her focus on the problem at hand.

They were near *Destiny II*, but still could not communicate with her. Avienne hoped they could at least grant them access. Jaru might recognize the ship from years ago or, with any luck, it was in the database. It would confuse them, but hopefully they'd click in soon enough.

That wasn't her main concern, right now. They were getting close to the sweeping field; ships littered the space before them. Avienne believed this ship might actually have a chance at avoiding detection. If she stuck to traveling in neat lines between fighters, far enough not to be spotted by eyes, and in the weakest section of their scanning field, the skiff's hull should reflect scans harmlessly. The skiff could reach *Destiny II* with little hassle, but the second they boarded and fired the engines, the Solarian ships would be on the Mirial flagship like a swarm of bees.

She checked and double-checked her own sensors. They had managed to escape detection still. This ship showed off Mirialer engineering at its best.

Her board clicked. Some ships were changing their sensors' sweeping formation. Her blood grew cold. They were entering the asteroid field. Not as dumb as she'd hoped they were.

If they didn't reach *Destiny II* before they had to escape or attack, it would make it almost impossible to board her. Avienne ignored the safety warnings as she pushed the ship even faster, racing against time and chance.

***

Larod left Patros with Clave, the ether creature obviously capable of handling the madman. Rose followed him up, cradling the sleeping child in her arms. Jaru had not said much, simply stating that it might be best if they came up to the bridge. He had not mumbled, not gone on, which worried Larod more than he wanted to admit. Rose didn't know Jaru enough to feel the worry, but he worried that they would all know their own limits soon enough.

The doors slid open to reveal the bridge. It was quiet—not even Jaru's quiet mumblings filled the air. Larod looked around with worry, finding the systems analyst sitting at the tactical station, Captain Avienne's favourite post.

"What is it," Larod asked, his voice hoarse. *What else will we face this day?* Jaru pointed to the viewport as he switched the direction of the screen. Just on the borders of their asteroid field, a fleet of ships was sweeping the area. And many of the smaller, more manoeuvrable ones were beginning to enter the field.

Larod was surprised to hear Rose swear, followed by an immediate apology to Ardice. Larod grinned. The chief engineer crossed the bridge and placed the child in a drawer, locking it half-closed and placing enough blankets around her to keep the baby in place. She worked fast. She moved a seatbelt from one of the less used stations and tightened it around the child, gently, but enough so that with the blanket protecting her, she shouldn't fly out.

"We have company," Larod said. She nodded and sat at the engineering console, right beside the sleeping child.

"If we gun our engines, they'll find us," Rose said. "And if they find us, we'll have to not only fight our way out of here, we might also have to leave without the Keeper."

Larod sat down in the captain's chair. He shifted to try and get more comfortable, but knew it was nothing to do with the chair. Captain Avienne would fight every single last one of them to the teeth, and then wash away her wounds with drink. But Larod was a more patient man. Sea sailors had to be. You couldn't control the sea like people seemed to believe you could control space. Sometimes, you had to wait and see if the sirens would attack, or simply pass you by.

"Let's wait for a moment and see how the Fates will favour us," he said, leaning back against his seat, drumming his fingers on the armrest.

Wait and see who would find them first, ally or foe.

***

Layela could feel the tension from Avienne, but didn't ask her why. If Avienne needed her, she would ask. She had enough to worry about already.

Layela sat beside Gobran. Thankfully this ship was big enough to allow for both him and Ardin to lie down, and still provide room for the others. Gobran's vital signs were more stable than Ardin's. She didn't know what had happened to his eyes, but didn't ask. There was enough sorrow in the air of the shuttle already to crush them all.

"Gobran," she said gently. A slight smile spread across the man's lips. He was much thinner than he used to be. Not because of his very short time in the slave camps, but rather because of his daughter. It was not a malnourished slenderness. He had opted for a healthier lifestyle, to live longer for her. Now that he'd found something to live for again.

Layela wasn't sure what exactly to ask. The pieces of the puzzle that had seemed to lead to Gobran were fuzzy in her mind, now. She had wanted to help Ardice, but she thought she had, already. Or so she hoped, as long as Clave had been stopped. Her pulse quickened.

Ardin. She wanted to save him, too, from the dark ether. She didn't know where to go next. Gobran had studied all known maps of the universe, some so old that their solar systems had long been forgotten or destroyed, based on rays of light that had been cast long ago and had taken millennia to reach their world. Like peering into the past.

"Gobran," she spoke his name again. "I need answers, and I don't know where to go. The dark ether has Ardin, and if I use Mirial's ether, I'm afraid I'll kill him." She bit her lower lip. She hated sounding like a desperate and lost teenager in love. She was Keeper, and Gobran expected more from her. She shifted gears slightly, to appeal to his loyalty to Mirial.

"I need to know how the others are affecting Mirial so. There's so much I don't know about Mirial. Why does she even need a Keeper? Can her ether be cleansed once it begins turning to darkness?" She took a deep breath. "Gobran, do you know where I could find these answers? You know this universe better than any other person I know. You've studied the maps, and the maps of legend. Can you please help direct us?"

The shuttle shook a bit and veered. Layela didn't need to look up to know they had entered the asteroid field, and Avienne wasn't slowing down enough to avoid rough turns and gravitational pulls.

Gobran's voice was a drugged whisper. She hoped he still had his wits about him. "There was one race, so old that it only featured in legend. I found enough bits, over several years, to triangulate a likely position for them. They're called the Seeders, and I think they were there when Mirial herself was created." He gave a short wheeze. "But sending you after them is like sending you after the Three Fates themselves."

Layela's heart sank. She had put so much faith into Gobran, it had never occurred to her that he might not hold the answers she needed. She swallowed hard and tried to say something to the old man, to thank him for his help, to leave him feeling as though he had made a difference and not simply that he had crushed her hope. Before she could think of anything to say, Litras spoke up.

"The Seeders are real enough. Met one myself, years ago."

"Really?" Layela perked up.

She nodded. "Right after the Ether Wars. They went around to the remaining ether races and, I don't know, collected something."

"Collected?"

She nodded. "I remember it vaguely. I was really young. But my father spoke to the Seeder. They warned that a Great Darkness was coming, and we needed to be prepared. And they needed to know about our DNA, ether abilities, and all that stuff. I guess they were cataloguing, maybe? If the Seeder hadn't been an herald of Mirial, it wouldn't have been well-received."

"Wait, they knew about the Great Darkness before it occurred?" Avienne practically spat. "Why did they do nothing to stop it!"

Litras shrugged. "I don't think he was talking about Mirial's Great Darkness. Not even about what the ether creatures suffered through while Mirial hid. I don't think it was for another few generations, from the way it spoke." She relented. "Or at least, the way my father relayed the information."

"There might be something worse coming?" Layela whispered. Litras just shrugged.

The shuttle fell into silence again.

Then the shuttle rocked back and forth. "They're blowing up asteroids all over to get ships to move," Avienne reported as she navigated around chunks of rock.

"Blood and bones, they see us, hang on!"

Layela strapped Ardin and Gobran down, barely securing them when the skiff shook with a hit, tumbling on her side before Avienne righted her.

"She can take a hit," Avienne announced as she avoided several others. Litras had managed to make it back to the co-pilot's seat, a huge grin as she glanced at the ships beginning their attack dance, fighters changing course towards them.

Layela clutched the armrest of a seat and pulled herself in, fastening her seat belt and hanging on for dear life as Avienne banked the skiff down and forward, pulling on every last ounce of its speed.

Layela took a deep breath filled with dust and sweat, and she focused on her daughter, unable to ignore the vastness of space that still separated them. And how it was riddled with fighters intent on keeping them apart.

***

Destiny II hung in space, perfectly quiet. Larod had only felt such tension one other time in his life, on the journey that had ended his sea career. He had shot his nerves navigating waters that should never have been navigated.

Thought space was safer, he mused, *with all the fancy equipment and endless places to escape to. Was wrong.*

The sensor chirped near Jaru. He pressed a few buttons as everyone turned to him. "They're firing at a ship, bearing a Mirial signature."

"Is it the missing shuttle?" Larod asked.

"It isn't. Still one of our own, though." Larod forgot from time to time that Jaru was from Mirial, too. He had lived in exile so long, but once a Mirialer, always a Mirialer, or so he'd heard. Sounded like a lot of trouble to him.

Larod stood up and stretched, walking to the navigations console, where Clave should have been sitting. He sat down and brought it out of idling mode, activating the engines.

"Charge up all weapons, Jaru. Rose, shields please." He smiled. He loved the sounds of the ship churning to life. One thing he could say with ease about Mirialers: they knew how to build a good sounding ship.

***

Avienne swore worse than a drunk sailor. She was failing to avoid both rocks and weapons. Three ships were tailing her, and two more were flanking. At least ten others were closing in, and she couldn't afford to slow down to fly more carefully, or they'd catch up. The hull buckled beside Litras, a great dent stretching inward.

She looked at Avienne, eyes wide. "Ya, that's not good," she mumbled.

Managed to escape the whole Mirial fleet, but can't escape this fleet!

The controls of the shuttle had been fine when she had been going slowly, but now that speed was required, there were some major differences between a shuttle like this one and a much newer model like the *Destiny II*. She fired thrusters and three would come on instead of five, and she had no idea how to fire the others. She needed at least five thrusters on each side to navigate with the required dexterity through this asteroid field.

Another bump, and a yelp from behind. They were being pelted by rocks large enough to strain the metal of the hull. At least it was built to stretch, not to crack, but still, the hull could only take so many hits.

"I can't stop weapons and rocks," Avienne shouted. "So I picked energy absorbent shields to stop weapons. One good hit of their weapons and we're dead, but we can take several hits from the rocks." The shields around them buzzed with energy as they absorbed another hit. Down to forty-two percent capacity. "So stop complaining!"

Avienne swerved down and around another large asteroid. The ship behind her fired at the rock instead, pelting the *Haven* with shards, the sound of straining metal echoing throughout the skiff. "Smart little buggers," Avienne muttered as she returned fire with little effect.

"Layela, anything you can do?" Avienne asked.

"Not without killing Ardin," she said, so low Avienne barely heard.

"Well, we'll keep that as a last resort, then."

She pulled the shuttle down and manoeuvred between two asteroids, firing at them as she passed through. *Two can play that game.* Only two ships showed up on the other side. "Take over the side guns, I can only do so much at once," Avienne told Litras.

"I don't know how to handle a ship!"

"I'm not asking you to handle the bloody skiff. I'm asking to point and click. Now do it!" Avienne reached over and activated the side gun controls. Litras nodded and studied them for a few seconds before her large fingers reached for them. For a second Avienne feared her fingers would be too big for the Mirial-sized controls, but she handled the controls with surprising dexterity. She aimed, pressed down on the trigger and fired a few unsuccessful shots.

"Aim at the fighters, please."

Litras shot her a look filled with venom. Avienne grinned. Her next shot struck a shuttle dead on, and she whooped with joy. Litras fired again, and again. Her aim was true enough, but there were more of them than *Haven's* guns would be able to take out.

Another rock struck the front viewport. A slight crack spread and Avienne activated the front shields, just in case. The shuttle's primary shields dipped down towards the fully drained indicator. Thirty-one percent capacity. They were losing power too fast. Two direct hits and they were dead.

"Layela, we may be getting to the desperate stage," she turned back as she said it, catching Layela's eyes. Her features were pale, but set. Avienne gave her a small smile, as much as she could muster. *It's okay,* she wanted to say. *Ardin would want us to live, even if he couldn't.*

The words rang true, but she couldn't speak them out loud. She turned back to her station, not glancing at her unconscious brother, trying her best to ignore the fact that her own breaths were growing shallower and she seemed unable to simply breathe through her nose any more.

Litras wisely said nothing.

***

Compared to the shuttle up ahead, *Destiny II* was a great lumbering beast. They moved as quickly as possible, but the larger asteroids needed to be avoided, and the ship couldn't turn on a dime. Almost, but not quite. With her size, there was much more she could hit at once. Jaru and Larod both worked on weapons control to plough the field, and still they hit more small asteroids than Larod would have liked. Her hull was strong and she could take the hits, but Larod hated taking an untested ship against such odds.

It spelled disaster.

"Their ship's not doing so well," Rose reported, her voice tense. "Docking might prove challenging."

"Can we reach them yet?" Larod asked Jaru.

"Almost done rebuilding, but weapons control is splitting my attention." Larod stared at Jaru's hands. One was controlling a bank of weapons, the other was rebuilding the database, his eyes darting from screen to screen. That man just wasn't normal. But abnormal was what they needed right now, apparently.

"We'll open the front shuttle bay and hope they see it to fly right in. I'll set some flares."

"They'll come in full speed," Rose said from her station. "Set the nets and spray her as soon as she comes in. If she goes from space to oxygen with little decompression, her metals might crack. More. And prepare the fire safety. She'll be of no use if she blows up!"

Larod nodded and ran to the lift, Rose heading to the navigations station. She could handle both defense and navigation at once. Space sailors, he had to admit, multitasked much more effectively than sea sailors. All those fancy machines required lots of attention. A sail was a sail, on a ship.

He preferred concentrating on one task at hand. In this case, it was ensuring Captain Avienne made safe berth in the *Destiny II*.

***

"Tell me I'm not delusional!" Avienne screamed to Litras, pointing forward.

Litras looked up and frowned. "Is that one of yours?"

Avienne laughed and looked back. "Layela, it's *Destiny II*." Layela exhaled sharply and returned Avienne's smile. They wouldn't need the ether, after all.

Destiny II lumbered along, pushing asteroids out of its way with weapons, shields, and even her hull. She was huge, and lit by the sun of Thalos IV, as beautiful as her namesake had been. Avienne's heart ached at the sight, both in relief and longing. She gunned their small ship towards her.

Her front berth had a square section light by red lights. *An entry bay.* They had opened the bay and were ready to take her in, even at the break neck speeds they were approaching.

"This is going to hurt!" Avienne screamed. "Hang on!" She pushed forward and tilted the shuttle's nose down a bit to correct entry. They were wrapped in the shadow of the ship. She aimed for the entry port and pulled up, so that the nose wouldn't hit first and send them tumbling. Space vanished as they entered, the sound of decompression whooshing around the shuttle.

Avienne hit the reverse thrusters as they struck the first net, made of fireproof materials and stretching as far as it could to absorb the impact. For a moment it seemed they would stop, but then the skiff snapped it and skidded sideways, almost toppling over before striking a second net. The net slowed them further but snapped, the skiff skidding against the wall, metal grinding against metal.

Avienne's stomach lifted, remembering the crash on Thalos IV that had sent her flying away from her brother. Her fingers grew numb but still she hung on, regardless of the fact that there was precious little she could do now.

The ship began to bank sideways, slid further, then stopped. Silence blanketed the interior of the skiff.

Avienne let go of the controls and wiped her sweaty palms on her pants. "No problem at all."

She turned to the shuttle bay to see another shuttle breaking through the door, snapping half of it off and skidding straight for their ship.

Her hands went back to the controls before realizing there was nothing she could do.

***

Larod saw a shuttle hurtling towards the shuttle bay, and already knew it wouldn't stop. He took the rungs faster than he had believed possible and jumped down. If he could close the secondary gates, they would all be safe. A fully staffed shuttle bay would be able to easily compensate for this by having the secondary station activate it. But he was alone, and the secondary station was far.

He struck the ground hard and ran past the silent ship that he was certain held the captain, his lungs burning as he kept the second station in sight, near the protective barrier that kept the oxygen in the bay. He had no time to worry about what might happen. He had to stop the second ship from destroying the first.

He reached the control station and hit the button. The great gate came down fairly quickly, but not quickly enough. The shuttle crashed into the half opened bay doors and ripped them most of the way off. It skidded in, towards the captain's ship. Larod jumped off the station and pulled his gun free, running past the second door, the heat of the ship searing his arms and face, its screeching metal echoing in his skull.

He fired at the controls of the bay door, far away on the other side, and managed to blow them up. The captain wouldn't be impressed. Well, another captain wouldn't be impressed, but Avienne Malavant understood and even appreciated the need for wanton destruction at times.

The bay door buckled and its shields failed. Space began tugging everything out into itself, the oxygen being sucked out, deafening Larod. The second ship wasn't in deep enough to escape the pull and it began sliding back, clearing the secondary bay doors just before they closed shut, securing everyone else beyond them.

The captain was safe.

Larod clung to the control station. *Everyone was safe.* He glanced back, tears stolen from his eyes and sucked into the void. His hands were growing numb, the metal freezing what little he still felt.

There were safety stations along the walls, but he was too far to reach them now. He felt the pull of the escaping oxygen grab him and tug him along. *A burial at sea.*

He closed his eyes and imagined he was falling into the sea, into the waiting embrace of a siren, welcoming him home.

CHAPTER 34

AVIENNE RAN TO the bridge, followed closely by Layela, after leaving quick instructions to Litras on the location of the healing quarters. The ship was jostling and the alarm was still on. Not good signs.

They jumped in the lift, Avienne pressing the right combination of buttons to access the bridge. The lift moved, but not fast enough for Avienne's taste. "Come on, you bloody snail."

She hit the buttons again and again.

"I would have done it, you know," Layela whispered. Avienne didn't turn to face her.

"What? Hit these buttons? You can if you want, but common sense indicates that won't increase the speed. I just don't prescribe to common sense."

"No, I mean used the ether. To save us. I would have done it, and killed Ardin."

Avienne sighed. For just one day without drama. Or at least one drink with drama. Stupid oath. Idly she wondered if Ardin's death would have allowed her to drink again. She allowed herself a slight grin. She had to remember to tell Ardin when he was moving again. He'd appreciate the humour.

"Look, Layela. He'd have wanted it. We'd have all been dead, otherwise, and what's the point of that? He'd have been dead, but the rest of us would have lived. Just like Larod chose to save us all by sacrificing himself." She turned back and pressed the buttons again, swallowing bile.

Layela was silent for a few seconds. "Would you stop hitting those buttons? That's really annoying."

Avienne grinned. She turned her head slightly and cocked it. "Make me."

For a moment she thought Layela might actually tackle her, but then the lift doors open, and Layela exited in a flash.

"Keeper!" Rose exclaimed, jumping up from navigation.

"Man your post!" Avienne screamed. Rose yelped and sat back down, navigating them past the last boulders that cleared them from the asteroid field. Avienne quickly gauged the situation. Ships gathered before them, everything from small fighter ships to large destroyers. Some models were older and probably would be easier to destroy, but others seemed fresh out of the builders' yards. Those would prove more challenging.

Avienne looked to Layela, who had found Ardice tucked away in a drawer, all blankets and baby snores. *Probably snot bubbles, too.*

Layela cooed but left her in there, staying near. At least the woman still had some semblance of sense. For now, at least.

Avienne walked to her station, relieving Jaru of tactical. He relieved Rose in turn, who returned to her station at engineering. Layela took the chair on the other side of Ardice. Avienne loved this ship. Its ability to fight was only hampered by the imagination of its crew. And Avienne didn't lack in imagination.

"Rose, cross our two main guns' energy sources, aim them at the flagship."

Rose turned to her, eyebrow raised. "You want me to sabotage our own ship?"

Avienne grinned. "I want a bigger, unstable explosion."

She turned back to her station, shaking her head. "Energy sources crossed. It'll be bigger, but we'll kill those guns."

"You got a better idea?" No one spoke up. Which was just as well. She'd have smacked anyone who had.

"Jaru, as soon as they're fired, gun our engines forward and bring us to the tunnels."

"Through the fleet?" he asked.

Avienne sighed. So many questions for such a simple plan.

"Through the fleet. They're in front of the tunnel, and I wouldn't expect that move, if I were them. Let's hope they don't, either. Oh, and prepare some mines to seed on our way. I don't want them to follow too closely, and I'm still mad over those rocks that almost destroyed our ship."

"Aye, Captain," Rose said, flipping on all necessary circuits to allow Avienne full control. She had done what was requested, and done it fast. The Mirial engineer could learn, after all. A good old fashioned space battle would do them all some good.

"Well, no reason to wait. Firing guns, Jaru, hit the engines." The motions were smooth and instantaneous. The crossed energy sources doubled the weapons' capacity and exploded outward, burning the two guns but providing an explosion which ripped through the flagship. *Destiny II* rode in behind, avoiding the chunks of ship and clearing the fleet before they were able to recover from the shock of the loss of their leader.

The ship rumbled and shook, screeching from deep within her belly. Avienne gently patted her station.

"Easy girl. Scars are beautiful, too."

She started seeding mines before they'd even cleared the fleet, a few ships instantly caught in the magnetic field and destroyed. She seeded quite a few, but kept some for later. Just in case.

"Activating tachyonic shields," Rose declared. The shutters closed and the familiar hum and steady flow of the tunnels carried them forward, as far as they could go using this system. Gobran would have to enlighten them a bit more than "go that way in the tunnels," eventually.

Avienne leaned back. Layela pulled Ardice free of the drawer, holding the child close. Avienne rose slowly, trying to find the words to express what needed to be said. Worse, what needed to be done.

She paused by the captain's chair and watched Layela gently holding Ardice, whispering words she could not hear, touching her face with the back of her fingers, letting small fingers grab hold of her pinkie and brushing them with a kiss. Avienne looked away.

She played multiple possibilities in her mind, and all of them lead to one firm, unavoidable conclusion. Ardice couldn't stay onboard the ship, not as long as she could freely draw on ether, not if they were to save Ardin, and not if Mirial's lineage was to be maintained.

Just in case Layela herself didn't return from her meeting with these Seeders. It was not a chance they could afford to take. Not when they knew so little of Mirial, still. Not when so much lay at stake, so much more than their simple lives.

But how could she ask Layela to give up her newborn daughter, to leave her behind, when so many dangers lurked and hunted them, still? She didn't even know how to utter those words. She didn't want to.

She looked back at Layela, and the different coloured eyes riddled with ether met hers with a steady gaze. Avienne knew immediately that Layela understood.

Avienne sat down and waited, relief mixing with her grief.

***

Layela held Ardice close, her daughter seeming even more fragile now that Layela had almost lost her. The ether danced calmly around the baby, who reached out with her small hands and grabbed a wisp in her hand, looking around with wide eyes as it separated in two and floated away.

"You'll be strong, someday," Layela murmured, kissing Ardice. She had only been reacting to Layela's ward and to the dark ether. Ardice had not been the cause of the earthquakes, of the ether creatures losing control—it had been the usurper all along, aided by Murl and Clave. They had set a careful trap to lay blame at her feet, and she had walked right into it like a fool. And her daughter had almost paid the price of her foolishness.

Dunkat. He knew her weaknesses well. How he had come back she didn't know, but she would kill him again and again. As often as necessary to live in peace with Ardin and Ardice. Or for the two of them to live long lives without her, if necessary.

Ardice would be fine without her. Ardice wouldn't have to draw on the ether, to defend herself against dark ether. She wouldn't have to feel it lashing at her, as she did when touching Ardin's wound. Ardice did not need her to save her, unlike Ardin, who needed her more than ever.

She reached the healing quarters, the scent of antiseptic wafting in the air. Litras was sitting quietly and Layela found herself hesitating at the sight of the Kilita.

She is an ally. She forced herself to continue, wishing she didn't feel so foolish. Litras perked up as she walked in. "Cute baby," Litras whispered, in tender tones she had never before heard nuance a Kilita's voice. Layela felt even more foolish for distrusting the woman.

She smiled and showed her Ardice. "This is my daughter, Ardice." Kilita smiled, showing sharp teeth. Layela concentrated instead on the Kilita's laugh lines, gathering around her eyes. A lifetime of laughter.

"She's beautiful."

"Thank you," Layela whispered. "May I have a moment with Ardin?"

Litras nodded and slithered out, shutting the door behind her. His vital signs were stabilized; it was only a matter of time before he would open his eyes again. No one could predict the state he would be in.

She leaned down and kissed his dry lips. "I wish you could be awake to say goodbye," Layela whispered. She stood beside the bed, holding Ardice, not sure what to do. She wanted to forge a memory for her daughter. What if they didn't come back? Would she remember them? Would she remember her father?

She knew that she probably wouldn't, but perhaps the ether worked differently. She could plant a memory inside of her and then, later on, it could bloom, but to use the ether might mean to kill Ardin…

"We'll see you again, buttercup," she whispered, kissing the child gently. She wanted Ardin to open his eyes just then, and sit up and take Ardice into his hands and coddle her, and reassure Layela that she was doing the right thing, the only thing she could do under the circumstances.

But the steady beeping of his vital signs were the only sound he made. She opened her mouth to say something, realizing that she was the only one forging a memory now. A memory riddled with pain and uncertainty, and scarring loneliness.

"I'll be back," she whispered to Ardin, and walked out of the healing quarters, heading for the shuttle bay.

***

Avienne patched as much of the ship as she could, glancing back to the large door that had sealed Larod's fate. She wiped away sweat with her sleeve, hoping she had removed all the tears, too. Rose worked silently beside her, checking the controls, then double-checking them. Everything was functional.

"Where will you go?" Avienne asked, desperate to break the graveyard silence.

Rose turned to her, her own face covered in sweat. "Somewhere safe." She turned back to work.

"Of course, don't tell me, just in case we're caught." She went back to work. Time was so limited.

"I'll find you, you know. Even if Ardin and Layela don't make it back. I'll find you."

"I hope so, Avienne," Rose whispered. Avienne wanted to scream. The most painful goodbyes were the quiet ones. What guarantee did they have that Rose would make it somewhere safe, manage to get rid of the ship, and hide safely? The possibilities of things going wrong were driving her mad with despair.

"I put money in the pilot box," Avienne said. "It's everything I had, and it should be enough to get you on your feet. Maybe even buy a house. Depending on where you end up." She pushed another trigger up, and the ship's main engine kicked in. Everything was functional. There was nothing left to repair. But Avienne fussed over settings anyway.

"And I put in some ID, for you. New name, new homeworld, the whole works. Study it. No one will ask questions. No one cares. But this is your daughter, not your granddaughter. You got a little too happy with in-vitro, had twelve children, only one of them lived, and your husband abandoned you. It's a sad story and makes you look crazy and desperate enough to be unpalatable. Again, in case anyone asks."

"Interesting story," Rose said.

Avienne shrugged. "Or you could go with the usual daughter abandoned the baby crap. I just thought the in-vitro story would be more interesting."

"I'll grant it that."

"Good. I've also put in some jewellery in there that I, um, came upon. I hid it around the ship. Don't pull it out—it'll attract too much attention. Get rid of the ship, sell it to the black market. That should be easy enough. They'll find some jewellery as soon as they start assessing her condition, and they'll tear her apart to find the rest. That'll take care of this ship. No trace of it. No Mirial to track you by."

"Good plan."

Avienne jumped. Rose was kneeling right beside her. "Blood and bones woman, you'll be fine! You're a stealth bomber in disguise."

Rose didn't crack a smile, but gathered Avienne in her arms instead. "I promise you we'll be fine, Avienne. I'll keep your niece safe."

Avienne was taken aback by the show of affection, but found herself returning the hug. "If you need me," she whispered, "find a way to contact me. I'll tear the Heavens apart to find you."

The shuttle bay door opened and the two women broke the embrace. Avienne stood up, embarrassed.

Layela walked towards them without hesitation, holding her daughter in her hands as though the child were more precious than the last jug of water in the universe.

Avienne swallowed hard and waited for her to join them.

She could really, really use a drink.

***

Rose and Avienne waited for her in silence. Layela knew her face was pale and tear-streaked, but she didn't care. No one here would judge her. Ardice was awake, gurgling happily in her mother's arms.

Do you even know I'm your mother? Of all the things she feared the most, she realized that she feared that Ardice would never know her, as she had never known her own mother. That Ardice would grow up an orphan, abandoned so young, always left to wonder why, never finding any answers. Unless the answers sought her out, as had happened to Layela.

She felt foolishly selfish. She should be worried about more than that. Who cared if her daughter didn't remember her, as long as she had a chance at life. That's what really mattered, above all else.

She stood before Rose, but didn't meet her eyes. "I don't think she'll use ether unless threatened by dark ether. You might see her playing with things you can't see—that's the ether flowing around her. Don't worry, she'll probably just play with it and won't harm anyone." She looked down at the perfect round pink cheeks. "Not unless she has to."

Layela looked at Ardice for a few moments, capturing every small detail, from the different coloured eyes that tended to cross, to the dark spray of hair on her head, to the little nose that formed a bridge between her eyes, and the ears that seemed a little bit too small still. Her lips parted and Layela imagined a smile.

You'll be okay. She felt the reassurance lay on her heart like a warm blanket, hearing a whisper of hope in the cold shuttle bay.

"Mirial will look after you," she whispered. Ardice had the advantage Layela had not had: a strong First Star to call upon when necessary. The ship slowed, and Avienne's comm unit buzzed. "Captain, we're outside the tachyon tunnel."

The low hum of the engine and the yellow bay lights buzzed ahead as Layela handed her daughter to the sister of the woman who had once taken her away from her mother, too. She held Rose's eyes and kept her cracking voice low.

"I promise, I will come for her."

Rose dropped her head as a sign of respect, than she turned and boarded the ship, closing the door. Layela wanted to scream after her, to run into the ship and go with her. But to do so meant abandoning Ardin, and possibly all of Mirial.

A Great Darkness. A greater darkness. *I'll not let you live through that.*

She stepped back, one step wrenching a sob from her throat.

Avienne placed her arm around her. "We have to step out of the shuttle bay. They'll have to decompress the whole thing to let her out. Too much damage."

Layela heard her own voice through sobs, as though it belonged to someone else. "You mean I can't watch her go?"

Avienne's own voice was but a whisper. "No. But you can look forward to greeting her again, soon, with Ardin at your side."

Layela nodded and let Avienne guide her out. The great doors closed behind her, and Avienne locked them down. She heard a whoosh from within. Layela closed her eyes, imagining the ship leaving the bay, flying to safety somewhere far away. She didn't even know which star systems were near. It didn't matter. She would find her daughter. Mirial would surely see to that.

"Captain," the comm unit beeped to life again. "Shuttle bay doors closed. Ready to proceed back into the tunnel."

"Thank you, Jaru. Please do so."

The comm link closed. Layela stayed leaning against the wall, her eyes closed, feeling as though she might throw up at any second.

"I'll be on the bridge," Avienne said.

Layela listened to her footsteps until she was gone, and then, when she was certain she was alone, she slid down the wall and spent her grief.

CHAPTER 35

ELSA FOLLOWED THE shadows into the cavern. She had seen this spread before, curious as a young child. Berganda were blessed with instant and lasting memories, so she found it fairly easy to navigate, despite the near darkness. Her biggest problem lay in the stones that had shifted during the earthquakes.

Noise from up ahead caught her attention. She drew back into deeper shadows and held her breath. She hoped it wasn't one of Braken's new guards.

A light appeared in the hallway, and a man followed it, looking over his shoulders frequently. She recognized him. The Court Advisor, Gresko Listan.

Curious, she slipped into the shadows and trailed him. She would never have imagined seeing his manicured kind in this area. He peered her way a few times, but his eyes were unaccustomed to darkness and he failed to spot her. Her soft leather booths betrayed none of her careful steps, but he kicked small rocks without meaning to. He was obviously shaken. Elsa imagined that he had never believed he would find himself in these tunnels again, after spending so much time within them during the Great Darkness.

He turned into a small room, on which hung an old unlatched door of iron bars.

A prison? Elsa slipped into the shadows. He was whispering to someone. She tried to get closer, to see the second individual.

"Who goes there?" A woman's voice rang out. Elsa recognized it, despite its raw quality. Gresko jumped to his feet and almost tripped back down, his mouth hanging in a silent scream.

"It's just me," she said, stepping into the light. "Elsa." Mirialers and humans sometimes had a hard time telling her and her sisters apart. She had never understood how, but apparently they only paid attention to hair, eye and skin colour as differentiating factors.

"Elsa," Loran said, leaning back down. Elsa chewed on her lower lip as she approached. Loran didn't look well.

"You should not be here, child," Gresko reprimanded her as he dusted his robes.

"I shouldn't be anywhere on Mirial, apparently." She sighed as she sat by Loran. She had always liked Loran. She seemed a bit cold and foolhardy, at times, but Elsa knew how much pain she dealt with every day, without letting it stop her. She couldn't help but respect that.

Loran smiled at Elsa. "Gresko's right in this case. We're in Braken's territory, now."

"I know," she whispered, grief washing her own voice. She furrowed her brow, imagining her own mother would not have abandoned her friends, and she didn't intend on doing so, either. Loran could be of great help to the rebellion. "I'm not leaving without you."

"I can't," Loran whispered. Elsa noticed how strained her features were. She looked down, where a blanket had been placed on her legs. She looked to Gresko. He simply shook his head.

"I can help," she offered. "I know my mother could heal. Perhaps I can, too?"

Loran shook her head. "No. If you heal the wounds fully, we'll never get prosthetics on." Elsa shrunk at the pluralization. She bit her lower lip to stop from crying. They had taken her other leg.

And Mirial did nothing to stop them. No more than Mirial had saved her beautiful sister.

"What can I do?" she asked, feeling young and foolish. Nothing of her peaceful existence had prepared her for this. She was no warrior, regardless of what her mother or her sister had been.

"You can hide and be careful," Gresko answered. "The Lady Layela will come for us."

Elsa nodded. "What about you?" Her voice sounded thin and frail in her own ears. No wonder they didn't take her offer of aid seriously.

"I will stay to keep an eye on things, and on Loran," Gresko said.

Loran gave a short laugh. "I can't exactly leave."

Elsa stopped biting her lower lip and stood up. They were so brave, both of them. She wanted to be that brave, too, no matter how frightened she felt.

"There is a resistance," she whispered. "About a hundred strong, nearby. If we combine forces, we could topple him."

Gresko and Loran exchanged a quick look. Elsa stood her ground.

"I know it's dangerous, but the dark ether he wields is dangerous, too. We can't expect Layela to save us from everything and everyone. We have to stand up for Mirial ourselves."

Loran gave a low chuckle. "Spoken like a true Mirialer."

Elsa flushed with pride.

"There's no harm in keeping in contact," Gresko said. "Tell their leaders to meet us here tomorrow evening. Can you see my palace window from one of your scouting spots?"

Elsa nodded. She had no idea what areas the scouts covered, but she could make sure they checked. *If they listen to me.*

"Good. If my curtains are drawn at midday that means the meeting is on. If they are closed, that means danger is near, and you should keep away."

Elsa nodded enthusiastically. She could make a difference, as her mother would have.

She ran back into the darkness, feeling hopeful. She kept a close eye out for any monsters or detonation. Her hand against the wall, she maintained a grip on the roots and plants, hoping they could tell her of any danger or rescue her if need be. Slita would be proud of her. Her mother would be proud.

Her daughters would sprout within weeks. On a free Mirial. And then she would tell them such wonderful stories of how their bloodline had secured Mirial's freedom.

***

Loran waited until Elsa was long gone before speaking again. Gresko was administering her antibiotics, though by now she knew very well he was also pumping painkillers into her. She chose not to call him on that, and let him believe he was getting away with it, while she could continue deluding herself that maybe she was strong enough to take the wounds.

"Will you really call a meeting?" she asked Gresko. The advisor's long drawn face sobered even more deeply. She had never envied his role. Under Adina, he had seemed fulfilled if flustered. Under Layela, it was a constant struggle to be heard and respected. And now, in the last few days, he had put on years. Loran knew Gresko was terrified of the new Keeper, and not certain why the man bothered keeping him around at all. She could see the worry in his eyes every day, and the lines etched deeper and deeper on his face that spoke of sleepless nights.

"Of course not. How would we fight the ether? We'd all be slaughtered, and there are so few of us left. At least Braken seems to understand that, even if…" He stopped himself short of finishing his sentence.

"Even if what, Gresko?" Loran propped herself up on her elbow, ignoring the pain. "Even if what?"

The advisor seemed angry with himself for having said too much, but then crouched beside her, keeping his voice low. "He invited Solaria onto our lands," he whispered. He hesitated. "He…he turned the soldiers into monsters, half men, broken and mindless. Walking corpses, tar-like, like the beasts that once invaded Mirial."

Loran sucked in her breath. Gresko's eyes grew wider. "And he took the minister prisoner, I don't know for what purpose. All I heard was that he would send a message to Solaria." He hissed. "Solarian ships surround Mirial, but they don't attack. They just…stay there! I don't know what he's planning, Loran, but he's ruthless, and far too much for us to handle."

Gresko looked up in the entryway, and even in the darkness, she could see the colour drain out of his face. She turned around. Braken stood in the doorway. His stature and cloak could not be mistaken.

She reached out to grab a weapon, anything, but she had nothing. Gresko stood up. Loran tried to grab his robe, to keep him near her, to keep him safe. He saw her attempt and looked down, a slight smile crossing his lips. "Three Keepers is more than enough for any Court Advisor, my friend," he whispered.

"Please don't!" Loran cried, hating herself for the sob that broke her last word.

She watched helplessly as Gresko walked to stand before Braken.

"I didn't think betrayal would come from you, Court Advisor," Braken said, his voice rumbling with unspent ether.

Gresko held himself tall. "My loyalty has always been, and will always be, with the Keeper, Braken."

He had barely finished the words before Braken tossed him aside like a rag doll, sending him flying on a wall past Loran. She heard several bones snap, and screamed. "Monster! Why don't you just finish me?"

Braken gave a low laugh. "It amused my sister to keep you alive. Don't worry, by tomorrow night, you'll have many more dead to keep you company."

He turned and vanished. Loran threw a rock after him, but it bounced uselessly not far from her. She screamed in frustration and pulled herself towards Gresko, ignoring the sound of her skin ripping open as she pulled away from the blankets, ignoring the burning sensation, screaming the pain away, no longer caring whether or not she was heard. Every rock was like a long sword through her, but she grabbed at irregularities in the cave floor and pulled herself forward, not allowing her head to fall.

She threw up a few times when the pain became unbearable, ignoring the white stars and dark mists that threatened to consume her consciousness. After what felt like an eternity, she managed to reach Gresko, her screams still echoing within the caves.

He had died on impact, his neck snapped. His open eyes did not betray terror as she might have suspected, but instead acceptance, and even pride. She closed his eyes and brushed his robes down and managed to smile between sobs. It would not do for him to be messy in death.

"You make Mirial proud, Gresko Listan. May it once again know the glory that you represented so well."

CHAPTER 36

LAYELA WALKED SLOWLY towards the healing quarters, wishing she was walking barefoot on soft grass, warmed by a gentle sun, surrounded by the scent of fresh blooms and those she loved—all of her loved ones, even those long lost and out of reach. She stopped and shook her head free of the fantasy. She needed to find out where they were going, and Gobran had the answers she needed. She passed Ardin's chamber and entered the next room.

Litras slumbered in a chair near Gobran. She had changed his bandages and cleaned his face. He seemed comfortable enough, resting on freshly fluffed pillows. Layela analyzed the Kilita for a few moments. She had dressed back in regular clothing and was mostly covered now. Her dark, coarse hair seemed more horse-like than human, pulled back in a ponytail. Her broad shoulders and orange tint were the main indications that she was Kilita.

Layela cleared her throat, and Litras' head shot up.

"Sorry," Layela said. "I didn't mean to frighten you."

The Kilita smiled, all sharp teeth. "Kilita are harder to scare than that."

Layela nodded, still feeling exposed in front of her and hating herself for it. "So I hear."

Litras seemed about to say something to Layela, but thought better of it and turned her attention to Gobran. "He's a tough old man, I'll give him that. The infection's healing nicely already, and I think he'll be up and about in no time."

Relief flooded Layela. She could not bare the thought of losing another friend.

"Thank you, Litras. Thank you so much."

Litras stood. "Not much else to do around here. Suppose you want to be alone with him now, too?"

"I'm sorry, but yes, please." She paused. "Perhaps you could head up to the bridge. You can monitor their conditions from there, and we're low on crew members. We could use your help."

She stared at Layela with wide eyes. "I never learned to fly."

Layela shrugged. "No time like the present. Don't worry, Avienne won't let you crash the ship."

A smile spread on the Kilita's lips as she exited the healing quarters. Layela turned her attention to Gobran.

"Gobran," she whispered in his ear. "I need you, Gobran."

He grunted. "Beautiful women tell me that all the time."

She laughed. It felt good. "We're in the tunnel, heading where you told us to go. Where do we go next?"

Gobran shifted slightly. "I feel better," he mumbled.

"That's great. I'm glad, really. Where do we go next?"

He gave a slight smile. "Grab a workpad. I'll dictate what I know." Layela scrambled and found one of the tablets in the drawer. It was paper thin, made to jot quick notes for easy referral later on. Layela activated it.

"Bring up a copy of a Solarian tunnel map." He instructed her.

She did as told, putting the tablet down and projecting the map up to make it easier to see in a 3D format. Worlds spread before her, a small chunk of galaxy, solar systems interconnected by a vast array of purple tunnels, leading all the way to Mirial, showing Solaria's plans of expansion. These tunnels were the key to trade, a functioning government, and tourism. Some were well-maintained and numerous, closer to the heart of Solaria, but here, on the borders of the empire, the tunnels were much more quiet, some falling into disrepair regularly, ships crushed to two dimensional states as the great braces guiding the tachyon particles collapsed.

"You see where we are?"

Layela did. The computer was showing their progress with a little red dot. They were in the tunnel leading from Thalos to Oot. A tunnel from a smuggling port to a very moral port, it was little-used, which was a blessing.

Layela quickly looked at the different routes they might have taken. Right now, if they were pursued, which she could only imagine they were, there were at least five different junctions into other tunnels, and about thirty space exits, like the one they had taken to drop Rose off. It made her feel more comfortable to know their progress couldn't be so easily tracked. And the tunnels, especially these far reaching tunnels, were not well monitored.

They were safe for now.

"Can you tell me where we are?" Gobran asked with a slight chuckle.

Layela flushed red. "I'm sorry. We're about three quarters of the way to Oot."

"Ah, Oot," Gobran said. "I once met this woman there…well, you're too young to hear these stories, but I promised my daughter I would…" He stopped, swallowed, and continued. Layela lowered her head.

"Solaria would like you to believe that the tunnels were their technology, but I've discovered they aren't. Several ether races, with longer memories than us, support this very fact." He cleared his throat. "The main difference is that Solaria can't replicate the original technology. It was smoother, by all accounts, and didn't require the braces. And you couldn't see them with a naked eye. Solaria first discovered them accidentally and lost many ships trying to chart the tunnels. Eventually they knew enough to replicate…but this is all boring to you, I know. You need answers."

Gobran reached up with his hand. "Bring my hand to where we are now." Layela did so, his hand casting shadows and cutting parts of the projection of the 3D model. "We're here, then the tunnel goes this way, correct?" His fingers perfectly followed the tunnel.

Layela nodded before catching herself. "That's right."

"Perfect. That means about here," he showed her an area maybe three hours outside of Oot. "Around here, you'll see there are braces missing. No one ever really notices because they're not paying attention. But I've studied this for years, while stuck outside of Mirial. Right here." His hand stayed still. Layela made note.

"Where the missing braces are should be a connector to another tunnel. Veer left into it."

Layela gave a short laugh. "You're kidding, right? Tachyon particles will cut right through us if we veer in them that way. Tunnels are one direction only. And if there's no tunnel there, we'll crash nose-first into the side of the tunnel, and more than likely be destroyed!"

She felt foolish lecturing the old man, but he had consumed large amount of painkillers. Perhaps they had dulled more than just his pain.

He chuckled. "I love that reaction. I really do. You'll feel it. A small deceleration at first. That's due to the tachyons splitting at the level of the tunnel. And ether creatures can actually see them. Green mixes in with the blue. It's another type of molecule, much more stable. But tachyons are all Solaria ever managed to cultivate into tunnels."

Layela wiped Gobran's forehead, where a small sweat had broken out as he grew excited.

"Okay, so we enter the mystery tunnel. Then what?"

"It will guide you." He settled back down, and was snoring slightly before she could ask for further elaborations.

A familiar voice spoke by the entryway. "I'd expect more from a map expert than 'it will guide you,' myself." Layela turned to see Ardin standing there, haggard looking but smiling.

She jumped up and hugged him, feeling the spark of the dark ether against her skin and not caring.

She never intended to let him go.

***

Avienne felt better than she had in a while. She would have been happier with a large drink, but she now understood that she couldn't have it all. Layela had called up to tell her Ardin was awake and give her very suspicious sounding directions, which involved invisible tunnels and ether creatures. She'd worry about that nearer to those particular tunnels, which were still about three hours away.

The Kilita leaned near a monitor, going through some pilot training courses. She wasn't a natural, but she wanted to learn badly. Besides, if what Layela said was true, in three hours she'd be piloting the ship for them. Or Patros. But he had shown not even a remote interest in ships, aside from some engineering, which proved helpful for Rose, at least.

With Ardin awake again and on his way up soon, it seemed the tides were finally about to change. All they needed was to heal Ardin, beat back the dark ether, get the usurper off the throne (or not, it'd be best if someone other than Layela was Keeper, really), and she could go back to flying the stars, and maybe convince Layela and Ardin to fly away with her.

She liked having them here, for the most part. A bit more drama than she cared for, but she herself could be accused of being a little too emotional of late. She blamed the kid. Bring a cute fragile life form, and everyone was reduced to blundering idiots.

"I think we're being followed," Jaru reported.

"Fun!" Avienne exclaimed. She hopped out of her chair and to Jaru's station. She had grown up with the systems analyst aboard the original *Destiny*, so he was used to her. Which probably spared his poor nerves.

"See here," Jaru said, pointing at an energy chart of the tunnel.

"No. It's all a big purple mass."

"Well, yes, but notice at the braces, where the tachyon flow is renewed? There's a slight disruption at each of them, a few minutes after our own wake."

"Ah, that I see."

"Well, I think we're being followed."

Avienne looked down at the images. She had no way of telling who was following them. Either the psycho, as the Kilita so fondly called Murl, or a Solarian ship. And whatever had happened to that invisible ship that had saved them? Maybe it still orbited Mirial, waiting for their return? It was probably the psycho following them. Solaria wasn't that motivated to find them. Solaria was barely motivated to find its own shadow, most days.

The lift door opened, and Avienne was surprised to hear Ardin's angry voice. Layela looked like she was trying very hard to hold herself together. Ardin turned on her. Avienne went to meet him. She'd rarely seen her brother angry.

"Nice to see you're still alive," she said as they came face to face.

"You let her send Ardice away." He pointed towards Layela. Layela looked more annoyed than hurt. Avienne thought she might very well slap him. Which would amuse her.

"I let the mother of your child use her best judgment to protect her, yes."

Ardin looked even more annoyed. Avienne sighed and put a hand on Ardin's arm. "Ardin, we're sorry you didn't get to say good bye. Layela tried, but you're the oaf who wouldn't wake up."

Ardin's eyes flashed with anger and he turned, walked past Layela, and headed back down the lift. Layela sighed heavily.

"That went well." Avienne arched an eyebrow.

"I didn't mean to hurt him," Layela whispered. Avienne suddenly felt the bridge was too crowded for her liking, between Litras and Jaru, both staring at them as though their heads were spinning on their necks.

Avienne pulled Layela into the lift and headed down, somewhere, anywhere.

"He's hurt. Not used to not being the hero. You know how men are." Avienne shrugged.

Layela gave a slight smile. "I should find him. Even if he wants to shout some more."

Avienne snorted. "You're a more patient woman than I am. Just tell him to shut up."

"Where would he have gone?"

The two of them looked at each other. "Does he know about Clave?" Avienne asked. Layela nodded. Of course she had told him.

Avienne sighed. "Well, he's too honourable to kill him. I think. Does that dark ether change a person."

Layela didn't have an answer to give. Avienne hoped Patros was still with Clave. She pressed the buttons over and over again to bring them to the brig floor.

***

Ardin didn't really intend to do much of anything, though part of him wanted to inflict a great amount of damage on the man he had trusted on his crew; the man who had betrayed him; the man who had almost stolen his daughter from him. He didn't believe he would kill him. He had never killed someone outside of a fight, having been brought up on a strict code of honourable conduct, mostly imposed by himself.

But today he might just breach that code.

The wound ached like a thousand shards of glass pricking from his skin. If he moved, it felt worse. And he wasn't about to lie still in bed.

He felt guilty for screaming at Layela and Avienne. They had done the best they could under the circumstances. But he felt so… *powerless*. He needed to do *something*. Though, screaming at those he loved was hardly the best plan he had ever come up with.

He punched in his code to enter the brig. Clave sat in the first cell, and Patros was just outside it. He stood when Ardin approached.

"He's contained," Patros said. Ardin believed it. Clave looked like he was about to pass out. Patros ensured his calmness by sucking ether out of him regularly. The Slont seemed unaffected, except for a darker tint to his skin. Ardin leaned against the bars. He liked the old fashioned feel of them. No need to waste extra precious energy on fancy items like force field doors.

Clave sat up and held his gaze for a few seconds before looking down.

"Want me to open the door?" Patros asked. Ardin decided right there that he really like thed Slont. Clave now stood, leaning against the back wall.

"Not so brave when not dealing with newborns?" Ardin said, standing straight. He nodded to Patros. Ardin felt better already, seeing the terror on Clave's face. He wouldn't beat him up, the man could barely stand. But he would scare him enough never to even consider betraying them again.

Patros leaned down and punched in a code, then opened the latch. The door swung open.

Clave's eyes darkened for a moment, and then he collapsed to his knees.

"He just tried to use his ether. I've made sure that would be hard for him."

Ardin nodded, looking at the Slont's dark skin. "It's not harming you?" he whispered.

"No more than you," Patros replied.

"If it does and you can't contain him, we'll pop him out an airlock." That, Ardin did mean. He had to look after the best interests of his crew, and he wouldn't let Patros wound himself to keep a traitor in check. His loyalties were clear.

"You wouldn't dare," Clave said, his voice low. Patros really had done a number on him.

"I would. Don't test me," Ardin said. The man was so pathetic it made him want to throw him out an airlock anyway.

Clave looked up. "How would you explain to Layela that you've killed her brother?"

Ardin shared a quick, surprised look with Patros. Avienne and Layela burst into the room. Ardin gave them both an apologetic grin. Layela leaned against a wall and Avienne bent over in two. "Stupid big ship," she said between gasps.

"Did you two run here?" Patros asked. Avienne gave him a look of death.

"We weren't sure…" Layela said, flushing an even deeper red as she realized what she was accusing Ardin of.

"Don't worry. We were just chatting." He paused and went closer to Layela, where Clave couldn't see them. Patros stood in front of the open cell. Avienne fell ungracefully to the floor beside him.

"I'm sorry," he whispered to Layela.

"Me too," she whispered back.

He bent down and kissed her quickly. He looked sideways, hesitated, then continued. "Clave says he's your brother."

Layela's eyes grew wide. It was as though he had turned on a bright light of understanding within her. He was surprised to see her smile.

***

Layela walked past Ardin and to the cell door. Clave remained seated, drained by Patros to keep him in check. She entered the cell, Ardin not far behind, Avienne grunting from where she lay.

She crouched in front of him, meeting his eyes. *Dark blue.* Like both of hers had been, long ago. She suddenly understood so much, or thought she did, anyway, that it made her feel light-hearted. She had family. Stupid, slightly evil family, but family regardless.

Which meant Dunkat had not returned to destroy her. She would not have to face him again.

Mirial danced around her, excited by her own understanding. In his eyes, Layela could see the night.

"You have a twin," she simply stated. "And he's the one you left behind on Mirial."

He looked surprised.

Layela stood back up, her legs already growing numb. "Stand up, Clave." He did so, without question.

"I was right," she allowed herself a grin. "They're just traditions, after all. Men can wield the ether as effectively as women. It's just a stupid system we can tear down."

Clave looked surprised again. "But…you'd do that?"

Layela shrugged. "Of course. Although you're going to jail, and if you don't behave…" she turned slightly to Ardin, with an arched eyebrow.

"Thrown out an airlock," he offered.

"Fun!" Avienne said from the floor, still catching her breath.

Layela grew serious again. "But why do you channel dark ether?

Why not something lighter, less dangerous? And why did you not approach me, instead of concocting this ridiculous plan?" She paused. "And why would you try and take my daughter away? After I trusted you so, and Ardin trusted you?"

Clave looked down before answering. "I…" He coughed. "It's all we have access to. You blocked us from the ether of light!" He argued.

"I don't think so. Did I?" She hesitated. "How would I have done that? I didn't even know you existed until mere moments ago."

"We survived through the Great Darkness thanks to my brother. He's stronger in ether. He shielded our little village, since he was just a little boy. It cost him dearly." He didn't elaborate. Layela didn't care to know—it wasn't an answer she currently sought. "But that's all he could ever draw. We figured that Adina was pulling the pure ether for herself, and soon we would have access to it as well, but then you showed up, and took it for yourself."

Layela shook her head. That made no sense. "My sister could pull on the ether at the same time that I could, and so could my aunt. Your theory is flawed."

It dawned on her like a pile of bricks. She saw Ardin look down beside her, and she closed her eyes. "It's the only ether you can pull. It must be something to do with the difference between men and women. It's why the males are always sent away."

Because they mustn't find out they could even draw on their powers. Layela followed the thought to its logical end, not wanting to speak the words out loud. That was why the tradition existed. To ensure the drawn ether remained pure, that no males would bring the dark ether into Mirial.

"You must be wrong," Clave said, looking dejected.

Layela hoped she was. "I may be. It's just a theory. I don't see why it would be so. It's kind of ridiculous, honestly, to have sexist ether." She relented. "But maybe the dark ether has its worth."

Ardin snorted.

"Can you heal him, Clave? Can you heal Ardin?" She heard Avienne sit up behind them. "We've never willingly done you any harm. Please?"

Clave hesitated, then slid back down. "I didn't mean for it to get that far," he said, running a hand through his hair. "I thought we would just speak to you in the throne room—well, that Braken would. But he wanted to ensure you couldn't draw on the ether safely, and figured if you broke our wards, you'd have something else stopping you."

Avienne jumped up and moved past Ardin and Layela so fast neither one of them could catch her. She grabbed Clave, pulled him up, and punched him in the chin. He flew against the wall and she managed to kick him in the ribs before Ardin and Patros pulled her off of him.

"Calm down!" Ardin told her.

"He made me swear off drinking!" She spat back.

"What?"

"Would everyone just calm down!" Layela's voice pierced the cell. Clave coughed.

Avienne shot daggers at Layela. "I don't like people messing with my family."

"Or her drinking," Ardin mumbled. Avienne broke into a grin as quickly as she had snapped.

Layela shook her head and turned back to Clave. "So they sent the useless brother to keep an eye on us." He flinched at the words. She forced herself not to take them back. "Was the hope that you'd die and not return?" The next words felt bitter in her throat. "You know one twin has to die for the other to be more powerful, right?"

Clave managed to sit back up and he lowered his head on his knees. "I was supposed to bring back Ardice, to pass down the bloodline."

Layela's blood grew cold. Ardin clearly didn't understand what that meant, or he would have killed him. But Layela did. Her own brother had just admitted he would have brought his niece to be murdered. And to pass down the bloodline, she would need to be eliminated, as well.

"You disgust me." She spat and walked out.

Whatever joy she had felt at meeting her brother had vanished into disgust and dread.

CHAPTER 37

"I T'S YOUR SHIP, not mine," Avienne said, keeping her voice low as she stood by the captain's chair, her fists at her side.

"If it's my ship," Ardin replied, his voice low and threatening, "then you'll follow orders. The bridge is yours, for now." She bit another protest at the plea in his eyes. His drawn features were offset by his auburn hair and the dark circles under his eyes. He looked like death stalked him still, and he just didn't trust himself to captain the ship.

But you can do this! she pleaded back, but he turned from her and sat at tactical.

"Approaching tunnel entrance," Jaru said, hesitating between addressing Avienne or Ardin. Ardin raised an eyebrow at Avienne and leaned back. She wanted to hit him.

"Fine. Great. Get ready for some fun." She sat in the captain's chair.

The reversal made her queasy. She liked being part of her brother's crew. She liked feeling like they were working together. *I suppose we are now, too*, she thought. It was just weird giving him orders. He was her older brother, and she'd always looked up to him, despite a healthy amount of bad jokes and pranks.

Litras sat at the navigation console with a big grin on her face. Avienne wished she'd stop. Those sharp teeth were making her uncomfortable.

Patros sat at the engineering station, and Clave and Layela were not far. Clave was well tied to a chair—Avienne had made sure of that herself. Larod would have been proud of her knot tying abilities. Avienne sighed, leaning back.

She missed the sailor, and captaining the ship deepened the grief. It had taken five years to find a single sailor willing to stick it out with her, and it would probably take twice as long to find another. He had been her second-in-command, her go-to crewmember, reliable Larod. And now she sat in the captain's chair, but he was nowhere in sight. Jaru still remained in her crew, but he came from Mirial, so he didn't count. Mirialers always stuck together. Or so she'd always thought.

"All right, everyone but ether creatures look down."

"Litras, are you sure you can handle her?" Avienne asked, for the twentieth time.

"I'm sure," the Kilita said. "This is really not as complicated as you make it sound. The computer does most of the work."

"True," Avienne conceded. As long as the computer worked, of course. At least *Destiny II* was a new ship, so her computers should hold up to a lot. On most of her other ships, if the sailor relied too much on the computer, they could anticipate a very bumpy ride.

"Opening shutters," Avienne warned, a second before punching in the command. The blue flickers of the tachyons filled the bridge, giving Avienne the impression again that she was underwater.

"It's beautiful," Litras exclaimed.

"Don't look up, Avienne." She could hear the laughter in Patros' voice.

"Once was fun enough, thanks," she replied, resisting the urge to do just that. One seizure wasn't too bad, but add too many on, and you'd be cursed with a case of tachyonic sickness that left you drooling for good. Not how she intended to spend the rest of her life.

"I see it!" Litras exclaimed. Avienne had to struggle to keep looking down. There were definite advantages to being an ether creature. Great disadvantages, too, but definite advantages.

"Turn us into it," Avienne said, praying it wouldn't doom them all. Tachyon tunnels were finicky in the best of times, but veering while inside of one was not a recommended move.

"Turning," Litras said. Patros sucked in his breath. Avienne closed her eyes on concentrated on the movements of the great ship. She was turning well, at an adequate speed. She couldn't feel her slipping or tail spinning. *Steady…*

The engines churned once, then twice, and were silent. Avienne couldn't hear their hum or the hum of the tachyons.

"Screw it," she looked up, her breath catching in her throat. They were in a tunnel of the purest light. The tachyons were bumps of light, a jumble of disorganized weak lights, compared to this smooth perfection. Like riding a wave of milk. The wave broke only slightly into pinpricks of light, and she could see the universe beyond it, moving at speeds so great she couldn't believe she wasn't feeling any force on her body.

"Are our engines still on?" she asked.

Litras shrugged. "I think so. Looks like it."

Avienne jumped off her chair and leaned over Litras, looking at her readings. They were still on, but on minimal power. The tunnels alone were doing the work of bringing the ship to their destination. She wasn't too pleased with the lack of control.

"You can look at the tunnel?" Patros asked.

"Looks like it. Not tachyons, then. I like this technology better."

Ardin and Layela were looking up, as well. Clave dared a bit, but mostly kept his head down. Avienne grinned at her brother. "Come on, admit it, you miss space travel."

He smiled back at her, but didn't answer.

The lift doors opened, and Layela jumped up to help Gobran. "You shouldn't be up here!"

"I'm old and blind. I can be wherever I want to be." She lead him to a seat and secured him in. He didn't seem to be in too much pain, though he still wobbled quite a bit.

"What does it look like?" he asked, his voice thin.

"Like sparkling milk," Avienne replied. "And we're riding it fast."

Gobran laughed. "We're not far. These tunnels are fast. Let's hope the Seeders are where I hope they are."

Avienne nodded before catching herself. "I hope so. How did you even know this was here?"

He leaned back in his chair. "I'm a mapper. I know everything there is to know about these skies."

"Really?"

He chuckled. "Or I followed a string of clues and legends, and mapped them with strange sensor readings over the past few centuries. I was very bored for a few years."

Avienne grinned and then forced a slight laugh for Gobran's sake.

The ship buckled and slowed. "What are you doing?" Avienne asked Litras. The Kilita turned to her with wide eyes. "Nothing. It's slowing down."

"We're here," Layela said, standing up and taking a step forward. Avienne hissed. Layela's eyes glowed blue and green, and were disturbing all around.

"Great."

***

Destiny II floated back out into normal space without even a shudder, purring back to life. The low hum of her engines kicked back in. Layela could hear Avienne giving some orders, and the others moving past her, but she ignored them as she gazed before her. Everything within her was coming to life, from the tips of her toes to the roots of her hair. She felt light, and content.

Only one other time had she felt that way. When she had died and become one with Mirial.

"Layela?" Ardin asked, standing near her.

"Look," Layela said, pointing ahead. Motion on the bridge ceased as the last of the milky bridge parted and revealed their full surrounding. The space around them was not littered with stars, but rather with pinwheel galaxies of various colours, from reds to greens and blues. To their left she could see a planet forming, great chunks of rocks rotating together, orbiting what would someday be its star.

She had never seen the birth of a star before. It was beautiful. Two great arms of light arched away, rotating around a common centre, like two great lovers becoming one. Gasses fused at its centre, with great sparks of oranges, reds and purples. The energy escaped in waves and rocked the ship.

"We're pretty close to this thing," Avienne said as she tried to gun the engines back. They wouldn't start. "Of course."

Layela ignored her. In the core of the forming star, she sensed ether. So much ether it made her want to weep. And even the pure ether of Mirial seemed dirty, compared to this.

She looked at Clave. "Can you sense that?" He nodded, his eyes gleaming blue and filling with tears.

The ether danced around the ship, wild and uncontrolled. The *Destiny II* rocked in its wake.

"What's that?" Avienne asked, still fussing with the engines.

"Ether." She paused. "I think they're forming a new Mirial." Avienne hissed.

Jaru yelped. Broken from her trance, Layela turned around. Beside

Jaru hovered a ghostlike being, translucent and tall. Within seconds the being had solidified and looked more human, though too tall and gangly to ever pass as one.

"My apologies," the being spoke, its lips not quite matching its words. "But I have nowhere adequate to receive you, Keeper of Mirial." It bowed its head slightly to Layela. "We are still in… renovations." Its lips parted in what Layela guessed was supposed to be a smile. She returned the gesture.

"Um, thank you for, for welcoming us." The Malavant siblings flanked her now, and the rest of the crew had backed away. "I'm afraid we're not quite sure where we are."

The being clucked. Layela hoped it was laughing. "We did not expect a visit from Mirial for perhaps another decade, when preparations were more advanced. But I suppose that times do change. This," it said, making a grand gesture with its long arm towards the star outside. "Is the new First Star."

"How can you have a new First Star?" Avienne mumbled. "Wouldn't that make it the Second Star?"

The being clucked again. "A First Star, meaning the first star amongst all stars. The most important." Layela struggled to assimilate the information. Ardin was faster than she was.

"What will happen to our First Star?"

"When the time is right, your First Star will stop producing ether, and all production will veer to this new star. We expected Mirial to last longer, but… recent events have polluted its core. We fear for the ether creatures, and it is our duty to protect them."

Layela took a step forward. "The dark ether is spreading." She implored with her hands, and pointed to Ardin's chest. "Can you help us cleanse it? It would buy you time for creating the new star, too."

The Seeder lowered its head and looked at Ardin's chest, and then at Clave. "You are surrounded by dark ether, Keeper of Mirial. But your ether cannot be polluted, have no fear."

"Yes," she repeated. "But that is not my concern. Can we fight the dark ether?"

The Seeder nodded slowly, as though its head was caught in a wake she could not see. "Of course. The First Star can be cleansed, so to speak. She will be less powerful if you do so, but she will be pure again."

Layela felt hope and she shot a grin at Ardin, who looked worried. "How do I cleanse it?"

The being narrowed its eyes. "Your knowledge seems…limited, Keeper."

Layela stood tall. "Recent…troubles have made the passing of information much more challenging."

"Of course. The temple of Mirial is the access point to the First Star, as created by us long ago. You can help cleanse it from there. The details are inscribed on the walls."

"The altar," she whispered. "I need to go to the altar."

"Of course." The being cocked its head, a very human gesture.

"So this star will be ready in a decade?" Avienne asked. "Will she need a Keeper?" Layela sucked in her breath. It was not a question she had dared think to ask, too close to her heart.

"Of course. The Keeper will be your descendant, Keeper of Mirial. Whoever your child is."

Layela bit her lower lip and reached for Ardin's hand. He grabbed it and squeezed it gently. "What if I have no child?" she whispered.

"Then a new line shall be established. The Three Fates will see to it."

"Thank you," she whispered. *A decade.* A decade, and they could all be free. But first they had to save Ardin, with or without ether. She could feel his pulse as he held her hand, and the clamminess of his palm. She could hear the shallowness of his breath. The dark ether was eating away at him. She couldn't stand to lose him and Ardice, too. If Mirial was where the cure to his disease lay, then Mirial was where they would go.

"So a planet and a sun, that's nice," Avienne said, looking out the viewport. "The work of millions of years in a decade? Ambitious."

The being managed something closer to a laugh this time. "Time is relative. And it's not just a planet and a sun. It's a whole galaxy." It pointed out past the star, and Layela suddenly noticed the small pricks of light, other stars forming all around them, popping into view as she watched. Great arms stretched out, dark matter collapsed on itself, white dwarfs merged…an entire galaxy. In a *decade.*

"Okay, lots and lots of work. I'm officially impressed," Avienne said, giving a low whistle.

"Your galaxy is far, but our tunnels have linked your world to ours. If you are willing to wait a few of your hours, we'll complete work on the tunnel linking to Mirial. As a formality, we were soon to visit your world, Keeper, to prepare for the passing of responsibility. Mirial has done well, in her day."

The creature lowered its head, as though embarrassed that it had failed to reach her, first.

"You will always be welcome on Mirial, of course," Layela said, returning the nod.

Without another word, the creature vanished. "Come and go as they please," Avienne mumbled. "I know the type."

Layela still held onto Ardin's hand. Clave wasn't moving, looking down at the floor, his eyes tightly shut. Layela didn't go to him, turning to face Ardin instead, placing her hand on his chest.

He took her hand into his and brought it to his lips. He captured her eyes with his and whispered: "I don't want you to die trying to save me."

She smiled. "I'll promise that, if you promise not to die as I'm trying to save you."

He gathered her in his arms and held her tight. She felt the dark wound striking her like electric shocks, but ignored it, concentrating on his warmth instead.

And on the new lease on life they had been given.

***

Murl hated these games. Cat games. Waiting to pounce. The second tunnel had been a surprise, but she had followed and reached them. She was amazed she had not lost them. A creature had popped up in her hull, and she had explained she was with the Keeper, improvising along with its questions. It had taken her word for it and vanished.

Useless. All ether creatures were useless, of that she had no doubt. But they were part of Mirial's wish, and so she put up with them. As infrequently as possible.

Destiny II's crew seemed too busy to notice her ship, so she circled to the front and settled into the broken shuttle bay. The secondary set of doors were latched closed, but a portion of the ship's bay was now exposed to space, an open invitation to any stray ship. She latched the ship down and killed her motor. They'd have to come looking for her to find her. She kept only life support active, ready to follow them wherever they went. Of course, her brother would make sure that was Mirial. He had prepared the perfect callback for Layela. She closed her eyes. When she did so, she could sense him near, as though he stood beside her. She could barely breathe, but she relayed what she knew. Layela had what she needed. Her instincts were so sure—she conveyed it to Braken. He conveyed in turn that Clave had made it, with the child in tow. Murl smiled. Every piece of the puzzle coalesced as planned. When the time was right, she would attack the *Destiny II* and end the chase.

For Mirial. For herself, and the years spent in the Great Darkness.

CHAPTER 38

ELSA STARED AT the drawn curtains of Gresko Listan's room. She stood in the shadows of a cave, the wind playing in her hair. Everything was so dry, including her skin, save for where the tears had freely streamed all day. The leaders had refused to listen to her. Even her sisters were too terrified to fight, their terror and grief so strong she could taste it through their telepathic link, despite trying to block them.

Differences, small but distinct, had always kept them apart. Layela had once told her that she most resembled her mother, in spirit and feistiness. Josmere had not fit in with the Berganda, either. But Loran and Gresko had shown faith in her, and she intended to at least show up and confess her own childishness. She felt more human than a Berganda. Not five in Berganda years, which was adult, but five in human years.

She sighed and slipped into the darkness of the caves.

***

Loran could move her arm, if she really tried. It was all she could do. She stared up at the rocky ceiling, the darkness clouded by her tears. She couldn't even sob properly, lying on her back again, where she had spent so many days.

Braken had unceremoniously dragged her back, then treated her with painkillers and antibiotics, cleansed her wounds himself and covered her again. To keep her alive a while longer.

Gresko still lay crumpled where she could not see him, and her internal clock told her the time of the meeting was near. Braken wanted to trap them all, the ones who dared lead a rebellion against him. And they had handed them to him on a platter, even though they had never meant to gather them all here.

She heard a familiar shuffling. *Elsa!* She wanted to scream her name, to warn her, but all that she managed was a choked mumbling. Her tongue would not work properly. What drugs had he given her?

"El..a," she managed to mumble, so low she herself barely heard it.

The Berganda stepped into the room, a petite outline against the slight light.

"Loran? Gresko?" she whispered and took another tentative step forward. The second she was in the room, Braken stepped out from behind her and grabbed her arm. Elsa shrieked, but Braken simply laughed.

"I needed just one of you," he said. "The firstborn to enter the telepathic field."

Loran managed to move her arm, barely. He had been after Elsa only. Loran had handed him a child!

She bit down on her tongue, tasting the blood and forcing her body to move.

Too slow to help Elsa, who screamed again.

The echoes pounded in Loran, speaking of a pain much deeper than simply a tight grip.

***

Elsa's mind exploded in directions she had never even known possible. She felt all of her two hundred sisters join her screams, collapsing in the caverns where they hid. The Berganda children withered where they still grew, only a few days away from sprouting, some pushing up before their time, gasping in the fresh oxygen their lungs were not ready to absorb.

Elsa cried out to them, to all of the Berganda, but it was not there that Braken directed her mind. He forced her telepathy to grow in scope, to reach out across the worlds, across all of Solaria, connecting with every single ether creature, leaving them fallen across worlds and space. And then he pushed her further still, so far from her own mind and body that she became pure consciousness, unable to understand physical form, only observing from without.

Safe. She watched the thought float near.

And then he pushed her further still, until even that floating form of herself was left behind, and all she could hear was silence, as deep and wide as all of space itself. She hovered in limbo for seconds and lifetimes. He pushed her further still.

And she stood before Layela, her mind too shattered to cry for help, just reaching out with arms that no longer existed, desperate to just be held.

"Elsa?" She heard Mother Layela say, and she was flung back to her body, riding on the love she had heard in that voice. Mother Layela would not abandon her.

She collapsed to the ground, not feeling the sharp rocks cutting her, not sensing her blood pooling, or her ether healing her, not even knowing how to close her eyes anymore. Images flashed before her: Slita's corpse and blood pooling uselessly, Patros' smile, Layela's flowers...

She lay there, not understanding as Loran appeared near, not able to comprehend the words or how to respond to them.

She was lost and she had no idea how to come back home.

***

"Elsa!" Layela shouted again as the Berganda vanished.

"There's no one there," Ardin said.

She turned to her brother. "Did you see her, too?"

He shook his head, his eyes wide.

"Elsa, a Berganda. A five-year old Berganda! What did your brother do to her!" She crossed the floor and punched him in the chin. He remained in his chair, the bonds holding him in place.

"I don't know," he spat, eyes blazing. "Braken said he had a plan to bring you back, and I know it involved the Berganda, but...I didn't ask!"

Layela trembled with fury. She turned before she could strike him again. "We're going back. Now." She turned to Ardin and Avienne. "Braken wants me back, well, he'll have me back." She fixed her gaze on Ardin. "We won't lose anyone else!"

"The tunnel isn't ready yet," Jaru responded.

"Seeder!" Layela shouted. "If you can hear me, open the tunnel! Mirial needs me, and I need to go to her!"

The Seeder appeared, making Jaru jump again, sending coffee everywhere. "The tunnel is not fully prepared, Keeper. The ride will be much bumpier."

Layela closed the gap between them. "But will it get us there in one piece?"

"That it will."

"Then open it. Please. And I'll see you in a decade."

The Seeder cocked its head sideways. "Or earlier, Keeper of Mirial." He glanced around the bridge, pausing on the ether creatures for a moment longer. "Who knows what the Three Fates plan for any of us." It vanished with a breeze.

Before them, the entrance to a tunnel opened, white with wisps of purple.

"Sorry Litras, but Ardin had best take control."

"My thoughts exactly," Litras jumped off and Ardin settled in. Avienne took over tactical, and Jaru engineering.

Avienne glanced around. "Lots of dead weight on this bridge."

Layela cast her a withering glance. Gobran chuckled. "I can navigate, if you'd like."

Avienne grinned and didn't bother answering. "Just like old times, Ardin and Jaru." Layela looked at Ardin. He was growing paler and his hands shook a bit.

Just hang on. You too, Elsa.

She would find a way to save them all, regardless of the price she had to pay.

***

Ardin directed the ship into the tunnel. The engines powered down again, but it was hardly the peaceful ride they had enjoyed on the way over. The tunnel's edges strutted out and *Destiny II* bounced off both sides. The base, covered with bumps of its own, acted more as a trampoline than a smooth surface. Everyone hung on without complaint. At least it didn't sound like the hull actually took damage from the hits. It was more like bouncing off a pillow.

He held onto his console and glanced back at Layela. Her mouth was set. He had seen that look before, when she had been willing to sacrifice everything to ensure her sister lived. Layela had many faults, and staunch loyalty was one of his favourites.

Still, he couldn't let her die trying to save him. But he knew they needed to try to save the Berganda. They had been like daughters to her, after all. He couldn't imagine getting in the way of her motherly instincts. Which made him feel even crappier for the way he'd treated her earlier. Accusing her of not putting his needs before those of his daughter, basically.

You're a fool, Ardin Malavant. He concentrated on not pressing against the wound. It hurt him more than he hoped he let on. Like fire, then ice, then all twisted muscle. He could feel his heart beating wildly, as though trying to fend off the encroaching darkness. Each breath ended before it was full, his chest compressed by the spreading wound.

It used to be so much easier, when he was second-in-command, or even captain of his own ship. The rules had been clear, the battles simple, the codes of conduct straightforward. But now, with Layela being the Keeper of Mirial, he always felt shoved back amongst the shadows. By Mirialers, anyway. He would never admit it to Avienne or Layela, but he missed space travel. He missed being able to be honourable on a daily basis, through small actions, not political deeds. He missed the simplicity of black and white, of good and evil, of heroes and villains. Being a smuggler had been so much easier than being the consort of the Keeper.

He smiled and looked down. *Consort.* He was glad his sister hadn't clued in to that name yet. He could live without the merciless teasing.

He could live. He loved Layela and wouldn't trade her for the life he had left behind. But even now, caught in an unfinished tunnel, being tossed around, he loved the uncertainty and clarity of space travel.

"We should be nearing," Gobran said. Ardin looked back and caught Avienne's eyes. She winked and grinned. She loved it, too. In a much more reckless way.

"Thanks, Gobran!" Avienne shouted. She didn't need to, the ship quiet despite being tossed about.

"Blind, but still a great navigator," Gobran replied. "Next thing you know, I'll be captain of my own ship again!"

Avienne laughed. Ardin looked at Layela, lost in thought.

The jostling stopped all of a sudden.

"Still got it," Gobran said, leaning back into his chair.

Avienne swore. The tunnel had brought them right to Mirial, even closer than the tachyon tunnel did, which both impressed and worried Ardin. But standing in their way of the home world was a Solarian fleet of at least three hundred ships.

And he didn't need Avienne's weapons count to know they were armed to the teeth.

CHAPTER 39

MURL ACTIVATED HER engines at the same time as her weapons. She reversed and fired, the blast pushing her the rest of the way out of *Destiny II*. She launched rounds of torpedoes right into the fragile belly, with nothing standing in her way. Explosion after explosion rocked the ship, fire bursting out from its shuttle bay.

She laughed and turned her ship around, staying within her shields to launch more torpedoes on the weak spots. She knew them all—Clave had given her a full list. Exposed guns, viewing ports, spacewalk exits…she fired on them all, not all giving way to her attack, some too fortified still to collapse. But a few did collapse, the satisfying rush of oxygen and flames pushing outward.

The ship was moving now, its crew trying to swat the annoying insect that pricked it. Murl headed for the engines, firing rounds into the starboard one, flames jutting from it as combustibles escaped into dead space. She would cripple her, until Layela begged to reveal everything she knew to her brother.

And then, she would destroy her.

★★★

"Starboard engines down! We're hit all over! Whatever this is, it managed to get inside our shields!"

"It's Murl," Clave said, looking up at Layela.

"What does she have to do with any of this?" Avienne shouted from her station. "If I wasn't so busy trying to swat her away, you'd be the one I was swatting!"

Layela looked at him from where she sat. "What is Murl to all of this?" Clave tried not to stare at her eyes. *Green and blue.* The sign of a true Keeper. His brother's eyes were sea green, like his were night blue. Like Layela's had been, before her sister had died and passed her link to the ether on to her.

One twin has to die in order for the power to be whole. How could he have been so blind? He had thought, at first, that this was a phase for his brother. He had even liked Layela on Thalos IV, as she let him see some of her vulnerability, a girl—and, unbeknownst to her, a sister—and not the most powerful being on Mirial.

She didn't even seem aware of her powers most of the time. Was that the sign of a true Keeper?

"Murl is our sister. She was born in the family that adopted us." He looked at her, eyes pleading. "She's not evil, just lost. She really cares for Mirial and her people, and believes she's doing what's best for her." He bit his lower lip and stopped himself. "Braken gifted her with some dark ether." He glanced at Ardin. "It's changed her. She's less patient, more dangerous, kind of like an adrenaline junky."

"Clave, you intended to kill Ardice and me," Layela said incredulously. He shook his head. How could he convince her?

"I'm sorry, I'm an idiot. I seriously believed the line could be passed easily, since we're your siblings. I honestly believed that!"

"You were going to kidnap Ardice!"

"To bring her back to Mirial, her home! Braken said—oh, Mirial—Braken said he'd just present the child to Mirial and ask that her powers be transferred to him. That's all he said! I swear, oh, what would I have done?"

"He could have killed us all, but he didn't," Patros offered from the side. "The ether is dark, yes, but connecting with him frequently, I didn't spot any great evil."

Layela looked back at Patros. "So you mean I'm related to an idiot, then?"

Patros inclined his head.

"Please, let me speak to her."

Layela glanced at Ardin and Avienne, both too busy trying to keep the ship functional to offer an opinion. "All right. Patros, keep him in check."

"With pleasure," the Slont said, removing his gloves. She undid Clave's bonds with some difficulty and Patros escorted him to the comm station. Avienne swore when she saw him, but was too busy to stop them.

He looked at Layela with wide eyes. She nodded down. "Do it."

He punched in key combinations and entered her access code. "Murl?" Clave said, hoping he remembered the right codes. "Murl?"

"Clave?" She sounded out of breath. "I'm almost at Mirial. Just giving the *Destiny* something to think about."

Clave closed his eyes. She thought he was on Mirial. She would only believe that if Braken had told her that. *Fool!*

"I'm not on Mirial, Murl. I'm still on the ship that you're shooting at."

"What?" She paused, and the shots stopped. She was checking the provenance of the call. Murl was nothing if not thorough.

"Braken said you were on Mirial with the child." He kept his head down, to not meet Layela's withering glance. He could feel her anger pummelling into him. It seemed every one of his siblings wanted him dead, right now.

"He lied, Murl," the words stung. "He needs me dead to get the full ether." He paused, bile in his throat. "I'm so sorry, Murl. I believed him, too."

She didn't respond, and he feared she hadn't believed him. But then her voice came back on.

"He was going to make me kill you." He knew that voice well, from when the toughest decisions had to be made. It was the calm voice of weighty decision. Murl was detaching herself from the situation so that she could do whatever was required next. She would become both awesome and fearsome, all at once. "What is he planning next?" Clave didn't answer, not certain what to answer. Layela answered for him.

"He's planning on channelling the dark ether, Murl. More of it, until it's all that remains. Mirial won't survive. Her pure ether is already weakening."

Even without pulling on it and risking hurting Ardin, Clave knew Layela could feel the damaged star, especially after having felt the power of the new star. Mirial was but a shadow of a former glory they had never known.

"Can you stop him without killing him?" Murl asked.

She bit her lower lip and cast a glance at the Slont, as though wondering how much ether he could safely absorb. Clave doubted it was much more. The slont's skin was sallow, a definite yellow quality mixing with the blue. His eyes were half-closed and his hands shook slightly. It was affecting him, whether he cared to admit it or not.

"Maybe," she answered. "I'll try. You have my word on that."

Clave looked up and met her gaze, giving her a slight smile. "She's our sister too, Murl, whether we like it or not. She's telling the truth."

Murl scoffed. "I know. She can barely lie to save her soul. Part of what makes her such a bad Keeper."

Layela didn't bite by responding.

"All right, I'll help you stop Braken. But those Solarian ships are still standing in your way," Murl said. The comm unit died.

"I won't tie you back up, but at the first sign of trouble, Patros will deal with you," Layela said. "Don't make me regret trusting you."

"I'm sorry, it was all for Mirial. To make her strong again."

Layela didn't answer.

***

Braken could feel the darkness closing in. The Keeper was foolish, as was Murl, to believe her. He loved Clave. He was his brother. But he was weak and foolish, too, and Braken needed him dead to gain full control of the dark ether.

Dark ether. He scoffed at the thought. It was still ether. It was the ether that courted him, that had kept him safe all this time. The ether that had protected his entire village during the Great Darkness. For Murl and Clave to fail to see that proved disappointing. If he could rake enough of the ether, he could help Mirial grow at such a rate that within a year, she would flourish. He would tend to all of her, not just the gardens surrounding the palace. From the largest lake to the smallest bug. It would all flourish.

And her people would be whole again.

His people.

Mirial had gifted him with a face too hideous to show, so that he would be forced to hide it. So that his people could focus on his words, and in them, hear Mirial. He understood and accepted the sacrifices he had borne for her.

He would gladly do it all again.

If Murl failed in her duties, Murl, whom he loved above any other, who understood him and never flinched at the sight of him, then

Solaria would finally become handy. And his message on this day would be clear. He needed all of Solaria to know and understand why Mirial could never, would never, be messed with again.

He opened the planet's hailing frequencies, reaching out to every ship in the vicinity, and their superiors in turn.

He closed his eyes and smiled, waiting for Mirial to inspire the words that would herald an era of change.

***

"Mirial is strong once more," Braken's voice boomed over the comm units. Avienne lowered the volume.

"He's opened all the planet's hailing frequencies. Everyone's getting this," Jaru reported.

"This should be good," Avienne mumbled.

The disembodied voice continued. "Solaria is weak. Solaria is a bastion of immorality, fear and hatred. You are not welcome here, on the sacred land of Mirial. We send a message on this day. Let anyone who wanders near fear the same fate."

Silence.

"He closed hailing frequencies."

"What's the message?" Layela looked down at Clave. Clave stood. "He's gathering dark ether, I can sense it. But I don't know for what."

"Shields at maximum strength!" Avienne cried.

Layela opened frequencies to Murl. "Murl, stay inside our shields, they're stronger than yours."

She didn't respond, but Layela took that as acknowledgement enough. Clave gave her an apologetic smile. For a second, she almost returned the smile, but turned away from him instead. Avienne and Ardin were her family, and Ardice, somewhere far away. She would fight for them, and needed no one else.

Warning lights flared on the consoles all around them, and would have almost given the bridge a festive atmosphere had they not signalled danger. Everyone on the bridge stopped and looked toward Mirial. The sun turned dark for a fraction of a second, casting them in total darkness. A cloud detached itself from the sun, passing by the planet without touching it, but then covered the entire fleet.

Layela glanced at Avienne. She shook her head. "I can't get a reading."

"It's graveyard quiet," Groban's voice sounded over their systems.

Clave closed his eyes and sat down, catching his head in his hands.

"What did he do?" Layela demanded. "Clave?"

The cloud dissipated before he could answer. The fleet stood just as it had moments ago, lights flickering on and off. Avienne adjusted the view screen settings to get a closer look at the ships. Tar clung to them, and all of their lights flickered out. A comm link flared to life for a half a second, flashing a distress signal, but vanished too quickly to be answered.

Silence and darkness cloaked the fleet before them. Avienne moved their view around, showing one ship after another being covered in tar completely. Layela exchanged a glace with Ardin.

Avienne sucked in her breath. The fleet began moving towards them.

"They're not raising shields, not charging weapons," Avienne said. "They're just…charging us!"

"They're dead," Clave said, his head still down. "They're just… animated by dark ether, walking corpses." He looked up, his eyes lined with grief. "We used them to help fight battles, but never turned actual living beings. We just used the dead that littered the fields. We needed help." He paused. "So many people, dead just on his command…" He lowered his head again, as though he might be sick.

"Avienne," Ardin asked. "How many hits can we take?"

"Small ships or big ships? We can't take that many, Ardin. They're loaded. Our shields took a hit in the asteroid field, and they're not fixed. Our hull, well, Murl did a number on that." She glanced at Clave.

Ardin turned to Layela. "You have to use the ether," he said. The bridge grew dead silent. "You have to stop them. Or we're all dead."

"Ardin…"

"I'll not have you die because of me!"

The first ship struck the shields, *Destiny II* rocking angrily.

Her freedom was so close. A decade away. And yet never before had she craved it less. She would be Keeper of Mirial forever if it meant not having Ardin's blood on her hands.

***

Murl watched as one million people died before her. Just like that, their life-force pushed out of their bodies by her brother's will, rendered into useless corpses, able to only perform the simplest tasks. Like ramming a ship bigger than their own. The great beast that was Mirial's flagship rumbled over her, hit after hit buckling her shields.

Murl had done good damage to *Destiny II*. Once the shields were gone, the ships would easily destroy the rest of her. *Which is exactly what he wanted.*

He had used her. She had been willing to kill for him, to die for him, but she would never kill Clave. He was her blood, as much as Braken, as much as her own parents. As much as the other siblings they had all buried during the Great Darkness.

Braken's voice rolled onto the speakers again. "Layela, if you come peacefully to relinquish your role as Keeper, with your daughter, then I'll spare the ship. Murl will give you a lift."

Murl flung back as though wounded. She was already moving towards the shuttle bay, she realized. He was controlling her, too!

And he would kill Layela, forcing the full ether to flow to her daughter. Then he would rip it from the innocent child Clave had failed to acquire. She realized that he had never needed Ardice without Layela. He had needed both. He had made her set up Clave to be killed, and then tried to get her to execute the final blow.

Anger boiled within her. She clasped the stone firmly implanted on her chest. She clawed at it, but only managed to make herself bleed.

Soothing waves flew up from it. *I will always be there for you.* The words, so often spoken amongst the three of them, in the dark, fearful, endless night. To use them now mocked everything they had survived for. Mirial could not be strong unless Mirialers stood strong. And they never would, when controlled and not free.

***

"He means to kill you," Clave said. "You and Ardice."

Layela glanced back at Ardin and said nothing. They didn't know that Ardice was gone, which meant she was safe. It was a secret she was willing to take to her grave.

The ship rocked as another small fighter ship skidded sideways and collapsed into the shields, flattening its port side before drifting uselessly away. "Impatient little bugger, isn't he?" Avienne mumbled, swearing as two more followed suit.

Jaru was running from station to station, trying to fortify the shields while mumbling about possible ways to stop the fleet, incapacitate the ships, anything to just give them an edge. Avienne's fingers danced as she fired at the ships around them, but as soon as she downed one, two more took its place.

Ardin went up to Layela and took her arms in his. "I love that you want to save me. I really do, even if it annoys me. You went to uncharted space to save me, but you can't. You have to let me go and save yourself." He stopped, his voice gruff. "You still have so much to live for."

Ardice. Of course, she would live for her, too, but…Another ship struck the shields. A much bigger ship. Avienne hissed. "Shields are gone. Next one's straight on the hull."

"I don't think I want to be a sailor anymore," a pale Litras exclaimed from a chair. Gobran held out his arm towards her, and she gratefully grasped it. Layela had forgotten anyone but Ardin existed on the bridge at that moment.

She reached up and kissed him full on the mouth.

"I'm sorry," she whispered, and walked to the centre of the bridge. She cast a look at Avienne, who didn't meet her gaze. But her fingers had stopped moving.

Layela closed her eyes and summoned Mirial, ignoring Ardin biting his cry, ignoring Avienne as she jumped over her console and almost beat on Clave for trying to catch Ardin, ignoring her sobs as she reached out, further and further, gathering the ether inside herself.

And then, she released it into the fleet.

***

Murl felt the tingling of the ether dance on her skin, not like the pinpricks of her ether, but like soothing velvet. It rode on her mind and freed the grasp Braken had on it. She watched it roll out towards the fleet, the ships shifting slightly as the ether cleansed them, too.

And then she watched another ship crash into *Destiny II*. The powers of Mirial were great, but perhaps not great enough to fight her own darkness.

She clutched the jewel on her chest.

She had lost this battle, she knew. There had been too many players, too many rules. But at least she could buy Clave a fighting chance. Perhaps he could in turn save his twin.

She veered her ship away from *Destiny II*. She wanted a bit more of a view. The Solarian ships ignored her as she broke their rank and stood behind them. She turned and watched the ships ramming into Mirial's flagship, the great beast standing her ground despite explosions wracking her.

She had been wrong all this time. Mirial's strength was not in its ether. It was in its ability to stand against adversity, without flinching, and survive.

She hoped her brothers would reach the same conclusion on their own.

And that someday, perhaps they could meet in Mirial once again.

***

Layela fell to her knees, the mists dissipating around her. She grabbed for them with all of her will, thrusting out towards them, her hands reaching out regardless of the fact that only her mind was necessary to manipulate the ether, to charm it into coming back, to plead and bargain for their lives. She reached and met empty, cold air.

Her hands dropped down uselessly to her lap. "It didn't work."

She looked at Avienne, who spoke gently to her brother, her face white as she leaned in to listen for a heartbeat. "Don't die yet, please don't die yet," she could read on the redhead's lips.

She placed her ear on his chest and listened deeply, her features wrinkling and then smoothing again. The ship lurched over and over again, but Layela ignored it, not even willing to move towards Ardin, just watching the reaction on Avienne's face.

Avienne's eyes opened and she gave Layela a slight smile and a thumb's up. Layela closed her eyes. She had almost killed him.

She *had* killed him. She had killed them all. Because she hadn't used all of the ether at her disposal, too terrified at the thought of losing him. Ardin would not die by her hand. They would all die by her inaction, but she could not, would not live with Ardin's death on her hands.

"I'm sorry," she mumbled to no one in particular. Sections of the ship were shutting down, Jaru listing them off until Avienne asked him to stop. They had no more engines, no more power in weapons, no more methods of fighting back. They were an easy target, and Braken either had other plans for Layela, or he had decided he no longer needed her.

The comm unit chirped over the destruction and warning sounds. Murl's voice sounded clear and crisp. "Don't take this as a sign that I'm still clinging to my duties to protect you, Keeper." She paused, but did not take back the honorific. "I'm doing this for Clave. Live, my brother."

Clave jumped to his feet and screamed, trying to punch in the right codes to speak to Murl, but she had cut him off.

"Murl? Murl!" He screamed over and over again. Not even

Avienne tried to stop him. A wave of darkness suddenly spread out and enveloped them. Silence smothered the ship, even her rumbling quiet for a few moments. Then they heard it, starting with a few thunks. Metal on metal, ships bouncing uselessly off *Destiny II*'s hull, a wind chime absorbed in the quiet of space. The thick blanket dissipated and they regained sight and sensors. The fleet of Solaria hung uselessly around them, the spark of dark ether that had reanimated the corpses extinguished.

"Murl," Clave said one last time before collapsing in sobs. Gobran softly began to sing the old Mirial song, greeting its sailors home to rest, still clutching Litras' hand. Layela did not join in. She stayed on her knees, watching the carnage around her and wondering how they were supposed to win the day if she was unwilling to sacrifice Ardin for Mirial.

***

She was gone. Just like that, her life snuffed out, as carelessly and easily as a candle. Braken remained standing, perfectly erect. Murl was gone. She had been more than a sister to him. He had always known that, but she had always favoured both brothers equally. She had been the laughter on dark days, and they had all been dark. The strength at gravesides, the sustenance of empty stomachs, the story on quiet nights.

She had never shied away from him, never tried to desert him, had been his protector and companion, had touched his skin without flinching, smiled at him and looked him straight in the eye. Held him after he had burned. Held him, the scars on her arms proof that she had not let him go.

His own brother had cowered, fearful of the ether. But she had stayed at his side.

Even as she sacrificed herself to save Clave, she had loved them both, still. She would have killed for him. She would have died for him.

He found comfort in that thought, knowing he had forced her hand, wanting to see if she would choose him over Clave. He looked over Mirial, the great planet spreading below him, still mostly desert. He would help it grow. He would help it adapt to the new, more powerful ether. An ether that was not fully reliant on an unreliable star. Ether he could draw from himself, if necessary.

But he needed to be whole. He had reached the limits of his

power, and Clave hoarded the other, smaller portion. He needed it now, and he needed Layela.

As though I'd have let her die, Murl. You know me better!

He felt angry at Murl for not having trusted him more. He would have saved Layela, and he could have saved Clave, too, if it had meant that much to Murl. At least for now.

He reached out and grabbed his brother's weak mind. He needed them, now.

The time for games had ended with Murl's choice.

***

Clave saw a hand move a split second before he realized it was his. He reached out without willing his body to do so, uncertain why he did. The hand was his, he knew, but it didn't *feel* like his. It jutted in the air before him, jerked back, its movements clunky and uncertain. He tried to move it himself, but his mind was trapped in a deep fog.

Then his right leg jerked up, like someone was testing his reflexes. The left one twitched but didn't jerk. His feet curled in and then straightened out, rocking back and forth until they were in unison. And then, in his haze, he felt himself stand.

He watched in panic as he took a step forward with uncertain footing, the ground seeming suddenly far away. He tried to reach out to brace himself, terrified he would fall, but the second step came more easily and the third seemed perfectly natural.

The panic had pierced some of the haze, and Clave now understood that he no longer controlled his body.

Braken! He had seen his brother's mind tricks before, but he had never dreamed that he would use them on him. He was his brother! His twin brother! What was he planning?

He wanted to warn them. Murl had died protecting him, and he didn't intend on going down so easily. But the more he tried to fight him, the tighter the grasp became. He heard soothing words in the back of his mind. Not to worry. That everything would be fine. That he would take care of him.

Clave didn't believe any of it as he walked towards Layela, who was standing again.

"I think I can get us enough power to fly to the planet and maybe land," he heard someone report.

"Good enough for me. Let's get this over with," Avienne responded.

Her voice was far away, like in a dream.

Layela turned to face Clave. She seemed shorter now. Was he looking through his own eyes, or through Braken's? *Braken! Let go of me!* He broke into a sweat with the effort of trying to break free. But he doubted Layela would notice a difference in him, not with grief still so freshly painted on his face.

She looked sideways and then back at him. "I am sorry, Clave, for what it's worth. But your sister died protecting us. You can be proud of that."

Clave found himself nodding, and felt a smile cross his lips. His stomach lurched. Victory was meant to be theirs, not Braken's alone. He felt the dark ether around them, pouring from his skin, coating everything and everyone around them. *Like ashes of the dead.* He gagged, bile slashing the back of his throat with betrayal. Not only had Braken killed Murl, but Murl's death had released dark ether and formed a trail. Now Braken was riding that trail, using it. Clave wished he could close his eyes or at least shed tears from them.

Murl, you tried so hard to save me, and you gave him the perfect opening.

He bent over and hugged Layela, who flinched at the touch. But she didn't push him away. She was too soft, too soft. His hands linked behind her back, and Braken's dark ether rode the wave of Murl's shattered ether all to way to them, snapping both him and Layela in one teleportation spell.

Clave managed to close his eyes then. Layela's scream was ripped away by the ether.

***

Patros jumped up as Clave wrapped his arms around Layela. He could sense the dark ether, having been so infused by it himself. He saw it gathering around Layela and Clave, like a great hand come to swoop them away. He threw himself into the circle of fingers just as it closed. Layela's and Avienne's screams mingled as he clutched Clave's exposed neck with his bare hands and squeezed to drain ether or life from him—he didn't care which, as long as he stopped him. The dark ether pounded his cells, but still he held on, unwilling to let go even though his skin burned with it.

Then the hand was gone and he fell to the ground, smelling of charred skin.

Avienne was beside him in a second, red hair spilling towards him.

"Blood and bones, Patros, are you all right?" Her eyes were wide with concern.

He smiled. "Did I stop him?"

She nodded, but he saw hesitation in her eyes. He propped himself up, his body aching, the top layer of skin on his hands burned clean off. Avienne helped him up, and he leaned against her as she guided him to the captain's chair and sat him down.

That's when he understood his mistake. Clave was on the ground, unconscious, possibly dead. But his goal should have been to save her, not just to stop him. Layela was nowhere to be seen. She had been swooped away as he fought her brother. He leaned back in the chair and closed his eyes.

He should have drained the dark ether from around her, not just from Clave.

He had failed to protect the Keeper of Mirial.

"Push her," Avienne ordered, all joke gone from her voice. "I want to be at that palace within minutes. I don't care what it takes."

No one argued as *Destiny II* lurched forward, as wounded as her crew.

***

A layer of skin had been scraped off Layela, and every part of her tingled with small bursts of flames. Clave's arms slipped away but still she was dragged down, resisting the urge to call on the ether, resisting the urge to continue screaming.

Solid ground materialized under her feet again and she stumbled forward, to be caught by a large man. She tried to back away, but he held her firmly. She looked up. Braken had lowered his cloak, his flesh as burnt as the surface of Mirial. She didn't flinch, keeping her gaze firm on his sea green eyes. *Like Yoma's.*

"I don't know how you managed to stop Clave from coming too, but that won't save you for long." Layela didn't answer, kicking up instead. She struck a knee and his grip loosened. She kicked again, higher, and he collapsed to his knees. Layela turned and ran, only to be grabbed by Solarian soldiers with dead black eyes, smelling like tar. *Rotting ether.*

Braken stood back up. The soldiers' hands dug into her arms as they turned her around to face him, their fingers at unnatural angles against her flesh as they squeezed to the bone.

"You use the same ether that almost doomed Mirial long ago," Layela said, trying to look brave.

He brought his face close to hers and she fought the urge to back away or to let disgust show on her face. "The ether that almost destroyed Mirial is what was supposed to protect us. Why? Because someone was too soft to let someone else die." He brought his face even closer. "Tell me, will you be strong enough to use your ether to save yourself and Mirial, even though it will mean your 'lover's' death." He practically spat the words out.

He grinned, his top lip curling high where part of it had been burnt off. She stood her ground silently.

"I didn't think so."

***

Destiny II entered the atmosphere at breakneck speed, shaking wildly under their feet. Avienne held onto her console.

"We're going straight to the palace," she said loud enough for everyone to hear. "He'll probably take Layela to the temple, not far from it. Clave, you're a dead man if you go anywhere near that madman, and we need you alive, at least for now." She gave him a look of warning. "Gobran, I hate to do this, I really do, but you're in charge of the ship. You know her controls as well as any of us." Gobran nodded and stood to move towards the navigation panel. He used the control stations on his left to guide him, and then moved straight to his right. He found it with barely any difficulty, giving Avienne heart.

Jaru looked relieved. If he could focus on a train of thought for more than a second, she would have left him in charge. But that was asking for greater disaster than leaving a seasoned captain in charge, blind or otherwise.

"Patros and Litras, you're with me." She glanced at her brother, still unconscious. "If he dies," she crossed the floor between her and Clave. "You'll suffer a much, much worse fate than what your brother has in mind for you, understood?" Clave nodded.

"Good." The ship's landing sequence was initiated. Jaru nodded to her. She bent in close to him and handed him a gun. "I know it's not your style, but if he gets out of hand, shoot him."

He took the gun and put it down immediately, his hands shaking. Well, it had been an idea, anyway.

She jogged for the lift, where Litras and Patros waited for her.

She glanced once more at Clave. "Much," she repeated as the doors closed.

***

As soon as the doors were closed, Clave knelt by Ardin. "Don't do that!" Jaru cried from his station as he finished the landing sequence.

"I won't hurt him, I promise," Clave said, knowing his promises held little weight in this company. "I set the wards on Layela," he explained. "I'm better at the subtle stuff than my brother is. I think I can ward his wound from her ether, kind of like a reverse ward."

Jaru seemed undecided. Gobran spoke up. "Let him try it, Jaru. Ardin's a dead man either way. Layela will have to protect herself, sooner or later."

Jaru nodded and returned to his work. Clave reached down into the wound. It was large, and growing still. He needed to stop it from spreading, and stop the ether from touching him. It was a large spell, and he still felt nauseous from Braken's mind grasp and the Slont's ether drain. He closed his eyes and forced all of his concentration on this one task: to ensure the ether of Mirial would never again touch Ardin Malavant.

CHAPTER 40

ELSA FELT THE whispers of her sisters goading her back. They were scared and wounded, and many of the children had perished. They were calling for each other, all of the missing ones, the broken links, the unanswered cries…She tried to move a hand, and it twitched. She felt it jump off the ground and land back down.

"That's the spirit," Loran said. A faraway voice. Cold water sprayed on her face. It felt good. Loran worked water on her arms and legs, too. Elsa had never realized the captain of the guards had paid any attention to the Berganda, but apparently she knew how to heal them.

The ether danced around her body, as though uncertain what to do. She had not been physically wounded, and her wound was not something the ether could heal. Loran trickled water down the Berganda's lips. It ran fresh down her throat.

"Can you move?" Loran asked, and Elsa tried to open her eyes. She couldn't quite figure it out yet. Her body was a foreign object, its operations difficult to understand.

She reached out with her mind. She soothed each of her sisters one at a time, each sproutling that remained, though there were precious few. It was easy for her mind to wander now, having been freed from its body too long.

She wandered the halls, ignoring Loran's questions. She could go anywhere, be anywhere. Away from the pain and loss. Her spirit danced the halls of the palace of Mirial, free and inhibited, twirling and jumping until something caught her attention.

She followed the light, not walking towards it, nor floating towards it, but rather appearing in front of it as soon as she had wished it.

Layela, she thought. She had found her, being dragged by those monstrous soldiers, towards the temple of Mirial. Elsa flickered in front of Layela.

What can I do? Layela did not hear her, too concentrated on escaping, or too afraid.

Elsa reached into the dead minds of the soldiers. She could see the consciousness just hovering there, a useless spark that could only animate joints. She leaned in and blew on it, and the soldier collapsed. She giggled and hopped to the side, doing the same to the second soldier.

As soon as he was down, Layela was off, running towards the temple where they had been taking her, regardless.

Confused Elsa tried to follow, but yelped as she was dragged back to her body, her eyes snapping open.

"Sorry," Loran said, sheathing her knife back up. "Although I'm glad that worked."

Elsa looked at the fresh green blood pooling beside her arm. The ether was already healing the cut.

She turned to Loran. "Layela is here. Near the temple."

"We have to help her," Loran said, pushing herself up to an almost seated position.

"What can I do?" Elsa asked, her body feeling small and useless.

"Behind that pillar," she indicated with a nudge of her head. "Gresko hid two legs for when I was healed enough. You'll have to help me put them on, and heal the wound around the synthetic, so it holds."

Elsa nodded and ran back, having to drag the legs back one at a time. They were both left legs—spares, she guessed—but they would do.

"Won't fusing the skin with the synthetic do more damage?" Elsa whispered.

Loran nodded. "But we need to fight, and I don't know how to fight like this."

"You seemed like you were doing a fine job to me," Elsa murmured. Loran smiled.

"Hook 'em up, Elsa. We have work to do."

***

Destiny II landed awkwardly, taking off a chunk of palace near her port. "Never liked that bit anyway," Avienne mumbled as she opened the rear landing bay doors.

"Coast is clear!" Patros announced. Avienne jumped out, gun in hand, her belt of knives well fastened. The Kilita had found her spear again and a couple of guns she enjoyed. Thankfully she had opted to remain clothed, this time.

"Where is everyone?" A shot rang by Avienne. She jumped sideways and hid behind a column, as did Patros and Litras.

"There!" Patros screamed as he shot a Mirialer. The man fell from the ramparts in a bloodied heap.

"Hold fire!" Avienne screamed.

Patros looked at her, stunned. A few shots rang by them. "They're the ones shooting at us!"

"I know! There are just so few Mirialers left…Isn't there another way?" She covered her eyes with her hand. "Gah, I'm turning into Layela!"

Patros grinned at her. "How attached are you to this palace?"

She shrugged. "It's pretty, but could probably use renovations."

He crouched down and placed both hands flat on the ground. He closed his eyes and the ground below him turned dark before dissipating. She heard screams from their attackers, but all shots stopped.

"What did you do?" She asked as they started running again. He grinned. "I asked the palace to absorb their feet, basically. Nifty trick, I'd say. Plus I got rid of some of that dark ether. Uncomfortable stuff. No wonder Braken is so cranky."

Avienne laughed and ran down the palace way, towards the temple, when the ground erupted beneath them and a large shadow loomed over them, grunting.

"Spread!" Avienne screamed as a giant animal leg came crashing down beside her head. She didn't bother trying to get a good look at the monster, too busy desperately avoiding its attack. She could no longer see neither Patros or Litras.

She ran and hoped no leg would crush her before she had figured out how to fight back.

***

Litras felt energized by the battle. Her body was young and strong

—she had selected it as such. The humans had no idea who she was, though the Seeder had almost given it away, had they been paying attention.

She avoided a blow easily and threw her spear up into the belly of the undead beast. It was a monstrosity from a time long ago, brought back at the whim of that false so-called Keeper. Litras laughed at the idea. Keepers were selected, not self-proclaimed.

The beast turned and headed towards the rest of the palace, its rotting tail detaching, the ground shaking. It had been a mighty beast once, and deserved better than this.

"Patros! It's heading for the palace! Free the Mirialers!" Avienne screamed, firing off her ether knives into the beast, running and screaming at it as Patros used the ether of the world around him to free the Mirialers again.

The beast turned, the redhead swearing as she avoided a leg. She was spectacular, and fun to watch. That had been a pleasant surprise from this journey. The only pleasant surprise. The beast was a bother, and they certainly had no weapons with which to destroy it.

"Get out of here!" Avienne screamed at the confused Mirialers, not certain who to shoot at anymore. The air was crisp and their cries echoed from the buildings. Litras jumped up, to finish it before it finished them.

***

Layela dashed into the temple and tripped on a stone, which sent her sprawling to the ground, chafing palms and knees. She scrambled back up to her feet and ran for the altar.

She needed to cleanse Mirial, to get rid of the dark ether and stop Braken. She ran up the steps and hopped over the deep river that served as bed to the temple. Her sister's resting place. Her steps faltered.

Yoma.

She grabbed the ceremonial knife, left here a long time ago, her blood and the blood of her sister still encrusted on the blade.

Wielding the knife with deadly efficiency, she brought it to her palm and cut through it. She bled into the altar and tried to steady her breath, wishing for Mirial to shed the ether.

Nothing happened. She felt no ripple in the ether, noticed no change. She glanced around.

"I was thinking more a cut along the neck." Braken stood beside her in an instant, grabbing both wrists and crushing them until she dropped the blade. She cried in frustration. "But first, I need to deal with my brother." He cocked his head sideways.

"Don't worry, he's on his way."

***

Avienne watched the Kilita jump maddeningly high and plant her spear in the creature's eyes. She wouldn't have believed that to be enough, except the creature grunted and toppled over, taking out another chunk of the palace.

Litras hopped off.

Avienne tried to catch her breath. "I…never realized…Kilita could jump…so high!"

Litras grinned. "We're born warriors, not soft, like Mirialers and Slonts."

"Won't argue that," Avienne said as she straightened. Patros stood near with his hands up. Avienne whirled around, but the Mirialers were surrounding them, guns held high. Avienne swore and dropped her weapons.

She recognized a few faces amongst them. Some of Layela's guards, and even maids. A gardener, she thought, to her surprise. There were a good number of them.

"You can relax," Avienne said. "I hardly intend to kill any of you. I think there are too few of us left, anyway."

That gave them pause, and they exchanged glances.

If I had a plan, Avienne thought, *I'd spring it right about now. Too bad I don't have a plan.*

***

The shuttle landed right outside the temple.

Clave stepped into the temple, his hands in his coat pockets, looking more like he was going for a walk then coming for his execution. His brother stood tall near the altar, holding Layela's two wrists in one hand behind her back. She tried to break free, dark hair spilling everywhere, but he was using dark ether as bonds. Without her own ether, she would never break free.

He stopped short of the stairs. His brother stood above him, towering. Satisfaction crossed his face. Clave almost looked away. It was not the scars that disgusted him, but rather the deformity of his spirit. His eyes had large pupils now, as though the darkness meant to conquer the pure sea green of Mirial.

"I want it to end, Braken," he said. "I want to go home, with you. I want to give Murl a proper burial. And I want to forget all of this ever happened." He meant every word. He wanted it so dearly it hammered his chest.

"That sounds lovely," Braken said. His voice was different, too. He was changing. The dark ether was changing him. "But I have other plans."

He raised his hands, and Clave just had the time to say "Sorry," before Ardin leapt out of the shadows and stabbed Braken straight through the heart. Braken turned on Ardin and tried to strike him with dark ether, but Clave's wards were strong. Ardin pulled his blade free and swung again, striking for the neck at a downward angle. Blood jutted and Braken's screams gurgled, the stench of iron coating the stale air of the temple. Braken took a step towards Clave, looking at him with panicked eyes, lifting his hand imploringly.

Ardin pulled his sword free and lifted his blade high for a third blow, screaming as he brought the blade down and severed the head from Braken's body.

Clave closed his eyes.

"Not in the water," he heard Layela say. "He doesn't deserve that."

Clave fell to his knees, knowing his eyes had changed, knowing that one was now of purest night, the other of purest day.

He lowered his head and allowed himself a smile of victory.

CHAPTER 41

AVIENNE WAS GROWING more and more annoyed. A tall man stood before her, clicking his teeth as he approached her with rope. From the way he held it, Avienne doubted he had ever tied a useful knot in his life. Other Mirialers stood near, shuffling in anticipation towards her.

"Can't we just figure this out? I mean, aren't we all fighting for the same thing?"

Nobody seemed to agree with her, even the ones she recognized. Litras growled at them as they came close. Avienne pulled her hands away from the man trying to bind her. "First of all, you're doing it annoyingly wrong. Second of all, don't mess with the Kilita. She has sharp teeth and she bites."

They stared at her sullenly.

"Well, you people lack spirit. What's wrong with all of you, anyway. You're like walking corp—" she stopped herself. She exchanged a quick glance with Patros. She looked more closely at the Mirialers who surrounded her. Their skin was pale, even for Mirialers, and clammy. Their pupils were bigger than they should have been, covering most of their irises.

They were being turned too, either on purpose or through exposure. "They stink," Litras spat.

"Don't move!" A shout came from the shadows.

"Now what?" Avienne mumbled as she turned around. Loran

walked towards them at an odd angle, each step clunky and awkward. Elsa strolled beside her, the girl looking left and right at shadows that Avienne couldn't see. The walls were covered in Mirialers, pointing weapons down at the other Mirialers.

"Looks like we're just in time," Loran said as she strolled up. Avienne looked down. The ripped pants revealed two prosthetic legs, both left. Loran flushed red when Avienne looked back up. The woman was pale, a line of sweat beading her brow, her skin almost gray beneath it.

Avienne grinned. "Impeccable timing!"

The earth rippled under them, sending most people to their knees.

"The temple!" Avienne gasped as she broke into a full run, not caring if anyone else was following her.

***

"The dark ether is loose now!" Clave exclaimed. "You have to cleanse Mirial, like the Seeder said."

Layela nodded and looked up at the walls. *The path is on the walls.* She gazed around to the deeply carved figures in the stone walls. She had never taken the time to see how beautifully the temple had been decorated. Animals, some that she had never even seen, ran or nurtured their young in grandiose strikes of the chisel. Flowers bloomed all around them, roots wrapping around bud, under the large symbol of Mirial, a great sun that turned into a flower.

Her gaze ran across the long walls covered by murals, yet nowhere did she see any indication of a Keeper. She turned around to look more closely when Clave screamed beside her. "There!"

Layela followed his finger to a short wall covered in shadows. She squinted to make out the details in the darkness, running her fingers on the fine lines, dust crumbling away and filling her nostrils.

A pictogram showed an empty star surrounded by a flower. *Mirial.* Layela was certain of it. The flower led away from it, its blossoms withering, petals falling until the vine was empty of any life. But then it wrapped itself around a fully chiselled star, deeply chiselled, as though showing it was full to brimming. The vine wrapped around the full star and then, on the other side of it, it bloomed richly, from one vine to more flowers than Layela could count, a myriad of details and petals.

From a lesser Mirial to a brighter Mirial. Layela stared at the pictogram, running her fingers along the vine that linked both stars.

From a lesser Mirial to a full Mirial, and the path showed a vine dying and then ripening…

"It wants me to destroy all of the plants of Mirial?" The realization struck her like a blow. Why would Mirial want her to destroy that which she loved best? That which they both loved best?

Clave nodded right away. "It seems that way. Plants have always been a big draw for ether and Mirial. Maybe so much so that Mirial can't be cleansed unless they unleash all of her ether, first."

Layela turned to Ardin, who had cleaned and sheathed his sword. "But if I use my ether, I'll kill Ardin!" She ran a hand through her hair, undoing what little remained of her ponytail. "And why would Mirial demand that I destroy something so beautiful to cleanse it! It makes no sense. It's downright ridiculous!"

Clave shrugged and indicated Ardin with a quick motion of his head. "I warded his wound. Same ward as the ward I had used on you. It kept you from accessing the ether, so it should keep your ether from accessing him. For a while, anyway."

Layela looked to Ardin for confirmation. He nodded. "I feel much better," he said. Layela reached out to touch him and see, but the ward pushed back on her. Clave looked embarrassed. "Sorry, that's temporary. I'll remove it as soon as the dark ether has dissipated." He gave a short, nervous laugh. "What am I saying, it'll be gone on their own!"

Layela glanced at Ardin, who smiled encouragingly. "If we get rid of the dark ether, in ten years, we can be free." The longing in his voice reminded her of her own hopes. She smiled and leaned on the altar for support.

She closed her eyes, letting everything wash away. The bells had not tolled for a while, and she suspected her fears combined with the dark ether had triggered them. Ardin would be safe, she knew with certainty.

She would not kill the plants. She would bid them sleep. If she, as Keeper of Mirial, was supposed to hold a deeper understanding of the mystical First Star than anyone else, than she needed to interpret her bidding herself. The plants were closest to Mirial, even more so than the Mirialers themselves. Layela had seen the ether dance around and within the plants, she had witnessed the eagerness with which the plants had sprouted back on Mirial with only the slightest of urgings.

If she was one with Mirial, than Mirial must reflect a part of her soul. And Layela would not undo all of the life that Mirial and she had cultivated again. Killing could simply not be the way to cleanse dark ether.

She reached out tentatively for the ether. When Ardin did not cry out, she welcomed all of it back to her, like a warm blanket on the coldest winter nights. Every nick and wound healed with the ether, Layela reached out and called the plants to sleep, for now. The leaves of the great trees of the temple turned yellow and red and began falling, brown before they hit the ground. The flowers of her gardens pulled back within themselves, the pink flowers of Ardice losing petals before shrivelling. The plants that guarded the remaining Berganda children folded in on themselves and collapsed.

Layela then drew deeper, into the underground, and the great gardens that had fed Mirialers during the Great Darkness. She snuffed the glow of the Lacile flowers and laid them to rest. She found every blade of grass, every seed about to burst, every bee about to pollenate, and asked them to rest. And they did. One by one, they followed her wishes and entered a deep slumber.

She was breathing heavily, the ether more demanding than anticipated. It didn't matter—she was almost done.

And then, she would soon be free.

***

Ardin watched Layela with concern as her breathing grew more laboured and sweat plastered her hair against her forehead and her shirt to her back. He couldn't help her. He hated the ether for that. It was so dependent on Layela, at his exclusion.

He looked over to Clave, who examined Layela with as much intensity as he did. Much more intensity, in fact. Ardin glanced at the room around him. He couldn't see anything out of place, but he gently placed his hand on his sword. The sword practically vibrated in his hand.

They were in danger.

He went to pull his sword free of his scabbard, but his arm was locked in place. He looked up. Clave was looking at him. He brought a finger to his lips and winked at Ardin.

***

Layela had recalled everything, every single thing she could find that was plant life. The closest thing to plants that remained were the Berganda sproutlings, the few that remained. If Mirial didn't understand the difference between an ether creature and a plant, they were in much deeper trouble.

She felt Mirial respond, as if expecting the gesture. Layela sent back soothing waves. She wasn't sure what was supposed to happen now. She turned to Ardin to see his hand on his sword, a quiet plea in his eyes.

She turned quickly, but Clave was already behind her. He struck her hard against the face and sent her reeling on Ardin. She collapsed at his feet. She struggled to remain conscious.

"That was useful, Ardin," she heard Clave say. "I believe I'll have you bronzed like that. Don't worry," he added as though an afterthought. "I'll have Layela bronzed at your feet, too. You do make a charming couple, and I'm sure Mirialers would love spitting at your statue for generations to come."

The ether around her exploded in darkness. Clave's hands were deep in the altar and, when he lifted them, blood flowed freely from both hands. Layela squinted into the thick, dark light, like liquid obsidian. A large, cloaked shadow surrounded Clave, hiding all his features, but Layela recognized him nonetheless.

Braken.

The two had managed to join, Clave's eyes shining blue and green in the darkness. Their souls had merged in a way Layela had never been able to with Yoma, who had left her for Mirial long ago.

Clave looked her way and grinned. The dark ether whipped around her, and she suddenly understood.

He was cleansing the sun, as she had meant to do.

But he was cleansing it with dark ether, destroying any of its remaining light.

***

Avienne ran to the temple, Patros and Litras right at her heels. She ran across the bridge, down the few steps, jumped through the threshold and then across the courtyard. She spotted Ardin immediately, his hand on his sword. Layela was at his feet, struggling to remain conscious.

At the altar stood Clave, bleeding. Mirial shook. Avienne stumbled to her feet, but pushed herself back up, praying her aim was true as she let three knives fly towards Clave. They all fell uselessly to the ground beside him.

Of course. She continued to run, jumping over the small river, ignoring the stench of rotten plants and dampness. Clave's hand shot back and Avienne felt as though it closed on her neck, even though he was nowhere near. "I really like you," he said. "Don't make me kill you."

She tried to break free, but had nothing to grasp at. The more she struggled, the tighter the grip became. Litras jumped up and struck the unseen arm with a short sword she had acquired somewhere. Clave looked insulted but concentrated on the altar.

"It's too late," Clave said. "I've already cleansed it of *your* ether. If you kill me now, Mirial will die and take half the universe with her."

Avienne went to jump forward regardless, but Litras held her back. "Careful! He speaks truth!" Avienne broke free of the Kilita.

"How do you even know that?" Before Litras could answer, Clave struck back again, sending both of them flying into the courtyard, Avienne hitting her head against a tree.

Patros went to Layela and helped her up. There was no one else who could fight this battle.

***

Layela stood up, the side of her head aching and her legs woozy under her. Patros was speaking to her, but she couldn't make out his words over the buzzing in her ears. He pointed at the altar. Layela saw the ecstasy on Clave's face, felt the dark ether surrounding everyone and everything, and she stumbled towards it. Her palm still bled.

She stuck her whole hand in the altar, letting her blood mingle with his, her head snapping back as Mirial called her home.

Nice move, she swore she heard her sister say, and she heard Clave scream as she forced the dark ether to be cleansed. But the sun…It was already so weakened. Could she truly save it now? Was it better to leave it be, and cultivate what little of the pure ether might remain?

What about the plants? What about Ardin? Would any of them survive? Would inaction be wiser than further action?

She smelled iron mixed with a whiff of oak. Earth and water licked her senses. She took a deep breath, letting them wash her clean and wipe away her indecision.

Layela thought of Ardice, far away, who would have to spend at least ten years without her or Ardin. She thought of how her daughter would have more choices, and how she herself would in a decade as well.

And how Ardin could live for so long still, as long as the dark ether was expelled from him.

Come back, she wished. *Please, Mirial. Yoma.*

Mirial heard her wish and answered.

The planet shook under her.

EPILOGUE

L AYELA STOOD BEFORE her throne. One by one, the citizens of Mirial walked up and bowed or curtsied. It was an old ritual she had never undertaken before. It had seemed silly.

She counted them, as they came. Three hundred and forty-seven, in all. Thee hundred and forty-seven Mirialers, and two hundred and thirteen Berganda. One Slont. One Kilita.

Only fourteen of the Berganda children had survived, and now, under the red skies of Mirial, they were preparing to leave, under the guidance of Elsa. They needed more light to survive. Somewhere away from Solaria and their slave camps. Layela's hands turned to fists.

She looked outside the window, above the temple which was under renovations. The sun had shed all of the dark ether, but by then, there had been so much, so much because she had failed in her duties as Keeper and not kept the sun free of weeds, that an entire layer had been expelled. The planet had been spared, protected by ether, but the system had reverted to a nebula, now governed by a white dwarf. A star too cold and dark to really hold the plants Layela so loved, nor the Berganda.

Ardin stood to the right of her throne.

Three hundred and forty-seven. When they had all come and gone, she still stood before it, reaching back for Ardin's hand. He grabbed it. His hand was cold. Clave's wards had protected him, all right. Protected him from being fully healed. He didn't complain, didn't say anything, but she felt the sting at night when she drew too close to him.

He could not hold her as he used to.

A decade. A decade of darkness to tend to the dying sun, to allow it to live long enough to know relief. A decade of not seeing Ardice, not mentioning her, in the hopes that the Seeders would leave her alone.

A decade without holding Ardin, unless the wards and dark ether somehow faded. But all her knowledge had been spent.

A decade.

At the back of the room, Avienne stood after everyone had left. She sent a kiss their way. Layela nodded to her, and Avienne stepped out. Who knew how long before they would see her again, too.

A decade.

A decade to learn to be a good Keeper, and to make any harm up to her people, who had already suffered far longer than a decade.

***

Avienne wanted to stay, but needed to leave. This place with its red skies was unbearable. Her heart hurt at the thought of leaving Ardin and Layela behind, but what choice did she have? They wouldn't come with her and space called to her. Beside, her brother had made his request clear. With the dark ether still clinging to him, he feared he'd be too easy to track, but her, she could hunt to the far reaches of the universe to ensure Ardice's safety. She *would* find her.

Patros and Litras waited for her at the palace docks.

"Well," she said, putting on what she hoped was a convincing smile. "This was fun, but I have many more things to do. Are you coming? Most of my crew is gone. Jaru and Gobran will come! That's good. But I could use you two, as well."

Patros smiled and nodded. "I know little of space flight, but am willing to learn."

Avienne held out her hand and he shook it. "You're hired. But that doesn't mean you'll get paid!" She quickly added. He laughed.

"What about you, Litras."

The Kilita smiled, showing her pointy teeth. Avienne was starting to like that smile. "Are you going to become a full-fledged sailor? You're already showing some good promise!"

Litras' grin deepened but then she shrugged. "Nah. Our paths part here, Avienne Malavant. At least for now."

"Too bad. Want a lift off-planet. I'm taking the Solarian Minister back to his retirement, so I can drop you off, too."

Litras shook her head again. "I'll be fine. I have a ride."

Avienne furrowed her brow. "There aren't that many ships around here," Avienne said. "You sure you didn't hit your head too hard?"

Litras laughed and handed Avienne a package. Avienne looked inside and saw a bottle of an astium-based liquor. She didn't know the name, but she liked the red colour. "It's okay. Some oaths are just a grain of salt on the vast beach of the universe. Go ahead and enjoy," Litras then turned and left, calling over her shoulder. "We'll meet again someday soon, Avienne Malavant."

"What did she mean by that?" Patros asked.

Avienne watched the Kilita leave, remembering her jump, her seeding the right information at the right time, the Seeder's pause and slight nod as he had looked at her…She shrugged. "I'm not sure, Patros. But either way, I'm drinking this tonight, with or without your help."

She looked back towards the Kilita, but she was gone. Seconds later, she heard a ship take off. Avienne looked towards the sound, but saw nothing, following it until it crossed the atmosphere, leaving a trail of smoke. *An invisible ship.* She doubted this would be the last time she saw the Kilita, too, though she hoped their next meeting wouldn't come too soon.

Avienne shook her head, opened the bottle and took a long, cool drink. She lowered the bottle, handed it to her new crew and walked back to the *Dessicate* under the red glow of the skies of Mirial.